Praise for
CARLENE THOMPSON

SHARE NO SECRETS

"Intriguing . . . brims with madness and creepy thrills."
—*Romantic Times BOOKreviews*

"Turns and twists make you change your mind about who the killer is and the ending is a real shocker. Get this one quick."
—*Rendezvous*

"Thompson knows how to write gripping suspense and keep readers enthralled throughout. A great mystery with thrilling intrigue."
—*Fresh Fiction*

"A chilling murder mystery with lots of twists, turns, and unexpected curves . . . one of the best romantic mysteries I have read . . . a great book that you don't want to miss."
—*Romance Junkies*

"A page-turner that will leave you on the edge of your seat . . . another wonderful thriller from Carlene Thompson . . . a must-read."
—*A Romance Review*

"An intriguing tale told in a wonderfully fresh voice. Thompson has a truly unique style that blends beautiful prose with compelling plots . . . this novel reads like lightning—and has the same effect on the reader . . . Thompson has created sharp, smart characters with motives that drive the story along. They are enough to keep the story moving at a quick pace. Her voice has a sense of rhythm and a rustic beauty that lingers in the reader's memory."
—*Romance Divas*

MORE . . .

"An action-filled read with plenty of twists and turns that will keep you guessing until the very end! This story is highly detailed with an array of in-depth characters that are smart, funny, and engaging."

—*Fallen Angel Reviews*

IF SHE SHOULD DIE

"A gripping suspense filled with romance. Ms. Thompson has the reader solving the mystery early in the novel, then changing that opinion every few chapters. [An] excellent novel."

—*Rendezvous Reviews*

"With engaging characters and intriguing motives, Thompson has created a smart, gripping tale of revenge, anger, and obsession."

—*Romantic Times BOOKreviews*

"*If She Should Die* is a riveting whodunit!"

—*The Road to Romance*

"In the tradition of Tami Hoag or Mary Higgins Clark, Thompson has created a gripping page-turner. The storyline is engaging and the characters' lives are multi-dimensional. This is literally a book the reader will be unable to put down."

—*Old Book Barn Gazette*

BLACK FOR REMEMBRANCE

"Loaded with mystery and suspense . . . Mary Higgins Clark fans, take note."

—*Kirkus Reviews*

"Gripped me from the first page and held on through its completely unexpected climax. Lock your doors, make sure there's no one behind you, and pick up *Black for Remembrance*."

—William Katz, author of *Double Wedding*

"Bizarre, terrifying . . . an inventive and forceful psychological thriller."

—*Publishers Weekly*

"Thompson's style is richly bleak, her sense of morality complex . . . Thompson is a mistress of the thriller parvenu."

—*Fear*

SINCE YOU'VE BEEN GONE

"This story will keep readers up well into the night."

—*Huntress Reviews*

DON'T CLOSE YOUR EYES

"*Don't Close Your Eyes* has all the gothic sensibilities of a Victoria Holt novel, combined with the riveting modern suspense of Sharyn McCrumb's *The Hangman's Beautiful Daughter*. Don't close your eyes—and don't miss this one."

—Meagan McKinney, author of *In the Dark*

"An exciting romantic suspense novel that will thrill readers with the subplots of a who-done-it and a legendary resident ghost seen only by children. These themes cleverly tie back to the main story line centering on the relationships between Natalie and Nick, and Natalie and the killer. Carlene Thompson fools the audience into thinking they know the murderer early on in the book. The reviewer suggests finishing this terrific tale in one sitting to ascertain how accurate are the reader's deductive skills in pinpointing the true villain."

—*Midwest Book Review*

IN THE EVENT OF MY DEATH

"[A] blood-chilling . . . tale of vengeance, madness, and murder."

—*Romantic Times*

THE WAY YOU LOOK TONIGHT

"Thompson . . . has crafted a lively, entertaining read . . . skillfully ratchet[ing] up the tension with each successive chapter."

—*Charleston Daily Mail*

LAST SEEN
ALIVE

Carlene Thompson

St. Martin's Paperbacks

LAST SEEN ALIVE

ISBN: 0-312-93731-8
EAN: 978-0-312-93731-7

Printed in the United States of America

St. Martin's Paperbacks edition / June 2007

St. Martin's Paperbacks are published by St. Martin's Press, 175 Fifth Avenue, New York, NY 10010.

10 9 8 7 6 5 4 3 2 1

To my canine and feline family
Who graciously appear in my books

*Thanks to Pamela Ahearn, Jennifer Weis, and
The Mason County Emergency Services*

Special thanks to Beverly Watterson

PROLOGUE

Sixteen-year-old Chyna Greer eased up her bedroom window. Hot July air washed over her face. Behind her, Chyna's best friend, Zoey Simms, squealed, "I can't believe we're doing this!"

"I don't think we *should* be doing this," Chyna said. "If I get caught going to the lake at night—"

Zoey grinned. "Absolutely nothing will happen to you."

"Mom and Dad aren't as laid-back as you think, Zoe."

"Compared to mine, they are. The two weeks I get to spend with you every summer are the only fun I *ever* have."

Chyna rolled her eyes. "You live in Washington, D.C., but your time in little old Black Willow, West Virginia, is the highlight of your year?"

"Getting to come here *is* the most fun I have all year because I'm with you. I'm going home day after tomorrow, so don't be a drag, Chyna."

Chyna looked into Zoey's large velvety brown eyes and sighed. Although Chyna was only a few months older than Zoey, she often felt years older. Sometimes she regretted never having been the ebullient sprite that was Zoey and tried to be less "sensible" all the time, but wishing couldn't change her personality.

Chyna didn't have a good feeling about this trip to Lake

Manicora, but then, Chyna didn't have a good feeling about a lot of things. Her older brother, Ned, always told her to "lighten up" and quit thinking so much. As dearly as she loved Ned, she had no idea how to stop thinking as he apparently did when he got that blank look on his face for days at a time.

Chyna pushed her long dark brown hair behind her ears, stalling. "We're upstairs, Zoe. One of us might fall and break a leg. How will we explain that?"

"Oh, will you chill out?" Zoey huffed. "Sometimes you sound really old, like thirty. Climbing down the rose trellis from the second floor isn't exactly death defying. Geez!"

Zoey was getting angry. She hardly ever got angry, but she'd fallen madly in love eight days ago and since then she'd turned into a mass of swirling emotions. Zoey wouldn't tell Chyna her beloved's name. Chyna thought this was either because Zoey knew Chyna wouldn't approve of the guy or because Zoey thought that secrecy made the romance more exciting. Whatever the reason, Zoey remained adamant about meeting her anonymous Romeo at the lake. "This is a romantic tryst, Chyna," she explained hotly, "and if you won't go with me, I'll go alone!"

Chyna noticed Zoey's false bravado. She was certain Zoey feared going down to the lake alone at night, but Zoey had made a promise to her mystery man and she intended to keep it.

Chyna closed her eyes and took a deep breath. She couldn't turn her back on Zoey. After all, Zoey had been Chyna's closest friend since forever. Their moms were best friends in college, and Zoey was even Chyna's godsister, if there was such a thing. Chyna felt it was her duty to look after Zoey.

"We're only going down the hill, and across the highway," Zoey persisted, her voice taking on that sweet wooing tone most people found hard to resist coming from such a pretty girl.

"But it's late at night and across the highway is Lake Manicora. It's a big place, Zoey."

"You make it sound like one of the Great Lakes."

"It's thirty-two acres."

"Leave it to you to know the exact size," Zoey snapped. "Let's see . . . that would be thirty-two acres of sharks, electric eels, octopuses—"

"Octopi."

"Excuse me. I forgot you *are* a genius."

"I'm not a genius."

"You just have an IQ that's in the stratosphere. There, did I say that right?"

"You're trying to charm me with compliments."

"They don't seem to be working," Zoey said glumly as she twisted a lock of her short sandy blond hair the way she did when she was nervous. She looked frustrated enough to cry. "Look, you're not gonna get caught. Your mom's in bed with a headache, your dad's working late in his study and he never checks on you anyhow, and Ned's in his room listening to music through his headphones. No one will notice we're gone, so are you going with me or do I go alone?" Chyna hesitated. "Okay, I'll go by myself," Zoey announced. "He said to, anyway."

"Who is *he*?"

"I'm not telling, but he's not a pervert or weird. He's romantic and wonderful. He also doesn't have anything in mind like getting in my pants. We'll just talk and maybe kiss, that's *all,* and I'm going!"

"Okay, I'll go," Chyna said reluctantly, realizing Zoey was intractable on this matter. "You knew I would."

"No, I didn't. Honest."

That was one of the many things Chyna had always loved about Zoey—her honesty. She might occasionally sneak around her overprotective parents, for which Chyna couldn't condemn her without condemning herself, too. But Zoey *never* lied to Chyna. They'd made a blood oath when they were five. They'd pricked their fingers with a needle and been horrified when tiny drops of blood popped out, but they'd endured the agony and rubbed their fingers together. They had never broken the oath.

"Well, off we go," Chyna sighed. "Together as always."

"Great!" Zoey almost shouted, then lowered her voice and hugged Chyna. "You're the best friend in the world, Chyna." Zoey drew away, her brown eyes beaming. "Now, you go first."

"Why do *I* have to go first?"

"You're more familiar with the rose trellis than I am."

"Yes, I always use the trellis when I come and go," Chyna replied sarcastically. "It's so much more convenient."

"Just *go*," Zoey said impatiently. "I'm gonna be late."

Chyna gave Zoey a hard look. "When we're old and gray, I want you to remember this, Zoe. I expect a really big favor in return."

"Okay," Zoey replied solemnly. "When we're in the nursing home together, I'll let you sit next to the cutest guy at the dinner table, the one who still has all his teeth."

"After tonight, we probably won't make it to the nursing home together." Later Chyna would remember that prediction with a chill.

Chyna swung her jean-covered leg over the window frame and hung on until she got one running shoe–clad foot placed firmly on a rung of the trellis. If her mother's rambler roses hadn't been decimated by the new gardener, this trip down the trellis would have been impossible.

Still clutching the window frame, Chyna stuck her left foot into a lower triangle of the trellis. Finally, she completely let go of the window frame and grabbed the trellis, which felt surprisingly solid.

"Hurry up!" Zoey hissed.

"Will you give me a chance to make sure I don't fall?"

Zoey subsided as Chyna began her descent, knowing she was driving Zoey crazy with her measured steps. At last, Chyna let go of the trellis and dropped about a foot onto the loamy dirt of the empty flower bed. Zoey looked down at her anxiously. "My turn?"

"Yes, but go slowly and be careful."

Zoey neither went slowly nor was the least bit careful and fell off the trellis, sailing the last seven feet of the trip through the air, arms flailing, before she hit the flower bed.

Chyna rushed to her. "Are you hurt?"

Zoey clambered up and shook off the dirt. "I'm fine." She adjusted her jeans and pale blue top. "Let's get going."

They crossed the front of the house, nearly tiptoeing past the living room and Chyna's father's office, where lights still burned, ran down the driveway and out to the asphalt road leading down the hill to the main highway.

When they'd traveled three minutes in silence, Chyna said, "I don't like this. It isn't a good idea—"

Zoey whirled on her. "Then go back to the house. I can take care of myself!"

"I've already climbed down that darned trellis, and besides, I am *not* leaving you out here alone in the dark meeting some guy you barely know—"

"This guy is not someone I *barely* know."

"You've met him in Black Willow before this trip?"

"Yes, but this time is different. Sometimes you just click with people, you know?"

"No," Chyna said. "I don't know."

"That's because all you think about is that jet pilot. Scott Kendrick. You talk about him constantly. You are *madly* in love with Scott Kendrick."

"I am *not!*" Chyna flared. "That's the silliest thing I ever heard. His mother and Mom are good friends. That's how I know so much about him."

"When he showed up at the Fourth of July barbecue today and said, 'Hi, Chyna,' you turned about five different colors and got choked on your lemonade."

"Zoey, you are so full of it! I've never thought twice about Scott and it wouldn't do me any good if I did, because I'm just a little hick-town teenager and he has about a dozen glamorous girlfriends all over the world and—"

"And you're getting so loud they can probably hear you back at the house," Zoey grumbled. "If you quit harping on me about what a bad idea this is, I'll stop teasing you about Scott."

They stamped on down the road, one in anticipation, one in anger. But anger isn't going to do me any good, Chyna thought. Nothing is going to stop Zoey and I don't want her leaving day after tomorrow mad at me.

The night was hot and languid. Chyna hadn't even noticed the weather last night when they were enjoying the annual Greer Fourth of July barbecue. She'd been having too much fun. Now, trying to calm down, she drew deep breaths of the sweet evening primrose growing amid the locust trees and sassafras on either side of the asphalt road. A few birds chirped in the darkness, but not many. By dawn they'd be going full tilt. The foliage beside Chyna rustled. Zoey jumped and clutched Chyna's arm before a rabbit skittered into the road, then vanished with lightning speed.

Zoey finally broke their silence by asking, "Who do you think will get married first? Me or you?"

The question was so nonchalant after their earlier quarreling, she took Chyna by surprise. Chyna tried to answer with the same offhand tone. "You. Guys don't seem to like me."

"Sure they do!" Zoey said enthusiastically. "It's your looks and your huge brain that scare guys off." Chyna gave her a sideways glance. "You're tall and slender and you're named after an exotic country, which is so cool, and you have that long, thick brown hair and those haunting gray-blue eyes—"

"Haunting?"

"Yeah. They're beautiful but mysterious, like you've got all kinds of secrets behind them. And I guess you do." Chyna looked at her sharply. "I didn't mean it in a bad way," Zoey said quickly. "It's just that ever since you were little, you started getting all those sixth-sense things going on, and they're kind of scary, especially because you're usually right."

Chyna could feel her face reddening even in the dark. Her life had been different for so long, sometimes she was able to forget she wasn't like everyone else. It had been nine years since she'd been out in their cabin cruiser, with her parents and Ned, and they'd traveled down the Ohio River with neighbors who owned a cruiser almost identical to theirs.

The adults had pulled both boats near the bank, keeping them running as they yelled back and forth about where they wanted to go next. None of them had seen seven-year-old Chyna, hot and bored, slip out of her life jacket and go to the edge of the boat to look at the opposite bank where she'd spotted a traveling carnival. Suddenly the neighbors, slightly drunk, had pulled away from the bank, banging into the Greers' boat *The Chyna Sea* and knocking Chyna into the river. Only eleven-year-old Ned had heard her scream and dived in after her. The boat pulled her under it and she opened her eyes in terror to see the razor-sharp propeller slicing through the water only a couple of inches from her face just before she banged her head on the bottom of the boat and everything went dark.

Ned, a remarkable swimmer for his age, became the hero of the day when he surfaced with his unconscious sister in his arms. Chyna hadn't returned to full consciousness for several hours. A week later, Chyna had begun to have flashes of events that would come in the future and of things that had happened in the past, things she could not possibly have learned about by any normal means. Sometimes she even knew what people were thinking while they were saying just the opposite.

The flashes had been vague at first, only slightly more clear than the "tingles" she'd felt before the accident. As she aged, they became stronger, clearer. By the time she was thirteen, she realized she was frightening people. It was then she had begun lying, declaring vociferously that she no longer had "spooky" thoughts. Only occasionally did she slip in front of Zoey, from whom she'd never been able to keep a secret.

"Zoe, you've never mentioned my visions or the voices to anyone else, have you?" Chyna asked, suddenly anxious about what people thought of her.

"No! Oh, I did a long time ago, but not after you made me promise not to tell *anyone,* not even my mom. I'd be thrilled if I had ESP, but I know it bothers you."

"If you really think I have it, why don't you believe my bad feeling about tonight?"

Zoey looked down at the ground. "Because nothing says you're *always* right. Sometimes you get being *careful* mixed up with having a bad vibe." Zoey rushed on. "But that doesn't mean I don't usually listen to you, and I feel superlucky that you're my best friend. You're my lucky charm. That's why I got us these four-leaf-clover necklaces last year." Zoey reached up and touched hers on its delicate gold chain. "Are you wearing yours?"

Chyna pulled hers from beneath the neck of her T-shirt. "I never take it off."

"That means I'll be safe forever. I've got on my four-leaf clover and I'm with the coolest friend anyone ever had."

Chyna blushed but said nothing, not wanting Zoey to know how much the compliment had touched her. Although many people would have said Zoey and Chyna couldn't be more different outwardly, inwardly something linked them that Chyna sensed was stronger than blood. She'd never told Zoey how she felt, but she was certain Zoey knew and felt the same way. What would I do if Zoey ever went away? Chyna thought. What would I do if I never saw her again?

Suddenly Zoey stood on her tiptoes and said excitedly, "There's the lake! The gazebo is right in front of us." She pointed to a fanciful wooden structure sitting on a tiny island in the middle of the lake and approached by a narrow wooden bridge. "I can see him inside, waiting for me! I won't be longer than thirty minutes; I promise." Chyna opened her mouth, but Zoey cut her off. "I won't be out of your sight and I'll be fine. Thanks for coming, Chyna. Hasta la vista!"

"Vaya con Dios," Chyna returned softly, although she really wanted to shout, Please *don't* go!

She stood until she saw Zoey cross the bridge and enter the gazebo. The guy stood up, and they hugged. Chyna watched as they sat down on the bench. The light from the moon on the water wasn't strong enough for her to make out the features of Zoey's heartthrob, but Chyna saw their faces come together. Ah, the passionate kiss, she thought. The "how do we get along without each other when you leave?" feeling that would probably last about a week at most.

You're jealous, Chyna thought. She'd had two dates all summer, unlike Ned, who usually had at least three girlfriends at one time. Always they found out about one another. An explosion of broken hearts ensued, resulting in a barrage of phone calls that set Chyna's parents wild. They would yell at Ned and things would quiet down for a few weeks before the next cycle began. Still, Chyna envied her brother's popularity.

Chyna yawned with such ferocity she thought she might unhinge her jaw. She wished she hadn't already taken her antihistamine pills. On summer evenings, her nose stopped up, her throat tickled, and she sneezed uncontrollably without them, but the medicine always made her sleepy and she'd already been tired from the long day at the barbecue.

Chyna sat down on the grass. After five minutes, her eyelids began to droop. She fought a losing battle with sleep. Soon her head sagged forward and almost instantly she tilted over onto the cool grass, peacefully unconscious.

"Chyna, wake up!" Chyna's nose tickled. Her body ached and she was damp with dew. She opened her eyes wider and looked up to see her mother standing over her as she still lay on the grass beside the road leading down from her house. "Where is Zoey?" Vivian Greer demanded.

Chyna jumped up, instantly alert. The sun, dimmed by mist, rose from the east. It was morning, she realized, ignoring her mother's loud, angry questions. Chyna began yelling for Zoey. Her voice sounded small, lost in the trees and the undergrowth between the house and the lake—the lake where Zoey had been going to meet her boyfriend.

Fear clutched Chyna's heart like an icy hand. Zoey was gone. Gone in the night, gone in the mist.

Even six hours later, when the police, Ned, her parents,

and a dozen friends and volunteers tramped through the woods looking for the girl while the police talked about dragging the lake, Chyna had known with sickening certainty she would never see Zoey again.

CHAPTER ONE

Twelve Years Later

1

Chyna Greer stood on the bank of Lake Manicora. The late October day was gray, the sun almost white, and the lake bank covered with faded, damp leaves brought down by a recent storm. She drew the belt of her black raincoat tighter. "Lake Manicora," she said aloud. "A *manicora*—a being with the head of a woman and a body covered in scales." She sighed. "I don't know who named this lake, but it doesn't seem they were in a cheerful mood that day."

Michelle, sixty pounds of husky dog with yellow Labrador mixed in her lineage, looked like she was frowning in concentration as she gazed up at Chyna. She seemed to absorb the information about the lake's name, then went back to warily studying the cold, dark water.

"Enjoying the day?"

Chyna looked up to see a tall black-haired man approach her. He wore jeans, a brown suede jacket, and a tentative smile. He also limped slightly and leaned on a walking stick. Her heart jumped at the sight of him just as it had done when she was sixteen. "Hey, Chyna, it's me—"

"Scott Kendrick," Chyna supplied quickly, too quickly, she immediately thought.

"Well, I must not have aged so much you didn't recognize me." He smiled, then looked at the dog. "And who's this?"

"Michelle. I got her last year at the pound."

Scott drew toward the dog slowly, stooped down with a slight grunt as he bent his right leg, and put out his hand for her to smell. Chyna immediately noticed healing scratches on his hand and wrist. Michelle sniffed, then licked his hand, and Scott smiled, showing even white teeth against a fading tan. The smile was nice, but it didn't have the rakish quality Chyna remembered from his younger years.

"She's beautiful," Scott said.

"She'd thank you if she could. I was lucky to find her." Chyna scuffed one of her black boots through a pile of sodden, molding leaves. It seemed to her autumn had gained an early grip on the town, although she hadn't been home in October for years.

"Maybe you don't care to talk about your mother right now, but I want you to know I saw her last week," Scott said gently, still petting Michelle absently as if he didn't quite know what to do with himself in this situation. "She looked happy and healthy. In fact, she stopped by the house with a cherry cheesecake. I couldn't believe she remembered my favorite dessert." He finally stood up, all rangy six foot two of him, leaning on the walking stick again. He'd always been slim, but he had the look of someone who'd recently been ill and lost weight. "She was a close friend of Mom's, but she was always especially nice to me, too."

To her surprise, Chyna had not cried one time in the thirty-odd hours since she'd learned of her mother's plunge down the stairs in the Greer home, a fall that had broken her neck. When Chyna had received the call from her brother, Ned, with the news, she'd simply packed a few clothes, stuffed a frightened Michelle in her carrier, taken the first flight out of Albuquerque, New Mexico, for Charleston, West Virginia, then rented a car and driven, arriving in Black Willow at dawn.

"The autopsy showed that Mom had suffered several minor or what they call 'silent' attacks and then a final, fatal attack. That last attack must be what caused her fall down the stairs. I didn't even know she had heart trouble," Chyna said, looking back at the lake, partly to hide the fact that she *wasn't* tearful. "And here I am a medical resident."

"She probably didn't want you to worry about it."

Chyna nodded. "Not even Ned knew Mom was sick. I'm not sure if she was getting treatment. She always avoided seeing doctors. You can imagine how that drove me nuts, because I'm in the medical profession."

"I guess it would." Chyna noticed the shadows and deepened wrinkles around Scott's dark eyes. He didn't look as if he'd been getting much sleep. "But I want you to know how sorry I am."

"Thank you." Chyna thought she sounded formal and insincere, but something inside her refused to let her emotions show, even in her voice. "So what brings you out here on this dreary day?" she asked abruptly, forcing herself to look directly into Scott's beautifully sculpted face and stop acting like a stiff, backward child, which was exactly how she felt.

"I didn't really want to come out. I just needed to think. To be alone."

"Oh." Chyna pulled on Michelle's leash. "Sorry to interrupt you. We'll be on our way—"

"I didn't really mean *alone*," Scott said instantly. "I meant alone from Irma Vogel, who's been helping out ever since I came home."

"I remember her," Chyna said. "When I was a teenager, she worked at our house. General cleaning. A little cooking. I always got the feeling she didn't like me. She left when I was about sixteen." She'd left right after Zoey's disappearance, but Chyna didn't want to refer to that depressing incident.

"It probably wasn't you she didn't like. It was your looks. Irma's no beauty and she's never very friendly to girls who are pretty." Scott smiled, but Chyna kept her face downturned, a bit taken aback by the low-keyed compliment. "I think she's just bounced from job to job all of her adult life. I know she means well, but she empties the ashtray every time I smoke a cigarette, grabs any magazine I lay down for three seconds and puts it in the rack, and tries to feed me every twenty minutes. While she's working, she sings in an indescribably awful voice. She frequently lets me know that she's still single at forty. *And* a virgin. I never know what I'm supposed to say about that last piece of information."

"Immediately propose."

"I guess so, but for some reason, I'm not tempted. I wish I could get rid of her, but I don't want to hurt her feelings. Besides, I guess I have needed *some* help the last few weeks, although not nearly as much as Irma is offering."

"I'm surprised your parents didn't come home when you did," Chyna said.

"They wanted to, but they've been planning this cruise to the Hawaiian Islands for twenty years. They were already three days out in the ocean when I called them about the . . . accident. I told them I didn't want them to come home now and Dad could tell I wasn't just being noble or polite. Frankly, I'd gone over the details with investigators so much, I couldn't bear talking about it anymore for a while, and you know Mom is like a pit bull when she wants information. I think I have Dad to thank for insisting they continue the trip. They'll be home next week, though. Then I'll have to go through a complete description again."

"Oh." Chyna felt absolutely stumped when it came to saying something comforting. After all, what simple words could comfort Scott, who had been piloting a jet that had crashed in Indiana five weeks ago, killing seventy-two people? Her mother had written to her that he'd been cleared of all blame, but he was deeply depressed and thinking of giving up his career as a commercial jet pilot. After over a week in the hospital, he was now on leave, recuperating from the wounds he'd suffered in the crash. "I'm sorry, Scott." Chyna colored, not knowing whether she should bring up the crash or merely leave the disaster unmentioned.

He jammed his left hand in his jacket pocket and stared up at the dismal sky. "I'd planned a trip home soon. I just didn't expect it to be under these circumstances. And the house is depressing. It's more like a museum than a home."

He smiled, but his incredibly dark eyes remained sad. His

gaze used to be confident, just charmingly shy of being cocky. She wondered if it would ever regain that look. The wind picked up a bit, blowing his black hair across his forehead. Chyna hadn't seen Scott for five years, but she spotted wrinkles above his eyebrows and the purple-yellow remains of a bad bruise. He also had a healing laceration down his high right cheekbone and another along his left jawline. Both bore thin Steri-Strips, and Chyna guessed that stitches had been removed recently.

"Do you mind if I walk with you?" he asked. "It might warm us up."

"Good idea. I'm afraid I'd gone into a trance standing here. Michelle is probably bored to death, especially with all these exotic smells around her to explore."

"Exotic? The rotting leaves at Lake Manicora?"

"To her they're exotic. She's used to the desert. Or rather, *looking* at the desert," Chyna said as they started out slowly, like two invalids. "She doesn't like to walk in the sand."

"Do you like New Mexico?" Scott asked.

"Most of the time. Occasionally the heat gets to me, but I'm usually inside in the hospital."

"Ah, that's right. What are you now? First-year resident?"

"Second year."

"And you probably know as much as a third year. Or more." He gave her that pleasant smile that never quite reached his dark eyes. "What do you plan to specialize in?"

"Pediatric oncology."

"Children with cancer? My God, Chyna, you're a lot stronger than I am if you can face that every day."

"I'm not there yet, Scott. I might find out I'm not strong enough, either."

"You will be. I have confidence that you can do whatever you set your considerable mind to." He smiled slightly. "And speaking of children, how are your niece and nephew?"

"Kate and Ian are fine. Ned says they're excited about trick or treat tomorrow night. I'm sure their mom is great at diverting them from dwelling on their grandmother's death. Beverly is a born mother, even though at five and three the kids are really too young to let a death in the family ruin trick-or-treat night anyway."

Michelle began sniffing around Scott's legs, and Chyna glanced down at the object of her curiosity. "That's a beautiful walking stick you have, Scott."

Scott looked slightly chagrined. "I could not stand using a crutch anymore, so I grabbed this at the house." He held it up. "It's one of Mom's antiques."

Chyna looked at the dark hardwood stick with its ivory head and frowned. "I can't quite make out the carving on the ivory."

"It's Henry the Eighth." Scott flipped the stick over. "The Tower of London is carved on the other side of the head. Mom would probably rather I wasn't using it, although right now I can get away with just about anything." He sighed. "It feels good being home, though. I never thought I'd say that about Black Willow, but for once, it's seemed like a haven. I'm afraid I'll never want to leave again."

When Chyna was growing up, she'd felt connected to this place, maybe because her ancestors had lived in or near Black Willow since the mid–nineteenth century. After Zoey disappeared, though, and the police had finally stopped looking for her day and night and even unsuccessfully dragged the lake, Chyna longed to escape this town and never come back.

She'd left a year later for college and been shocked to realize she yearned for the town. She'd tried to suppress the yearning, tried to obliterate it, but she never could. The pull of Black Willow and the pull of the lost Zoey were too strong. Still, Chyna had managed to confine her trips to Christmas. She couldn't bear to look at the lake in the summer when it appeared just as it had the night when Zoey had seemed to walk off the face of the earth.

"You'll want to leave," Chyna told Scott. "If you don't leave, you can't be a commercial pilot."

"That's the problem, Chyna. I'm not sure I want to be a pilot anymore."

"But it's what you've always wanted to do!" Chyna burst out. "You told me that when I was just a teenager."

Scott shrugged. "Time and experience can change you, Chyna."

They had reached the spot on the shore where a wooden bridge used to lead to the gazebo on the tiny man-made island set picturesquely in the lake. At least, Chyna had once thought the gazebo was picturesque. Now it looked shabby, the wood weathered, a shingle dangling off the top of the structure, and fallen leaves blowing through it. Chyna had a feeling she was seeing the true face of the gazebo—bleak, lonely, and shabby. And something beyond those minor failings. Something dangerous and malevolent. Something that laughed in the night when bad things happened.

Chyna couldn't force herself cheerfully to assure Scott that of course he'd want to return to piloting. If she'd had his experience, she'd probably never again want to look at any airplane, particularly a commercial jet. To fill the silence, she gazed at the gazebo and said almost angrily, "That place looks like hell."

Scott nodded. "I agree. That storm we had late Friday night didn't help. It even tore loose the gazebo bridge. Irma, who seems immediately to know everything that happens in this town, tells me the city council is debating on whether to repair the gazebo or tear it down and build a new one."

"They can't possibly be cheap enough to just patch up this one!" Chyna said fervently. "The bridge is barely hanging on and the roof is in bad shape. Good heavens, I can see holes from here and most of the shingles are gone. I'm sure the floor isn't safe."

"I wouldn't want to go in it if they only spring for repair work. I don't think most people would, either, especially those with children. It's always been a big draw to the area, though. Tourists love it and it wouldn't cost a fortune to replace it. I'll bet Ridgeway Construction would do a beautiful job, and *since* they're located in Black Willow, they might even be talked into charging only for materials." For the first time, Scott seemed to brighten a bit. "I think I'll talk to Gage Ridgeway about that. He used to be a friend of your brother's and mine. He'd listen. Now his dad—"

Suddenly Scott glanced at his watch. "I lost track of time. I have an appointment with a rehab therapist. I'll be late if I don't leave right now," he said abruptly, a shadow falling over his face as the memory of the plane crash came back to him. "It was great seeing you, Chyna, even under the circumstances."

"Do you need a ride?" Chyna blurted, then realized that of course Scott hadn't walked to the lake. Her face reddened, but Scott ignored her silly question.

"Thanks, but I'm parked right over here." He pointed to a white sedan. "Old car of Dad's I've been borrowing. I'm sure I'll be seeing you again. Don't stay out too long. It's chilly." He looked down. "Nice meeting you, Michelle. Bye, you two."

Michelle knew the word "bye" and held out her big paw. Smiling, Scott bent slowly and shook it. "You're a doll," he said with some of his old liveliness. In a few minutes, he waved to Chyna as he pulled out of the Lake Manicora parking lot and headed back for town.

2

Chyna thought of the crush she'd once had on Scott, remembering her fantasies about him showing up at the door one day announcing he'd realized she was the love of his life. She sighed. It had never happened, but to her he looked just as he had when he was in his twenties, only older and world-weary. I'm sure I look more world-weary than I did twelve years ago, too, she decided. That's what time did to you.

Unfortunately, time didn't always erase bad memories. I wish I could look at this lake and not immediately think of Zoey, Chyna thought. Zoey with her freckled nose, her bouncy blond hair, her vibrant spirit—they'd all vanished on a warm summer night while Chyna had lain on the grass and slept like the dead. The thought chilled her. *I* slept like the dead while Zoey was probably being murdered.

If I hadn't been sleeping so deeply, Chyna thought guiltily, maybe I could have saved Zoey. Chyna had always believed that when it was too late, Zoey had recognized danger. If she'd been able to call out before the end, maybe Chyna could have gotten to her in time to do *something* to save the girl who'd meant more to her than a sister.

No condemnations from her parents or Zoey's parents for the girls' foolishness or for Chyna's irresponsibility had compared to the guilt with which she'd lashed herself like a whip. She hadn't been the person who'd no doubt killed Zoey, but Chyna couldn't have felt worse if she'd run over the girl with a car or pushed her off a cliff. And Chyna couldn't forgive herself for not listening to her own instinct warning that Zoey was walking into peril that night. For years before Zoey's disappearance Chyna's life had been ruled by her instincts—instincts that had rarely been wrong—but that summer evening she'd let her desire to please Zoey overrule her intuition, and Zoey had paid the price. Not her—not Chyna—but dear little Zoey.

As usual when Chyna let herself think deeply about Zoey, coldness and nausea almost overwhelmed her. I have to stop dwelling on this. My own mother just died, she chastised herself, and all I'm thinking about is Zoey. There are arrangements to be made, dishes of food already being delivered for which I have to make a list so the empty dishes can be returned and thank-you notes written. I haven't even picked out an outfit for Mom to wear for burial. And will the coffin be open or closed? Ned and I really haven't had time to make any decisions.

While Chyna's thoughts whirled, she'd let go of Michelle's leash. The dog made for the edge of the lake, looked at it for a long moment, then took two tentative steps into the cold water. Michelle wasn't fond of swimming, in spite of her part-Labrador background. She took one more step into the water until her paws were covered. Then she stood rock still and the hair along her backbone rose.

"What is it, Michelle?" Chyna asked, going forward to retrieve the leash.

The dog completely ignored her and stared out at the

lake. Michelle had gone rigid and her nose twitched furiously. A dead fish? Chyna wondered. Maybe a dead animal?

"Michelle?" she urged, gently pulling on the leash. "Michie, come with me. Don't be stubborn."

Michelle remained taut, her ears standing up, the hair on her back stiff. Michelle was an obedient dog, violently attached to Chyna, but now Chyna felt as if the golden dog didn't know she existed.

"Michelle?" Chyna drew nearer, even taking a step into the edge of the pond. She didn't mind getting her leather boots wet—they weren't new, anyway. "Michie, what is it?"

And then Chyna heard it. Soft, far away, and blurred, but a singsong voice. "Star light, star bright . . ."

Chyna whipped around, expecting to see a child nearby, but there was no one.

Chyna shook her head. I've gone too long without sleep, she thought. I'm hallucinating.

Then she definitely heard a voice. A familiar voice.

"Chyna? Chyna, it's Zoey."

Chyna felt that if she had hair on *her* back, it would be as stiff as Michelle's. Instead, Chyna's neck tingled as the skin all over her body seemed to tighten.

"Chyna, I'm lost in the dark. Lost and lonely."

Chyna's gaze shot all around the lake. On the other side, a family with two adolescent children walked, the parents talking animatedly, the children looking bored. At the far end, two boys around seventeen sat under one of the picnic shelters, sipping out of cans. In the parking lot, an elderly man walked toward a car. No one else lingered near the lake.

"Chyna?"

"I'm listening," Chyna said, helpless not to answer what sounded like Zoey's voice. "What is it?"

"You're the only one who can help."

Chyna closed her eyes. She was tired. She was filled with sorrow over her mother. She was imagining things. She shook her head as if to clear it. "Come on, Michelle. We have to go back to the house," she said briskly.

"No, no, *listen*," the voice from the lake pleaded, louder, clearer. "You have to find me, because there were other girls like me. There will be more girls like me if you don't do something. Chyna, help me. Help *them*."

"I . . ." Chyna suddenly felt frozen inside. Her hands shook and she could barely breathe. Clutching Michelle's leash, she turned and ran from the lake, the long-lost Zoey's voice still calling after her.

CHAPTER TWO

1

Chyna slammed the front door behind her, locked it, then leaned against the varnished wood as she drew long, ragged breaths. Michelle, also breathing hard, looked up at Chyna and pawed her leg. The dog is as scared as I am, Chyna thought, then decided no one was as scared as *she* was.

She nearly staggered over to one of the wing chairs in the living room and sat down with a grunt. The chairs were elegant. They were also hard as rocks, made for looks, not comfort. But Chyna thought if the chair hadn't been so close, she would have been lying on the floor by now.

Chyna felt her heart pounding in her chest. Okay, you have to calm down, she told herself. This is ridiculous, especially for a woman who's known for her unflappability. Of course, she wasn't as imperturbable as she usually let on, but she was far from nervous, squeamish, or easily frightened. She knew that at the hospital some of the nurses called her Woman of Steel behind her back. She'd never let on that she knew, sort of liking the feeling that colleagues thought she was strong.

Her breath was slowing and so were her thoughts. She closed her eyes again and reviewed recent events. Tuesday evening, before her night shift, she'd taken a nap. After an hour, she'd jerked awake from a dream of being chased through a wooded area. The dream had left her with a thumping headache for which she'd taken aspirin throughout a particularly rough night. She'd been unable to sleep most of the next day, and Wednesday's night shift had been even worse than Tuesday's. When she'd come off-shift, she'd been home only an hour when Ned had called to say their mother—their beautiful mother whom Chyna had adored—was dead.

Stunned, Chyna had called the hospital to cancel the next few days—days she had coming to her for skipped vacations and extra shifts. She'd stuffed clothes in a suitcase, found Michelle's travel cage, and headed for the airport, deciding simply to wait for "standby" on the next flight that would get her near Black Willow.

After hours of pacing the airport terminal, eating a candy bar that tasted like cardboard and pretending to read instead of staring at fellow travelers, she'd boarded a flight, then endured a long layover and a change of planes before reaching Charleston, West Virginia. On both flights, she'd settled in her seat and found out that although she was exhausted, she couldn't sleep even with the help of a vodka tonic to calm her nerves. The same was true when she reached the Greers' beautiful stone house atop the hill overlooking Lake Manicora.

By then, she'd managed to drift into a brief, dream-torn nap. When she awakened stiff and fuzzy-minded, she'd decided to take a walk, and even though she hadn't planned it, she'd ended up at the lake, the last place she'd ever seen Zoey. That was smart, Chyna, she thought. That was damned brilliant. No wonder you imagined you were hearing her voice.

Hearing *Zoey's* voice. Chyna had heard voices before, but they were barely above whispers. "Don't do this." "Pick that one." Phrases that when she was young she'd thought of as coming from a guardian angel. *Never* had Chyna heard a familiar voice. *Never* had she heard someone call her name and beg her to listen. The accumulation of events had thrown her imagination into overdrive, she decided. That's why she thought she'd heard Zoey beseeching for her help.

But I didn't imagine the way Michelle went rigid and the hair on her back stood up, Chyna reminded herself with a dull, inexorable fear that no amount of levelheaded reasoning could banish. The dog had been terrified down at the lake.

Michelle was not an aggressive dog, but she wasn't timid, either. She wouldn't have frozen at the sight of another dog or of a duck on the lake, even if there had been any other animal life around except a chipmunk or a squirrel Chyna hadn't spotted. And Michelle wouldn't have stood rooted with her paws in the cold water while Chyna pulled on her leash. The least tug had always immediately brought her to Chyna's side. But today Michelle had refused to move. And when Chyna had "thought" she was hearing Zoey's voice, Michelle's ears had lifted stiffly, just as they did when she was listening with special intensity.

The phone rang and Chyna literally leaped from her chair. Michelle cringed, bracing herself for flight, when Chyna rolled her eyes and said, "Just the phone, girl. At this rate, between the two of us, we should be dead by sunset from pure nerves."

Chyna crossed the tapestry rug covering a pale cream-colored carpet and picked up the phone. "Greer, here."

"Well, hello, Greer." The voice was light and feminine.

Chyna relaxed. Beverly, her sister-in-law. "Sorry, Bev. I answer to 'Greer' at least a hundred times a day at the hospital. Sometimes I forget I have a first name."

"Well, you do, and it's beautiful, so get used to being Chyna again for a few days. You got here so quickly you must be exhausted."

I'm exhausted to the point of losing my mind, Chyna almost said, then forced a bit of liveliness into her voice. "I'm tired, but I'm used to long hours. Michelle and I just got back from a walk along the lake. We ran into Scott Kendrick."

"Really?" Beverly sounded surprised. "I thought he hardly ever left the house. How did he seem?"

"Physically, recovering nicely. Emotionally? Trying hard to pull himself together and maybe not doing so well." She wished she hadn't mentioned seeing Scott, feeling as if discussing his mental state even with Beverly was a betrayal of him. "How are my niece and nephew?" she asked abruptly.

"A handful, but healthy, so I should count my blessings instead of my gray hairs, right?"

"On my last visit, I didn't see one gray hair," Chyna teased. "You looked as young as you did the day you got married."

But I don't know about me, Chyna thought. She glanced at herself in the gold-framed mirror over the marble mantle and decided she looked bedraggled, dry-skinned, sunken-eyed, and at least ten years older than she had two days ago.

Beverly took a breath, then said compassionately, "I'm sorry about Vivian, Chyna. I know how much you loved her."

"I just can't believe Mom had a heart condition I didn't know about," Chyna burst out. "I mean, that's a hell of a thing to hide from your daughter, especially when she's a doctor."

"Vivian didn't tell anyone," Beverly said soothingly. "I think she'd probably been seeing a doctor out of town. About six months ago when I was at her house, I saw an appointment card from a doctor on her desk."

"Do you remember the name of the doctor?"

"Not right off the bat, but it will probably come to me. I'm fairly certain the card gave a Huntington address, although I didn't really get a good look at it because Vivian walked in and started talking so fast I could hardly keep up with her. Now I'm sure she was trying to divert my attention from the card. I feel bad for not mentioning it earlier, but it didn't seem important at the time." Beverly sighed. "Anyway, there was nothing you could have done about her health even if you'd known she had heart trouble."

"I could have arranged for her to see some of the *best* cardiologists in the country." Chyna paused and swallowed. "And I certainly could have come to see her more often. She was seriously ill and I stayed away because . . ."

"Because of Zoey. I know. Your mother knew, too. She didn't blame you."

"For what? Not coming home often? Or for Zoey's disappearance?"

"She didn't blame you for either one." Beverly must have heard the tears gathering in Chyna's voice, because she said, "I think you need some rest right now. Drink one of those herbal teas that are supposed to be relaxing and get a couple of hours' sleep. Ned and I are getting a babysitter tonight. We thought we'd come over about seven so you don't have to stay up late with us. I hate to intrude on you when you're so tired and upset, but we have to talk over funeral arrangements. We'll make it as quick as possible."

Chyna closed her eyes in dread. She didn't think she could make even one suggestion about funeral arrangements, but she couldn't shove off everything on Ned, either. "All right, Bev. I'll see you around seven."

"Want us to bring you some food?"

"No, there's plenty of stuff in the kitchen. Obviously Mom wasn't expecting something to happen, and she must have been to the grocery store day before yesterday." Chyna felt her throat beginning to close with trapped tears. "If you'll just stop by a convenience store and pick up a bag of Gravy Train for Michelle, I'll be forever grateful."

"Gravy Train it is, then. Turn on the TV or some music. It sounds quiet as the grave over there." Beverly caught herself. "Oh, that was awful! I just meant—"

"I know what you meant and music would cheer up the place. Mom always kept on the television, or she listened to music. This silence is creepy."

"I'm sure it is. We'll be there as soon as possible, Chyna."

The grandfather clock in the hall chimed five times. Five o'clock. Chyna wondered how she was going to keep herself occupied until her brother and his wife came to this house she'd always loved, especially when she was in it alone and could pretend it belonged to her?

Chyna stood and walked over to the portrait of her parents, Vivian and Edward Greer. The portrait had been done nine years ago. Vivian sat on a velvet chair, her mahogany-colored hair—just like Chyna's—touching her shoulders and gleaming with gold and red highlights pouring in from the window behind her. The artist had really done an excellent job of capturing Vivian's hair, Chyna thought, although in real life Vivian had usually pinned her hair into a casual French twist, never visiting the beauty shop more than a couple of times a year for a trim. Her gray-blue eyes, also like Chyna's, gazed from the portrait with a hint of amusement, as if saying, "Isn't it silly for Edward and me to be posing here like royalty?" She wore a simple grayish blue dress that exactly matched her eyes, an eighteen-inch string of Tahitian pearls, and small pearl earrings.

Vivian's left hand reached up to touch her husband's draped over the back of the chair and showed her antique engagement ring, a three-carat center diamond with four small sapphires placed in platinum filigree on either side of the reigning gem. Chyna had always loved the ring and her mother had told her how Great-grandfather Greer had bought it at Cartier's, the first of the great jewelry houses to use platinum in jewelry. "Someday this will be yours, Chyna," Vivian would say as the child held it in place on the ring finger of her own left hand. "I'm sure your husband will pick out something for you, but you must tell him kindly but firmly that *this* will be your engagement ring. If he balks at your wearing a ring he didn't pick out, just remind him that he doesn't have to pay for one. That should settle the matter," she'd laughed.

Even at eight, Chyna was certain her mother knew everything and she began preparing herself for her future beloved to balk—maybe even have a temper fit and shout like Uncle Rex did sometimes—but she knew she would hold firm on the issue of the ring because that was what her mother had told her to do. Besides, she knew she could never like another ring better than this one.

In the portrait, her father stood tall and handsome with his prematurely silver hair, his strong jaw, slightly aquiline nose, dark blue eyes, and kind smile. Chyna had loved her father's smile, although there had been a trace of seriousness in it, even when he laughed. He was soft-spoken, dignified, and beautifully mannered—the perfect bank president. He never looked mischievous like Vivian or his younger brother, Rex. But then, Edward rarely looked angry or even annoyed, either, while Vivian and Rex were quick-tempered and moody. Chyna had always thought of her mother and Rex as the ocean churning up for a storm, and her father as a cool, gentle wave rolling gently onto a beach at night.

Edward Greer had died only three years after this portrait was painted. Chyna had been crushed, unable to stop dwelling on how handsome yet solemn her father had looked at Ned's wedding just two weeks before his death. He'd smiled at the reception, said all the right things, acted happy for his son, but Chyna had known something was troubling him. Her "second sight" hadn't helped her at all, though. She knew her father loved her, but she'd always felt that he held her at a distance, so when finally she'd asked him what was wrong she wasn't surprised when he'd kindly but firmly brushed aside her questions.

After he died, though, when she'd tried to talk to people who might tell her what was bothering him, they would answer abruptly, "Chyna, don't make your father's death more upsetting than it already is for your mother." Yet her mother, as usual, had been rock, and she and Edward's brother, Rex, had gotten everyone through the tragedy with as little interruption to Chyna's young life and Ned's new marriage as possible. Although to Chyna's knowledge her mother had never had so much as one date after Edward's death, she had expected Vivian to outlive her husband by a long time, even to see Ned's children grown and married.

Chyna stepped away from the painting, gazing at it as if she'd never seen it before. Had her father's blue eyes always held that trace of sadness? Or was it longing? He'd been a quiet man, calm, even-tempered, and self-contained although somehow assuring both his children of his love for them without being outwardly affectionate. He seemed the exact opposite of his younger brother, Rex, who was upbeat, expansive, funny, charming, and still a handsome ladies' man at fifty-four. Rex had been married four times, but Chyna had never met the wives. He always seemed to be divorced at Christmas when they were both in Black Willow. Chyna suddenly felt as if she knew Rex, but she'd never really known her father. Because Edward was so taciturn, so private, her only chance of really knowing him had died with her mother, a mother who'd kept secrets about something as serious as her own impending death. And now both were gone and at twenty-eight Chyna suddenly felt as bereft and alone as a little orphan who'd never known her parents at all.

2

Fifteen minutes later, after Chyna had dragged herself away from the portrait and put on music to give the empty house some life, her stomach growled loudly and she realized how hungry she was. She hadn't eaten anything except the tasteless candy bar since yesterday morning. She walked into the huge kitchen with oak countertops and walls painted a bright coral. In the spring and summer, windows all around offered a beautiful vista of a giant terrace with a modest fountain and a plethora of flowers in every color. Right now, the terrace looked bleak with dying leaves lying everywhere, including in the fountain, which clearly needed a good cleaning. Chyna knew her mother always had the place sparkling by holiday time, but apparently her handymen hadn't yet begun their autumn duties.

Chyna opened the big chrome refrigerator and studied the contents. Yes, Vivian had definitely gone to the store within the last two days. Every shelf was packed and Chyna knew local people would be taking the usual food offerings after a death in the family to Ned's house because they hadn't known when she would arrive home. Chyna wondered if her mother had planned a small gathering. She even spotted chocolate and coconut for her mother's specialty—German chocolate cake.

Chyna's gaze kept returning to the two T-bone steaks on the second shelf. She pulled out one for herself, then looked down at Michelle—Michelle her loyal dog who she told herself loved her beyond measure and would fight to the death for her. At least that's what Michelle's expression seemed to be saying. Chyna pulled out a second T-bone. "Phooey on Gravy Train," she said to the dog, who immediately stood up, tail flying. "My girl deserves the best!"

Chyna rummaged through the refrigerator until she found a container of macaroni salad from the deli her mother loved—an untouched container—and in the freezer a package of baby peas and a loaf of French bread from the bakery. The date tab told Chyna the bread was very fresh, which meant Vivian had bought it the same day she bought the steaks. All this food meant that she had planned on having a guest to dinner. Only one person, though, or there would have been more steaks. But whom had Vivian invited?

Soon Michelle was wolfing down her broiled T-bone and Chyna was almost keeping pace with her. Chyna then fixed the coffeemaker and turned it on. In minutes, the fragrance of a gourmet blend floated through the kitchen. She knew she'd be making another pot before Ned and Beverly arrived. Sipping the first steaming cup, Chyna looked over at the messy kitchen and thought, I haven't enjoyed a meal this much for weeks. What's wrong with me? How can I be so sad and so hungry, too?

Soon after Chyna cleaned up the kitchen and put on a second pot of coffee, the doorbell rang. When she opened the door, Beverly and Ned stood on the front porch holding a twenty-pound bag of Gravy Train. "Since when do you ring the bell instead of walking right on in?" Chyna asked Ned.

"We didn't want to startle you," Beverly said.

"*She* didn't want to startle you," Ned retorted, seeming annoyed with his wife. "I knew you wouldn't faint if we walked in and called your name."

Chyna smiled at Beverly. "The house does seem empty and strange tonight without Mom here. I think ringing the bell was considerate of you."

"Thank you," Beverly said. "Did you hear that, Ned?"

"Yes, dear," he called sweetly. "I'm not deaf."

Chyna helped Bev out of her navy blue trench coat. Beneath it, she wore neatly tailored jeans and a delicate lavender sweater set. Her short, pale blond hair fell in flattering layers and her makeup blended perfectly with her outfit. Chyna was always amazed at how Beverly could put in a mind-rattling, body-draining day with two youngsters and always manage to look like she'd just showered, dressed, and completely redone her face and hair.

"I'll take this to the kitchen," Ned said, indicating the bag of dog food. "I'll bet Michelle is starved."

"Uh, not really," Chyna said. "I fixed her a steak."

"A *steak*!" Ned burst out. "And I got some awful tuna casserole a friend of Mom's made and brought to the house?"

Chyna smiled. "You'll live. Besides, Michelle deserves it. You didn't spend hours in a cage in the baggage compartments of two planes."

"No, I didn't, but a *steak*!"

Beverly shook her head. "You'd think he'd never had a steak in his life." She paused and studied Chyna closely with her big, brown eyes. "You look exhausted, honey."

"I'm okay."

"You always say that."

"All right, I know I look awful. I'm tired and, most of all, shocked." She wrinkled her forehead. "Mom was only fifty-two, Bev. She had so much energy and just plain joie de vivre, I was certain she'd live to be at least ninety."

"She told me once she was aiming for one hundred," Beverly said, "and then she wanted to have, in her words, 'one hell of a party.'"

"I know. And I *so* wish she could have." As Ned carried the dog food into the kitchen, Chyna whispered to Beverly, "How's he doing? And why is he favoring his right leg?"

Beverly closed her eyes briefly. "Last week he tripped over a water hose at the dealership, fell down, and pulled a muscle in his thigh. It didn't seem too bad at first, but we've been gone for three days to my sister's wedding in Pennsylvania and I could tell it was just killing him. He refused to see a doctor, of course."

"He should. He might have pulled a tendon or ligament."

Beverly nodded. "I know, but he's as stubborn as your mother. As for his mood, all I can say is that he seems okay today, but yesterday was awful for him." Her eyes filled with tears. "He dropped by to see your mother after we got back from Pennsylvania. The next morning he said he had a funny feeling about her and he was going to come by again and check on her. He absolutely wouldn't just call. He said he had to see her. Isn't that strange? It's the kind of thing the family has told me you used to do. Get weird feelings."

"That was a *long* time ago," Chyna said sharply, then, seeing the startled look on Bev's face, softened her tone. "It was a phase I went through as a child. An embarrassing phase."

"Oh, you shouldn't be embarrassed. Kids go through a hundred phases," Beverly said dismissively.

"Yeah. So go on about Mom."

"Well, Ned wasn't supposed to stay long," Beverly continued in a quick, low voice, obviously trying to tell her story before Ned returned. "He'd arranged to take an extra day off to help me unpack and maybe go on a picnic together—you know he hardly ever takes a vacation. Anyway, when he didn't come home after almost two hours, I called. Ned answered and told me he'd found Vivian dead at the foot of the stairs. I said I'd be right over, but he said no, he was handling everything. The Emergency Service was here and so was the coroner." Beverly closed her eyes and almost shuddered. "Chyna, his voice was so weird. It was flat and almost robotic. I was shocked about your mother, but at that moment I was more scared for him, for what kind of emotional state he was experiencing.

"Kate was in kindergarten and I took Ian to a neighbor's," Beverly went on. "Ned finally came home and moved around like an automaton all day. He livened up when the kids came home, but it was an act. Tonight he's grumpy. He doesn't talk about your mother at all. He only says he's irritable because his leg hurts." She shook her head. "I don't know what to do for him."

Ned entered the room, favoring his right leg. He gave his sister a tight smile. "I can tell Michelle had a steak for dinner. She literally turned up her nose at the Gravy Train."

"It'll look better to her tomorrow when she's hungry again," Chyna said. "But a dog can't live on Gravy Train alone. An occasional bite of people food won't kill her."

"A whole steak is a bite?"

"Oh, quit griping," Chyna said lightly. Beverly was right. Ned looked thin-lipped and pale, his posture stiffer than usual. Chyna's instinct was to make him relax. "Well, we're all standing around like we're in someone else's house. Sit down. I made fresh coffee."

Ten minutes later, they sat in the familiar living room, coffee cooling in china cups. Ned's blond hair was cut slightly shorter than usual, probably because of the wedding he'd recently attended, but his blue eyes were as bright as ever, although they lacked their usual twinkle.

"Ned, Beverly said you came over here the morning you found Mom because you had a bad feeling about her," Chyna burst out, surprising herself. "You knew she was sick and you didn't tell me!"

"I did not know she was sick." Ned looked at his hands. "I mean, I didn't know she had heart trouble. When I saw her the day before, she just didn't look or act quite like herself. Frankly, I thought something was bothering her mentally, emotionally, not physically. I thought there was something wrong in *your* life she wasn't telling me and I couldn't get hold of you, so I came back the next day and . . ." Tears rose in his bright blue eyes.

"Oh." Chyna felt ashamed of herself for attacking her brother. "No, I've been fine."

"Well, I know now the problem wasn't you and I'm relieved. I worry about my little sister being so far away," Ned said with surprising kindness as he blinked back the tears.

"I'm sorry, Ned. I . . ."

With a quick sweep of his hand, he waved off her apology.

"We're all on edge. This has been a terrible shock, but here we sit stiff as strangers. No one wants to, but we have to deal with this."

Chyna nodded. "I guess no one knows how to sensitively broach the subject of Mom's funeral, so we might as well just be direct. Shall we hold her service at the church or the funeral home?"

Ned looked at her in surprise. "Mom wanted to be cremated and to have *no* service."

Chyna blinked, then shook her head. "No, she didn't. Oh, I know she mentioned cremation sometimes, but no service? She never said anything about not wanting a service."

Beverly, sitting next to Ned on the couch, reached over and pulled an envelope from her purse. "Actually, she did. She wrote these directions for her burial arrangements about two months ago, Chyna. She even had them notarized. We were startled when she gave them to us, but she just laughed and said, 'You never know when something might happen.'" Bev paused. "The directions are very explicit."

"But she didn't say anything to me!" Chyna realized her voice had risen. She sounded like a little girl who'd been left out of a secret. She lowered her tone a bit. "I mean, it seems she would have said *something*."

"I know. I assumed she had." Beverly handed Chyna the envelope. "But you can read these papers for yourself if you have any doubts."

"I don't doubt you." Chyna took the envelope with a slightly shaky hand. "I'm just startled. And baffled."

Ned nodded. "I was, too, but when she told us what she wanted and gave us that document, she said, 'I *really* don't want a funeral. I want to be cremated and I don't want a service. Just a little notice in the paper, maybe, but *no* service. Promise me.'" Ned looked at Chyna. "And we did. But we didn't rush to the phone to call you because you were really busy during that time and we didn't want to bother you over something we thought she'd either change her mind about or that wouldn't be an issue for at least twenty years."

Chyna stared at the envelope, but she didn't remove its

contents. She didn't want to think about her mother giving instructions for her funeral, or lack of it, much less look at them written in her mother's handwriting. "She knew then she was going to die soon and she didn't say a word. That hurts."

Ned nodded. "I understand. But you weren't the only one left out, Chyna. *I* didn't know she was sick, either, and I still don't believe she thought she was going to die any time soon, even if she had heart trouble and didn't tell us about it." He sighed. "I also believed even if she didn't change her mind about cremation, she'd decide to have her urn buried next to Dad's grave."

"She didn't want the urn buried next to Dad?" Chyna asked in shock.

"She said she wanted you to keep it."

"Me!" Chyna uttered shrilly. "Well, that's just ridiculous! Maybe she didn't want to be buried, but you live here, her home. She hated Albuquerque!"

"I don't believe she was thinking of the local sightseeing," Ned said with a trace of his old humor. "Besides, you were always her favorite."

Chyna nearly shouted, "I *wasn't*!"

"You *were* and it's all right, Sis. It never bothered me once I got past age seven." Ned smiled at her. "Besides, things get pretty rough-and-tumble at our house. Maybe Mom was just afraid the urn would get turned over and her ashes spilled all over the carpet."

"Oh, Ned, that's dreadful!" Beverly exclaimed.

"Well, it's a definite possibility," he insisted, although Chyna knew he wasn't serious.

For the next half an hour they talked about when the family attorney had told them the will would be read, when Chyna would return to New Mexico, what they would do with this house and the property.

By nine-thirty Ned and Beverly said they'd promised to be home by ten to release the babysitter and bade Chyna tired good-byes. Beverly hugged and kissed her, and both Ned and Beverly asked if she wanted to spend the night in the house alone. "You could stay with us if you think you'll be lonely," Bev said, although Chyna knew she had meant scared instead of lonely. Ned had once confided to Chyna that spending a night alone was one of Beverly's greatest fears.

"I won't be lonely," Chyna reassured her. "I have Michelle with me, remember? And she's always my only roommate in New Mexico."

"I'll bet," Ned leered.

"Ned Greer, you keep your salacious thoughts to yourself!" Beverly chastised, pushing him out the door. "Honestly, Chyna, he's terrible!"

"You don't think a woman who looks like Chyna studies *all* the time, do you?"

Chyna smiled with relief that her brother seemed to be acting more naturally. She watched fondly as the couple walked to their car, still quarreling yet holding hands the whole way. Beverly, four years younger than Ned, had drooled over him hopelessly for years. Then one day, blinders seemed to drop from Ned's eyes and he discovered the pretty blonde. They'd been together ever since and seemed to have as close to a perfect union as marriage could get. Chyna envied them, but she didn't see the same kind of relationship ahead for herself—another of those certainties she hated but couldn't shake. She knew her own life would never be like Ned's.

Chyna watched the red taillights of Ned's car crawl down the asphalt drive to the main road running beside Lake Manicora. Then she gathered up the coffee cups and saucers, carried them to the kitchen, and rinsed them before she put them in the dishwasher. The strain and lack of sleep she'd suffered the last two days caught up with her and she finally felt tired enough to fall on the floor. She turned on the dishwasher and had her hand on the kitchen light switch, wishing she didn't have to climb all those stairs to her bedroom on the second floor, when the phone rang.

She groaned, but habit would not allow her to ignore the call. She automatically hurried to the phone on the kitchen counter and glanced at Caller ID. No number was listed—simply the words "Unknown Name." Chyna was mildly puzzled and hoped this wasn't a sympathy call as she picked up the receiver. "Greer here." She caught herself. "I mean, hello."

The sound of wind blowing in the distance seemed to tingle against her ear for a moment. Long ago, that sound wasn't unusual for a long-distance call, but this was the twenty-first century. Calls hadn't made that sound for over fifty years. "Hello?" she said again.

The sound grew louder. Chyna glanced at the window, wondering if she really was hearing wind, only coming from *her* end of the connection. The tree limbs she saw through the kitchen windows, though, remained perfectly still. After one more attempt at a greeting, Chyna was ready to hang up when a faraway voice asked, "Zoey?"

Chyna went completely still. Her hand clamped on the receiver. "Zoey?" A female voice was clearer this time, but still sounded unlike a voice on a modern phone.

A joke, Chyna thought. Someone was playing a cruel joke on her at night, thinking they could rattle her nerves. After all, there were still people in this town who thought she'd had something to do with Zoey Simms's disappearance.

"This is Chyna Greer," she said in a loud, firm tone, trying to sound as though she wasn't frightened. "No one by the name of Zoey lives at this number."

"Zoey?" This time the voice was even clearer. And familiar. "Zoey, darling, is that you? It's Mom!"

Chyna's hand began to shake. Caller ID had said " Unknown Name," but the woman sounded exactly like Anita Simms, Zoey's mother, whose voice Chyna would never forget even if the woman had refused to see or speak to the family after Zoey's disappearance. "Mrs. Simms?" Chyna asked, then could have kicked herself. If someone was playing a joke, she was giving them their money's worth.

"Chyna? Is that you, honey? My, you sound so grown up!" Chyna's mind spun back twelve years to the last time

she'd talked to Anita Simms on the phone. She'd said that
very thing: "My, you sound so grown-up!"

"I . . . Mrs. Simms?"

"Yes, Chyna." Chyna stiffened as she heard Anita Simms'
tinkling laughter that had sounded just like her daughter's.
"Are you girls having a good time this visit?"

A chill ran down Chyna's spine and her hand stiffened on
the receiver. Michelle sat vigilantly at her feet. Once again,
the hair on the dog's back was raised, her ears perked to attention.

All right, calm down, Chyna thought. There's something
wrong with Mrs. Simms. She'd refused to talk to the Greers
for twelve years. Anything could have happened to her. They
did know she'd suffered a nervous breakdown after Zoey
disappeared. Maybe she was having another one. Did she
believe it was twelve years ago and her daughter was here?

"Mrs. Simms, if this really *is* Mrs. Simms—"

Again that all-too-familiar laugh. "Bubble Gum?" Chyna's
old nickname from when she was four and had gotten bubble
gum so badly tangled in her hair, it had to be cut short. "Bubble Gum, of course it's Anita Simms. What kind of game are
you girls playing?"

"No . . . we're not playing a game. I just don't understand
why you're calling."

*Asking for your daughter who's probably been dead for
twelve years.*

"I think you *are* playing a game, Chyna." Still good humor in the voice, but the laughter was gone. "Is my daughter
nearby?"

"Zoey?"

"I only have one child!" A bit of laughter. Then a pause.
Next Anita spoke in a voice edged with suspicion. "Chyna,
Zoey *is* there with you, isn't she? You're not covering for
her, are you?"

"Covering?"

"She hasn't gone out late at night to meet some boy, has
she?" The voice was beginning to grow fainter, the sound of
wind coming back. "I strictly forbade her to do any single dat-

ing on this trip. A double date with you and your boyfriend was allowed, as long as you were home at a decent hour, but no going out *alone.* You don't know what might happen to a young girl going out at night alone. I've told her that a hundred times. There are dangers young innocent girls like Zoey have never thought of, but I'm sure *you* know better. Chyna, you know I count on you to look out for my little girl when she's visiting you. . . ."

By now Chyna's entire body felt like a column of ice and she couldn't hide the shaking of her voice. "Mrs. Simms . . ."

"Where is Zoey?" The voice grew alarmed just as the windy sound grew louder. "Chyna, has something happened to her?"

Chyna stood with her dry mouth slightly open. The room started to spin as the voice on the other end of the line cried in hysteria over the wind, "Chyna, where is my little girl? Something's wrong; I know it! Oh God, where *is* she?"

The line went dead.

Chyna closed her eyes. Then, slowly, she nearly pried her hand from the receiver and hung up the phone. She turned and, placing her back against the wall for support, sank to a sitting position on the floor. Michelle, only a step away from Chyna, placed a big blond paw on her thigh and licked her face.

"It's all right, Michie," Chyna said. "It's all . . ." She fell silent, then began to vibrate all over. It was not all right. Nothing about that call was right.

3

Chyna sat on the cool vinyl floor for what seemed an endless time until finally she felt she'd calmed down enough to stand. She put her hand on the dog's strong back, using the strength of her legs and a bit of the dog's steady weight to raise herself to a standing position.

All right, what do I do now? Chyna thought. Call the police and tell them Zoey Simms's mother had just called asking for her daughter who'd been missing for twelve years? They'd think she was drunk. Or nuts. She already knew many of the local law enforcement officers thought she'd had something to do with Zoey's disappearance and maybe her probable death.

Ned. She'd call Ned. He was the only family she had left, and he'd never laughed at her, even when she was a little girl claiming to know things from the past, have premonitions, even occasionally read minds. He'd always taken her seriously, even when she'd lied and told him she never had "visions" anymore, a lie she'd never retracted.

She dialed Ned's number and was relieved when he picked up, obviously reading the number on Caller ID. "Hey, Sis," he said teasingly before she'd uttered a word, "I'm not gone half an hour and you can't wait to hear my voice again."

"Something happened—" Chyna burst into tears.

Immediately Ned's voice turned serious. "Sis, what is it?"

"N-Ned, I'm scared."

"I was afraid you might be, there in the house all alone."

"That's not it." She grabbed a tissue from a nearby box and wiped her wet face. "Ned, Anita Simms just called here asking for Zoey."

Ned went silent for a moment. Then he said with forced calm, "Chyna, someone was playing a bad joke on you."

"That's what I thought, too, but the Caller ID read: 'Unknown' and the woman called me Bubble Gum and there was this sound of wind blowing in the background and then she got hysterical and . . ." Chyna drew a deep breath. "Ned, did anyone let Anita know Mom just died? Has Anita had another breakdown? She sounded so weird. . . ."

After a moment, Ned said, "Chyna, I think you're really tired or, like I said, someone is playing a joke—"

"I'm not that tired and it wasn't a joke!" she snapped, torn between frustration and fright. "Ned, I remember Anita Simms's voice. Her laugh. It was just like Zoey's. And she knew my nickname and . . ." She drew a deep breath. "Ned, I know you. You're keeping something from me. What is it?"

After about three beats of silence, Ned said gently, "Chyna, it *couldn't* have been Anita Simms on the phone. Mom and I didn't want to tell you because we knew you'd blame yourself, but Anita couldn't accept that Zoey was gone. She kept having breakdowns."

"So she's had another one and thinks Zoey is alive? Has she called before? Recently?"

"No, Sis." She heard Ned draw a deep breath. "Last year Anita's sister finally called Mom, but it was to tell her that Anita had another breakdown, only this time she slit her wrists. They found her too late. . . ."

Chyna's hand began to shake violently. "No, it couldn't have been too late. There was a mistake. Ned, she *called* me—"

"No, she didn't," Ned said firmly. "There was no mistake—Mom went to Anita's funeral in Washington last year without ever telling you." His tone softened. "I'm sorry, Chyna, but Anita Simms is dead."

CHAPTER THREE

1

Chyna jerked awake, bitterly cold although she lay under a down comforter. She'd even pulled it over her head. She struggled out of the tangle of silky sheets, the comforter, and a duvet that had come unfastened. After she'd crawled from the nest she'd made for herself, Chyna went to the window and looked at the day. Sun. She could actually see the sun trying to pierce through gunmetal gray clouds. Thank God, she thought. She didn't believe she could have endured another day as desolate as yesterday.

And she certainly couldn't endure another phone call like the one from Anita Simms.

Except the call couldn't have come from Anita Simms. If Chyna hadn't drunk two glasses of brandy, she would never have relaxed enough to go to sleep. This bright morning, it seemed easier for her to believe the whole thing had been a macabre joke and she would expose the prankster by looking at the numbers from which the Greers had received calls yesterday. If she hadn't been so shaken, she would have thought to do so last night. Instead, she'd checked locks on all the doors and windows and turned to booze, she thought. Her father would have disapproved. Her uncle Rex would have probably emptied the decanter and become boisterous, telling jokes, making her laugh in spite of everything. She certainly wished he had been able to get here yesterday.

Still, she'd finally slept deeply and felt normal, or as close to normal as she could under the circumstances. Thank goodness, she thought. She had a lot to do today. She couldn't wallow in the fear struck deep into her by someone's cruel prank.

Michelle thundered down the stairs behind her toward the kitchen, obviously deciding she was starving. Chyna fixed coffee and cinnamon toast for herself, and, unusually hungry just like last night, she felt like she couldn't get everything down fast enough. Michelle was another matter. She looked at her bowl of Gravy Train with disdain, then stepped away from it and stared up at her mistress with an expression Chyna could only interpret as insult.

"You can't have T-bone steak *every* day," Chyna told the dog. "Just eat this now, and I'll get something you like better for dinner. Deal?"

Michelle took three sips from her water bowl, gave Chyna one last reproachful glance, and walked out of the kitchen with stiff dignity. Her behavior and posture were so much like Vivian Greer's would have been, Chyna was torn between laughter and tears. "Mom might not have been a dog lover, but she would have liked *you*," Chyna called to a sullen Michelle.

Chyna guiltily fixed two more pieces of toast, wondering what had triggered her voracious appetite of the last two days, then decided to check out the telephone as she should have done last night. She picked up the handset and scrolled back to see the latest calls made to the number.

The last number recorded was Ned's. Chyna frowned, thinking. Had Ned or Beverly called her back after her hysterical call to them last night? No. Ned had talked to her for about twenty minutes, trying to calm her down, urging her to let him pick her up to stay with them, but when she'd refused, pretending to be getting herself under control, he'd given up and said good night. She'd then drunk the brandy and gone to bed.

The secret of the caller's identity must lie in the next

number. Chyna's heart hammered, both because she wanted to know who'd called and because she didn't want to think that someone out there was trying to frighten her. But if she had an enemy, even a harmless one who took pranks no further than phone calls, she needed to know. The next name and number came up. Her uncle Rex. She'd already listened to his message on the answering machine saying he would be here today. Before that, a call had come from a telemarketer. The telemarketer was preceded by an elderly lady who lived close by asking no one in particular if there were any way she could help after dear Vivian's "passing." That was the last call listed.

Chyna sat down at the kitchen table and rested her forehead on her hands. During the last four years, her episodes of what most people called ESP had lessened. She didn't know if it was because of her tremendous workload, the change of scenery, or simply a matter of "growing out" of it. Whatever the reason, she'd been unutterably relieved. But now it seemed to have kicked into gear again. First, there had come the voice at the lake. Next, she'd gotten the strange, windy phone call from someone sounding remarkably like Anita Simms. Chyna could put both down to heightened imagination caused by grief over her mother if Michelle hadn't acted so strangely, too. But Chyna had to admit that the dog was deeply attached to her. Perhaps Michelle had been reacting to her heightened adrenaline levels. Maybe the dog's two bouts of alarm yesterday were the result of Chyna's fear, not Zoey speaking to her from the lake or Anita calling her on the phone.

Chyna shook her head, deciding not to dwell on the subject further right now. At eleven, she had an appointment at the funeral home. She took a shower and washed her hair, then rooted through her suitcase to find she'd forgotten to pack her blow dryer. She went into her mother's room to find another. At the time of Chyna's father's death, the room had been decorated in beige, light brown, and fern green. Over the years, Vivian had added some saffron yellow, pale apricot, and watermelon pink—small touches that had both enlivened the room and made it more feminine.

Last Christmas when Chyna had come home, her mother had insisted on doing "my little girl's hair" for the annual Christmas party. Chyna hadn't looked in the mirror as she felt her mother whipping through her long strands of hair with hot rollers and curling irons. She's making me look like a twelve-year-old with ringlets, Chyna had thought with dread. Then Vivian had chirped, "All done!" Slowly Chyna had forced herself to look in the mirror to find that her mother had indeed added curls to the hair, but big, loose curls. She'd pulled the top part to the back of Chyna's head, teasing it a bit for height and using an antique gold and pearl clasp to hold it in place, then draped the lower part seductively over Chyna's right shoulder.

"You look like a Greek goddess," Vivian had said with complete love and admiration, not with a tinge of jealousy over the fact that lovely as she was, she dimmed in comparison with her daughter. "Now go out there and socialize. Don't hover in a shadowy corner like you usually do," Vivian had instructed. "You seem to feel like you should hide if you're not wearing those horrible scrubs from the hospital. You have a fabulous figure. Show it off. By the way, Scott Kendrick might be here tonight."

Chyna's heart had beat faster at that thought, and throughout the evening her spirits had drooped along with her curls when he hadn't shown up. "Weather got my Scott hung up in New York," Mrs. Kendrick told her around ten o'clock, her voice slightly slurry from too much spiked eggnog. "He should be here tomorrow and I'm sure he'll be sorry he missed the party. He's probably stuck alone in some shabby motel room watching *It's a Wonderful Life* for the thirtieth time."

Chyna had smiled stiffly. She had no doubt Scott was in a motel room. She was totally certain he was not alone watching *It's a Wonderful Life*. That night she'd vowed she'd get over this ludicrous crush she'd had on him since she was a teenager.

But seeing him at the lake yesterday convinced her that she hadn't really made much progress since last Christmas.

She still thought he was the most charming, handsome—
downright sexy—man she'd ever seen and her heart had
beaten just as fast eighteen hours ago at the sight of him as it
had when she was sixteen.

"Oh, Chyna, you're hopeless when it come to Scott," she
said aloud as she pulled herself from her reverie and headed
for her mother's bathroom, stubbing her toe on something
barely sticking out from under the bed. Chyna bent down and
pulled out an album, once white, now ivory with age. She
opened the cover and on the first page saw a cut-out newspaper article titled "Sixteen-year-old Girl Goes Missing."

Zoey. Chyna read the first article written in the *Black Willow Dispatch* about Zoey, who had vanished in the night
"while with her friend Chyna Greer, 16, of Black Willow."
"But she *wasn't* with me," Chyna burst out, just as she had the
first time she read the article twelve years ago. "She wasn't
with *me.*" She turned the album pages, every one of them
containing an article pertaining to Zoey, some from the local
newspaper, some picked up from the Associated Press from
newspapers as far away as Washington, D.C., Zoey's home.
They reported details about the search for Zoey, and they reported when she'd been given up for dead.

Chyna turned the page and gasped when she saw the
headline of the next article: "Another Local Girl Goes Missing." The newspaper was dated December 28, nineteen
months after Zoey's disappearance, while Chyna was home
on Christmas break from college. The article stated that
Heather Phelps, 17, a senior at Black Willow High School,
cheerleader, and member of the student council, had taken
her parents' car around 7:00 P.M. to Baker's Drugstore,
where she'd been last seen alive. The Phelpses found their
car parked near the drugstore around 11:00 P.M. Heather had
not been missing long enough for the police officially to list
her as a missing person, so the family had organized their
own search team.

The next day local police became involved sooner than
protocol strictly required. They learned that while no one in
the store had seen Heather talk to anyone except the checkout

girl, a few people on the street had seen Heather after she left the store. They said she was alone and looked untroubled. She'd wandered on foot up the street, apparently window-shopping for Christmas gifts, although no one had spotted her entering any stores, and no one working in the stores had helped her or even noticed her looking around. The search had continued for months. Then the case went cold.

Chyna's hands turned icy. In fact, she'd begun to shiver all over as she read the newspaper accounts. She remembered when Heather Phelps had gone missing. Ned had mentioned it to her, although her parents said nothing, and every evening their newspaper disappeared before Chyna got to read it, stuck in the trash by her mother, no doubt. She hadn't wanted Heather's disappearance to remind Chyna of Zoey's, yet Vivian had kept accounts spanning for months of the search for Heather Phelps. Why? Because she thought Heather's experience was linked to Zoey's?

Chyna sat down on the bed and flipped pages until she came to an article dated in May—the May she had come back to Black Willow to attend her father's funeral. The article concerned Edie Larson, aged 16, whose backpack had been found about a mile north of town and brought to the police station by two thirteen-year-old boys. When police contacted the parents, Mr. Larson claimed Edie had been gone for two days, but he hadn't reported her missing because he thought she'd run away with her boyfriend, Gage Ridgeway, age 19, also of Black Willow.

Ridgeway, however, had never missed a day of work at his grandfather's construction company and told police that for the past few days he had thought Edie was home with the flu, although her father, who did not approve of Gage, would not allow him to speak to Edie when he'd called twice to check on her. Once again, a search was launched, although this time the number-one suspect had been Ron Larson, Edie's father, who had a juvenile record, two DUIs, and a history of domestic abuse. Three times when police had arrived at the Larson home, they'd found Mrs. Larson sporting black eyes and split lips. Each time, though, she'd come up with elaborate, if unbelievable, excuses for her injuries and never pressed charges against her husband.

At the time of Edie's disappearance, though, Mrs. Larson finally admitted that her husband had refused to let her tell the police Edie was missing even though the girl, who'd been alone and on foot as far as Mrs. Larson knew, had not returned from a play rehearsal held one evening at the nearby high school. The teacher conducting the rehearsal confirmed that Edie had attended the rehearsal and left the school alone, refusing a ride from a student who needed to stay later to practice another scene. Edie had said she would get in trouble at home if she were late.

Later Ron Larson defended not reporting his daughter missing by telling police he thought Gage Ridgeway had "knocked up Edie" and she'd simply run off, thereby disgracing the fine name of Larson in town. Larson also suggested that instead of hassling him, police should arrest Ridgeway for "stationary rape," a quote the town's newspaper editor couldn't resist including in the article.

Chyna laid the album on her lap. She remembered Ned mentioning Edie when Chyna had come home that summer, and her mother quickly changing the subject. The last newspaper article in the album, dated May 25 of eight years ago, said police were continuing the search for Edie, who had been missing for ten months. "But I'm sure they didn't find her," Chyna said aloud. "Just like they didn't find Zoey, just like they didn't find Heather." Three girls in less than four years. What had the voice coming from the lake said yesterday? "You have to find me, because there were other girls like me." Chyna knew Zoey was telling her Heather and Edie had suffered the same fate she had.

Chyna slammed shut the album and placed it on the bed beside her. Three girls had died because someone had come to Black Willow twelve years ago, someone dark and deranged, and he'd roamed the area for four years, then . . . then what? Died? Been killed?

Decided to move on to greener pastures?

No, definitely not the last. The voice coming from the

lake, Zoey's voice, had told her, "There will be more girls like me if you don't do something." Chyna closed her eyes in dread and fear that there was some great plan at work. Was that why her mother had died? To bring Chyna home before more girls vanished to suffer horrors in evil hands?

"Yes," a voice seemed to whisper coldly through the room. "You're their only hope."

2

With a shudder, Chyna stuffed the album of newspaper articles back under her mother's bed, pushing it as far against the wall as she could, hiding it, hoping she could forget about it. She didn't want to think of her mother clipping out those articles year after year and carefully centering them on pages, slipping vinyl covers over them, preserving them. Preserving them for what? For me to read, Chyna thought. Vivian had always expressed worry about Chyna claiming to have "visions," but Chyna had sensed that perhaps Vivian was acting, and she really believed her daughter had powers beyond normal. Once, when Chyna was around eight and Vivian had drunk too much wine at a Fourth of July barbecue, hadn't she told Chyna about her own two aunts and her younger, deceased sister who'd "sensed" things?

Later Vivian denied she'd ever told Chyna such a thing, but she'd always had a guilty look on her face during her denials. Chyna guessed her father had overheard Vivian telling the story and for once put his foot down with her mother, insisting she refute her "fairy tale." But Chyna was certain, just as she was certain of so many things for which there was no proof, that her mother was telling the truth about her sisters.

Her mother did believe in second sight, Chyna thought. Vivian had gone along with her husband when he wanted to take Chyna to doctors after the boating accident and Chyna had begun to make predictions, recall incidents from the past she couldn't possibly know about, find things no one else could find, but her mother was only trying to please Edward. She had believed in ESP because she'd seen it at work in her own family, and she'd left this album full of details about the missing girls knowing Chyna would find it because she was meant to save other lives, and not by medical means.

The obligation seemed too much. Chyna felt crushed by the burden she feared was hers. She hung her head. She wanted to cry. She wanted to grab up Michelle and get away from Black Willow as fast as she could. She wanted to abrogate responsibility for any lost girls, past or present. But she knew she couldn't.

Slowly, Chyna raised her head. The only answer for now was to get hold of her emotions, she thought. She went to her mother's dresser and looked in the vanity mirror. "I will not think about this again today," she told herself sternly. "I will not think about the album or that bizarre phone call." And she would especially not think about the haunting voice at the lake, Zoey's voice, singing, "Star light, star bright," which for some reason had frightened Chyna more than anything else that had happened since she came home. She knew she could not run from responsibility. She also knew from experience that if answers were to come, they would come in their own time, in their own way. She could not force them.

Chyna glanced at her watch and saw that she'd spent more time looking at the album than she'd realized. The morning was almost gone and she had errands to do in the afternoon.

She began moving around briskly, found the blow dryer, finished her hair, pulled it back into a long ponytail, and slid into brown slacks and a red sweater. At least she'd remembered to bring the jacket that matched the pants. After all, she wanted to look presentable at the funeral home. Some blue-gray powder on her eyelids, bronze blush, and matching lipstick brightened her face. She stood back and studied the result. She decided she looked almost normal. Almost if you didn't know she wasn't usually so pale or cursed with mauve shadows beneath her eyes.

When Chyna took the blow dryer back to her mother's room, she heard scraping against the back of the house—not the gentle scraping of leaves in the breeze but the definite scrape of wood or metal against the stone. She also heard a voice. Someone singing. She froze, listening. The melody was something she'd never heard before. The notes were flat. There was no real rhythm or timing. Michelle, standing beside her, perked up her ears. Oh God, no, Chyna thought. Not another voice out of nowhere. Not another voice telling her . . .

"Satisfaction . . . oh no, no, no! I can't get no . . ."

Was she hearing a voice from the "netherworld" mangling with loving gusto "Satisfaction" by the Rolling Stones? No, it couldn't be. Chyna had heard many odd and frightening things through her sixth sense before, but nothing quite this wacky.

She went to her bedroom window, glanced out, then raised the window. A slim, brown-haired man stood on a towering ladder, his gloved hands raking at leaves in the gutters as he sang with passion, bobbing his head to a beat that was unfathomable to anyone but himself. Chyna looked at him for at least a minute as his voice grew louder and his head bobbed faster. He finally came to the end of the song, whooped in ecstasy, looked over at her, and almost fell off the ladder.

"Good God!" he shouted.

"Sorry to scare you," Chyna said, trying not to burst into laughter. "I was drawn by the music."

His good-looking face flamed, his ears so red they looked like they were going to catch on fire. "I didn't think anyone was home. I clean out Mrs. Greer's gutters every year and I didn't think this year should be any different. I know she's passed on, but people will be coming to the house and she'd want everything to look perfect." Then he squinted through the bright sun at her with clear green eyes. "Chyna? Is that you?"

"Yes. I flew in yesterday. My rental car is in the garage."

"Well, geez. I gave us both a fright. I haven't seen you for at least ten years. Gage Ridgeway."

"Oh, I remember you, Gage," Chyna said, still smiling. In

fact, I just read about you in a newspaper article, she thought. You were the boyfriend of Edie Larson, one of the girls who vanished. He would be about Chyna's age, now, and he'd grown into a striking-looking man. But then, he'd also been a striking-looking teenager, with no shortage of girlfriends. She continued to smile.

"How are things with you, Gage?"

"Fine. Still working at the construction company. Grandpa's dead, so it belongs to Dad and me now. My grandfather built this house, you know. That's why I do the handy work around here. Grandpa thought a lot of your grandfather and of this house. He said it was the best one he ever built and as long as there was a Ridgeway alive, *we* were going to take care of it, not some amateur who'd cobble up the place and do more harm than good." Gage removed one of his gloved hands from the gutter and brushed at some leaf flakes on his face and hair. "I'm really sorry about your mother, Chyna."

"So am I. Her death was a complete surprise."

"No kidding. I saw her last Saturday. That storm we had nearly demolished your brother's old clubhouse. He was in Pennsylvania at his sister-in-law's wedding and your mom had me come out here and finish tearing down the place and haul off the scraps. She acted okay that day. Oh, maybe a little pale and quiet, but I put that down to her being shook up over the storm and worrying about tearing down Ned's clubhouse without asking him first. You know how he was about the place."

"He was ridiculously possessive of that stupid building. It should have been torn down years ago—it was a ramshackle eyesore on an otherwise beautiful back lawn." Chyna sighed. "I'm glad to know Mom didn't look sick earlier in the week. I've been beating myself up for not being here when she died, but I didn't even know she was sick."

"I don't think anybody did." Gage looked away awkwardly and added, "Considering the circumstances, I'm sorry I was out here bellowing, too. Grandpa would slap my face for that show of disrespect."

"I certainly wouldn't want him to slap you for singing

while you work." Chyna tried to smile. "It's just that I've never heard that particular rendition of 'Satisfaction.'"

Gage grinned. His skin was weathered and he looked older than his years, but Chyna didn't believe anyone could say he wasn't still ruggedly handsome. "Guess you know why I got kicked out of a garage band when I was sixteen and another one when I was eighteen," he laughed. "Just because you've got music in your soul doesn't mean it's gonna come out of your mouth."

Chyna laughed. "I'll think of that every time I'm singing along with music in the car and wondering why the dog is howling." Gage laughed, too. He looked so normal, so happy-go-lucky, so . . . innocent, she thought. It was almost impossible for her to think he had anything to do with the disappearance and possible murder of a girl.

And then Chyna remembered Zoey seeing him downtown the summer she disappeared and nearly swooning in teenage admiration when Gage smiled, winked, and said, "How're you doin', Zoe? Lookin' good these days." That final night Chyna had asked Zoey if on an earlier visit she'd met the guy with whom she was having her pathetic romantic rendezvous at the lake. "Yes, but this time is different," Zoey had said. "Sometimes you just click with people."

Chyna could easily believe that Zoey had been so taken with Gage, nothing could have stopped her from seeing him that night if he'd later called her and asked her to meet him. She could also believe that Zoey would have delightedly walked into the dark woods with Gage for a passionate kiss, Chyna thought in abrupt horror. "Well, I have business downtown," she said sharply. "I'm late already."

"Nice seeing you," Gage got out before she slammed down the window. She might have just been bantering with the killer of three girls. Or you may have been talking to a perfectly nice man who now agrees with most of the town that you're crazy, she thought. Oh well, too late to worry about her image. And who cared, anyway? She only came back to Black Willow for a few days once a year anyway.

Chyna had startled Gage out of singing, she thought as

she grabbed up her purse and raincoat and dashed from the room. When she pulled her car out of the garage, she rolled down her window. Complete silence. If Gage had felt like singing earlier, he didn't anymore. He was probably up on his ladder pondering what could be wrong with the notorious Black Willow "seer."

Driving toward town, Chyna called Ned on her cell phone. "I'm going to the undertaker's to pick out an urn for Mom. Do you want to meet me there?"

"To pick out an *urn*? God, no," Ned burst out.

"Well, don't sound so horrified. It has to be done."

"I know. I hate to push this off on you, but . . . well, you know Mom's taste better than I do."

Chyna rolled her eyes. "That's about the weakest excuse I've ever heard." Ned was silent. "Oh well, I understand. I'm not exactly looking forward to this particular type of shopping myself."

"No one would be." Chyna could tell Ned was walking outside the showroom of the Greer Lincoln-Mercury Agency and on to the car lot, his business that had been doing well for the last five years.

"Ned, I still can't believe Mom didn't want to be buried next to Dad or to not even have a funeral service. Was she acting weird lately?"

His voice grew louder as he talked to someone out on the lot looking at a car. "That's a fine model there. Got every bell and whistle a person could want. We could probably work you out a good deal on that one." His voice lowered to normal. "What do you mean, was Mom acting weird? Sick? Or crazy?"

"Not crazy. Unusual. Strange. I mean, I'm still floored by her insisting on not having a funeral service and wanting me to take her ashes back to New Mexico with me. It feels all wrong—"

Chyna slammed on the brakes at a red light. The old man in the crosswalk gave her the finger. I deserved that, she thought, her face growing warm. She hadn't been paying enough attention to her driving.

"I know her final request seems out of character for her, but she gave that envelope to Bev months ago and never asked to have it returned. She wasn't acting on impulse, Sis." Ned yelled something unintelligible to another potential customer, then lowered his voice as he spoke into the phone. "Did you read the letter we gave you last night?"

"Yes. It seemed purely businesslike. Maybe I missed something peculiar about it, though. I was still fairly shaken by that call from Anita Simms."

"It wasn't Anita Simms," Ned said flatly. "It was a hideous joke someone was playing on you and I want you to put it out of your mind, although I know that's easier said than done." He took a deep breath. "Chyna, I'm sorry to give you the dirty work at the funeral home this afternoon, but we're having a big day. I've really got to go. I'll talk to you this evening. And you're a sugarplum for doing this."

"Thank you. I've always wanted to be a sugarplum," Chyna said drolly, but Ned had already hung up.

Chyna pulled into the parking lot of Burtram and Hodges Funeral Home. She remembered coming here with her mother when Edward had "passed away," as the funeral directors kept saying. Edward Greer had died as he'd lived—quietly and with dignity. Vivian had simply awakened one morning and found Edward lying beside her, dead of a stroke. He had not made one sound loud enough to wake her.

Rex Greer, his younger brother, had been in France at the time, and for some reason Vivian had asked Chyna to help with the arrangements because Ned refused. Ned once shamefacedly confided to her that death terrified him. His actions seemed to prove his truthfulness. When people carried on conversations about the dead or dying, he quietly left the room. If he went to a wake, he signed the guest register but never looked at the body if the coffin was open, and left as soon as possible. When he attended a funeral, he stood far away from the proceedings and usually focused his gaze at a tree or flower arrangement near the funeral tent. Once Chyna had followed his line of sight closely and discovered he was watching a mole tunneling beneath the earth.

The day was bright and at least ten degrees warmer than yesterday. Chyna got out of the car, looked up at the baby blue sky and pale yellow sun, and drew in a deep breath of crisp air. Immediately she felt better, a little less heartbroken, a little bit cheerier. Then she opened the heavy door of the funeral home, stepped in, and her spirits seemed to hit the floor with a thud.

Mahogany walls. Navy blue carpet. Frosted glass over muted light fixtures. Mournful organ music floating through solemn halls. And a faint scent of once-fresh flowers now gone slightly stale. A slender man somewhere in his midthirties with sculpted features, medium brown hair, and slightly downcast eyes approached Chyna.

"How do you do?" he said with cool formality. "I'm Russell Burtram. May I be of assistance to you?"

Russell glanced up, seemed to catch a glimpse of her bright red turtleneck, then immediately looked down again, making Chyna immediately wish she'd dressed differently. Perhaps navy blue would have been advisable. She would have looked like Russell, whose suit matched the carpet. She noticed the sprinkling of gray at the temples in his brown hair and the hands clenched tightly, as if he were nervous or holding a pose that didn't come naturally. Russell seemed aware of Chyna's quick assessment of his looks and stiffened, looking up at her again with gray eyes.

"My mother died," Chyna began. "Apparently she was suffering from heart trouble the family didn't know about. She had a heart attack and fell down the stairs. Her neck was broken," Chyna said in a rush before her throat tightened and the next words came out in an unintelligible bleat. "I have to make arrangements."

"You don't have to explain. I know all about Vivian Greer's death." Russell Bertram's gaze softened in sympathy. "You don't remember me, do you?"

"What?" Chyna nearly choked past her tight throat.

"It's Rusty Burtram, Chyna. I was in Ned's class in school."

Chyna swallowed and tried to hide her surprise. She took a deep breath. "Rusty! My goodness, I'm seeing all kinds of people from the past today. You've . . . changed."

"The acne cleared up; I got contacts, did a little body-building." He smiled almost apologetically. Chyna, having done a rotation in plastic surgery, also guessed he'd had a nose job and chin implant. "I hope it all helped."

"Oh, it helped immensely!" Chyna burst out with unflattering enthusiasm, then realized how insulting she sounded. "I mean, you looked fine before—"

"I looked like a nerd and I was always self-conscious about it. The transformation came right after I graduated and decided I wouldn't go off to college looking like I did." Someone approached them and Rusty's face immediately became sober again, his voice softer. "This is Dad's business, but I guess you know that." Chyna nodded. "We handled your father's funeral."

A tall black-haired man stopped in front of her, nearly pushing Rusty aside. "Owen Burtram, Miss—or should I say Doctor?—Greer." Rusty's father, Chyna thought. Vivian Greer had thought he was a ridiculous stuffed shirt. "Your mother talked about you a great deal."

"She did?" Chyna wondered where Vivian had done all this talking to Owen. She didn't like him and usually tried to avoid him at social functions. "Well, I miss Mom very much already," Chyna said. "She was only fifty-two."

"Ah, yes. I know fifty-two seems far too young for one to depart, but we do not always comprehend the ways of the Almighty. His is a power far greater than ours, and it is He who decides when it is a person's time to pass." After finishing this sententious pronouncement, Owen finally smiled slightly, showing a row of perfect teeth. Too perfect, too white. Porcelain veneers, Chyna thought. She was also certain that a man in his fifties must have at least one gray hair. Owen's was a lusterless black, the color obviously derived from a bottle. "Won't you come into the office, Chyna?" He turned to Rusty and said dismissively, "*I* will handle Dr. Greer's needs."

"Yes, sir." Rusty's voice was meek, but Chyna saw the twinkle in his eyes, gray like his father's but much warmer.

"Would you care for tea or coffee?" Owen asked, walking briskly down the hall as if to show her how spry he was.

"Coffee, please." Chyna followed Owen toward the back of the building, noting that he was just a shade taller than his six-foot son was and only a bit heavier. The hall was long and shadowy. She guessed that most people would find it somber, but it somehow struck her as sinister. The two-inch heels of her shoes sank into the deep navy carpet, giving her a feeling of descending into quicksand. A particular piece of organ music that sounded like a dirge droned in the background, and Owen stooped to pick up a shriveling white rose petal that had obviously fallen from a funeral arrangement, sniffing it before he crushed it in one of his large hands. The air was so cool, Chyna wished she had worn a coat instead of a blazer. I would go crazy in here, she thought. Absolutely raving crazy. I don't know how Rusty stands it.

At least the office was a bit brighter than the rest of the funeral home, although Owen kept the vertical blinds half-shut. He motioned toward a tapestry-upholstered chair and while Chyna sat, noting that the chair had an unusually vertical back that allowed no slouching, Owen poured coffee into a dainty cup and added a dash of milk and a heaping teaspoon of sugar. Chyna had not asked for milk or sugar and wanted neither, but she accepted the cup with a polite smile and immediately took a sip. At least it was hot.

Owen sat down behind a large desk, folded his big hands with their manicured nails, a slender gold wedding ring on one hand and a large onyx ring set in platinum on the other, and turned a practiced, compassionate look on Chyna. "I assume you are here to make arrangements for your mother's funeral."

"Yes. I know it should have been done sooner, but my brother just can't face . . ." She didn't know what to say. Places like this. People like you. Death in general. "I would have been here sooner, but I had to come in from New Mexico."

"I believe Vivian said you're training in a hospital in Albuquerque."

"Yes. I'm a second-year resident. I'm glad I worked so many extra shifts and skipped so many vacations so I could take off time for this event." She smiled. Owen stared at her. Event? God, I sounded like I'm here for a holiday, Chyna thought in horror, and quickly stopped smiling. "Anyway, I have almost two weeks off."

"How convenient for you," Owen said, gazing fixedly in the direction of her breasts. "Now, first I suppose you would like to look at our selection of coffins. We have a wide price range, but I'm sure you'll want the very best for your mother."

"Well, no, we don't want a coffin." Owen's eyes sliced up from her breasts to her face. "I mean, my mother wanted to be cremated."

"Cremated!" Owen repeated as if Chyna had just said her mother had wanted to be thrown into an electric woodchopper. "Vivian Greer wanted to be *cremated*?"

"Uh . . . yes," Chyna said weakly, feeling like a toad under the suddenly frosty glare of Owen Burtram. "We were surprised, too. The family, I mean. But she made her wishes quite clear to my brother and sister-in-law. And she wrote a letter giving directions. She had it notarized."

"A notarized letter?"

"Yes. I didn't bring it with me, but I could show it to you. . . ." Chyna felt like a little girl sitting across from the principal for some hideous school-related infraction. She sat a bit straighter in her chair, pulled her jacket over her breasts, and fought to compose her face, which she knew looked guilty and embarrassed. She didn't have to prove anything to Owen Burtram. "You do handle cremations, don't you?" she asked, forcing herself to sound stronger and more confident.

"Well, yes, on occasion," Owen said with distaste, "although it somehow goes against the grain. It doesn't quite meet the standards, the dignity, the decorum for which Burtram and Hodges has become known—"

Or the money the usual funeral costs, Chyna almost said snidely. Burtram and Hodges would make at least seven thousand dollars less for a cremation than for a regular funeral.

Maybe more, if the family decided to go all out on this final good-bye to Vivian. Chyna realized Owen had stopped talking and was looking at her hopefully, perhaps thinking he'd shamed Chyna into asking for a funeral with all the frills. "What matters to me is following my mother's wishes," Chyna said, glad her voice sounded cool and firm. "If she wanted to be cremated, then she will be cremated. However, if you'd rather not be associated with cremation—"

"We'll do it," Owen said swiftly. "You still have to pick out an urn, though." He paused. "You *do* want an urn, don't you?"

No, a shoe box will be fine, Chyna had an urge to reply solemnly, but bit back her retort. Vivian would have gotten a huge kick out of the reply to this haughty man, but Chyna's father would have been embarrassed, believing you should always be polite even to people you don't like, and Chyna was not here to take down Owen Burtram a peg.

They spent what seemed like hours studying urns. Owen relentlessly tried to convince Chyna a service was crucial—what would people in town think?—but her refusal remained firm. When they finally finished, Chyna felt as if she'd run a race in the Olympics, and during the ordeal she'd managed inadvertently to insult Owen at least four times until he'd begun looking at her with barely concealed dislike. Chyna remembered an older man who must have been Owen's father taking her and her mother back to his office for a quiet chat and more refreshment after they'd arranged Edward's funeral, but Owen couldn't get rid of her fast enough.

As they walked toward the front door, Owen's gait was even brisker than it had been when Chyna arrived. Chyna tried to make conversation but got only "yes" or "no" in response. Owen even seemed to be breathing harder, no doubt waiting to vent his frustration about cheapskate Chyna Greer to some unlucky underling who worked at the mortuary.

Halfway down the hall, just such an underling appeared—a young man asking obsequiously if he might interrupt Mr. Burtram on a pressing matter. Owen couldn't hide his smile of relief. He looked at Chyna. "So sorry, but I'm needed. I'm sure you can find your way out—down the hall, turn right, and the doors are straight ahead of you. There will be a *lovely* funeral in about an hour in the slumber room to your left, so I'm sure you won't blunder—walk in there and disturb anything. Just go straight out the front doors. I'm glad we could help you in some *small* measure."

"Thank you." And sorry I broke your heart with my mother's cheap funeral requests, Chyna fumed inwardly, but I don't care what anyone in this town thinks.

As Owen marched away talking in hushed tones with the assistant, Chyna began her longed-for escape from the funeral home. Down this hall, Owen had said, and then to the right. Chyna made the turn and slowed down slightly when she saw the blessed front doors ahead of her. Outside there would be fresh air. Birds. Sunshine. Her deluxe rental car and a Coldplay CD to fill it with music she loved. Maybe a trip to Bev's to see her nephew, Ian. Kate would be in kindergarten at this hour.

As Chyna neared the door, the aroma of flowers became stronger. Fresh flowers, the scent sweet and enticing. As Chyna walked on, she remembered Owen's words: "There will be a *lovely* funeral in about an hour in the slumber room to your left . . ." Owen had nearly told her to stay *out* of the area, as if Chyna's very presence would cast a blight over the intended dignified and proper service. But as Chyna passed the room, she came to a complete stop without even realizing it. She peered in at the rows of chairs set up for mourners, the intricately carved pulpit for the minister and eulogists, the flower baskets and wreaths—good heavens, there must have been over fifty of them—grouped most densely near the cherrywood coffin. The open coffin.

I should walk right out of here, Chyna thought. I should head straight for that front door. But she couldn't. She felt as if she were being pulled into the room, her free will quashed by something much stronger than she was. Chyna looked over her shoulder. The hall was empty. Then, with the stealth worthy of a burglar, she entered the "slumber room."

Here the horrible organ music had been shut off.

Mozart's beautiful Clarinet Concerto: Adagio played softly through wall speakers. Chyna walked closer to the coffin, noting the opalescent torchères at either end casting an almost mystical light over the white silk interior. And within the coffin, her head on a lace-edged pillow, lay a girl of about seventeen in waxen perfection, her long ash-blond hair arranged in soft waves around her pale face and expertly combed over her shoulders and down the front of her dainty lace and pink organza dress. One small, perfectly manicured hand had been crossed over the other at her waist. A star sapphire and diamond ring on her right ring finger glinted in the light from the torchères.

Desolation filled Chyna at the sight of the girl. A week ago, this had been a giggling teenager full of dreams and secrets and probably boundless energy. And now here she lay, all her dreams and secrets, all her energy, all her future, gone forever. Gone to a place called Heaven? Chyna hoped so, although she'd never been particularly religious. In fact, the last time she remembered wishing fervently that Heaven existed was when Zoey never came home and Chyna had known her friend was dead.

"Good night, sweet princess," Chyna whispered to the oblivious girl, her eyes filling with tears she feared might drip onto the silk and organza.

Abruptly the Mozart ended and before another song began, Chyna heard a girl's sweet young voice, a voice remarkably like Zoey's, coming from the coffin. "Star light, star bright, first star I see tonight . . ." Chyna gasped, rubbed her hand roughly over her eyes, clearing away her tears, and looked at the girl's motionless mouth.

"Beautiful girl, wasn't she?"

Chyna nearly screamed. Rusty Burtram had come in so quietly she hadn't even heard him.

"The family will be arriving soon."

Chyna tried to swallow and couldn't. She looked at the girl, motionless as a statue, then back at the inquisitive gaze of Rusty. He couldn't miss seeing the fear in her eyes, the panic on her face. What could she say?

"I . . . the room looked so beautiful . . . you did a wonderful job. . . ." Rusty tilted his head a fraction. "I couldn't help being drawn in . . . the music, the flowers." She nervously twisted her hands together. "I didn't touch anything."

"I'm sure you didn't, Chyna. You don't have to look at me like I'm going to strike you or something. It's just that Dad doesn't want anyone in here before the service—" He broke off awkwardly and blushed. "I mean, he always wants things perfect for a service and thinks someone might disturb the setting. It's not just you."

"It *is* me and it's all right, Rusty. I rubbed him the wrong way." Chyna knew she should leave as quickly as possible. She had no doubt that Owen Burtram was capable of wielding considerable wrath if disobeyed, and Rusty would probably be the victim. Still, she couldn't make herself move.

"Who is she?" Chyna asked.

"Nancy Tierney," Rusty answered. "Didn't you read about her in the newspaper?"

"I didn't arrive in Black Willow until yesterday." Chyna heard the tremor in her voice and she tossed her jacket over her hands to hide their shaking. "I haven't read a newspaper and no one mentioned her to me." She paused, looking at the girl again. "She was so young and pretty." And she talks even though she's dead, Chyna almost added.

Rusty looked at her closely and she knew he saw the leftover tears in her eyes, the paleness of her face. Both his posture and his voice softened. Apparently, he was more swayed by Chyna's obvious emotion than he was by fear of his father.

"Nancy was my cousin, Dad's niece," Rusty said with a catch in his voice.

"Oh, Rusty, I'm so sorry for your loss!" Chyna exclaimed. Then she grimaced. "I hate that phrase. It sounds so automatic and canned. I apologize for intruding. And I'm truly sorry about Nancy."

Rusty reached out and put a surprisingly large hand on Chyna's shoulder. "Calm down. You're trembling. I frightened you—" No, *she* frightened me, Chyna thought, trying not to look at the lovely Nancy Tierney, who spoke even in death. "This has been a hard time for us," Rusty went on. "Nancy was such a beautiful girl. Everyone adored her. She was the darling of the family." Chyna averted her gaze from Rusty. Had she imagined it, or was there a trace of resentment in his voice? "Unfortunately, her death has been the talk of the town, which makes it even harder for her parents."

What happened to her? Chyna wanted to shout. She glanced at the girl again. Nancy's lips had been painted petal pink, and they didn't move. Of course they didn't move, Chyna thought. They were sewn shut, a gruesome thought but the custom when the corpse lay in an open coffin. "She doesn't look like she'd been ill," Chyna ventured.

"Oh, she wasn't." Rusty gazed over at the girl, a mixture of frustration and puzzlement in his eyes. "Nancy liked to run in the evenings. Tuesday evening, she went out later than usual. Her parents tried to stop her. They didn't want her out alone after dark, but Nancy did as she pleased. Always. I suppose quite a few people would consider her spoiled." Including you, Chyna thought, trying to keep her face blank.

"Anyway, when she didn't come back after an hour and a half, my aunt got worried," Rusty continued. "She and Nancy's father went looking down the trail Nancy usually took. After two hours, a couple of neighbors and their teenage son joined them. The boy went off on a different path and he found Nancy. Apparently, she'd stepped in a hole hidden by leaves, fell, and hit her head on a large rock. Her ankle was broken, a bone in her neck cracked, and she had a subdural hematoma. I'm told sometimes they can reduce those hematomas, but Nancy's was extremely bad and she'd lain there around three hours." He took a deep breath. "She died on her way into surgery."

So she wasn't another lost girl, Chyna thought immediately, ashamed, but also relieved. Nancy had been gone for only about three hours when they found her dead because of an accident. She'd fallen. She hadn't been spirited away and probably murdered. Rusty was looking at Nancy, and Chyna closed her eyes. But the girl had *spoken* . . .

Or had she? Chyna would have sworn she heard a voice,

Zoey's voice, just like she'd heard at Lake Manicora, but she *knew* Zoey couldn't have been speaking to her at the lake. And Chyna hadn't seen Nancy's lips moving as Zoey's voice flowed from her. The dead girl had not been rattling out a child's chant about stars. Chyna was simply imagining voices. She *had* to be.

"My aunt is heartbroken," Rusty was saying. "I'm afraid this will be the emotional end of her. And for the first time, I'm glad my grandfather died last year. Nancy was the apple of his eye. He loved her more than anything."

"Oh, how devastating . . . ," Chyna said faintly.

"Yes." Rusty's father appeared in the doorway, and Rusty suddenly became all business. "The service will begin soon. People will be arriving. I'm afraid I must ask you to leave, Dr. Greer," he said coolly.

"Oh, of course. Once again, I'm sorry . . . ," Chyna babbled as she moved toward the door of the "slumber room." "So tragic. Such a shock. . . ."

"I'm sure you've said all that already," Owen Burtram snapped. "Thank you." Sunlight poured into the dark hall and Owen glanced at the open front door. "Here are the first of the mourners. Her parents. I wish you wouldn't—"

"I'm on my way out," Chyna assured him.

Owen had stepped forward to embrace a smaller, feminine version of himself, clearly his sister and Nancy's mother, as Chyna fled down the hall and out the door before it had fully closed behind Nancy's parents. Outside, Chyna leaned against the brick wall of the mortuary and tried to draw deep breaths, although her lungs felt shut off, as if they refused to accept air. For a moment, everything went dark and Chyna thought she was fainting. Then the crisp air hit her like a slap in the face and suddenly she became almost frighteningly alert.

Dear God, she thought, what's happening to me? Throughout the years, Chyna had heard voices before, but they'd always been gentle, warning voices: "Don't step into the street" right before a drunk driver careened around the corner. "Read Chapter Sixteen again," and sure enough, several important test questions would be drawn from Chapter 16. "Your earring dropped off three steps back," and when she looked behind her she would see the earring sparkling in the sun. The voice was like a little guardian angel, never loud, never frightening. But rhymes? A rhyme seeming to come from a lake, and the same rhyme seeming to come from a dead girl?

Panic shot through Chyna. Schizophrenics heard voices. Had she finally gone around the bend into schizophrenia? Could it come on so quickly? She hadn't even heard the little warning voice for nearly a year, much less the voice of someone she had known, like Zoey. Chyna tried to remember if she'd heard the rhyme in both ears or in just one. True schizophrenics heard voices in both ears. What were some of the other symptoms of schizophrenia?

Chyna was aware of people trickling into the mortuary, some looking at her curiously, some warily, but she absolutely could not move. She kept her hands pressed against the brick wall, feeling as if it were the only thing holding her up. Certainly her legs weren't. They felt as if they were vibrating under her brown slacks. I can't stand here forever, she thought, plastered to the wall like a mashed bug on a windshield. I have to pull myself together. At *least* I have to make it to the car.

She briefly closed her eyes, telling herself there was nothing wrong with her legs and she could move if she'd just try it, when a deep male voice asked, "Chyna?" She opened her eyes and looked up into the dark, penetrating gaze of Scott Kendrick. "Chyna, are you all right?"

Chyna ran shaking fingers over her upper lip and forehead and felt a sheen of moisture. "I guess making arrangements for Mom's funeral was harder than I thought it would be," she said lightly, then slumped. If Scott hadn't reached out strong arms, she would have dropped to the pavement.

"Where's your walking stick?" she asked vaguely, aware of mourners looking at them, then quickly turning away their gazes, obviously believing they were seeing an extreme reaction to grief and embarrassed by it.

"I was only walking to and from the car," Scott was saying to Chyna. "I don't need the walking stick for that. Do you want me to help you inside?"

"No!" Chyna nearly shouted.

More surreptitious glances, more blushing and shifts of heads away from Chyna. "I think it's that Greer girl," Chyna heard someone mutter. "You know how strange she is."

Chyna turned her gaze to Scott. "I'm sorry," she said in the most even voice she could manage. "I'm making a fool of myself and causing you to feel awkward."

"Coming here alone was too much stress after your mother's death." Scott sounded certain. Then he asked in faint annoyance, "Where's Ned?"

"Ned is at his car dealership. I didn't ask him to come with me because . . . well, it's not important." Chyna slowly drew back from Scott, noticing how handsome he looked in his charcoal suit and burgundy tie. "He has his reasons for letting me handle this part of the ordeal."

"I think your mother would have something to say to him for pushing this entirely off on you," Scott said sternly. "You're a mess."

Chyna tried to smile. "Thanks, Scott."

"I just meant—"

"I know what you meant. I *am* a mess." Chyna still worked at a convincing smile. "You're obviously here for Nancy Tierney's funeral. I'm okay now and the service will be starting soon. You should go in."

Scott shook his head. "I barely know the Tierneys and I didn't know Nancy at all. Mom asked me to come, but I'm sure Nancy's parents won't notice if I'm here or not. There's a gourmet coffee and pastry café on the next block. Want to get something to eat and drink, take a little time to pull yourself together before you go home?"

Suddenly the thought of coffee and pastry sounded irresistible to Chyna. She knew she shouldn't drag Scott away from a funeral his mother wanted him to attend, but Chyna still felt too shaken to go to the café herself. "All right, if you're sure you don't want to attend the funeral."

"I am *very* sure a funeral is not what I need these days," Scott said firmly. "Oh God, I see Irma Vogel coming. Let's just walk away. Fast."

Scott took Chyna's arm. As he led her away from the mortuary, they heard Irma calling, "Yoo-hoo! Scott!"

"She sounds like she's yodeling," Scott grumbled. "I wonder if she practiced that dulcet tone."

Chyna smiled. "Let's hope so. If she was born with it, her mother must have gone insane by the time Irma was three years old."

Scott burst out laughing. It was the first time Chyna had heard him laugh since she'd come home, and she'd forgotten how charming that deep mixture of rumble and chuckle could be. Irma glared at them. "Guess she knows we're talking about her. Let's go before she comes over here and does us bodily harm."

CHAPTER FOUR

1

They walked to the relatively new, fashionable café L'Etoile, owned by one of Scott's best friends growing up, Ben Mayhew. The noon crowd hadn't arrived yet, and only two other couples were seated. Still, Scott picked a table in a corner under a print of Renoir's *Luncheon of the Boating Party,* one of Chyna's favorite paintings. Sun shone on the print, the café was bright and cheerful, and she felt better almost immediately. Almost.

A pretty, auburn-haired waitress around eighteen appeared at their table. "Hello, Mr. Kendrick," she said, her amber eyes lingering on his face. She fumbled with a tablet and pencil.

"Deirdre, you've known me all your life," Scott teased. "It's 'Scott' and I'm fine."

Chyna remembered Ned talking about a Ben Mayhew, just a few years older than Ned was, getting married while he was still in high school because his girlfriend was pregnant. Ned had said a lot of people thought Ben was an idiot, because he could have had a great future with the football scholarship that was a sure thing until he'd quit school to get a job and support his new family. He was throwing away everything, they said, for this girl and their unborn baby, who could have so easily been made to vanish at an abortion clinic.

Ten-year-old Chyna had thought those people must certainly be right until she'd seen Ben, his young wife, and their baby Christmas shopping a year later. His wife had tenderly carried the baby, swathed in a pink blanket and wearing a crocheted hat with a pom-pom on top. Ben had looked at both his wife and baby with such adoration, Chyna had known he hadn't thrown away anything he cared about as much as those two. And now she was talking to that baby he'd loved so much.

"How are you these days, kiddo?" Scott asked as he laid his walking stick on the chair beside him.

"I'm doing great," Deirdre said with what Chyna thought was forced enthusiasm. "Considering."

"Considering?" Scott asked.

"Well, Nancy Tierney . . ." Tears rose in the girl's beautiful eyes and she swallowed hard. "We were really good friends and you know what happened to her. Her funeral is going on right now, but I just couldn't attend. I saw her last night, at the wake. She looked so pretty and so . . ." *Dead.* The girl's thoughts seemed to scream into Chyna's head. Nancy had looked lifeless as a mannequin, Deirdre was thinking. One of the tears in her eyes trickled down her cheek and she wiped it away with the back of her hand. "I just couldn't go," Deirdre ended flatly.

Scott nodded. "I understand. One of my good friends died in high school—a car wreck—and I went to the funeral. I had nightmares about it for months. I wish I hadn't gone. He would have understood."

"I hope Nancy does," Deirdre answered dolefully. "Lynette Monroe is going. The three of us were good friends even when we were little. Lynette said Nancy would know she was attending for both of us." Deirdre shrugged. "I guess it sounds childish."

Scott said softly, "Stop worrying about it, Deirdre. Life is too short for regrets over not attending things like funerals." Then he smiled and said in what Chyna knew he meant to be a cheery voice, "Your dad told me you graduated with straight As."

Deirdre blushed. "Yes, but I had to attend summer school in order to finish this year because I needed to make up some credits. I wasn't able to take a few classes during the school year because I had to help out with Mom." Vivian had mentioned to Chyna that Anna Mayhew had died of cancer last March. "I didn't finish in time to apply for college this year," Deirdre went on. "Besides, I couldn't decide what I wanted to do, so Dad said I could work here this year since he only has Irma Vogel, who works part-time."

"Irma Vogel?" Chyna asked Scott. "Doesn't she work for you, too?"

"She's at my place three days a week and here three."

"Busy woman," Chyna said.

"Yes. She's a big help to Dad when she isn't eating up all the pastry." Deirdre blushed again. "Oh, that wasn't nice."

"But true, if I know Irma," Scott agreed, pulling a face.

"Anyway, when I decide what I want to major in, I'm definitely going to college next year," Deirdre said with a wide smile and a gay, sweeping gesture of her hand that brushed against Chyna's long hair lying across the shoulder of her jacket.

You're not going to college, you know it, and it's breaking your heart, Chyna thought with a jolt as she looked up at the fair-skinned girl with a small dimple in her chin who was apologizing profusely for messing Chyna's hair.

"You can't mess up hair that's just hanging limp as a rag," Chyna laughed.

"Oh no, it's not!" Deirdre exclaimed. "Your hair is beautiful, so soft and shiny and . . ."

Deirdre ran out of words, looking almost as if she were going to burst into tears. But your tears wouldn't be over my hair, Chyna thought. They'd be over the future you've just been reminded you might not have.

"Chyna's hair is still intact and I'm sure you'll get into any college you want next year," Scott said to Deirdre, then nodded at Chyna. "Oh, sorry I didn't introduce you. Chyna Greer, Deirdre Mayhew." They said hello at the same time, although Chyna was certain Deirdre already knew who she was. Deirdre's cheeks grew pinker. Young and bashful, Chyna thought. "Chyna is a medical resident," Scott went on. "Maybe you'd like to talk to her about the medical profession."

Deirdre's face turned redder. "I've always dreamed about being a doctor, but I'm probably not smart enough."

"Your grades say you are." Scott grinned. "Your dad told me you were invaluable in helping out a lot with your mother when she was so ill."

"That's not exactly the same as being a doctor, Mr. Kendrick—I mean Scott—and, well, I wasn't able to do anything for Mom anyway."

"No one could have saved your mother, Deirdre," Scott reassured her. "You're good in chemistry, aren't you?"

"It was my favorite class."

"Wonderful. And I'll bet you have a strong stomach, too."

Deirdre raised her eyebrows at Scott, clearly puzzled. "Is that important?"

"If you're going into medicine, it is," Chyna interrupted. "Unfortunately, few med students don't know until they're actually faced with a cadaver. I remember the first time I was in an anatomy class where we were going to see an autopsy. Some of the guys were *so* patronizing, telling me not to be ashamed if I got sick and that I'd probably have to work hard at being able to watch an autopsy, but they'd try to 'help me through' the ordeal. Meanwhile they bragged about how nothing gory bothered them." She grinned. "I was unforgivably thrilled when three of them ran down the hall to the restroom with their hands up to their mouths fifteen minutes into the autopsy."

Scott and Deirdre laughed. "Consider medicine anyway, Deirdre," Scott said. "I'm sure Chyna wouldn't mind talking with you about it in more detail, would you, Chyna?"

"Not at all," she said, noticing the adoring look in Deirdre's eyes as she looked at Scott before she dropped her pencil and order pad on the floor, her face turning even pinker as she retrieved them. I know exactly how you feel, Chyna thought. I blushed and fumbled around him all through my teenage years, too. And I still do, she thought in frustration. "If you're really interested, Deirdre, give me your home phone number and a good time to call. I'll get back to you this week."

Deirdre smiled. "That would be great, but I wouldn't want to put you out."

"You wouldn't be. I'm always happy to talk about the medical profession."

The girl quickly wrote down her name, as if Chyna would forget it, a phone number, and "any time after 8:00 P.M." on an order sheet. She tore the small piece of paper off the pad and was handing it to Chyna when a heavyset man behind the counter called, "Hey, Deirdre, you considering taking their order?"

"Sorry, Dad," Deirdre said over her shoulder, and turned back toward them with a face an even darker shade of red. There's nothing like being yelled at by your father in front of the man of your dreams, Chyna mused in sympathy.

"Give the girl a chance to be sociable, Ben," Scott called. "You want to get a reputation for being a slave driver?"

"Already got one," Ben answered with a barely there smile.

"Well, knock it off. It can't be good for business." Scott's voice was light with a serious undertone. "With those extra pounds you've gained, you should be playing the jolly innkeeper."

Ben finally laughed. "Keep your remarks about my figure to yourself, Kendrick. I just look healthy."

"Who told you that? Someone wanting free food?"

"Can you believe people used to think he was charming, honey?" Ben asked Deirdre, who giggled politely, clearly at a loss for something to add to the banter between men whose once-lively friendship had grown distant but certainly not dead.

"Dad's great," Deirdre finally got out.

"Yeah, he is," Scott said. "And he adores you, no matter how cantankerous he sounds sometimes."

Chyna folded the sheet of paper Deirdre had given her

and put it in her purse. "I won't forget to call her; I promise," she told Scott.

He grinned. "Am I being accused of criticizing you when I haven't said a word?"

"No. I can just tell you like her and I don't want you to think I'll let her down."

"She's a great kid."

"I can tell that, too."

Five minutes later, Chyna sipped a cappuccino and nibbled a chocolate biscotti. Scott drank espresso and ordered two pieces of cheesecake. "Is the cheesecake good here?" Chyna asked drily.

Scott flushed. "Well, yeah, and cheesecake is my ultimate weakness." He leaned across the table and said softly, "It's good, but not as good as your mother's."

Chyna smiled. "She'd be so pleased to hear you say that."

"Maybe she can hear me."

"Ah, a believer in the afterlife?"

"Definitely." He paused, looking at her intently. "And you?"

Intellectually, *no,* she wanted to say. But how could she take that stance when she'd been hearing voices from beyond the grave since she was seven, and particularly the last two days? "I'll take the Fifth on that issue," she answered lightly.

Scott sipped his espresso and looked at her with his depthless dark eyes. "Why were you so shaken at the funeral home? And don't tell me it's because death always frightens you. I won't believe that one coming from a doctor who deals with death every day."

"I try to stop death every day."

"That's very noble. It's also evasive."

"How about the time-honored expression 'it was meant to be'?"

"That won't work, either."

Chyna picked up her cappuccino, saw that her hand was shaking, and immediately put down the cup. "Do I have to tell you what frightened me?"

"No. You don't *have* to tell me anything. But I think confiding in me might make you feel better. I don't know why I think that—we're not exactly best friends—but I've known you all your life."

"You've barely known me."

"I've known you better than you think. Our mothers' friendship, remember? I've heard a lot about you. Besides, I've had an interest in you since you were a teenager. If I hadn't been seven years older than you . . ." Chyna raised an eyebrow and Scott's cheeks reddened. "Well, that sure didn't come out right. I sound like a pedophile. What I meant was that you've never been invisible to me. Not even when you were only seven or eight. I always thought you were . . . different."

"Different? Is that because people thought I was a kook?"

"Different because you were special." Chyna stared at him. "Oh, forget it," Scott said. "I can't explain how I felt. I didn't understand it myself."

"Well, that's helpful." Scott looked at her closely, as if he expected her to be offended, but she smiled at him. "I'll take 'special' any day over 'a kook.'" Chyna finally felt calm enough to lift her cappuccino cup to her mouth. "Your mother will be angry when she finds out you didn't attend the funeral."

"My mother hasn't gotten even miffed with me since the plane accident. I'm beginning to feel like a hothouse flower. She even lapses into baby talk over the phone."

"She's grateful you weren't killed, Scott."

"I should have been." He looked at her with such sudden sadness in his eyes, Chyna felt overwhelmed. His voice was so sincere, his gaze so full of pain, she knew his feeling of guilt ran even deeper than she had imagined.

"Scott, the crash was in no way your fault," she said softly, even though no one sat near them. "I read everything I could find about it. I know what the investigation revealed."

"The fan on number three engine failed, slicing through the plane's hydraulic lines," Scott said, his voice emotionless. "Without hydraulic fluid, the plane was almost totally out of control—jerking, shuddering. No elevators to control the pitch. No aileron control."

"Aileron?"

"It's a movable surface at the edge of the wing that controls maneuvers like banking. We were losing altitude; we couldn't turn right. We'd lost the steering. Without hydraulics, we had no brakes."

Scott's eyes stared at her without seeing her. They were lost back on that horrible day. She could literally feel his panic, his fight for inner control, his mind scrambling for a way to get the plane down without crashing. He couldn't know it, but her heart was probably beating as hard as his had during those awful moments as the plane dropped inexorably toward the ground. She knew it had hit, risen again, then nose-dived and split into four pieces.

"Scott, you saved one hundred and four people," Chyna said gently.

"And killed seventy-two."

"*You* didn't kill them. The plane malfunctioned. You're not omnipotent. You couldn't control what happened to the engine fan. The newspapers said it was a miracle everyone wasn't killed and that miracle was due to your skill."

"My *luck*." Scott looked out the window. "We were over flatlands. If we'd been over a city, mountains, an ocean, there would have been no survivors."

"Maybe it wasn't luck. Maybe it was destiny."

Scott looked back at her, a bitter smile on his face. "Then destiny was awfully cruel to those seventy-two people who went up in flames when the plane crashed. Ten of them were children, Chyna. Children under twelve. They never really got a chance at life. But here I am. I was thrown clear of that inferno with some lacerations, a pulled ligament in my leg, and first-degree burns." He hesitated. "I ask myself a hundred times a day if I should go back to being a pilot, and I don't think I can."

Chyna paused, absorbing what he'd said, trying to come up with a comforting line, but she couldn't and be honest, too. "I wish I had answers, Scott. I wish I knew why those people died, but I don't. I haven't a clue any more than I know why the innocent children I treat so often die of cancer. I wish I had faith that everything happens for the best—it would make death so much easier to accept—but I don't have that kind of faith. So I simply do what I can to prevent even more sadness in the world than there is, and that's exactly what you *did*, Scott. You saved one hundred and four people. That's more than I've saved. Many more."

Scott continued to look at her, but his bitter smile faded. "I'm ashamed of myself for sitting here whining to you. Your job must be incredibly draining. Your mother has just died. You're still grieving over her and I could see guilt about Zoey in your eyes down at the lake yesterday." She lowered her gaze. "You can't hide your sense of responsibility for Zoey or for your mother, Chyna. You don't have to hide it. I understand." She glanced up. He looked at her with a softness and compassion in his eyes. "I told you at the lake, I know you better than you think I do."

"That's because you've heard so much about me from your mother."

"I'm fairly sure it's something deeper than that."

"I don't know what it could be," Chyna returned. "Do you know this is the longest conversation we've ever had?"

"I guess it is." Their conversation had become gloomy, and Chyna sensed Scott wanted a change. Eyes twinkling, he looked at her and said, "It seems strange that we've never really talked, considering all the intimate stuff I know about you."

Chyna almost choked on her cappuccino. "All the intimate stuff you know about me? Like what?"

"Well, I can't go into it *here*." Chyna played along, staring at him with wide eyes. For at least thirty seconds he stared back solemnly. Then he laughed. "I'm teasing, Chyna, although that horrified look you just gave me has made me wildly curious."

She set down her cup casually. "I'm really very boring."

"Uh-huh."

"Well, I *am*."

"Do you know you're the first woman who has ever tried to convince me she's *boring*?"

"Really?"

"Yes. Absolutely."

"Oh. Well, I guess there's a first time for everything." Chyna paused. "But I *am* boring."

"Whatever you say."

Chyna was on the verge of going into details about just how boring she was, suddenly perplexingly bent on proving she wasn't worth his interest, when she realized Scott's smile was genuine. She thought of the misery that had been there only minutes ago and decided she'd say just about anything to keep that look from returning. "Well, all right, you've found me out, Scott. I stay on the down low here in Black Willow, but I'm an absolute wild woman in Albuquerque."

"I've always suspected it, no matter how hardworking your mother claimed you were."

"Oh, I'm not really a medical resident. Actually, I run a call girl service."

"I'm impressed. You're so young to be a *madam*."

"Well, you said I was smart."

"Not to mention enterprising." Scott grinned, motioning for the waitress. Deirdre had appeared beside them again, this time looking slightly more composed.

"Would you like something else?"

Scott nodded. "I'd like another espresso."

"And more cheesecake?" Deirdre asked in amusement, looking at his two empty cake plates. Chyna couldn't stifle a snicker.

"No, I think I've had enough, Deirdre. It was delicious." He looked at Chyna. "Another cappuccino or biscotti?"

"Another cappuccino," Chyna said.

After Deirdre left, Scott looked at the white silk rose on the table for moment, then raised his dark eyes to Chyna. "I've poured out my heart to you for the last twenty minutes. Why don't you tell me why you looked like you were going to faint outside the mortuary?"

Chyna immediately stiffened. "I don't like mortuaries."

"Here we go again. You're trying to evade my questions, but you're not getting off that easily, Chyna." He leaned across the table and spoke softly. "There was definitely something wrong when I came up to you, and as disagreeable as arranging your mother's funeral must have been, I don't think it would have left you looking near death yourself."

"I was just tired, nervous. . . ." Deirdre brought the cappuccino and left with a whiff of vanilla-scented cologne—the same scent Zoey had worn twelve years ago. Chyna felt the color drain from her face.

Scott reached out and took her hand with a firm grip. "You're like ice and it's not cold in here." He frowned. "Chyna, what's wrong?"

"I . . . I don't know." Let go of my hand, she thought. Let me go home and be alone. I don't want to talk about my feelings. "I'm just sad and I feel like I don't know what I'm doing. . . ."

"You're not the helpless type," Scott said sternly. "And no, I'm not turning loose of your hand so you can run away." She looked at him in surprise. "I didn't read your mind. You're trying to pull your hand out of mine and you're looking desperately at the door."

"Oh. The master detective."

"Just observant." He seemed to scrutinize her face, his hand still firmly holding hers. "I can't let you leave and drive home when you're so obviously upset. Come on, Chyna; humor me. I've just been through a terrible experience, remember? Humor me and tell me what's wrong."

Chyna glanced down at his hand holding hers, a hand much larger than her own, with a light dusting of black hair on the back, and two Band-Aids. The stitches have been removed, she thought absently, but the wounds still need protection.

"Chyna?"

When she was thirteen, Chyna had vowed she would never discuss her ESP with anyone except Zoey, a vow she'd kept. She realized she still harbored her old attraction to Scott, but that didn't explain why she now had the urge to tell him the thing about herself she'd kept secret for years. Abruptly Chyna made up her mind. She felt as if she *needed* to open that secret part of herself, to tell her secret, and she wanted the recipient of that secret to be Scott.

"All right." Still looking down, she began to talk. "Scott, have you ever thought you heard voices?"

She lifted her gaze. His face had become expressionless and she thought she saw wariness creeping into his eyes. "You mean those voices that say, 'This isn't a good idea,' or, 'Maybe I should check this lock, just to be sure'? That kind of voice?"

"Well, yes," Chyna said carefully, not wanting to immediately lose Scott's attention by describing the kind of voices she *did* mean. "I guess you'd call them thoughts, only loud thoughts."

"*Warning* thoughts."

"Yes," Chyna nearly pounced. "Not just the usual stream-of-consciousness sort of thing, but thoughts that seem to leap out from the rest to get your attention."

"I have those," Scott said slowly.

"Do you think *everyone* has them?"

"Yes." Chyna noticed he was rubbing the Band-Aids on his hand again. "I don't think they're unusual, Chyna. I believe some of them are the subconscious repeating warnings you've been given in the past. I think the rest of the voices are really instinctive thoughts for self-preservation that all normal people have."

"That makes sense," Chyna said. "I believe that, too. But what if the thoughts are . . . stronger?"

"Stronger?"

"What if they manifest themselves as voices?"

Scott waited an instant before answering. "I'm not an expert or anything, Chyna, but it seems to me a particularly strong thought could *seem* like an actual voice coming from someone besides yourself."

"Even if it isn't warning you about something?"

Scott stopped scratching his hand and leaned closer to her, frowning. "Why don't you just *say* what you're talking about instead of circling it like a plane circling the runway? Because you *are* talking about a particular experience, Chyna. I can tell. And I think it happened to you in the mortuary."

Chyna looked up at the Renoir print, tucked her long hair behind her ears, and finally said softly, "Nancy Tierney spoke to me."

2

Scott stared at her in obvious shock for a moment before blurting out, "*What?*"

Chyna drew back, offended. "I knew you'd react that way!"

"And other people wouldn't?" Disbelief, chariness, and an urge to flee crossed Scott's face all in the space of less than a minute. Then he seemed to use all his strength to compose himself mentally, gave Chyna a tolerant, if not understanding, look, and said quietly, "Tell me exactly what happened."

She hesitated, furious with herself. She was certain he didn't believe her, but she'd blundered by telling him about Nancy instead of keeping her mouth shut as she should have. Now she'd backed herself into a corner and couldn't just leave things hanging without explaining the incident.

Chyna began slowly, being careful to keep her voice calm and her manner composed. "After we'd discussed the arrangements for Mom, Owen Burtram was walking me to the mortuary door when someone came saying they needed him immediately. Owen told me not to go into the 'slumber room' where a funeral was to be held in about half an hour. I was leaving when I passed that 'slumber room.'

"I didn't know anything about Nancy Tierney or her death. I was just drawn in, almost against my will," Chyna plowed on, not quite meeting Scott's eyes for fear of what she might see. "There was a mountain of flowers, classical music playing, and lighting that threw everything into a soft glow. I looked in the casket and there was Nancy, beautiful and looking as if she were asleep. And then I heard a voice. She said," Chynna's own voice changed slightly as she imitated the singsong quality of the voice that had seemed to come from Nancy, " 'Star light, star bright, first star I see tonight . . .' Nancy's mouth wasn't moving, of course, but the voice sounded like Zoey's down at the lake—"

"Down at the lake?" Scott interrupted.

"I'll get to that later." Chyna's gaze finally met Scott's, challenging the guarded expression in his eyes. "Anyway, as soon as Nancy had finished speaking, Rusty came in."

"But he didn't hear her."

"I told you she'd already finished speaking. No. Rusty didn't hear her. By then, the only sound was music. I asked Rusty about the girl in the coffin. He told me she was Nancy Tierney, his niece, and how she'd died."

"I see."

Chyna looked at Scott in disappointment. "You don't believe me."

He fidgeted with a Band-Aid, then said carefully, "Well, I won't say that I believe Nancy spoke to you."

"You don't have to tiptoe around me, Scott. Just say what you mean."

"You've been through a lot, Chyna, and after all, Nancy *is* dead. But I do think you heard something or *thought* you heard something." Chyna stared at him, frustration rushing through her. "It might have been a hallucination. Wasn't Nancy the same age and coloring as Zoey Simms?"

"Yes, but—"

"Couldn't you have been projecting your sadness about Zoey onto Nancy?"

"I *could* have, but I *wasn't*." For the first time, Chyna thought of the incident with absolute assurance. She *had* heard the rhyme coming from Nancy. "I told you it wasn't the first time I've heard that rhyme," Chyna said, wishing she could stop talking but unable to stem her flow of words.

"The day we were at Lake Manicora, I heard the same thing. You'd already gone to your rehab session. I was still standing by the pond and I heard: 'Star light, star bright . . . ' "

"Was that a favorite rhyme of yours when you were young?"

"No. I've heard it, of course, but I never went around saying it or even thinking of it. And there was more." Scott gazed at her steadily and kept scratching his bandaged hand. "The voice at the lake—Zoey's voice; I'd know it anywhere even now—said, 'Chyna, I'm lost in the dark.' I looked all around. No one was near me. Hardly anyone was at the lake that day, if you remember, Scott. When I heard the voice, I'm ashamed to admit my impulse was to take off like a coward, but I was too scared to move."

Chyna took a sip of her cold cappuccino before going on. "The voice asked if I was listening; then it said, 'You're the only one who can help me.' Then I *did* try to leave, but Michelle wouldn't budge. Usually one little tug on the leash and along she comes, but not that day. The voice went on. 'You have to find me, because there were other girls like me. There will be more girls like me if you don't do something.' "

Scott's fingers tapped the white tabletop. Finally, he said, "My mother told me you only come home at Christmas and you haven't been to the lake since Zoey disappeared. It was probably the influence—"

"Zoey disappeared in July, Scott, not October," Chyna flared. "The lake doesn't look anything like it does in midsummer. And I'm not even going to mention the gazebo, which used to be pretty and is now a wreck. The atmosphere was completely different the day we were there from the last time I saw Zoey at the lake, so don't tell me I was influenced by being in the place that looked just like it did when Zoey vanished."

"Okay."

"And another thing," Chyna rushed on hotly. "I wasn't the only one who heard that voice. Michelle did. I told you she wouldn't move when it started. As it went on, she stepped into the water, which was highly unusual. I think she's the only yellow Lab in the world who hates water. Her ears perked up. The hair on her back stood up. She *heard* something, Scott Kendrick, and it scared her!"

"All right," Scott said mildly. "You don't have to get so mad just because I offered a suggestion. Besides, you're getting loud, your face is red, and everyone is looking at us."

"I don't care!"

But Chyna did care, embarrassed and hoping everyone would experience immediate memory loss. No such luck, though. Deirdre approached the table cautiously, gave them each a tentative smile, and asked, "Would you like anything else?"

Scott suddenly acted casually amused. "Not unless you have something to calm ruffled feathers. Seems I said the wrong thing." Chyna glared at him, but his gaze was fixed on pretty, young Deirdre. "I'll have a glass of milk this time. It's supposed to be calming. One for the lady, too."

"I don't want a glass of milk," Chyna hissed.

"Get her one anyway, Deirdre. She'll thank me for it later."

As soon as Deirdre left, Chyna said, "Well, aren't *you* the big, strong man trying to settle down the little lady having a tantrum!"

"Please don't get mad again. Almost everyone has stopped staring at us, and a glass of milk won't kill you."

"I hate milk. I won't drink it!"

"You sound very grown-up, Chyna. At least five years old. You might have to be sent to bed without supper."

Chyna glowered at him for a moment, then lowered her gaze in shame. She'd sounded about as mature as her niece and nephew. Most men would have walked out on her. This one had merely tried to tease her out of her anger. "I'm sorry," she said reluctantly.

"Okay." He smiled at her. "So, you're *sure* you heard the voice at the lake."

"I don't want to talk about this anymore."

"Well, I do and you owe me for embarrassing me in one of Black Willow's classiest joints. Now, tell me about the voice at the lake."

Chyna sighed. After all, she'd brought up the subject, she reminded herself. The least she could do was finish her story. "All right." She began quietly. "Honestly, Scott, at first I thought I imagined the voice. I thought about how tired I was, how upset I was over Mom's death, how little I'd had to eat, on and on." She paused. "Then I considered how oddly Michelle had acted. She was frightened, Scott, and I don't think dogs imagine the dead speaking to them."

"But they react to their master's—or mistress's— emotions. It all has to do with their being able to sense your adrenaline levels, and if my guess is right, yours was soaring."

"Yes, I'm sure it was, but she's never acted that way before."

Deirdre arrived with the milk. Scott gave her a dazzling smile. Chyna managed a weak tremor around the mouth. She knew a smile wasn't going to change the girl's opinion of her now. When Deirdre left, Scott leaned across the table and said, "You can lift your head. I don't think you're the center of attention anymore." She looked at him, still self-conscious but encouraged by the good-natured humor in his eyes. "You think I was dismissing you as overimaginative," he said. "Maybe I was a little, and I'm sorry. Apology accepted?"

After a pause, she nodded. "Yes, if you don't make me drink every drop of this milk I don't want."

"Deal. But take a few sips. It's good for you and you're looking on the thin side to me. Now, has anything else strange happened?"

She took a sip of the milk and decided it wasn't so bad, after all. "Yes, and I'll tell you if you promise not to dismiss me as a high-strung nut."

"Wouldn't dream of it. I haven't dismissed the other two things, either, although I might have sounded like it."

"You did. But here goes." Chyna told him about the call

from Anita Simms—the strange, windy sound behind Anita's voice, Anita sounding as if she'd just called to check up on Zoey—and finally about calling Ned and having him say that Anita had killed herself last year. She also described Michelle's behavior during the call. "I know you're going to say she was just reacting to my fear," Chyna said, "but there was one more thing. The woman on the phone called me 'Bubble Gum.' No one else ever did."

"Couldn't someone else have heard the name?"

"Besides Zoey and my mother? Anita only stayed for the night when she came to pick up Zoey. I don't think she ever even met anyone around here. And Mom never used the nickname."

Scott sat almost rigid in his chair, staring at her. She met his stare, determined not to act as if she doubted herself. She knew if he rejected her accounts of voices and phone calls, no matter how politely, she would be humiliated. Even worse, she would be deeply hurt, which was silly, because Scott Kendrick was not even a real part of her life. He was nothing but a guy she'd had a crush on for years when she was young.

Scott leaned forward, making a temple of his fingers, and asked without a trace of derision, "Are you sure you didn't dream Anita Simms's call?"

"I am absolutely sure," she returned firmly. "And I wasn't dreaming or hallucinating when I heard the voice at the lake or the voice in the mortuary."

Scott looked at her steadily, then nodded. "When you were younger you heard voices. My mother told me you did."

"Yes. When I was much younger. Then I told everyone I didn't hear them anymore. Actually, I was just embarrassed by the way people looked at me and treated me, so I disciplined myself to shut out the voices, and I was fairly successful. In fact, in the last few years, I've only heard them a handful of times. But they weren't voices like these. There was no tonal quality—I couldn't tell if the voice was male or female—and they certainly never chanted nursery rhymes or called me by old nicknames or begged me for help, like Zoey's did."

Scott lowered his gaze, staring at the white silk rose in a bud vase on the table. He thinks I'm a lunatic, Chyna thought. Either that or he's trying not to laugh in my face out of respect for both of our mothers. But when he looked up, his dark eyes were serious, his expression grave. For a moment, Chyna thought he was being extremely cautious with what he considered an unbalanced woman and getting ready to say she needed professional help. But when he spoke, he surprised her.

"Chyna, I don't believe in ESP. I've never even thought it might be possible, then rejected the notion. But what you're telling me . . ." She nearly stopped breathing while she waited for what he would say. "I don't understand myself right now, but for some reason, I believe that everything you've told me *has* actually happened."

She was stunned. "You do?"

"Yes. I can't explain why something I've always dismissed as overimagination or plain trickery suddenly sounds possible to me." He gave her a humorless look. "I said *possible,* not *probable.* But coming from you . . ."

"But coming from me . . . what?"

"You've always struck me as so levelheaded, so sensible, that I'm considering it might actually *be* possible. I have to keep in mind that I don't know everything. Phenomena I never thought about can, probably do, exist in the world."

Chyna's breath came out in a rush. "Thank you, Scott, for taking that attitude." She paused. "I wish my father had thought the same thing." She heard the slight pain in her voice. "He believed there was something wrong with me. That's why I stopped telling anyone except Zoey when I had a vision or a premonition."

"Zoey said my *gift,* my *power*—whatever you call it— would be our secret," Chyna went on. "Everyone else, including Ned, thought I was just going through a phase of wanting to get attention by making up stuff. That didn't explain how what I said about the past had actually happened or what I said about the future came true, but sometimes people don't want to accept what frightens them. When I stopped mentioning my visions, people thought I'd outgrown my need for attention or my vivid imagination. The visions didn't stop coming, but they became rare. The voice, however, never stopped. I just tried to ignore it."

"But you said the voice was different now."

"Well, yes." Chyna was still reluctant to discuss the issue, although Scott seemed to be taking her seriously, and she began slowly. "As I said, in the past, the voice didn't belong to anyone, certainly not Zoey or Anita. It was always flat, anonymous."

Scott curled and uncurled his fingers, his gaze turned inward. I've lost him, Chyna thought. He thinks I'm a lunatic and he's trying to come up with a graceful way of escaping me. As she sat there, feeling ludicrous for caring so much about having lost his good opinion of her, he said, "Chyna, I'm going to keep an open mind about all of this because you've always struck me as being an extremely smart and rational woman."

"Oh," Chyna said simply, dumbfounded. Was he sincere? Or was he merely flirting with the girl who'd had a crush on him since she was twelve? "Well, if you do believe me—"

"I said I'll keep an open mind, not that I'm convinced."

"Pardon me," she snapped, suddenly angry. He was making fun of her. She was sure of it. "I do so appreciate your open mind."

"Now you're mad again."

"I'm not."

"You are."

"Okay, I am. I never claimed to have ESP, and I don't like to be laughed at."

"Who's laughing?"

"Certainly not me."

"Not me, either," Scott said. "Give a guy a chance to wrap his mind around an idea he's rejected for thirty-five years."

"All right," she said. "I'll settle for an open mind, if not enthusiastic belief."

Scott smiled broadly. "Thank you. And will you do something for me?"

"That depends."

He suddenly looked serious. "You gave me the impression that you don't confide these visions, voices, all of it, to Ned or Beverly or anyone."

"I don't."

"Then keep it that way. From now on, tell these experiences only to me. I promise not to dismiss them as silly imaginings. I also promise not to confide in other people. What you tell me will be strictly confidential, just between us. I think it's important that you only tell me."

"Why?"

He shrugged. "I just do." He forced a grin. "You don't want people saying the things they did about you when you were a teenager, do you?" She shook her head. "Then promise me."

Was his request merely a kindness? Was he just trying to get her to shut up so that everyone in town wouldn't think she was crazy? Maybe. But even if it were, he was showing her great consideration. He was willing to listen, just as Zoey had done so long ago. Finally, Chyna said softly, "All right. I promise."

Scott nodded, his face solemn. "Don't worry, Chyna. I take promises seriously."

Five minutes later, it was time for Scott to leave for his rehab. "A week more of this and I'm done, thank God," he said, reaching for his cane. "I'm sure it's good for me, but I've had enough. It's just another reminder of the crash."

Chyna was trying to think of something profound to say when Deirdre Mayhew appeared beside them. She was so pretty with her auburn hair and amber eyes. "It was a pleasure meeting you, Dr. Greer," she said shyly.

"It was a pleasure meeting you," Chyna said. "I'll see you later this week and we can talk about college, even medicine.

Don't doubt yourself, Deirdre. I'm sure you're smart enough
to be anything you want to be."

Deirdre blushed and smiled in delight. Later, Chyna was
thankful she'd made the girl happy, even for a moment.

CHAPTER FIVE

1

Although the house was stocked with food for people, all that remained for Michelle was Gravy Train. Chyna stopped at the grocery store on the way home and chose a variety of moist food and Michelle's favorite treats. On a whim, Chyna also bought the dog a small rubber baseball that squeaked—one of Michelle's favorite toys at home that Chyna had forgotten to pack—and a small, fuzzy teddy bear for the times when Michelle seemed to want to be a mother. At least, that's what Chyna thought.

Afterward she thought of stopping by Beverly's to let her know all the arrangements had been made for Vivian's cremation, but Chyna decided the fear she'd experienced in the mortuary still showed on her face. Beverly would immediately spot it and ask questions Chyna was determined not to answer, partly because she didn't want to think about the terrifying incident anymore and partly because she'd promised Scott she would only talk with him about anything strange that happened. She'd promised immediately, without thought, and now she wondered both why he'd wanted her to promise and why she'd done so almost without the slightest hesitation.

"I'm losing it," she said aloud. "Thinking I hear voices, making promises I haven't given any consideration." At a red light, she closed her eyes for a moment. "I'm done for the day," she said. "No more analyzing, no more confiding, not even small talk with Beverly."

Chyna opened her eyes just as the light turned green and she headed right, toward the Greer house, away from Ned's. She needed to be alone, she thought. She needed to spend the rest of the afternoon in the house she'd grown up in and loved, and she needed her dog for company. Only her dog. After all, Michelle never asked many questions.

When she pulled into the driveway, Chyna saw that the big white truck with "Ridgeway Construction" written in red on the side was gone. Gage had finished his work, or he'd been so freaked out by her behavior this morning, he'd simply abandoned the job for the day. In either case, she was glad she wouldn't have to think of anything normal to say to him after she'd just remembered the way he'd flirted with Zoey the last week of her life. Chyna could just unload her shopping bags and not be troubled by his very presence.

Vivian Greer had never liked a quiet house. Chyna remembered her younger years when the house was always filled with the sound of television newscasts coming from one of three televisions, music coming from their state-of-the-art stereo system, or Vivian herself playing the grand piano in the living room. Walking into her dead-silent former home now gave Chyna the creeps, as if she could hear the empty house breathing death and sorrow all around her. She nearly ran for the television and turned on an afternoon re-run of *Law & Order.* At least it's one of my favorite shows, she thought, turning up the sound as Detective Lennie Briscoe interrogated a "perp."

Michelle, who'd obviously been napping, thundered down the stairs to Chyna's side. She gave her dog a powerful hug. "I absolutely could not stay in this house if you weren't here to keep me company," she told the dog, who fervently licked Chyna's cheek. "It's been another one of those days, you know, when you have dead people talking to you?"

Michelle tilted her head and looked as if she were frowning, making Chyna laugh. "I guess you never have dead dogs talking to you, but you wouldn't tell me if you did."

Chyna unpacked everything she'd bought downtown, muttering a curse when she realized she'd forgotten to get candy. After all, tonight was trick or treat. Although they were never inundated with trick-or-treaters willing to climb the hill for a piece of candy, there were always a few hardy souls who made it. She'd seen at least half a bag of candy when she searched the cabinets last night. Maybe that would be enough. Otherwise, she'd have to turn off all the lights and pretend not to be home. That move should earn her at least a few nasty messages written in soap on the windows.

Pushing the candy crisis out of her mind, Chyna placed the canine paraphernalia she'd bought for Michelle on the floor. The dog sniffed all of it intently, making Chyna think of dogs trained to sniff for drugs, returned with special interest three times to the stuffed bear, then gently picked it up and carried it into another room. Chyna knew Michelle would bring the bear to bed tonight and try to snuggle both her and the toy. If I get her more stuffed animals, I'll have to buy a bigger bed, Chyna thought in amusement.

But it wouldn't be her bed upstairs. Within two weeks, she would be heading back to New Mexico. Although Chyna had always loved this house, she had to admit that this time she was anxious to leave and didn't know if she could ever make herself return to a place where she'd lost her father, her mother, and, of course, Zoey.

2

Gage Ridgeway turned off the highway and drove his truck over the dirt and gravel road, past the old barn, beyond the aluminum equipment shack where he stored a ride mower, a tractor, and a Harley-Davidson Electra Glide motorcycle he'd had since he was eighteen. He finally stopped in front of the white farmhouse he'd lived in for the past ten years. His parents said he was crazy to buy the place. He didn't farm the surrounding twelve acres of land, he kept no animals and therefore had no use for the old barn, and after a brief, tumultuous marriage that ended six years ago with his declaration that he would never marry again, he certainly didn't need a rambling five-bedroom house constantly in need of repairs. Or so his parents told him repeatedly. Gage, however, loved the privacy the house afforded him, no matter how old and impractical it was. He'd bought it with money left to him by his grandfather, money Gage knew his father thought he should have largely invested in Ridgeway Construction.

Gage glanced at his watch. It was only midafternoon. He could have stayed two more hours and finished his work on the Greer house, but the more he thought about the way Chyna had looked at him before slamming down the window, the more agitated he felt. Finally, he decided he could not be there when she returned. He wanted to be alone. He wanted to think.

He unlocked the front door, slammed it behind him, went straight to the kitchen, and opened the refrigerator. Not much food in it—he usually brought home unhealthy meals from fast-food restaurants—but at least he'd had the good sense to buy a twelve-pack of Michelob beer. Had he experienced a premonition yesterday that urged him to buy more beer when he already had a few cans left? No, premonitions used to be Chyna Greer's specialty, he thought sourly, or so she'd claimed. He'd merely bought the beer because it was on sale. He wondered for a moment if it had been on sale to encourage him to buy it. Then he decided the day had shaken him into harebrained thinking. He'd also been shaken into unwanted memories of certain people.

Particularly, Zoey Simms, Heather Phelps, and Edie Larson.

When Zoey Simms disappeared, no one bothered him beyond asking the usual questions about the last time he'd seen her, because someone had reported his speaking to her downtown one day when she was with Chyna Greer. He had a girl to thank for making the cops back off immediately, a girl he'd been with the night Zoey disappeared, who told the police her date with Gage had lasted until nearly 1:00 A.M., hours after Chyna said Zoey had met her mystery man. The girl had added, "Who'd think Gage would even *look* at Zoey Simms when he's dating *me*!"

Over a year later, Heather Phelps had vanished, and once again, the police questioned him, because he'd done work at the Phelps house for Ridgeway Construction. The questions were cursory, though, especially when Mr. and Mrs. Phelps said they'd never seen Heather even speak to Gage.

But two years later, Edie Larson became a different matter. Edie had been his girlfriend. His mother had dragged him to a community production of *Our Town* and he'd spotted a sixteen-year-old Edie who'd mesmerized him, not just because of her beauty but also because of her talent, a talent that had earned her rave reviews in every newspaper within a hundred-mile radius. He'd immediately asked her out and she'd accepted.

But other people didn't understand their relationship because Edie was three years younger than he was. Townspeople immediately thought it was suspicious that he'd date a girl—a minor—when he *should* have been with a girl his own age. Edie was quiet and kept to herself, so those people didn't know how mature she was for her age, a consequence of growing up in a home where just getting through each day was a physical and mental challenge. They didn't know she was smart and funny and upbeat. Edie never let her miserable life destroy her optimism or her dreams of becoming a movie star. In most of the locals' opinions, Edie was just a pretty girl from a bad family, who'd happened to make a splash in a small-town play, but who was definitely too young for a man two months shy of twenty.

And then she went missing just like Zoey Simms and Heather Phelps had.

The continual police questioning, the sudden linking of Edie with Zoey and Heather, the growing suspicion of and antipathy toward Gage, had almost driven him out of town. He supposed that's why when his grandfather Henry died, he'd left him so much money and a percentage of the business, a fact Gage's father still resented after all these years. Henry Ridgeway didn't think his son, Peter, had what it took to run Ridgeway Construction. Henry thought Gage did. He'd known that if he passed over his son, Peter, and left everything to Gage, townspeople would be appalled that the mild-mannered, ever-pleasant, malleable Peter had been cheated and would take out their indignation on Gage and the business. So, Henry had left the bulk of the construction company to Peter. Henry had left Gage enough of the business he loved, though, to make sure he wouldn't abandon Ridgeway Construction.

So Gage had stayed, every day enduring his father's ill-concealed seething resentment, and bought a place where he could be close enough to his job to make commuting easy but still have plenty of privacy, which was what he craved.

Gage popped open the can of beer, walked back into the living room, and dropped onto the old brown vinyl recliner. In places the vinyl had split and white stuffing stuck out, but he didn't mind. When *Architectural Digest* came to do a spread on his home, he'd claim the stuffing-spouting tears in the vinyl added to the chair's charm, he told himself, laughing. So did the faded hooked rug, the sagging couch, and the cheap plastic molding of a conquistador he'd bought at a yard sale and hung over the fireplace.

He picked up the television remote control lying on the folding metal table beside the chair and flipped on a game show. He hated game shows, but he decided to make himself watch it, shouting out answers between gulps of beer. But his mind wasn't on the show or the beer. It was on Chyna. She'd looked even more beautiful than ever. And when she'd opened the window, she'd seemed delighted by his mangled version of "Satisfaction." She'd been friendly. His heart had soared. And then he'd seen the doubt in her eyes. The suspicion. Even the fear. When she slammed down the window, his wrath had been so great he'd seen nothing but black for a moment. He'd hung on to the ladder, fighting for control, willing relief for the sudden, stabbing pain in his head. Finally, his vision had cleared and he'd seen her tearing out of the driveway. "Get away, little Chyna!" he'd shouted. "Get away before big, bad Gage Ridgeway drags you into the void, just like he did your friend Zoey and poor little Heather and Edie!"

He now took another slug of beer, realized he'd already drained the can, went back for a second one, then decided to bring a third and fourth along because the second one would be gone in less than five minutes. Maybe by the time he finished the fourth beer, he would be able to wipe the image of Nancy Tierney out of his mind. Nancy, with her long blond hair and voluptuous body. Nancy, who in spite of all his better instincts he'd picked up in his car a couple of nights when she'd told her parents she was going to study with one of her friends. How unfortunate that one of those nights, when he was dropping her off a block from her house, they'd been seen.

He couldn't believe no one had even questioned him yet about her, that the person who'd seen them together hadn't said anything or didn't recognize him. But eventually they would, even though Nancy had probably been with at least twenty older guys like him during the last year. She didn't like boys her own age, she'd told him. They *were* just boys, and she liked men. Unfortunately, right before she'd died, she'd decided Gage was the flavor of the month, and as usual, he couldn't say no to a pretty face and dynamite body.

He'd been a fool to mess around with Nancy. A damned, stupid fool. Hadn't age and his experience with Edie taught him anything? Apparently not. And now Nancy was dead.

Gage thought about going out to the equipment shed, getting his Harley, and going for a long ride. After all, the powerful motorcycle was in excellent condition. He only took it out every couple of months, then washed it, covered it with canvas, and left it propped up by its kickstand on the clean concrete floor of the shed.

But he never rode it when he'd been drinking, not because he was worried about his own safety but because he feared damaging the machine he'd loved almost as much as he'd ever loved a person. Perhaps even more.

No, there would be no ride this afternoon, Gage thought. He took another gulp of beer, knowing that not even four beers would help him today. Maybe six beers and a little bit of bourbon. Or a lot of bourbon.

He was in that kind of mood.

3

Chyna was always so used to the fast-paced life of the hospital, she hardly knew what to do with herself on break. She'd taken Michelle for a walk, this time hiking up the gentle hillside behind the house, not downward toward Lake Manicora. Chyna had wiped down the kitchen, which was already spotless, and rearranged the spice rack because the bottles were slightly out of alphabetical order. Finally, she tried to play the piano the way her mother liked to do. Michelle loyally sat by Chyna's side, but when she looked down into the dog's unhappy face she had to admit that the years had not improved her talent. "Better hope I make it as a doctor," she told the dog. "I certainly can't support the two of us as a pianist in a restaurant."

When she rose from the piano bench, Michelle jumped up happily. "Glad the ordeal is over?" Chyna asked. "I promise I won't play again. I'll put on some real music."

She flipped through the box of CDs and picked out one by the Carpenters. Chyna could remember Ned rolling his eyes whenever his mother played the Carpenters' music—they were far too all-American apple pie for him—but Edward liked the music and Vivian always sang along with Karen. Vivian's voice was nowhere near the quality of Karen's, but at least she didn't mangle the songs as Chyna did when she used to wail out "Superstar," setting their ancient hound dog howling.

It was too early for dinner, especially after the biscottis Chyna had had earlier, so she decided to read. After flipping through a *National Geographic,* then a *Vogue*, then a *Newsweek,* choosing articles, reading one page three times and not remembering a word, she gave up. Next, she tried television but had no better luck with concentration there, either.

Finally, she looked out the windows. At five forty-five, already yellow had faded from the sky, replaced by pale gray that would soon turn to a depressing shade of granite. "Well, I'm not hungry yet, but I'm sure you are," she said to Michelle, who lay at her feet.

Chyna fixed a heaping bowl of dog food—more than Michelle should have, because she already needed to take off at least five pounds—but reasoned that Michie didn't need to be dieting on a vacation. And sadly enough, this would be their vacation for the year. As Chyna set the bowl on the kitchen floor, her eyes finally filled with tears for her mother. "Oh, Mom, why did this have to happen?" she asked aloud, wiping at her face with her hand. "You were so young, so full of life, so much my *mommy*, even when you were a thousand miles away."

Michelle didn't touch her food but sat looking with what Chyna interpreted as concern at her mistress. "I'm okay," she said to the dog, giving her a teary smile and one of the beef-basted biscuits she loved. "You know how humans are—a big mess of emotions."

Chyna wandered around the kitchen, wishing a biscuit could lift her spirits, but she'd finally hit earth, she thought. Her mother was gone. She'd never again play the piano, laugh, gripe at Ned for hanging on the phone too much, or call Chyna her "glorious girl." Vivian was gone forever, or at least the rest of Chyna's life, which to her was forever.

"Your bedroom."

Chyna whirled around at the sound of Zoey's voice. But of course Zoey wasn't in the kitchen. No one knew where Zoey was or, rather, where the remains of Zoey were. Chyna hated the thought of her mother at the mortuary, perhaps in the hands of Owen Burtram with his breast-seeking eyes and unctuous manner, but even that was better than thinking of the horrors Zoey's missing body might have endured.

"Chyna . . . your bedroom."

Chyna spun again, looking at the other end of the dining
room. Nothing except the kitchen table, shining cabinets, a
hanging fern, and the kitchen door leading outside, which
was securely locked. No voices spoke to her in this room.
But Michelle had stopped eating and her ears perked up, her
gaze roaming around the kitchen just like Chyna's.

"Zoey?" Chyna almost whispered, half in fear, half in
disbelief. Then, much louder, "Zoey?"

"Don't be afraid," Zoey's voice soothed.

Chyna's heart raced. "Don't be afraid? Zoey, I know
you're dead. You can't be here just like you weren't at the
pond and your mother wasn't on the phone and Nancy Tierney didn't speak to me at the mortuary."

A lighthearted giggle. "Please go to your room."

Chyna slapped her hands over her eyes just as a child
would during the scary part of a movie. No one is there, she
told herself. Dear God, what's wrong with me?

Michelle had moved away from her food. She stood beside Chyna, the hair along her backbone raised, her legs
rigid.

The dog is just reacting to *me,* Chyna told herself, but she
began to feel dizzy, desperately wanting to leave the room
but too scared to move. "I won't hurt you." Chyna's heart
seemed to slow to almost normal as her eyes closed in a remembered sense of camaraderie and love she and Zoey had
shared.

"Chyna, your bedroom. Look at everything; *feel* everything."

Chyna decided to stop fighting what she thought she
heard. The situation was ridiculous, impossible, maybe even
laughable. But she was too tired, too confused, too afraid, to
argue with the disembodied voice of an old, beloved friend.
Besides, there was no one here to care *how* ludicrous Chyna
was acting.

Her hands icy, her breathing fast and deep, Chyna turned
away from the kitchen, passed through the living room, and
climbed the stairs to her bedroom. Night had fallen—a chill,
moonless night that wrapped the house in silky darkness—but

Chyna didn't bother turning on lights. She knew this house like the back of her hand. She could walk through it blindfolded and never bump into anything.

Now the house seemed to guide her directly to the staircase. She began climbing the stairs with what seemed like bodiless ease. All she heard was Michelle's heavy panting, her big paws padding along behind Chyna through the house.

She stood at the door of her bedroom for a moment, expecting to see the girl in white inside. But there was only darkness. Finally Chyna turned on the overhead light. After all, Zoey had told her to look at *everything*. She couldn't do that in the dark. She stood in the doorway for a few moments, scanning the room. All seemed as usual—carpet the same color as her blue-gray eyes, muted blue and crisp white satin bedspread, sheer voile curtains beneath tieback draperies, shining cherry furniture, a jewelry box, a Tiffany lamp, a ceramic ballerina figurine . . .

An eight-by-ten photograph in a silver frame. A photograph that had not been on her dresser this morning.

Chyna stood perfectly still. Michelle rubbed against her leg and she looked down to see the dog's raised hackles. Chyna wondered again if she was causing the dog's fright, then knew with complete certainty she was not. The house seemed to be breathing heavily in anticipation, pushing her, vibrating in its anxiety for her to cross the room and look at the picture she was sure she'd been drawn here to view.

Even before she could see the picture clearly, Chyna recognized the frame. She hadn't seen the framed picture for many years, but she remembered every line of it. Now it sat—the picture clear, the frame dust-free—on Chyna's dresser and she had not moved it.

Chyna had always loved her bedroom, which was delicate without being frilly and in the daytime seemed to soak up every bit of available welcoming light. But now the room didn't seem welcoming. It felt as if it had drawn in on itself, thrumming with silence, full of shadows.

It seemed to be waiting for her.

Her steps almost dragging, Chyna neared the picture, then picked it up and looked at it closely under the glow of artificial lighting, not that she had to look at it to know what it was. For a while after Zoey's disappearance, it had sat in this exact spot on her dresser. Chyna, though, couldn't even glance at it without crying. Without saying anything to her about it, Vivian had removed the framed photo. She never told Chyna where she'd put it—only that it was safe and someday she'd return it when Chyna could look at it with joy, not sadness.

The photo had been taken at the Fourth of July barbecue the Greers held every year. No invitations were sent out. Word had simply spread over the years that anyone who just wanted to have good food, lots of fun, and see a fireworks display at night was welcome. Only twice over the past twenty-five years had anyone been removed for bad conduct—Edie Larson's father, Ron, who'd had too much to drink when he arrived, drank more at the barbecue, and began sliding his hands over women's breasts and buttocks while bragging about the astonishing size of one of his body parts. Chyna remembered her and Zoey watching in teenage excitement as Uncle Rex corralled Larson while someone called a cab. In ten minutes, Rex and two other male barbecue guests stuffed a bellowing Ron into the back. Chyna remembered being glad Ron had come without his wife and daughter Edie, both of whom Chyna knew slightly from the Larsons' fresh vegetable stand, which Vivian frequented every year.

The color photo had been taken that evening, just as the sun had set. Chyna and Zoey had stood with their arms around each other's waists, smiling happily, as a star-shaped golden firework lit up the pearl gray sky behind them. They'd each worn their four-leaf-clover necklaces, cutoff jeans, and cotton T-shirts, Zoey's tighter than Chyna's to show off her late-blooming curves.

Their arms and legs were tanned, their faces lighter because Vivian had lectured them about preventing wrinkles by wearing sun block. Chyna's hair hung long and loose, but humidity had caused Zoey's short blond hair to transform from waves to the curls she hated. Looking closer, Chyna could see they each wore pink lipstick and she'd dabbed on blue eye shadow, which Vivian forbade. Zoey, with her round face and freckles and big brown eyes with naturally curling lashes, looked a year or two younger than Chyna and . . . and what? Chyna frowned, trying to figure out what seemed different about the girls so close in age. It was their expressions, she finally decided. Already Chyna had begun to look slightly sophisticated and worldly-wise. Zoey looked far more credulous. Innocent. Approachable.

Vulnerable.

Oh my God, Chyna thought. Zoey looks so open, so trusting. Suddenly Chyna's hands began to jitter because although there was no one else in the photo, Chyna could feel a gaze that had been trained on them that night, the night before Zoey vanished. Not the gaze of an amused adult. Not the gaze of an admiring but harmless teenage boy. The gaze of a predator, someone out of the camera's range who had scrutinized them, analyzed their personalities on the basis of their expressions, and coolly judged their susceptibility.

In horror, Chyna realized at that exact moment, as the camera flashed, Zoey had been chosen as the trusting, reckless victim.

CHAPTER SIX

1

"Fond memories?"

Chyna whirled around, nearly dropping the framed photo. She let out her breath in a gust when she saw her uncle, Rex Greer, standing in her bedroom doorway, smiling.

"Oh, Uncle Rex!" she cried, rushing toward him. He was a big man—at least six foot two—with a solid build. Chyna felt his strong biceps beneath his jacket when he hugged her, and she was certain he was only a couple of inches larger around the waist than he had been ten years ago. His older brother, Edward, on the one hand, had always looked his age—handsome, yes, but a bit stodgy, with prematurely white hair and rare smiles. Rex seemed to have stopped aging at forty, with dark brown hair silvered only at the temples, brilliant blue eyes like Ned's surrounded by laugh lines, and a smile most women couldn't resist. And hadn't.

"Did you bring your wife?" Chyna asked. "Let's see, would this be number seven or eight?"

"You're just as sassy as ever." He grinned at her. "It would have been number *four* if she hadn't flown the coop a couple of months ago." Rex held Chyna out in his arms and looked deep into her eyes. "Honey, I am *so* sorry about your mother. Everybody loved her, but *you* . . . " He paused, pressing his lips together. "You meant the world to her. I want you always to remember that, Chyna. You were her dream child. She adored you."

Chyna's eyes filled with tears and he hugged her again. "I'm so glad you're here, Uncle Rex. Ned is just devastated, but you know how he is about death and funerals—"

"I'll bet he didn't even help you make the funeral arrangements," Rex said in irritation. "You don't have to say you didn't mind doing it by yourself. I'm sure you did mind, no matter how much you protest. I wish I could have gotten here sooner, but I was down with the flu when I got the news about Vivian."

"I told you not to move to Maine."

"I will be leaving soon now that I'm a bachelor again. I long for sandy beaches and rushing waves—"

"And girls in bikinis."

He laughed. "At my age, all I do is look, but looking wouldn't be bad. After two winters in Maine, I've seen all the boots and bulging down-filled jackets I care to for a while." He glanced at the photo she still held. "I remember the day that was taken. I thought it was the best Fourth of July barbecue we'd ever held here. Your dad got all ruffled over that drunk pawing the women—"

"Ron Larson."

"I didn't remember his name—just what a buffoon he was. I could have gotten into a good fight with him if your father hadn't stepped in and stopped me."

"Dad was always good at diffusing bad situations."

Rex looked again at the photo. "You and dear little Zoey. God, you look young. Not to say you aren't aging slowly— I'd never guess you were twenty-eight—but you still had that innocent look in your eyes back then."

Chyna tensed, considering that she'd just been thinking how much more innocent Zoey had looked and that very night, while the photo was being taken, so much more innocent and malleable that the abductor had picked her rather than Chyna. "Rex, do you think Zoey looked younger than I did?"

"Younger?" He peered at the photo. "Well, not exactly

younger, but somehow different. Maybe a little more . . ." Chyna almost stopped breathing, waiting. . . . "open, child-like. Gullible. She never struck me as being the savvy girl you were, Chyna, even before you started having your visions."

"I haven't had a vision since I was about thirteen," Chyna lied without a qualm. "I wasn't fibbing back then, but I think I might have had some slight brain damage they didn't detect at the time of the boat accident that caused the problem. Anyway, it healed on its own." She was repeating the same falsehood she told everyone who'd known her back when she used to divulge innocently the fact that she had visions. "I'm just your average woman now."

"Nothing about you is average, Chyna."

"I disagree. Anyway, I was looking at this photo and thinking about Zoey. She was taken the next night and we all assumed she was abducted by the guy she went to meet at the lake. But just now, thinking about how many people were at that barbecue who saw how cute she was and sweet and, well, gullible like you said, maybe she wasn't taken by the guy she met at the lake. That night I saw her meet someone and then I went to sleep. I didn't see what happened, but maybe she and the guy parted company and then she was coming back up the hill and someone—maybe even someone who'd seen her at the party or someone who was mad because she'd met that guy—was waiting for her. Maybe that person dragged her off and . . . and . . ."

Rex reached up and put his fingers to her lips. "Poor Chyna, still obsessing over this. I'd hoped that with time the pain would begin to dull."

"Rex, there were other girls! It wasn't an isolated incident. Besides, the pain over losing Zoey will *never* dull for me. Maybe if I knew what had happened, it would help, but not knowing is just intolerable!"

"I know, honey. You've always felt things so deeply, but try to calm down. I didn't mean to sound patronizing when I said I thought time would make the pain dull. I guess it was more of a wish than a belief." He sighed and Chyna realized he looked paler than usual and his eyes were slightly blood-shot. He'd said he'd had the flu. He was probably worn-out from the trip. "You look like you could use a drink and a rest before a hot fire," Chyna said. "The family room is so much cozier than the living room and the wood in the fireplace is all ready to go. I'll fix you a vodka martini—it won't be as good as Mom's, but I'll try. You go relax, and we won't say another word about Zoey."

He smiled at Chyna and she thought of how alike yet how different he and her father had looked. The shape of the eyes was the same; the spirit behind them was completely different. "You're every man's dream, Chyna. If you weren't my niece, I'd ask you to marry me," Rex said warmly.

"So I could be number five? No thanks," Chyna returned with a teasing tartness. "Oh, you'll find I brought a companion with me when you get to the family room."

Rex raised a dark eyebrow. "A young man?"

"No, a young woman. Blond. Beautiful. Smart."

Rex smiled. "She sounds wonderful."

"And she loves playing Frisbee and fetch-the-stick." Suspicion crept into Rex's expression. "Her name is Michelle. I'm sure you two will hit it off famously."

Ten minutes later, Chyna carried two vodka martinis into the family room, where Rex sat on the couch beside Michelle, speaking to her in French. "Is she answering you?" Chyna asked.

"Most passionately. I think we're engaged." Chyna handed him the martini. "She's adorable."

"I know. And Mom would have a fit if she saw her sitting on the couch like this."

"Vivian only had one old-maid quality—no animals on the furniture."

"Oh, is that quality restricted to old maids, Mr. Sexist?"

"Guess I did slip up there. I try to keep my tiny bit of sexism a deep, dark secret." Rex sipped his drink. "Almost as good as your mother's, Chyna."

"Thanks. I know she was the master, which is funny, because she came from a teetotaling family."

"With whom she didn't get along and whom she decided to be as different from as possible."

Chyna nodded. "I'd forgotten that you met her even before Dad did. Wasn't it when she was twenty?"

"Nineteen. We met at one of those keg parties fraternities throw on Friday evenings." Rex smiled. "Every girl there was jealous of her. She was not only gorgeous, but she could drink them all under the table and act not only totally sober but classy as hell."

"So you asked her out."

"Of course." Rex took another sip of his drink. "We had a lot of fun for a while, and then I introduced her to my older brother. I never had a clue he would fall for her. Frankly, as much as I admired Edward, at the time I thought he was one of the stodgiest guys in the world—smart and strong and honorable and all that, but stodgy."

"And Mom didn't."

"Well, I guess that wedding ring she let Edward put on her finger six months later proved she didn't. Sometimes I wonder if things would have lasted if I'd married her instead. It takes me about one minute to figure out the answer. *No.* We were too much alike. Each of us needed a stabilizing influence. She found hers in Edward. And as much as I love you and Ned, as much as I love visiting here, I don't think I could ever have fit into this life. I would have been a lousy father. I *have* been a lousy husband. Four times."

"Maybe because all of this—the house, the children, being president of the bank like Dad, and belonging to at least five community clubs, life in general in a small town—just wasn't for you, Rex," Chyna said. "And it still isn't. That doesn't make you an awful person. Just different from your brother. And wouldn't the world be a boring place without diversity?"

"I suppose so, although I've made a lot of mistakes in my life."

"Oh," Chyna said as if disappointed. "I didn't know that. How odd of you. I'm sure no one else has."

Rex laughed. "And they say geniuses have no sense of humor."

"I'm not a genius and if one more person calls me that, I'm going to hit them over the head with a frying pan."

"Your rather heated reaction to being called a genius is why everyone keeps calling you one. They're pushing your buttons, Chyna dear, although you *are* a genius."

"I'm certain if you asked Owen Burtram at the funeral home, you'd get a different reaction. He wasn't too impressed with me today."

"I went to school with Owen. He always was a creep. And proud as a peacock. Was he mean to you, honey?"

"No. He just acted like I was being a cheapskate for having Mom cremated."

Rex's eyes widened. "You're having Vivian cremated?"

"It was a surprise to me, too, but it's what she wanted. Ned and Beverly gave me a letter she left requesting cremation, no ceremony, and for me to take her urn back to New Mexico." Rex stared at her. "I'm not making this up. It sounds as crazy to me as it does to you, but I can show you the letter."

Rex shook his head. "I know you're not making it up, Chyna. I don't need, or want, to see the letter. I'm just surprised that Vivian didn't even want a ceremony, much less not want to be buried beside Edward." He sighed. "What doesn't surprise me is her leaving explicit instructions for *you*. I'm not saying Vivian didn't love Ned, but it was you she trusted more than anyone. She might have been afraid that Ned wouldn't do as she asked. I don't know what's wrong with him, but we nearly had to drag him to your father's funeral. Leaving her *cremation* in his hands—" Rex lifted his arms. "She probably thought he just wouldn't have the strength to make arrangements for something he'd consider so drastic. To him, being buried would be bad enough. Being burned to ashes . . ."

Chyna winced, then nodded. "I suppose you're right."

"Honey, I'm always right."

"Except when it comes to picking wives," she said sweetly.

The phone on the end table beside Rex rang. Smiling, Chyna motioned for him to answer while she went to pour him another martini. When she came back, he held out the receiver to her. "It's your lovely sister-in-law, Beverly." He spoke into the receiver again. "Here's Chyna, Bev, but I assure you, I'm a much more charming conversationalist."

When Chyna took the receiver she could hear Bev giggling in the background. She adored Rex's cosmopolitan style and wit. "If my wife ever runs away with another man, I'll know immediately who he is," Ned said lightly. "Wish I had a little bit of Rex's savoir faire myself."

"Hi, Chyna," Beverly said almost gaily. "I'm glad Rex finally made it in."

"Me, too. We've been having an interesting talk—"

"And a few martinis."

"One. I have had *one* martini!"

"Okay, Chyna, don't get jerked out of shape. I was just teasing you."

"And I was teasing back."

"Good. I'm glad we're not having a fight because I have a favor to ask."

Oh no, Chyna thought. She was tired. She was rattled by what had happened at the mortuary. She wanted to spend more time with Rex, who could always make her forget her troubles. "Name the favor."

"Well, I was placed in charge of a gaggle of children, including Ian and Kate, to take out trick-or-treating. Ned was going to hand out candy at our house, but he just called and said he has a guy coming in around seven—trick-or-treat time, naturally—who wants to look at a new Lincoln for himself and a used Mercury for his son. The man who stays at the dealership until eight tonight is sick, so Ned has to go back. He can't pass up selling *two* cars."

"No, he can't. So what do you want me to do? Sell the cars for him?"

Beverly giggled again. "No, silly, although you might be more of a salesperson than Ned when it comes to men. Oh, don't tell him I said that, but you *could* roll around on the car hoods in sexy poses to really grab male customers' attention."

"Yes, I'm notorious for posing on car hoods."

"So I've heard," Bev laughed while Rex raised eyebrows at Chyna. "What I had in mind was giving you an option," Beverly went on. "You take out the kids—"

"The gaggle of children in costumes?"

"Yes. Oh, Chyna, they're very sweet. Or you could stay here and hand out candy at our house. I know you get hardly anyone at your place, but we get tons of children all loaded with toilet paper to lace in your trees if you don't give them candy."

"Children certainly are wonderful creatures," Chyna said drily.

"I hate to ask, but—"

"You take the gaggle around the neighborhood and I'll hand out the candy."

"You will? Oh, Chyna, thank you so much. We have plenty of candy. It'll be fun."

"That's what they told people who reserved a room on board the *Titanic*."

"Don't be silly. The kids are darling, the weather is supposed to be mild, and trick-or-treat time only lasts two hours. I'm sure Ned will be home to relieve you before it's all over."

"Sure he will, Beverly. I don't even believe there's a man wanting to buy two cars. Ned just wanted the evening off, and he knew old softie here wouldn't be able to decline helping you."

"Oh, Chyna, don't be a sourpuss." Bev sighed. "I'm *so* relieved. You work with children all the time. I'm sure you're very good with them. I have several different kinds of candy. Be sure to bring a blazer or light jacket in case it's a bit chillier than the weatherman predicted."

Three hours later, Chyna mentally cursed the weatherman as she stood freezing in the open doorway wearing a corduroy jacket as the temperature steadily plunged fifteen degrees lower than expected. As group after group of skeletons, ghosts, vampires, and werewolves arrived at the door holding out their baskets for treats, Chyna mentally composed a scathing letter to the weatherman she intended to write as soon as she got home and send out in the morning.

When she noticed a child dressed as Little Red Riding Hood staring at her with a mixture of fascination and fright, Chyna realized she'd begun to talk to herself, or rather to the weatherman, conveying how angry she was because his temperature prediction had been so inaccurate. Half of these children would be sick tomorrow because they weren't dressed warmly enough. The little girl in a red cape looked at Chyna with huge blue eyes and finally asked, "Are you talking to someone invisible?"

Chyna forced a wide smile and said cheerfully, "You caught me! Did I scare you?"

"Well, yeah," the little girl said, "although some of the kids down the block said you've been talking to invisible people for a while. I wanted to see it for myself." Oh, wonderful, Chyna thought dourly. I'm the talk of the neighborhood. Beverly will be thrilled. Chyna gave the little girl an extra peppermint patty and Tootsie Roll, another bright and hopefully normal smile, and cursed the weatherman again.

She'd left Rex at home to cover any trick-or-treaters they might get. "But we only have half a bag of butterscotch balls and they look at least a year old," he'd complained.

"Uncle Rex, we get about ten trick-or-treaters a year. They don't want to climb the hill. If any hardy souls do, give them one of your martinis. I guarantee they'll leave happy."

Chyna could have cried with relief when at eight thirty Beverly arrived home with the children, Kate sulking because her mother had made her put a denim jacket over her "princess" gown, Ian crying because some "big kids" had made fun of his Donald Duck costume.

To top it off, on the way home Kate had popped a piece of unwrapped candy in her mouth just to defy her mother. As Chyna was rooting through her purse, looking for her car keys, Kate suddenly turned white, broke into a drenching cold sweat, and threw up in the hall before even making it to the bathroom. In a panic, Chyna and Beverly loaded both children into Chyna's rental car and rushed them to the local hospital emergency room.

They would probably have been relegated to the waiting room if Kate hadn't gushed forth again and Beverly wavered, "I think she's been poisoned," before nearly passing out. The two people ahead of them urged that Kate be taken in next. "Stay out here with Ian," Beverly told Chyna, who looked at the terrified little boy in a Donald Duck suit and felt helpless despite always feeling in control when she was on duty at the Albuquerque hospital, where she was not dealing with her own family. "I'll call Ned," she said to Beverly, ready to rush down the hall with a nurse and a heaving Kate. "What's his cell phone number?"

"I saw his cell phone on the bedroom dresser recharging, and I can't think of his private office number." Beverly started to cry. "Oh God, I'm just blank!"

At the sight of his mother's panic, Ian began to howl. "Never mind." Chyna waved for her sister-in-law to follow the nurse, a heaving Kate in tow. Then Chyna bent down to her nephew. "Ian, you know I'm a doctor and I promise you that everything is going to be fine," she said in what she hoped was a convincing voice.

"Kate's gonna die," Ian insisted. "She ate poison canny."

"We don't know that the candy was poisoned. Maybe she was just allergic to it."

"What's 'lergic' mean?"

"'Allergic' means it didn't agree with her. It made her sick."

"But it could kill her and then who'm I gonna play with? The boys don't like me anymore 'cause I'm a duck." Ian sobbed harder, then burst into a siege of hiccoughs.

Chyna didn't know whether to be annoyed or amused that Ian was mainly concerned over the possible loss of a playmate. She decided on amusement when she reminded herself he was only three years old. He could get away with being selfish at three.

She started to suggest they get something from the candy

machine, then decided that was the worst idea possible after
Kate's experience with candy. Instead, Chyna picked up Ian
and said, "Let's look out the window at all the pretty lights
across the street," the pretty lights coming from the house of
a family who left Christmas decorations up all year long. Ian
sniffled and agreed. In a moment, he stared mesmerized by a
giant sleigh pulled by remarkably lifelike deer and carrying
Santa. Three large artificial trees in the front windows were
draped with glittering ornaments and strings of old-
fashioned lights, and every eave of the house looked as if it
bore dozens of glowing white icicles.

Ian smiled and pointed. "Pretty!"

Chyna stared until all the lights began to blend, forming a
swirl of bright color. "Forever," she muttered. "Forever and
ever and *ever.*"

Ian ignored her, his attention captured by Rudolph's huge
red nose. Chyna didn't see the garish nose. Chyna saw tall,
dark shrubbery. She reached out and touched a leaf, strong
and green. Then she saw white. Just a flash. "A ghost?" she
murmured.

"What?" Ian asked with a mixture of excitement and fear.
"Ghost? Where?"

Chyna gasped. Pain shot through her head, as if she'd
been struck. She threw out her arms, leaving Ian to drop
straight down onto his heavily padded duck bottom. She felt
herself flailing, something scratching the flesh on her arms,
stinging badly, something closing around her neck. Then she
smelled a sweet odor. Don't breathe, she heard in her mind.
From a long way off, she heard Ian crying, but she couldn't
concentrate on him—only on not breathing. Don't breathe!
Don't breathe! Can't help it. Can't help . . .

"Are you all right?" Someone had taken hold of her
shoulder and was shaking her gently. "Ma'am?"

She struck out with her left arm and a man's hand closed
around her wrist before it made contact with his chin. "Ma'am,
what's wrong? Ma'am?" Suddenly his weather-beaten face
sharpened into Chyna's view. "Nurse? Somebody?" he yelled.

Chyna shut her eyes for a moment, then snapped them

open. A woman held Ian, her gaze fastened on Chyna with outrage. "You dropped him!"

Chyna staggered and the man helped her to a chair. "Lady, what's wrong?"

The waiting room, the man with the weather-beaten face, the woman with the furious eyes, poor sobbing Ian in his ridiculous costume, all came into focus. "Oh my God," Chyna gasped. "I don't know what happened. I . . . Ian! Ian, are you hurt?"

"No, he isn't, no thanks to you!" the woman snarled, squeezing Ian so tightly he could hardly breathe. "What's wrong with you? Are you drunk?"

"Drunk? No! My niece. She's back there. . . ."

The man still hovering over Chyna gave the woman a hard look. "I was here when this woman came in with her sister. Her niece has probably been poisoned. I think the shock just hit her."

"Yes. The shock . . . ," Chyna mumbled, knowing very well she wasn't suffering from shock. She'd had a vision. A soul-shaking vision more vivid than she'd had for years. "I'm all right now." She looked up at the woman. "May I have my nephew?"

"*No*," the woman snapped truculently. She glared at Chyna with her cold, narrow eyes. "What are you going to do next? Throw him against the wall?"

Ian struggled in the woman's death grip. "Aunt Chyna," he managed almost breathlessly. "Want Aunt Chyna!"

"Give her the child," the man said. The woman looked at him defiantly. "Give her the *child*, lady," he said forcefully. "He's her nephew and she's all right now." The woman glared at the man, then at Chyna, then back at the man. "Ma'am, do I have to call security?" he asked the woman in a low, stern voice.

"Oh, okay, but if she hurts him, it's *your* fault!" The woman thrust Ian at the man, who gave him a reassuring smile, then set him gently on Chyna's lap. "You looked like you were going to pass out and I couldn't get a nurse in here to help you," he said to Chyna.

"I don't need a nurse. I'm fine now. Really."

"All right. How about a cup of coffee instead? It's only that vending machine stuff. . . ."

"That would be wonderful," Chyna said with a shaky smile. "And thank you for your kindness."

Twenty minutes later, after the narrow-eyed woman had loudly told every newcomer to the waiting room about Chyna dropping Ian, a nurse arrived and asked Chyna to join her sister in an examining room. Chyna clutched Ian and fled the waiting room, still shaken by her experience but more worried about Kate. Oh God, she thought. Don't let that vision have anything to do with her. Let her be all right.

And she was. Although Beverly still looked as bleached and frightened as if her daughter had nearly died, the doctor told them that Kate had merely ingested that famous vomit inducer ipecac. "A large dose can be fatal, but your daughter swallowed just enough to make her sick," he told Beverly. "It's a dirty trick some people like to pull on kids at Halloween, but not uncommon." Then he assured everyone that Kate would feel better in the morning.

The four of them dragged out to the car. Beverly and Chyna were both limp, although giddy with relief, but Kate was another matter. She'd ruined her princess gown, which set her howling in heartbroken tears all the way home. Ian wailed right along with her just to keep his sister company.

Ned arrived at the house shortly after they did. "Where in the world have you been?" Beverly demanded. "It's almost ten o'clock!"

Ned looked tired, frustrated, slightly disheveled, with the lines between his eyebrows deeper than when he'd left for the car lot. "I never worked so damned hard selling two cars in my life! Father and son wanted the same new Lincoln and I thought they were going to come to blows before the spoiled kid gave in and *allowed* his father to buy him something else." Then he saw his two tear-stained children and shouted, "What the hell happened here tonight?"

Exhausted and shaken by her experience at the hospital, Chyna left Beverly to explain the disaster of the evening and drove quickly through town, where a few beyond-curfew trick-or-treaters wandered, then up the badly lighted asphalt road to her own home. This was the first night without daylight saving time, meaning darkness had fallen an hour earlier than usual, and she suddenly wished the lighting along the road were better even though the stars seemed especially bright.

As soon as she opened the door to the house, Michelle bounded toward her with a mixture of ecstasy and fear. Heart sinking, Chyna yelled, "Uncle Rex," a couple of times, but she knew he was gone even though she hadn't looked in the garage for his car. On a table beside the door and under a lamp lay a note from him saying that as of eight o'clock they'd had not one trick-or-treater, so he'd decided to go visit an old friend who'd recently lost his wife. They might go out for a few beers together.

Chyna shook her head as she put down the note. Typical Rex—charming and unreliable. Just because no one had come to beg for candy didn't mean a few of the town's teenage troublemakers wouldn't decide to do some damage to a large, dark house on All Hallows' Eve. "But Rex would never think of that," she told Michelle, who was nervous at having been left alone in unfamiliar territory and clung closely to Chyna. "Uncle Rex thinks mainly about having a good time. He always did." She quirked a smile at Michelle. "But you can't teach an old dog new tricks."

Michelle huffed in agreement.

Still shaken by what had happened earlier, Chyna circuited the house, making certain every door and window was locked. Then she fixed a vodka tonic and sat down on the family room couch to watch a movie, but she couldn't relax and concentrate. *Don't breathe!* The words she heard in the hospital waiting room kept echoing in her mind in a slightly familiar voice. Certainly not Zoey's. Then there'd been the flash of white, the stinging of her arms, then an overpoweringly sweet smell. None of it fit together. It was a jumble, nothing but a jumble. *Random images like a dream,* she told herself. *I was tired and upset and cold and . . .*

"And something is wrong," she said aloud in a hopeless voice. "I can't escape it. Something awful has happened tonight."

Chyna waited until one o'clock, but Rex never came home. If she'd known what friend he was visiting, she would have called; that's how desperate she was. Tonight the house seemed large and lonely and—she hated to even think it—haunted. Michelle, sensing Chyna's distress, cuddled close to her in bed. She hugged the big dog close to her, grateful that tonight of all nights she wasn't completely alone.

2

Deirdre Mayhew stepped out of the house for a cigarette. Her father would have a fit if he knew she smoked. He would have a fit if he knew she drank, even sparingly during a Halloween party at a friend's house. He really didn't even want Deirdre to go to the party, but after the necessity of making her work at his café, L'Étoile, while she finished her senior year of high school and helped with her dying mother, then watching Deirdre's pain when she'd learned she'd finished summer school too late to attend college this year with her friends, he'd been unable to deny all of her pleasures. Not that this party was as much fun anyway. Not without Nancy, who was always the life of any party. Deirdre knew a lot of the partiers felt the same, but those who attended the university just two hours away had come anyway because the Halloween party was a tradition.

For Deirdre, this one wasn't only bad because of Nancy's absence, though. Deirdre felt years older than the people she knew from high school. The parents of the girl having the party were gone for the evening and everyone had expected this festivity to be especially fun because it was the first one held in any of her friends' houses not chaperoned by hovering parents, but no matter how hard they tried to act as if they were having a ball, their gaiety was obviously forced. Oh well, Deirdre thought, even this event was better than sitting at home with her father watching educational programming on the habits of the wildebeest, one of his favorite episodes. How much happier he'd been, how different everything had been, before her mother's death from cancer last year.

Deirdre took another puff on the cigarette, listening to the laughter and bantering of the few inside who had actually managed to get drunk. Honestly, the people her own age sounded like a bunch of adolescents. She tugged at the silly balloon-skirted party dress of her mother's she'd worn as a costume and thought about Chyna Greer. Deirdre knew Chyna's mother had also just died, but her life wouldn't change as Deirdre's had when her own mother died. Chyna had already left home and was well on her way to a successful, admirable career. And she was so beautiful, so smart.

Throughout the years, Deirdre had heard all about Chyna and even seen old pictures of her winning numerous science contests while a teenager and a picture in the high school showcase of her as senior class president, but she was so much prettier in person. She'd gotten even lovelier with age. She didn't look like a teenager anymore. She looked womanly and somehow slightly exotic even in a turtleneck sweater and slacks. No wonder Scott Kendrick gazed at her the way he did. The day they were in the café, he didn't see anyone in the room except Chyna. Not even me, Deirdre realized glumly, although he was polite enough to talk to me and introduce me to Chyna. But that was Scott's way. Good looks, good mind, good manners. He was a prize, the kind of man women dreamed about having as a husband.

But he'd never be hers, Deirdre mused. He was in his thirties, just a year or so younger than her father. And Scott didn't think of *her* as a woman. He called her *kiddo,* for heaven's sake. Besides, even if he were in his twenties and he'd never met her before, if Deirdre was any judge of potential romance, what she'd seen today told her he'd like to end up with Chyna Greer rather than Deirdre Mayhew.

Besides, I'll be at L'Etoile next year, not in a fancy college like the one Chyna attended. Even Lynette will be leaving for college in September, although neither her grades nor her ambition can compare with mine, Deirdre thought guiltily. After all, Lynette was her best friend.

Although she'd had an excellent school record, Deirdre hadn't even applied for a scholarship. Daddy won't find any help to suit him, she'd thought. If I left, he'd miss me. He'd forget to eat. He'd already lost twenty pounds he didn't need to lose since her mother died. Deirdre understood his intense grief. Her parents had met in grade school, "gone steady" since they were fifteen, and been married since they were seventeen. Ben Mayhew had spent over half of his life with Deirdre's mother. He won't go out with friends, Deirdre added to the list of ways in which her father wouldn't try to help himself. He'll just work and come home to watch television until he dies. Or until he gets so lonely he lets Irma Vogel force herself into his life. That thought almost made Deirdre ill. She couldn't stand Irma, who'd circled like a vulture waiting for Deirdre's mother to die so she could swoop in and snatch up Ben Mayhew. No other man in his right mind would have Irma. Only someone so devastated or crazy he didn't know what he was doing would marry Irma with her little mind and sneaking ways.

No, I'm Dad's only lifeline, Deirdre decided. I'm his only protection against someone like Irma. So how can I ever go blithely off to college and leave him? I'll just stay here in Black Willow forever. Forever and ever and *ever.*

She took another deep drag off her cigarette and wished she'd brought a beer outside with her. It would be nice to sip it and look up at the clear, star-studded night all alone even though it was cold. Going back into that den of raucous music and whooping teenagers earnestly trying to have as good a time this year as they usually had seemed unbearable.

Deirdre tossed down her cigarette and walked to a hedge of rhododendron that stretched across the back lawn. In the spring, the bushes towered over seven feet tall and were laden with white and bright pink flowers. The bushes bore no flowers now although they were still heavy with leaves. Deirdre reached out and touched one of the thick, leathery leaves that would stay on the shrubs, sturdy and green, until warm weather returned.

Her mother had been an excellent gardener. The Mayhew lawn used to look beautiful all through the spring, summer, and autumn thanks to her. Neither Deirdre nor her father had the knack, though, and it seemed to Deirdre that their lawn had died along with her mother.

The weather was much chillier than the newscaster had predicted. Deirdre drew her sweater tighter around her, wishing she'd worn a jacket instead. Oh well, she planned to go home in fifteen minutes or so anyway. Deirdre was reaching out again to touch a rhododendron bud that would be a flower in the spring when she heard a scratching noise, the sound of shrubbery branches brushing together. She dropped her hand, standing still. Again the sound. She tensed. Then she smelled a caramel-coated apple and saw a flash of white.

Deirdre immediately relaxed. "Oh my!" she exclaimed dramatically. "Is there a scary *ghost* hiding in these shrubs?"

She thought she heard a stifled giggle. Obviously, a child was in a ghost costume trying to scare Deirdre. She'd play along. "Gosh, I'm *really* afraid of ghosts. I always have been. I sure hope one doesn't jump out at me!"

Another rustling in the bushes. Something ran past her legs so fast she almost let out a scream, stepped backward deeper into the tangle of branches, then realized the runner was just Lynette's small black cat. Deirdre smiled. How pleased the child must be that a black cat happened to be available to add to the suspense of the moment. Halloween was just *made* for black—

Suddenly everything went quiet. The air around Deirdre stilled as if suspending itself, waiting, waiting. . . . Then, in an instinctive flash, Deirdre knew danger was upon her. She heard an intake of breath just behind her, followed by the quick rushing noise only a few steps might make—adult steps. In one blinding, terrifying instant, Deirdre realized it was not a child who stood hiding in the leafy growth behind her. As she started to run, something hard crashed against the back of her head. Deirdre crumbled, hitting the cold, hard ground with a thud, still conscious but stunned by pain in her scalp, feeling a trickle of warm blood running through her hair. A clump of dead grass and dirt fell into her mouth when she opened it to scream, but she still tried and managed a ragged grunt just as an arm circled her throat, jerking so hard she couldn't make a sound. She flailed her arms, but even through a sweater the strong rhododendron branches painfully scraped her arms. She fought for footing, once digging the heel of her shoe into the moist earth near the bushes, but the heel broke and the shoe slipped off as someone dragged her over dew-laden ground.

Abruptly the pulling stopped. Deirdre struggled to free herself from the strong arms, but almost immediately she heard a grunt, then something that sounded like a macabre snicker before a sweet-smelling cloth completely covered her mouth and nose. She tried not to breathe but couldn't help herself, her need for air even greater because of her struggle. Her lungs filled with the sweet scent of what she recognized from science class as chloroform.

Dizzy after one breath, she tried not to inhale again, but she'd fought so hard she was starved for oxygen. Don't breathe, she thought. Don't breathe! But her need for air was too great. She tried to take as small a breath as possible, but even that was too much. She managed one last twist of her head, feeling a searing pain in her earlobe. The cloth held firm, though, and she was forced to take another breath. The fight slowly draining out of her, she caught one quick glimpse of a face before the cool, star-studded world went spinning into darkness.

CHAPTER SEVEN

1

Scott's heart thundered in his ears. He clutched at the wheel as the plane bucked and shuddered. He tried to turn right. Nothing. He tried the brakes. Nothing. He looked out the window and saw flatlands—no city, no mountains, no ocean, only flatlands. Thank God, because they were losing altitude fast, diving unfalteringly nose first to the ground, where he was sure the plane would explode. What would it feel like to have flames consume his living body?

Scott slammed facedown against the floor and a woman shouted, "Scott, Scott! Wake up! It's just a nightmare! Wake *up*!"

Scott opened his eyes. He didn't see dirt and grass or feel his own body bathed in sweat and stinging from a dozen cuts or a throbbing dislocated leg lying unnaturally at a right angle from his pelvis. He didn't hear the grinding of metal against metal, fuel exploding followed by vicious, crackling flames, the screams of people in agony. Then he felt someone bending over him, pulling on his shoulders, chattering in a shrill voice.

"My land, you nearly scared me to death when I came in this morning and heard you up here shouting something about hydraulics. By the time I got to your room you were flying out of that bed onto the floor and—Scott Kendrick, don't you own a pair of pajamas?—and I heard your head hit and if you didn't give yourself a concussion it'll be a miracle!"

Scott groaned and focused on the face that shot words at him like a machine gun. Irma Vogel. She'd used her own key. Last night he'd forgotten that this was one of Irma's days to clean but mostly to follow him around talking, singing, hovering, and generally making his life miserable. Oh God, he thought almost desperately, closing his eyes again. Please make her go away.

"Get up. No, don't get up until I can help you. You might have broken something. Where's your robe? Don't you have a robe, either? Why are you in bed so late? It's ten o'clock. You never sleep this late. Here, wrap up in the blanket and I'll call the Emergency Service."

"I don't want the Emergency Service," Scott growled, sitting on the edge of the bed while Irma draped a blanket over him. "You don't have to fuss, Irma. I'm not hurt."

"Tell that to the lump on your head, young man. And your nose is bleeding."

Scott touched his forehead and indeed found the beginnings of a fine bump. He ran his finger under his nose. A tiny trickle of blood, no gushing.

"Put that phone down, Irma," he said. "I don't need the emergency squad. I just fell out of bed."

"And if you were a well man, that wouldn't be dangerous. But you, with all your injuries—"

"My injuries are almost healed. I'm fine. I just need a cold cloth for my nose and some," he'd started to say "peace," but that would hurt her feelings, "coffee. Please fix me a cup of that wonderful coffee of yours, Irma. If I don't feel better after I have that, I'll go to the hospital. Deal?"

"I'll *take* you to the hospital." Irma, five foot eight, broad shouldered, and thirty-five pounds overweight, probably because she worked at L'Etoile and frequently sampled the cuisine, rushed into the bathroom, came back with a dripping washcloth that she tried to hold beneath his nose before he snatched it away from her. "Irma, coffee, please," he said, sounding as if he had a bad cold. She leaped up with all the grace of a buffalo and thundered down the stairs so fast, Scott feared she would plunge headfirst.

After a minute, Scott held the cloth away from his nose, took a deep breath, ran his hands through his thick, black hair, and looked at the sun streaming through one of his bedroom windows. Usually he woke up early. But this morning he'd slept late and badly. He hurt everywhere and all he wanted was a hot shower, because he felt dirty, almost grimy. He remembered walking through the cold night—exhausted, shaken, afraid someone had seen him.

Abruptly he forced the memory from his mind. He whipped off the blanket Irma had wrapped around him like a shroud and hoped he could shower and put on a robe before she arrived with coffee.

He stepped behind the shower curtain to a cloud of steam, moaned, and turned his back to the showerhead. Hot water rushed over his rigid neck and shoulders. As he lathered, the soap stung dozens of scratches on his arms. He'd taken off all the Band-Aids and Steri-Strips yesterday because some of them itched and some were already coming off. The lacerations and scratches beneath them were mostly healed, anyway. All except for a few.

"I'm back with the coffee!" Irma trilled. Scott jumped, almost sliding to the slippery wet floor of the tub. Through the shower curtain, he could see Irma's sturdy form standing in the doorway.

"Thanks, Irma. Would you just set it beside the bed for me?"

"Sure." He listened to the clatter of cups on a tray but no thump of steps going back down the stairs. Great. Irma intended to stay in the bedroom along with the coffee. He thought she'd had that *look* this morning, the look that usually meant she had important information to divulge.

Scott stepped from the shower, toweled his body and hair, and slipped into his heavy terry cloth robe. When he came out of the bathroom, he cringed to see Irma sitting on the delicate chair accompanying an ornate desk that supposedly once belonged to Prince Albert. Scott's mother cherished

the antique set and insisted on placing it in front of the
French doors in Scott's room. She also insisted he never sit
at the desk. She would prefer he not even look at it for fear
of damaging it. Scott sighed. This was just one of the joys of
having a mother who had once been a museum curator.

Irma began pouring coffee into dainty china cups—Scott
preferred insulated mugs—and he couldn't help noticing
that in the sunlight her thin, naturally whitish-blond hair
looked like a wispy cobweb covering her scalp and her
bluish-red lipstick was smeared. Aside from the lipstick, she
wore no makeup, a first in his experience. She was also pale,
her light blue eyes red-rimmed and seeming to bulge even
more than usual. She obviously had a bad-news bombshell
to deliver.

"What's wrong this morning, Irma?" he asked.

"I guess you haven't heard what's happened."

"I just woke up, remember?"

"Well, brace yourself."

Scott set down the silly china cup with a bang. "Is something wrong with my parents?"

"Your *parents*?"

"Are they all right? They're supposed to be back in three
days. Dad has a heart murmur . . . Mom exercises too much.
Are they hurt? Sick?" Scott demanded loudly.

Irma looked alarmed enough to jump up and flee the
room. "No, Scott, your parents are fine. My land, if I'd
known you were going to get so upset . . . It must be that
post-traumatic stress syndrome or something. . . ."

Irma was exactly right. Six months ago he would have
heard her out instead of immediately imagining disasters.
But six months ago, before the plane crash, he'd been a different man. "I'm sorry, Irma, but will you just tell me what
the hell is wrong?"

Irma's hand had flown to the area of her heart, which
Scott imagined was beating as fast as a hummingbird's. "It's
Deirdre, Scott. Deirdre Mayhew."

"Deirdre? What's wrong with her?"

"She went to a Halloween party last night. Ben didn't

want her to go, but I . . ." Irma's big, pale eyes began to fill with tears. "I told him she worked hard and a girl should be allowed to have a good time once in a while. So he agreed. *I* talked him into it!"

Scott's breath began to calm. This was probably nothing more than Deirdre drinking too much beer, Ben blowing his top and firing Irma, whom he would rehire next week, to her vast relief. Scott was certain Irma had her eye on Ben as a potential husband. "So whose party did Deirdre go to?"

"Her best friend, Lynette Monroe's."

"I don't know Lynette."

Irma's expression turned sour. "She's Deirdre's age. I've heard people say she's pretty, but I think she's just a lot of bleached blond hair and makeup and tight clothes—you know, the trashy type," Irma said with disdain. "If I were Ben, I wouldn't let Deirdre hang around with her. I've told him she's trouble, but he doesn't listen."

Scott doubted that Ben listened to any of Irma's character judgments but said nothing. Irma continued. "Anyway, the party was supposed to start at eight and I heard Ben tell Deirdre to be home by eleven. At twelve-thirty, my phone rang and woke me up. It was Ben looking for Deirdre. I said, 'Well, what in the world do you think she'd be here for?' And he said, 'Because she's not here and I thought she might have drunk liquor when I told her not to and came to your house to sleep it off.' Imagine that! Like I take in drunken teenagers all the time!" Irma demanded indignantly. "I told him to call where they were having the party. . . ."

Irma seemed to drift away for a moment and the tears that had been gathering for so long finally made it over the slopes of her fat cheeks. "He did and she wasn't there, Scott. Nobody saw her leave. The kids that were left at the party started looking for her. At last, the parents came home—Ben nearly had a stroke when he realized there'd been no parents around—and then neighbors came and finally . . . finally. . . ."

Scott was on his feet, fully aware that his robe hung open and just as aware that he was on the verge of strangling the information out of Irma. "Finally *what*?"

"At the back of the yard there's a rhododendron hedge and beside one of the shrubs they found signs of a struggle. There were broken branches, the ground was scuffed up, and . . ." Irma took a deep breath. "And they found just *one* of Deirdre's shoes!"

Irma abruptly burst into full-fledged crying. Scott slowly pulled his robe around him and sat down on the bed, his hand automatically going to the new scratches on his wrist as Deirdre Mayhew's pretty amber-eyed, dimpled face flashed in front of him.

"It's always the same," Irma sniffled. "I've already talked it over with some people and they agree with me."

Scott felt as if he were slowly returning to the reality of the sun-filled bedroom. "You told people that Deirdre was missing and you talked *what* over with them, Irma?"

"That Deirdre's disappeared just like all those other teenage girls throughout the years. We never saw *them* again and we'll never see *Deirdre* again." Her red-rimmed eyes looked directly into Scott's. "And I know whose fault it is! Every time Chyna Greer comes to town, a girl goes missing. Zoey Simms, Heather Phelps, Edie Larson, now little Deirdre Mayhew."

Scott drew back, his gaze hardening, but Irma didn't seem to notice. Her voice rising, she leaned forward, her ugly eyes filled with malice. "I'm telling you, Scott, Chyna Greer is bad news. She's worse than bad news, because nothing on this earth can convince me, and a whole lot of other people, that there is *not* a connection between her and all those poor, lost girls."

2

"I used to babysit for Deirdre Mayhew," Beverly said as she sat in the big, sunny kitchen of the Greer home. Ned had brought her and the children for a visit with Rex, but anyone could tell Beverly was more concerned with discussing Deirdre's disappearance with Chyna, and Rex had kindly taken Ian, Kate, and Michelle into the backyard, where the children threw a Frisbee for the dog.

"When Irma Vogel called this morning with the news that Deirdre had been taken, I just couldn't believe it," Beverly went on. Her brown eyes were red and she held a tissue damp with tears in her hand. "I'd hardly gotten any sleep last night because of Kate, and then I heard Deirdre was gone and I just lost control. I love Deirdre, and the Mayhews have had such a hard time of it the last couple of years. Now this. Ned helped me get hold of myself so I wouldn't scare the children. I know you're exhausted after last night, too, but he suggested I come over here. I told him I was too nervous to drive, so he dropped us off while he goes on the search for Deirdre."

"Good lord," Chyna murmured, a strange, sinking feeling in her stomach. "She's only been gone since last night, though. There could be a lot of reasons why she didn't come home. . . ."

"Such as? Chyna, she's devoted to Ben. She'd never scare him by staying out all night without calling. I just hope the police can find her."

"The police? Deirdre hasn't even been missing for twenty-four hours. Are they looking for her anyway?"

"Unofficially. After all the missing girls we've had around here, no one is taking lightly another one going missing, especially a mature, responsible girl like Deirdre."

Chyna slowly nodded. Her hands felt icy although she had them wrapped around a steaming mug of coffee. She'd had a bad night but not for the same reason as Beverly. Chyna's experience in the hospital waiting room had deeply upset her, and she couldn't stop thinking about it—not the flash of white, not the feel of something scratching her arms, not the sweet scent that had sent her into oblivion. Or rather, sent someone else into oblivion. Could Deirdre's experience have been what she felt last night? She'd wanted to believe time had changed things for her, that she would never again live someone else's life if only for an instant, and she still wasn't quick to embrace the possibility that she could exist in another person's reality.

"We don't know Deirdre has disappeared like the other girls," Chyna said determinedly, as much to herself as to Beverly.

"Then what's happened to her?" Beverly demanded.

Chyna immediately felt herself placed on the defensive. Beverly clearly thought her formerly clairvoyant sister-in-law was holding back information, and Chyna flushed although her hands remained oddly cold. "I don't know any more than you do," she said, feeling as if she were telling a half-truth. "Deirdre was at a party. You said she'd stepped outside, but there were over a dozen people just a few feet away. She wasn't alone."

"Heather Phelps, the second girl who disappeared, wasn't alone, either. She was downtown," Beverly argued almost aggressively.

"But it was bitterly cold that evening and town was nearly deserted. Besides, Heather was in a large space. She could have gone north on Main and then somewhere else. Or south on Main, or across the street to Elm. . . ." Chyna raised her shoulders in bewilderment. "What I'm saying is, she wasn't confined. From the little bit you've told me, the backyard from where Deirdre seems to have vanished is small. The party was downstairs, where there are sliding glass doors leading into the yard. If someone took Deirdre, he would have stood a good chance of being seen by at least one of the teenagers looking out the doors."

Beverly fired back, "It was lighted inside and dark outside. Besides, I doubt if a bunch of drunken teenagers at the party were gazing out at a starlit lawn. And what about the broken branches of the hedge? Or the scraped ground? Or her shoe? Did she leave on a cold night wearing one shoe, for God's sake?" Beverly glared for a moment, then ran her hand across her forehead. "Oh, Chyna, I'm yelling at you like this is your fault. I'm so sorry. I'm worried about Deirdre."

"I know—"

"Mostly, though, I'm scared because I have a daughter who'll be a teenager someday and this kind of thing just keeps happening!" Beverly rushed on, tears spilling onto her cheeks. "What if this happens to Kate?"

"Don't even *think* such a thing!" Chyna shot back, surprising herself. Beverly jumped, startled, and Chyna closed her eyes. "Now it's my turn to apologize for snapping, but here you are, working yourself into a fit because you're certain something terrible has happened to Deirdre and anticipating an awful fate for Kate when maybe nothing bad has happened to Deirdre at all. For heaven's sake, Bev, Deirdre was last seen at the party at about ten o'clock last night. It's not quite noon today. There could be a lot of reasons why no one has seen her for fourteen hours."

"Such as?"

"She went off with a boyfriend."

"That's what everyone said about Edie Larson. They thought she'd run off with Gage Ridgeway, but she hadn't." Beverly had been slowly shedding her tissue and now grabbed up all the damp pieces in a bunch. "But Deirdre wasn't the type to go off with a boyfriend even if she had one, which I don't think she did. Her father depends on her *so* much since her mother died. She's his whole world."

"Maybe that's why she would run away, with a boyfriend or all alone," Chyna suggested, struggling not to sound as agitated as she felt. "I met Deirdre yesterday. She's pretty and obviously smart. I could tell she was disappointed that she wasn't going to college this year, although she downplayed her feelings. I believe the girl has a lot of dreams she's terrified she won't get to live out, either this year or any other."

"That's what she was thinking when you saw her yesterday?" Beverly asked anxiously.

"What she was thinking?" Chyna stiffened. "I'm not a mind reader, Beverly."

"Yes, you *are*."

"A long time ago I seemed capable of knowing what people were thinking. I'm not capable of that anymore. Not at all," Chyna lied without an ounce of guilt. Letting Beverly believe she still had her "special powers" could only lead to trouble, she thought, trying to keep up her facade of being perfectly ordinary with everyone except Scott. "And even years ago, I didn't *always* know what was going on in people's minds," she firmly told Beverly. "All I'm saying is that yesterday I got a feeling from Deirdre that she felt trapped. That's all it was—a feeling any halfway perceptive person would have picked up on." Beverly was still looking at her doubtfully. "Also, I've heard how attached Ben is to her," she added almost desperately.

"Ben wouldn't have made Deirdre stay with him, Chyna," Beverly pounced. "He's not a selfish man."

"I'm sure he wouldn't have *consciously* done it, but you said she's his life. Apparently, he hasn't rebuilt a life of his own without his wife, and Deirdre struck me as the kind of girl who would try to fill up all the holes in his."

"Then why would she run away?"

It was hard to keep arguing doggedly with Beverly when she was making so much sense, but Chyna couldn't stand to see Bev growing distraught. Chyna's need was so strong that words seemed to flow from her effortlessly, words she didn't believe. "Yesterday, Scott and I were in the café. She talked about wanting to go to medical school. Maybe thinking about what she'd like to do with her future, or being with her friends last night, most of whom are probably going to college, or even drinking too much caused her to act on a moment of impulse. She thought if she didn't leave *now,* she'd never leave."

Beverly frowned. "So she took off for parts unknown with no clothes except what she was wearing, no money, and one shoe?"

"You told me earlier that the shoe had a high heel that was broken," Chyna said. "Maybe she was in a bad mood, or a little tipsy, like I said before, thought to hell with an old, broken shoe, and left it behind on purpose."

"But Ben said she had no money—"

"She might have had money saved up, hidden away. Teenage girls don't tell their fathers everything. And even if she didn't have money of her own, she might have left with someone who *did* have money."

Beverly looked stubbornly angry. "Chyna, you're making up ridiculous excuses because you're as worried as everyone else but trying not to show it. Either that or you're just trying to get me to shut up, in which case I resent you dismissing me as if I'm just a silly kid getting all worked up over nothing. And furthermore—"

Kate saved Chyna from hearing what else Beverly resented by dashing into the kitchen, her cheeks rosy from the crisp air outside, her long curly blond hair bouncing on the shoulders of her wool jacket. No one could have guessed that last night she'd been pale, sweating and vomiting. Chyna knew Beverly still shuddered at her brief terror that the child had been poisoned. Chyna was certain Kate cared more about her ruined princess dress than what her mother had thought was a brush with death.

"Mommy, can me and Ian and Michelle go for a walk in the woods with Uncle Rex?" Kate asked breathlessly.

"Do you feel up to it?" Chyna asked.

Kate looked at her, puzzled. "Sure. Why not?"

"Well, you were sick last night—"

Before Chyna had finished, Kate put her index finger over her mouth and let out a gigantic hiss. "That's a secret. I don't want other kids to know about me making such a big mess."

"I haven't told a soul," Chyna assured her solemnly, "except for Uncle Rex, and he won't tell."

"I know. I made him take an oaf."

"*Oath,*" Beverly corrected while Chyna's mind spun back to the oath she'd taken with Zoey. "And I'd rather you kids stay on the terrace."

"But we're *sick* of the dumb terrace!" Kate had sounded loudly petulant. Immediately seeing her mother's expression hardening into a definite *no,* though, Kate changed her tone. "Mommy, *please.* We won't get in trouble; I promise. We'll stay right beside Uncle Rex, I swear, double swear, three times swear. . . ."

Kate shot Beverly her sweetest, most pitifully beseeching expression, and Chyna knew Bev was a goner.

"Okay, you can go on the walk," Beverly relented. "But don't go too far, and keep your promise to stay with Uncle Rex. No running off and hiding. After all, you don't want him to get mad if he has to look all over the place for you. Maybe it would be best if you and Ben held hands with Rex. And I want you back in twenty minutes."

"Me and Ian don't have watches."

"Ian and I," Beverly corrected again. "Uncle Rex does. Tell him I said twenty minutes. Well, twenty minutes to half an hour. No playing hide-and-seek. And don't take off your coat."

"Why would I do that?"

"I don't know. You might run and get hot and . . . just don't take off your coat. And did I say not to run off and hide?"

Kate rolled her eyes. "Yes, Mommy, about seventeen times." Kate had become very loose with numbers lately, trying to show how many she knew. "We'll be good as gold, like Grandma used to say."

Good as gold, Chyna thought. Yes, her mother had used the phrase so frequently it had gotten on Chyna's nerves. Now she wished she could hear Vivian say it just one more time.

"Okay," Bev said reluctantly, managing a weak smile. "Have a good time, Katie."

Kate walked sedately out the door and shut it quietly behind her before they heard her yell, "She said we can go, Uncle Rex! Let's find that lost girl!"

For a moment, Beverly looked stricken. Then she almost whispered, "We've been so careful not to mention Deirdre around the children."

"You mean, you talked about Deirdre when you *thought* the children weren't around," Chyna returned. "If I remember correctly, eavesdropping on adults is one of the major joys of childhood. I certainly did it constantly."

Beverly sighed. "I guess I did, too. I think when you become a parent you forget all the forbidden things you pulled off when you were a kid, in the hope your children won't do the same." Her gaze drifted to the door that Kate had just closed. "Hope for your children. Most parents have so much. Hope that they'll be happy. Hope that they'll be well." Her eyes filled with tears. "Hope that nothing bad will happen to them."

Chyna was determined not to let Bev drift back to the topic of kidnapping. "Speaking of bad, do you know who doctored Kate's candy with ipecac?" Chyna asked quickly.

"We're pretty certain it was Mr. Perkins down the street. He's in his eighties and mean as a snake since his wife died. Several other children got sick, too. He's also conveniently out of town today. Yesterday he told everyone he was leaving early this morning to visit his daughter in Florida. I guess he couldn't resist staying last night to do one final bad deed before he left. He's moving to Miami around Christmas to be near his daughter and seems pretty happy about it."

"I wonder if *she* is," Chyna said drily, earning her a smile from Beverly. "Whether or not she is, at least he won't be around to cause trouble here next Halloween." Chyna reached out and touched Beverly's hand. "We should be grateful for small favors."

"Do not use some hackneyed phrase to get me to stop worrying about Deirdre!" Beverly lashed out so unexpectedly that Chyna drew back. "I resent it and it won't work anyway." Her eyes narrowed slightly. "Maybe you're *not* the psychic after all, Chyna. Maybe *I'm* the psychic, because I *know* something awful has happened to that girl!"

3

Thirty minutes later, when Rex returned with the children, Chyna suggested they go to McDonald's for lunch, mainly to divert Beverly's thoughts from Deirdre Mayhew and lower her anxiety level a couple of rungs. Sitting here talking about the missing girl was doing nothing to help either of their moods.

The children were delighted, especially when Chyna suggested they take Michelle, pick up the food at the drive-through window, then eat at the little picnic shelter about a block away from the restaurant. Rex begged off, claiming he needed a nap after his long night (he hadn't returned until around three in the morning), so the children and Michelle loaded noisily into the car for a lunchtime treat while Chyna and Bev tried to act as if there were nothing in the world they'd rather do than go to McDonald's.

After a brief squabble over lunch selections at the drive-through speaker, punctuated by a few barks from Michelle, they collected their bags of food and ten minutes later drove into the small picnic area across the street from the library. Chyna remembered how as a teenager she'd often made up excuses for library work that would take her most of the day just so she could come here, buy a hot dog and soft drink from the vendor in residence May through September, eat in the park, and enjoy the view.

The library, with its colonial lines and surrounding wrought-iron fence, looked beautiful, like something that belonged in the restored town of Williamsburg, Virginia. The big clock on the courthouse kept perfect time and the chimes always sounded loud, in perfect tune, and, somehow, haunting. The sun shone on a fountain erected in the town square in the early 1900s, and sometimes an ancient character named Billy Newhouse played folk songs on his guitar for donations. In spite of the chill in the air, Billy was singing "Puff the Magic Dragon" today, and the children were delighted.

Chyna and Beverly unpacked the food, including a serving of Chicken McNuggets for Michelle, and sat down at one of the picnic tables. The little ones dived into the fast food as if they'd never eaten in their lives. "Hard to tell Kate was vomiting her head off last night," Beverly mumbled. "Kids are so much more resilient than we are."

"Thank goodness," Chyna said. "Otherwise, they'd never make it to adulthood."

The temperature couldn't have been more than forty degrees, but at least the sun was out. Beverly seemed to lose some of her nervousness as she sipped a Coke and watched the children eating voraciously and feeding bits of food to Michelle. But all Chyna could think about was Deirdre Mayhew. Was her father sitting in the café, paralyzed with fright that he might lose his daughter after just losing his wife? Even though Chyna had only seen him once in years and hadn't even talked to him yesterday when she and Scott were in L'Etoile, she had felt an aura of helplessness about him. He was the type who expected the worst and usually got it, she thought. Unlike Scott, whose tenacity would never allow him to stop fighting, Ben would give up easily, not because he wanted to but because he simply lacked faith.

"I shouldn't have ordered this fudge sundae," Beverly said, jerking Chyna's thoughts from Ben Mayhew. "I need to lose a couple of pounds. Or more like six or seven."

"You look fine," Chyna answered.

"You would say that if I were twenty pounds overweight."

"No, I wouldn't." Chyna looked into Beverly's pretty brown eyes. "Honestly, I wouldn't. If you needed to lose weight, I'd try to be tactful—"

"Not call me a tank or a whale?"

"How about a *baby* whale?"

They both burst into laughter when Ian, who'd suddenly appeared by his mother's side, demanded, "Where's the baby whale?"

"Right here if your mommy doesn't stop eating fudge sundaes," Bev answered.

"But I like baby whales," Ian protested.

"Well, your daddy doesn't. At least he doesn't want to be married to one."

Ian frowned and looked at his mother in complete puzzlement. "Is Daddy gonna marry a baby whale?"

"I'd like to be at *that* ceremony."

Chyna and Beverly turned around to see Rusty Burtram from Burtram and Hodges Funeral Home behind them. He wore jeans, a tan parka, and running shoes. His gray-kissed light brown hair partly covered his forehead rather than being slicked back as it was at the funeral home. Chyna thought that in casual clothes and away from that atmosphere, he looked at least five years younger.

"Mommy says Daddy's gonna marry a baby whale," Ian informed Rusty in injured tones, "but I don't think it's true 'cause Daddy doesn't know any baby whales."

Rusty frowned ferociously at the sky, then looked back at Ian and said solemnly, "You know, I don't think I know any, either."

By this time Kate had stopped stuffing her mouth long enough to address Rusty. "Don't listen to Ian," she said witheringly. "He's just a baby and not very smart."

"Am *too* smart!" Ian burst out, throwing a French fry at his sister.

Beverly adopted her severe look. "All right, you two, that's enough. Both of you leave the table and play with Michelle. Don't get carried away and start yelling. Don't go into the street. Don't let the dog go into the street, either. And no bickering!"

Kate threw her mother a harassed, melancholy look and mumbled, "*Okay.*" She left the table, pulling Ian along behind her as she repeated to her little brother every instruction Beverly had just given.

"Looks like they're a handful," Rusty laughed.

"Just between you and me, there are days I think I'll cry if I have to listen to one more demand or quarrel," Beverly told him. "Then when they're visiting my grandparents in Iowa for a week each year, I'm so lonely I can hardly stand it."

Rusty smiled. "I think most parents feel that way. At least that's what I'm told. Being a lifelong bachelor—"

"I know several nice women I could fix you up with," Beverly pounced.

Both Rusty and Chyna turned red, knowing Beverly was a relentless matchmaker and they were each single. Rusty was the first to regain his composure. "I've always thought love hits by coincidence. You can't arrange it or plan for it. It just happens."

"Me, too," Chyna said hastily. "I feel exactly the same way."

Beverly looked at each of them, amusement in her eyes. "You two are hopeless. I'll bet neither one of you weds and gets to enjoy married life and darling children—"

At that moment, Kate screamed. Everyone jumped up; then she yelled, "Ian pulled my *hair*!"

"Ian Greer, you stop that!" Beverly stalked toward the children. "If you two can't play nicely together . . ."

Rusty looked at Chyna and raised an eyebrow. "See what we're missing?"

"My heart is breaking."

Rusty laughed and again Chyna was struck by how time and plastic surgery had improved his looks. He was still no heartbreaker, not like Scott Kendrick, she thought. Nevertheless . . .

"I'm sure you've heard about Deirdre Mayhew," Rusty was saying.

Chyna pulled her thoughts away from Scott. "Yes. I'm hoping for the best, but even my brother Ned is out searching for her."

"You probably think I'm a jerk because I haven't joined the search party," Rusty said. "She hasn't been missing all that long, though, and she *is* eighteen, not a kid."

"I wasn't thinking you're a jerk. No one considers that she might have voluntarily run away." Chyna sighed. "But if she hasn't turned up and her father hasn't heard from her by this time tomorrow, then I'd say there's a reason to worry."

"I agree. And I will be helping search for her if that's the case, but God willing, it isn't." Lines formed between his eyebrows and his gaze took on a faraway look. "For now, though, I have a million errands to run. We have a funeral scheduled for the afternoon, but Dad insisted on handling it, just like he did Nancy's."

"Oh yes, Nancy Tierney," Chyna said, realizing her voice suddenly sounded a bit shaky. No wonder, she thought. She'd been sure the dead girl was saying, "Star light, star bright, first star I see tonight." Chyna had been terrified and she was certain Rusty had seen the terror in her expression, but he'd been kind enough not to say anything. "Did her funeral go well?" Chyna asked lamely.

"Well, there were no gaffes," Rusty said easily. "The minister said nice things, although I don't think Nancy had been to church since she was a little girl. Her mother cried like the dickens, but she didn't faint. We were all worried about that. She usually faints, or pretends to faint, when she gets upset. And best of all, none of the pallbearers dropped the casket. When that happens, it's always a disaster. Crashing sounds, mashed flowers, gasping from the mourners, sometimes a scream. Last year old man Simpkins—he must be around ninety and frail as a stick—insisted on being a pallbearer for one of his friends. He took two steps holding that heavy coffin, fell down, and yelled, 'Hell's fire, Arthur always did weigh a ton!' "

Chyna burst into laughter. "How did the guests react?"

"Most of them tried to stifle giggles. Some laughed outright. A few were appalled and said Mr. Simpkins should never have been *asked* to carry the coffin, as if we would do such a thing. Dad didn't take it well, to say the least."

"No, I guess he wouldn't. He's also not pleased that my mother is being cremated instead of having a traditional funeral."

"He told me." Rusty looked at her with kindness in his gray eyes. "But that's not his decision. It's your family's."

"No, it was Mom's. I didn't know about it. Frankly, I never thought about it. I believed she would just always be around. Isn't that silly?"

"No. Who wants to dwell on death? I certainly don't, but I can't escape it because I'll inherit Burtram and Hodges since Hodges is dead and left no heirs."

Chyna ventured gently, "You don't like your job, do you, Rusty?"

He lowered his gaze, paused, and clenched a fist. "I hate it," he said with quiet venom. "I absolutely hate it."

"Then leave."

Rusty's gaze shot to hers. "Leave? Just like that?"

"Why not?"

"Well . . . I . . ." He looked around. "My father counts on me."

Chyna thought of the way Owen Burtram had pushed Rusty aside when he thought he was going to be arranging an elaborate funeral for Vivian Greer. "Maybe he doesn't count on you as much as you think. If nothing else, I'm sure he'd want you to be happy, and if you're not happy working at the funeral home—"

"But I'm the heir to Burtram and Hodges." Rusty colored slightly. "That's what Dad calls me. The *heir*."

"Well, if you feel you must, stay until he dies. Then sell the place."

Rusty looked at her, his lips quirking in a half smile. "Chyna, you saw him. He takes such good care of himself, he'll live to be a hundred."

"Who's gonna live to be a hunert?" Ian burst out beside them.

"All of us," Rusty said gaily. "Maybe a hundred and ten. Wouldn't that be cool?"

"I guess. Would I have to be a duck on Hal'ween?"

Rusty looked confused, but Chyna shook her head. "You could be anything you wanted, Ian."

"I wanna be Spidey-Man."

"Okay, at a hundred and ten you can be Spiderman." Beverly had come up and heard the exchange. "You will let him be Spider-Man on Halloween, won't you?" Chyna asked.

Beverly smiled. "Certainly, but I'll still insist on going with him to make sure he's safe. Let's see, will I push Ian's wheelchair or will he push mine?"

They all laughed, all except Ian, who didn't understand why anyone had to be in a wheelchair. Abruptly he stopped trying to figure out adult logic and ran over to play with Michelle.

"I'd better get to the hardware store," Rusty said. "It's not

my favorite hangout. I'm not very handy, but I give it a try
every so often. It's been nice seeing you, Beverly. The kids
are adorable."

"Thanks, Rusty. You should come over and have dinner
with us soon. You're welcome to bring someone."

"Dad?"

"I was thinking of a female companion." Beverly smiled.

"Guess I'll have to get a rent-a-date for the evening,
then." Rusty laughed, but Chyna heard the trace of sorrow in
his voice. You poor thing, she thought. You must have spent
thousands of dollars trying to improve your appearance and
God knows how many hours working on shedding your shyness and insecurity, and you're still alone. And you always
will be, Chyna realized in one of those inconvenient flashes
of insight.

"Are you okay, Chyna?" Rusty asked.

"Fine," she answered edgily.

"Okay. Didn't mean to pry. You just looked a bit mournful there for a second. But I guess it's natural under the circumstances. Once again, I'm sorry about your mother."

Rusty put his hand on Chyna's shoulder. Abruptly the
picnic table, the children, Michelle, and Beverly all disappeared from Chyna's sight. She seemed to be standing near
a clump of trees, most of them still bearing a few fading
leaves. Then she heard the sound of running and she stepped
behind one of the trees, holding her breath as she looked out
at a narrow path. In a moment, a girl dressed in a navy blue
running suit ran up the path. She was a serious runner, her
steps and breathing measured, her face—her beautiful
teenage face—intent and determined, her long ash-blond
hair pulled back in a ponytail. I've seen her before, Chyna
thought dimly even though she was still lost in the vision.
I've seen her . . .

In a coffin.

Nancy Tierney with her carefully arranged hair, folded
hands, and shell-pink mouth sewn shut but still saying, "Star
light, star bright, first star I see tonight . . ."

"Great seeing all of you." Rusty lifted his hand from

Chyna's shoulder and the vision vanished. As he bade them a cheerful good-bye Chyna barely managed a smile, knowing that for a split second she had not been seeing through her own eyes but through Rusty's—Rusty's as he had watched Nancy on the evening run from which she had never returned.

CHAPTER EIGHT

1

Beverly seemed in a better mood when Chyna dropped her and the children off at their house. Kate and Ian begged to let Michelle spend the afternoon with them, but Chyna explained that Michelle didn't feel comfortable with anyone except her. Beverly looked at Chyna in gratitude. Chyna knew Bev felt more relaxed than she had earlier, but not enough to handle two children turned hyper by the presence of a dog.

As they drove home, Michelle let out a huge yawn. "I believe you showed every tooth in your head," Chyna laughed. "But I know how you feel. I think I could use a nap, too."

All thoughts of naps vanished, though, when Chyna reached Lake Manicora. At least fifty people must have been gathered level with the area where the tumbled-down gazebo stood, and someone had parked a gigantic SUV at the foot of the hill leading to Chyna's house, blocking the road. She pulled up behind the SUV, stopped, and got out of the car with Michelle. Several people looked Chyna's way, then quickly turned their heads. Baffled, she took a few steps forward, looking toward the gazebo, and nearly bumped into Scott Kendrick.

"Scott!" she said in surprise. "What's going on?" She paused, her face draining of color. "It isn't Deirdre, is it? Have they found her?"

"No, it's a bunch of townspeople whipped into a frenzy over Deirdre because they're certain she's been kidnapped, just like the other girls," he said grimly. "I let Irma bring me out here, mainly because I need to see you."

"Me? Why do you *need* to see me?"

"Where's Deirdre Mayhew, Chyna?" a man shouted from the crowd. "Got her stashed with all those other young girls who've disappeared?"

"Why don't you shut your big mouth, ignoramus?" Scott shouted back, then turned to Chyna, whose face had slackened in disbelief. Scott looked at her. "*That's* why I needed to see you."

Fifteen minutes later, they entered the Greer house. Chyna could walk the hill in ten minutes, but she'd gone slowly because of Scott's leg, even though he didn't seem to be favoring it as much as when she'd first seen him. The guy driving the SUV had refused to move, and Scott and Chyna had been forced to walk. As soon as they entered, Scott said, "I've already called the police on my cell phone. They should be here any minute to get that horde out of the middle of the road."

Chyna had said little coming up the hill except to ask Scott if his leg was all right. She was still stunned not only that someone had blocked the road and refused to move, but also that someone else had asked her if she'd taken Deirdre Mayhew and had her "stashed with all those other young girls who've disappeared?"

When they reached the house and went inside, Scott locked the door behind them. "You don't think any of those people are going to follow us up here and come in, do you?" Chyna asked.

"I wouldn't put it past a couple of them. More like a few of them." Scott looked out the window, then turned and gave her a solemn gaze. "You'll have to be careful from now on."

"Scott, what in the name of God is wrong with that gang at the lake?" Suddenly Chyna looked at him, appalled. "When

Zoey vanished, a lot of people thought *I* had done something to her. And now they think I've done something to Deirdre, don't they?"

Scott's expression combined pity and anger. "Some of the stupid ones."

Chyna stared at him. "Does that go for Heather Phelps and Edie Larson, too?"

"I wasn't around when they vanished, but my mother said a few people mentioned that it was fairly odd that *you* were here—once over Christmas, once for your father's funeral," he said reluctantly. "Mom was outraged, of course, and both times you were in Black Willow only a couple of days. I also think you stayed close to home."

"I did. That Christmas I never went downtown, and Edie's disappearance wasn't reported until the afternoon after my dad's funeral. I left the next morning. That's why I never heard any of this gossip, never knew people suspected *me*—" Chyna's eyes filled with tears as Michelle moved close to her legs, sensing that her mistress was upset. Chyna simply dropped her purse on the floor, then knelt and hugged the dog. "I can't believe people think I'd hurt these girls, Scott. Zoey was my best friend. I barely knew Edie. Heather came to a couple of my parents' Christmas parties when she was in her midteens. And Deirdre? I met her *once*. What's made people believe I did something to *her*?"

"Better to say *who* made people believe you did something to her." Scott gritted his teeth. "Irma Vogel."

Chyna gaped. "Irma Vogel! Scott, that's ludicrous! I know when she worked here and I was a teenager she didn't like me, but I haven't seen her since . . ."

"Since Zoey vanished." Scott walked to the couch, his limp slightly worse than usual from the trek up the hill, and dropped down with a small groan. "She hated you because she was envious of you, and I'd bet my last dollar she was spreading rumors about you even then. I know she's never let up on that ESP business."

"I haven't talked about that with anyone except you for years!" Chyna exclaimed.

"But people around here remember, Chyna. This isn't a big city with a helluva lot going on. People rehash old scandals, old gossip, old mysteries, few though they are. Zoey's disappearance is a mystery, and Zoey was your best friend who vanished right under your nose. Now, you take all that, mix it up in the head of Irma Vogel—homely, far from smart, violently jealous of any woman she thinks is a contender for any single man over twenty-five and under sixty, a dangerous gossip, and superstitious to boot—and you end up with a mess like we have down at the lake today. She's been keeping the phone lines hot since dawn."

"Beverly did say Irma is the one who called this morning and told her about Deirdre being missing," Chyna said faintly.

"See? She probably sat down and made a whole list of people to call. Then she zipped right over to my place and rousted me out of bed to deliver the news. She wouldn't even give me a chance to get dressed."

In spite of everything, Chyna couldn't help smiling. "You can't say she doesn't know when to take advantage of a situation."

"You're changing the subject."

"You're blushing."

"Guys don't blush, Chyna." Scott's dark gaze avoided hers. "I hate to ask, but since you didn't offer, may I have something to drink?"

"Oh, good heavens, where are my manners? Do you want a soft drink or something with a bit more kick?"

"I would like a beer."

"A Corona is coming right up if Uncle Rex hasn't drunk it all."

"Rex is here?"

"He got in yesterday," Chyna said as she headed for the kitchen, trying desperately not to think of the crowd outside, the crowd she could still hear yelling her name along with a few obscenities. "When Rex heard about Mom, he was down with the flu, so he got delayed in coming."

"I'm glad you're not staying here alone." Chyna realized

Scott had followed her into the kitchen. Scott *and* Michelle.
Chyna found a new six-pack of Corona beer in the refrigerator, poured one for Scott, fixed herself a glass of ice water,
then gave Michelle a biscuit. Scott sat down at the kitchen
table, looking out onto the dreary terrace. "That place is always so pretty in the summer."

"Beautiful. Or at least it used to be. Mom wasn't much of
a gardener and always hired a landscaper out of Huntington.
There were blooming shrubs and banks of vivid flowers
draped over arbors. And the fountain was always spotless."

"I remember. I came to quite a few barbecues here when
you were just a little thing."

"You make me sound like I was a toddler, Scott. You're
only seven years older than I am."

"Well, when I was seventeen and you were ten you might
as well have been a toddler as far as I was concerned."

"I seem to remember your coming to one of the Fourth of
July parties when you were in your twenties." Chyna smiled,
recalling him at a party wearing tight black jeans, a black
T-shirt, and a small gold hoop in a pierced ear. His mother,
on the one hand, had been horrified, particularly by the earring, and had loudly told him he looked like a hoodlum.
Chyna, on the other hand, had thought he looked breathtak-
ingly sexy, like a rock star. And then she remembered—that
party was the day before Zoey disappeared. Chyna's smile
abruptly disappeared.

"Yeah, I wondered when you were going to remember the
last Fourth of July party," Scott said. "Sorry. I shouldn't
have mentioned it."

"That's okay. I think about it a lot, although I try not to. It
was one of our best parties, what with Ron Larson getting
thrown out by Uncle Rex." She smiled. "Zoey and I thought
that was terribly exciting."

Scott grinned. "It was pretty funny. Larson made a fool
of himself, but then, that was his specialty. Do the Larsons
still live around here?"

"I don't know. I never kept up with them." She sighed. "I
wonder if they still look for Edie."

"Maybe Mrs. Larson does, if she gets a chance between beatings. Somebody should have thrown Ron in the slammer a long time ago." Chyna nodded, thinking of what a sad life Edie must have had with her one spot of joy being Gage Ridgeway. Please don't let him be the one who hurt her, Chyna mentally asked no one in particular. She remembered seeing them together once. Edie had looked at Gage as if she adored him.

Scott glanced at Chyna's solemn face and asked, "Hey, where's Rex? You said he'd finally arrived."

Chyna frowned. "He did, but the garage door is up and his car is gone. He must have left for a while."

"No wonder, considering the crowd down at the lake."

"Oh, he wouldn't have run from the crowd," Chyna said, finally able to smile. "He would have called the police and enjoyed seeing the rabble kicked off the property. No, Rex has always been restless. I doubt if in all of his adult life he's simply hung around the house all day. He's has to be on the go, talking to people, having a good time. I'm sure he left before that bunch of fun lovers arrived."

Scott grinned. "Rex Greer suffers from nervous energy?"

"I never thought of it as that. I always just believed he was outgoing."

"There's *outgoing* and there's *obsessive*. Rex's behavior sounds obsessive to me."

Chyna looked at Scott with mock sincerity. "I'll be sure to tell Rex you've diagnosed his problem."

"And knowing Rex, he'll find me and punch me in the nose. As I remember, he didn't used to take criticism well."

"He still doesn't." Chyna sighed. "I wish he were here, though. With that crowd down at the lake, I don't like being left in the house alone."

Scott raised an eyebrow at her. "Am I invisible? Or do you just not consider me a person?"

"Oh, Scott, I didn't mean to insult you!" Chyna burst out. "It's just that you're injured—"

"I was *injured* weeks ago. Now I'm just having a little trouble with my leg." His hands clenched into fists. "I can still knock the hell out of anyone who tries to bother you, and I will, too!"

Chyna maintained control for a moment, then lost it and burst out laughing. "What's so funny?" Scott demanded.

"You sound like my three-year-old nephew Ian blustering."

"I was *not* blustering—" Scott broke off, his face reddening slightly. "Well, maybe I was."

"There's no maybe about it, Scott."

"All right. So I sounded like a three-year-old. I'll accept that, but I *can* protect you." He waved the beautiful hardwood walking stick in the air. "I still have this, you know."

"I'm very glad and I thank you, Scott," Chyna said solemnly. "I appreciate it, although your mother might commit battery on *you* if you damage that thing."

"You're probably right. I'm about to give it up, anyway. My leg is getting stronger every day."

"Well, I'm glad you had the stick with you today. That walk up the hill couldn't have been easy for you."

"Unfortunately, I'll probably have to get out the Bengay tonight—I just love the smell of that stuff—but I *am* getting better. Much better."

"That's great, Scott. The last few weeks must have been awful for you—" When she saw Scott's face cloud, Chyna broke off and abruptly changed the subject. "I wonder if that crowd is still down at the lake? What do they think? That I abducted Deirdre and have her stashed in the basement?"

"I don't know what they think," Scott said in disgust. "I only hitched a ride with Irma because when I was getting dressed I heard her organizing this little bash here. I wanted to get to the house to protect you. Then I called on my cell phone and no one was home, so I had to hang around with all those merry souls until you got back."

"Irma is probably furious with you for coming up here with me."

Scott's face tightened. "I don't intend to ever speak to Irma Vogel again. When she started all that crap about you and the lost girls and urging me to come and meet people up here, people who intended to do something about you, I only kept my mouth shut because I needed a ride and Black Willow's fleet of three cabs seems to be in service elsewhere. Maybe the drivers are hanging out with the city cops, who *still* haven't shown up."

"Why didn't you come in your own car?"

"My car is in New York, Chyna. I spent a week in the hospital after the accident; then I was flown here to Black Willow. I still wasn't considered fit to drive, but I've used Dad's old car for the last few days. Naturally, today when I really needed it, it had a flat tire, and I'm not up to tire changing, yet. I wouldn't be surprised if Irma flattened it so I'd have to ride with her." Scott paused. "You know, even before the accident, I was thinking of buying a new car. I believe I will, now. Think Ned will give me a good deal?"

Chyna smiled. "I think Ned will let you have a car at cost. He'd probably *give* you one!"

"No gifts. I just want a new car. Having a few dollars knocked off the price wouldn't insult me, though."

"Do you have a model picked out?"

"No," Scott said slowly. "I thought I might get this girl I know to help me select one. I hear she's smart and has excellent taste."

"If you mean me, I have to warn you that I know a lot about how a human body works but very little about how a car works. I purchase automobiles on the basis of their looks."

"Fine with me. We'll have Ned there to tell us all about the car's more technical points."

Suddenly something seemed to explode in the living room. Chyna and Scott jerked in their chairs. Michelle ran from one end of the kitchen to the other, barking fiercely.

Scott jumped up and barely limped as he dashed to the corner of the living room, Chyna right behind him. She could have cried when she saw the beautiful bay window smashed, glass everywhere, and a rock the size of a cantaloupe lying beside the fireplace, where it had broken off a corner of the carved Italian marble mantle before falling to the floor.

A man shouted, "Get away from here, Chyna Greer! Disappear just like you made all those other girls disappear or face this town's wrath!"

A babble of voices followed, some raised above the others, one woman screaming, "You're death incarnate, Chyna. Go away! Leave innocent, God-fearing people alone, or so help me—"

"*That* was Irma," Scott said in quiet fury. "Innocent and God-fearing, my ass. *She's* the danger to this town." He turned. "Go back into the kitchen."

"Do you think they'll try to come in?" Chyna asked incredulously.

"Maybe," Scott said as he headed toward the telephone. "I don't know why the police haven't shown up earlier, but they'd better get up here *now* before one of those fools does some real damage!"

2

Deirdre Mayhew needed to urinate. "Urinate"? she wondered. What had made that word come to her mind instead of "pee" or, as her mother used to say, "use the bathroom"?

It's because I'm so scared I don't even sound like myself, Deirdre thought. I don't even *think* like normal. I want my father. I want to be safe in my bedroom. I want to dream about going to college. I want to have at least one more Christmas. Hell, I'd even settle for watching Irma flirt with Dad.

Instead, I'm probably going to join Mom, and much as I loved her, I don't want to be with her now. She's dead. Tears stung Deirdre's eyes. Oh God, Mom, I'm sorry, but I don't want to die, even to see you again. I'm only eighteen.

Deirdre's head throbbed from the blow that last night had cut her scalp. She lay on a blanket, but beneath it she could feel a gritty concrete floor. Also tape—what she feared was strong duct tape—had been plastered across her mouth and eyes. When they pull it off, my eyebrows and eyelashes will go with it, she thought. That was a certainty. Whether or not she would still be alive when they removed the tape was another matter.

Deirdre wasn't sure why the image of her face without brows and lashes made her want to cry even more. After all, that was the least of her worries now. Nevertheless, she knew how expressionless her face without its arched eyebrows and long lashes would look. Dead or alive, she wouldn't be Deirdre Mayhew anymore.

Maybe her taped eyes wouldn't release her tears, but her nose was running over her upper lip, yet another indignity. Yesterday she'd felt sorry for herself. She'd seen Chyna Greer, beautiful, a doctor, obviously the center of Scott Kendrick's interest. She'd been unhappy because she had to work instead of going to college. She'd missed her mother.

Right now, though, Deirdre would have given anything to have back her old life, no matter how many hours she had to work at her father's café, no matter that she hadn't been able to go to college next fall like her friends, no matter, awful as it seemed, that she'd lost Mom. She had died young, but at least she'd had *some* life—and the romantic love of a man. Even yesterday, Deirdre had been certain that she, too, would have love and at least one child. Right now, though, she wasn't so sure.

Deirdre had been in a chloroform sleep when someone dragged her away from the party and put her in this cool, dusty space. Was it a garage? she wondered. She might have been rendered blind and mute with duct tape, but she'd still possessed her sense of smell, and she'd detected no odor of gasoline or motor oil. The only scents she could identify were of dust, mildew, and mouse droppings.

Her captor had been thoughtful enough to throw a wool blanket under her and fold the extra part over her, but the chill of the concrete floor seeped through the blanket, sending ripples of cold over her naked body. He'd stripped her. The thought made her cringe even more than the realization that duct tape securely bound her ankles and held her wrists behind her. She writhed for a moment, knowing the movement was useless but feeling like she had to do *something* to free herself, not just lie here helplessly . . .

Waiting for him to come back.

The phrase shook Deirdre to the core. "Waiting for him to come back." And then what would he do to her? Rape would be bad enough, but somehow she knew rape was not the objective of her captor. It might be a prelude to the goal, but it was not the goal itself.

The goal was death.

Deirdre let out a helpless moan beneath her duct tape, a moan she knew no one could hear. After all, she had heard nothing for hours—no voices, no starting of cars, no barking of dogs. Absolutely nothing because she was all alone.

Waiting.

3

Ten minutes later the police arrived at Lake Manicora and quickly dispersed the angry crowd that had formed. Most of the people huddled near the water, but a few intrepid souls had begun climbing the hill toward the Greer house, one of these being Irma Vogel. Scott spotted her first, her wispy blond hair sticking out in all directions, her eyes even bigger with excitement, her mouth partially open as she drew in deep breaths. For the first time, Scott didn't feel Irma's ugly appearance wasn't just the luck of having unfortunate genes. They were a window into a flickering, hateful soul looking for a target that could fan it to life.

Scott marched to the front door. "What are you doing?" Chyna asked as he pulled open the door.

"Stay out of the way," he ordered.

"But Scott, some of those people could have more rocks!"

"Chyna, go in the other room." His voice was firm, and while Chyna didn't retreat from the living room, she did move away from the windows and the door. By now, Scott had the door completely open. He stood tall and unmoving, not even supported by his walking stick. His dark eyes fastened on Irma, whose pace up the hill slowed to a near halt.

"Irma, get . . . off . . . this . . . hill." His voice was so icy even Chyna felt its chill. Irma stopped but continued to stare at him.

"Scott, you don't understand—"

"I said, get off this hill."

"But Chyna's in there. And Deirdre's missing. There's a connection—"

"Chyna Greer didn't do anything to Deirdre and you know it. You've just found a good time to take out your jealousy on Chyna. But you don't fool me, Irma, and I'm sure you aren't fooling anyone else except for a few crazy zealots." An angry murmur arose, although quite a few people were looking at one another blankly, not knowing what a *zealot* was. All they knew was that they were being insulted. Scott's voice rose even louder. "Now Irma, I want you to gather up your dim-witted flock, go back down the hill, go home, and don't you *ever* come near Chyna *or* me again!"

"You?" Irma nearly squawked. "This doesn't have anything to do with you, Scott. It's all about *her.*" She'd started to sob. "Besides, you *need* me!"

"I don't need you for anything, Irma. Now go. And the next time you come into my house uninvited, I'll have you arrested for breaking and entering."

Scott slammed the door before Irma sank to her knees, wailing pitifully. Scott could tell part of her actions was an act for the audience behind her, though. In truth, she probably was already planning how she would get back at both Chyna *and* him.

CHAPTER NINE

Twenty minutes later the crowd at the lake had been dispersed by the city cops. Scott had stood at the window drinking beer from a bottle as he watched Black Willow's finest, if slowest, order people to move along or they would be given tickets. He'd expected the police to come up to the house to see what damage had been done, but instead the four cops who'd shown up had simply driven their two cruisers away as if nothing had happened. Well, something *had* happened, and Scott intended to call the sheriff, who was a personal friend of Mr. and Mrs. Kendrick, and not likely to ignore a complaint by their "hero" son, Scott.

Chyna had lingered in the kitchen and he found her there, sitting on the floor sipping a Coke and petting a clearly unnerved Michelle. "Excitement too much for her?" Scott asked, nodding toward the dog.

"The excitement was too much for both of us. Scott, this is insane. Are those people still out there?"

"No."

"Thank goodness. They looked like they were out for blood. If I'd been here alone . . ."

"But you weren't alone, and it's my guess that most of them wouldn't have come close to the house. They were just trying to scare you."

"Irma wasn't just trying to scare me."

"Wait until Mom hears about Irma," Scott said drily. "She won't have a thing to do with Irma again. And if it was Irma who threw the rock that chipped the Italian marble mantel in the living room, then God help her. Almost nothing makes Mom angrier than vandalizing antiques."

"Are you sure Irma's gone?"

"Definitely." Scott stood watching Chyna for a few minutes, then said, "Well, are you going to get up or spend the rest of the day on the kitchen floor?"

"I'm not sure."

"Oh, come on, Chyna," Scott said sternly. "You've never been a coward. I can't stand to see you huddled up like a . . . like a . . ."

"Coward?"

"Well, yeah."

"Okay," Chyna said in a lackluster voice before rising. "I'm up."

"You're still leaning against the kitchen counter."

"Oh, for Pete's sake, Scott," she snapped. "Do I have to stand at attention?"

"That would be nice. Makes you look brave."

"Also shows off her figure," Rex laughed from the kitchen doorway. "You don't have me fooled, Kendrick."

Scott smiled, but Chyna felt unreasonably annoyed that Rex had not been present earlier. "Where have you been?" she nearly snarled.

Rex looked taken aback. "I went to visit a friend."

"My, my, but you have a lot of friends around Black Willow lately." Chyna heard the bitterness in her voice. "And how convenient that you left before the hate crowd congregated outside. Otherwise, they would have blocked the road and not let you by."

Rex frowned. "The hate crowd? What crowd? Here? Why?"

Chyna took off fast and furious. "You'd know if you would bother spending one hour in the house where your sister-in-law died this week instead of acting like this is a vacation, gallivanting all over town drinking and socializing with God know who—"

"A bunch of people gathered at the foot of the hill," Scott interrupted, his voice loud enough to drown out Chyna's sudden shrillness. "They blocked the road to the house. I'd gotten wind of the little gathering planned to scare Chyna and hitched a ride with someone. When Chyna returned and they wouldn't let her drive back to the house, I walked her up the hill. Then someone threw a rock through the front window and broke a piece off the mantle. I called the police and they finally arrived and dispersed the crowd, although they didn't seem to take the whole thing too seriously."

Rex looked dumbfounded, his skin paling under its perpetual tan. "There was a crowd here? Someone threw a rock into the living room? *Why?*"

"Because Deirdre Mayhew is missing," Chyna said raggedly. "Because the people of this town have decided that a girl *always* goes missing when I come home, so I must be responsible."

Rex gaped. "That is . . ." He closed his eyes and shook his head. "That is the most ridiculous thing I've ever heard!"

"Not everyone in town subscribes to this brilliant theory," Scott said scathingly. "Just a few people led by one deeply disturbed—oh, hell—one green-eyed monster masquerading as a do-gooder but who has a magnificent talent for agitating her fellow fruitcakes."

"Name, please?" Rex asked calmly.

"Irma Vogel."

"Sounds familiar," Rex said.

"She used to work here when I was a teenager," Chyna shouted. "And you've probably dated her. You've dated every other woman under fifty in Black Willow!"

She then burst into tears. Rex took three swift steps toward her and enfolded her in his arms. "Honey, I haven't dated *quite* all of the women under fifty. There aren't that many places to go with one where you won't run into another, and you know how embarrassing catfights can be."

Chyna cried and laughed at the same time. "I'm sorry. I was just so scared."

"She didn't consider me adequate protection," Scott said drily.

"Yes, I did. Honestly I did, Scott. But Mother's mantle, you know how she loved that mantle, Rex, and it's ruined all because of me—"

"Yes, I know how you begged someone to throw a rock through the window and break your mother's marble mantle," Rex said soothingly. "It's all perfectly clear, now."

"I need a tissue," Chyna nearly wailed.

"You certainly do." Rex produced a handkerchief from his pocket, and grinned. "So what are you most upset about, honey? The crowd that thinks you abducted the Mayhew girl, your mother's damaged mantle, or your nose dripping in front of your boyfriend?"

"He is *not* my boyfriend!" Chyna sniffled into Rex's monogrammed handkerchief.

"Of course he's not. He's taking the news very well, too, all stoic and manly, not an ounce of desolation showing on his face." Chyna was well aware of the two men smiling at each other, but she couldn't make herself look at either. Rex took her arm and quickly led her from the kitchen. "Now let's go take a look at this mantle you're so worked up about."

Chyna knew Rex wasn't allowing her time to be embarrassed about her outbreak of tears. She'd never been the nervous type, but then, she'd never just lost her mother, either, and Rex was feeling guilty for not being there when a crowd appeared to accuse her of involvement in the Deirdre Mayhew disappearance.

She heard Michelle panting along behind her, then the tap of Scott's walking stick on the vinyl floor in the kitchen before they strode across the carpet through the dining room and into the living room. Rex walked over and looked at the piece of marble, approximately two by three inches, lying near a much larger, rough-edged rock. "Yeah, Vivian would have a fit about this," he said after turning it over a few times. "You say Irma Vogel threw it?"

"We were in the other room when we heard the crash in here," Scott said. "We didn't see Irma do it, but she was closer than anyone else."

Chyna frowned. "How do you know Irma Vogel, Rex?"

"I don't really *know* her; I'm just acquainted with her, thank God. A couple of months ago when I was here, I stopped in at that little café downtown. She waited on me and when she brought my order she sat down, uninvited, and introduced herself. Seemed to think I'd remember her."

Chyna and Scott finally looked at each other. "Husband hunting," they said together.

"She said she'd never gotten a chance to talk to me when I was visiting or say hello at the Fourth of July parties because she was always with, and I quote, 'a *very* possessive date.' I said that was okay because I'd always been with a *very* possessive wife."

"Which one?" Chyna asked wryly.

Rex smiled. "I don't remember all of them, honey. There have been so many, as you invariably remind me. Anyway, all I could think about was Irma staring at my left hand with those bulging eyes of hers. I swear, if she'd had a microscope, she would have been searching for tan lines on my then ringless third finger. At that point, her boss asked her if she'd forgotten she had other customers."

"That would have been Ben Mayhew," Scott said. "He's the father of the missing girl, Deirdre."

"Would Deirdre have been around seventeen or eighteen? Auburn haired?" Rex asked. Scott nodded. "She came into the café that day, too, but headed straight for the kitchen. She was very pretty. She also seemed shy." His gaze seemed to turn in on itself. "What a shame. Her father must be frantic."

"We don't know that anything has happened to her," Chyna said defensively. "She hasn't even been gone twenty-four hours yet and everyone is going crazy!"

Rex seemed to come back to them and gently stroked her hair. "Okay, honey. You're probably right. It's not like she's been gone two or three days. Something perfectly harmless could have happened to keep her from coming home or calling. Just settle down, Chyna."

She could feel some of the tension leave her body as Rex spoke soothingly. "It's just that the crowd down there suspecting *me* of having something to do with Deirdre's disappearance upset me more than I would have imagined." Chyna paused. "And I have to admit, only to the two of you, that the coincidence of another girl turning up gone when I've come home isn't lost on me."

Rex put his hand under her chin and lifted her head, looking deep into her eyes. "Chyna, you can't possibly think the same thing a few nuts in town do."

"Quite a few 'nuts' thought I had something to do with Zoey's . . . disappearance. Even her mother did."

"Anita Simms didn't think you'd *hurt* Zoey—"

"But she blamed me for not taking better care of Zoey!"

Rex nodded. "I'm afraid she did, which was silly. Zoey was your age, not a tyke for whom you were babysitting. And Zoey was the one who insisted on sneaking out that night. You kept saying she wouldn't have gone without you, but I think she would have if that boy she was meeting meant so much to her. Anita ignored all of that, but then, Anita wasn't the sharpest knife in the drawer. I never understood why she and Vivian were such good friends."

"Anita might not have been as bright as Mom, but she was sweet and kind and—"

"Adoring. Anita thought your mother was wonderful, and Vivian just couldn't resist people who looked up to her."

"Rex!" Chyna chided. "That's an awful thing to say."

"But it's true, and you know it."

"I know no such thing and I think it's terrible of you to accuse Mom of cultivating friendships with people just because she thought they admired her!"

Rex smiled calmly. "I'm not saying that Vivian's only reason for forming friendships was to gather a bunch of groupies around her, but not even you can deny that she craved adoration. Maybe we all do, just not as much as Vivian did, but I'm not going to argue with you about your mother's foibles, Chyna. You're far too upset as it is. Besides, I hate to burst your bubble, but I'm not quite perfect, either." He leaned over and gave her a light kiss on the cheek. "I'm going to take my unwanted candid remarks upstairs and leave you to visit with Scott. If any of those people come back here to harass you, give me a yell."

Rex turned and headed for the wide staircase, throwing up a hand in farewell. Chyna and Scott watched him in silence until he reached the top of the stairs and disappeared down the hall. Then Chyna turned on Scott, saying hotly, "I don't know what's gotten into him. My mother did not *use* people!"

Scott took a step closer to her, the cool gray light from the broken front window falling on the chiseled, aristocratic lines of his face from the intense dark eyes to the strong chin with its indentation. "Rex didn't mean to insult your mother, Chyna," he said softly. "I believe all he was saying was that your mother was extroverted and charming and beautiful and sometimes that kind of person attracts others who aren't so blessed." He smiled. "Hey, even when I was a teenager, I thought your mother had it going all over the place."

"And what exactly does *that* mean?" Chyna asked, not knowing whether to be offended.

"It means she was good-looking, friendly, dressed in clothes that showed she had a great figure without looking trashy, acted younger than her age—" He stopped, then said laughingly, "Chyna, your mom wasn't like my mother or the mothers of any of my friends. She was hip and, well . . . sexy. If she'd been a few years younger I might have had a crush on her."

"Oh really?" Chyna pictured her mother—beautiful, laughing, somehow seeming younger than all the other mothers she knew—and suddenly understood what Scott meant. But Chyna couldn't let him off with a simple "Oh." Instead, she cocked her head and said, "I thought when you were a teenager you had your eye on *me*."

Scott flushed and said loudly, "I thought you were an interesting *kid* who'd grow up to be an interesting woman. God, Chyna, I'm not a pervert!"

"I see," Chyna answered as if in deep thought. "You thought I was an interesting seven-year-old. What did your other friends think of me?"

By now, Scott had regained his composure. "They thought you were a pretty little smart aleck." He grinned. "And you grew up to be a pretty adult smart aleck. No, let me amend that. You grew up to be a gorgeous smart aleck." He winked at her. "How about getting me another beer, *chérie,* and I'll call Ridgeway's and have them bring over a piece of plywood big enough to cover that front window until you can get it fixed?"

Ridgeway's. Chyna thought of the expression on Gage Ridgeway's face yesterday when he'd been up on the ladder cleaning gutters and he'd clearly seen the sudden fear in her eyes when she remembered he'd been Edie Larson's boyfriend. Edie, one of the lost girls. Was Deirdre another one?

Scott followed Chyna into the kitchen, and while he flipped through the phone book, looking for the number of Ridgeway Construction, Chyna opened the refrigerator. She bent down to the bottom shelf and started to pull out a bottle of beer when suddenly she could smell dust and mildew and feel her arms trapped behind her, wrapped with duct tape, just like her ankles. She was cold in spite of an old, scratchy blanket that had been thrown over her, and she was terrified of death that might come any minute.

But she knew *she* was not having this experience. She was psychically linked to someone else having this experience. Aloud, she muttered, "Deirdre?"

Scott looked at her. "Chyna? Chyna, what's wrong?"

Slowly, the feeling of duct tape, the smell of dust and mildew, and the feeling of imminent danger faded away. Slightly dizzy and weak, Chyna mentally returned to her mother's shining clean kitchen, holding a bottle of cold beer as she looked up into the dark, alarmed eyes of Scott Kendrick.

"Chyna?" he asked again, softly, as if he didn't want to scare her. "What is it?"

She swallowed and choked. Her heart must be going at least a hundred beats a minute, she thought, and her chest felt so tight that at first she couldn't speak.

"I'm calling nine-one-one," Scott said, picking up the phone receiver. Chyna shook her head violently and reached out for him. His hands closed on her upper arms, and he pulled her up, then drew her close to him. So blessedly close, she thought, clinging to him for reassurance and safety. She couldn't stop looking into his eyes, calming herself with the sensation of his strong hands on her arms, of the nearness of his face to hers, of the comforting feel of his warm breath on her cheek.

Finally, Chyna took a deep breath. "Deirdre Mayhew is alive."

Scott gently pushed Chyna a step away from him although he still clasped her arms. "You kept saying she'd been gone such a short time, there was no need for everyone to panic. Did you really think she was alive?"

"Yes," Chyna said, barely above a whisper.

"I *knew* you were being far too calm about her, far too insistent that people shouldn't panic," Scott said slowly. "Now I realize you were afraid—"

"That if I said she'd been taken by whoever took the other girls, it would be true." Chyna drew a deep breath. "She *has* been abducted, but now I *know* she isn't dead. She's being held a prisoner, though. Her ankles and wrists are bound. I think her mouth and eyes are taped shut, too. She's terrified. And *so* cold. I think there's a blanket over her, but underneath, she's naked." Chyna shuddered and desperately looked up at him. "Scott, I don't know where she is, but I *do* know that the person who abducted Deirdre is torturing her by making her wait for her own murder."

CHAPTER TEN

1

Scott stared at her for a moment. "You're sure she's going to be murdered?"

"I don't know if that's what's she thinking right at this moment, but it's what she *has* been thinking. Or rather, she's certain of it and I've been almost sure of it ever since this morning when Beverly told me about Deirdre going missing. If I had the slightest doubt before, I don't now. Deirdre is another one of Black Willow's lost girls, just like Zoey, and Edie, and Heather, and . . . and maybe Nancy Tierney!"

Scott looked at her in shock. "Nancy! Chyna, Nancy Tierney died because of a fall."

"I know, but there was more to it than a simple fall."

"More? What do you mean? Was she pushed?"

"No. She did trip. But—"

Chyna broke off, seeing Scott's look of growing uncertainty, and knew she was losing his faith. "You don't believe any of this, do you?"

Scott closed his eyes for a moment, then looked steadily into her eyes. "It's not that I think you're lying or delusional, Chyna. But you went through quite a bit outside with those people yelling things to you about Deirdre. Isn't it possible you let that bunch of lunatics scare you into believing all sorts of things, even about Nancy Tierney? Nancy doesn't have anything to do with Zoey or Deirdre or the others."

"Yes, I think she does." Chyna began to feel the warmth of confidence trickling back into her. "Scott, I'm not impressionable. Not at all, although sometimes I've tried to convince myself I am. I'll admit that crowd outside unnerved me, but they didn't scare me into a belief about Deirdre I didn't already have. And they didn't say a word about Nancy."

Scott took Chyna's arm and led her to the kitchen table. "Sit and relax," he said gently. "Tell me what you mean, Chyna. I don't think you're crazy and I'm not humoring you. I really want to know what you're feeling about Deirdre *and* about Nancy."

Chyna pulled one of the chairs away from the shining oak table, turned it sideways, sat down, and looked at Scott's earnest face. "Are you sure you *really* want to know? After all, you never told me you believe in second sight."

"But I said I'd keep an open mind. That's what I'm trying to do. Please, Chyna. I want to believe you. Help me."

She sat still, took a couple of deep breaths, and tried to compose her roiling emotions. Finally, she gave Scott what she hoped was a patient look. "You're right. I've given you no proof that Deirdre has been taken just like the other girls because I have no proof. All I have is my belief based on an incident I haven't told you about earlier because . . ."

"Because?"

"I was going to say because I haven't had a chance," Chyna said reluctantly. "But that would have been a lie. And I'm tired of lying—to myself and to everyone else. For some reason, especially you."

Attention flickered in Scott's eyes. Then he asked softly, "What have you been lying about?"

"How much I see, how much I know." Chyna felt despair and relief wash over her at the same time. "Scott, I've told you about the voice at the lake and a few other things I've felt. But I made it sound as if I wasn't certain about what I've heard or sensed. But I *am* certain. I don't care if you think I'm raving mad; I can feel my power, my second sight, whatever it is, more strongly than I've ever felt it in my life." She glanced at him defiantly. "Well, aren't you going to tell me again I'm just upset because of that crowd yelling at me earlier?"

The trace of a smile appeared and vanished from Scott's face. "No, I'm not, Chyna. I'm relieved you've finally admitted what you've been feeling, and I'm glad you admitted it to *me*."

"Oh," she said, somehow feeling deflated. "You aren't going to try to talk me out of it, make me see reason?"

He shook his head. "Every Tom, Dick, and Harry thinks he sees reason. You're the one who sees *beyond* reason."

"I thought you were a skeptic."

"Maybe I'm not as much of a skeptic as I led you to believe." Scott leaned toward her. "I'm not humoring you, Chyna. I'm not trying to make you say things I think are silly. In fact, I believe when I expressed doubts in the café, I was only trying to hide the fact that I was a little afraid of what you can do with your mind. It is a tad scary for just regular guys like me."

"You're not a regular guy."

"Yeah, I am. But I'm not the subject right now. At least I hope I'm not, considering you believe someone abducted Deirdre with plans to kill her."

Chyna nodded and murmured, "All right."

"Tell me every so-called weird thing you've felt in the last couple of days," Scott said, then exclaimed, "No, wait!" He walked to the kitchen door and glanced up the stairs where Rex had gone. Then he came back. "Okay, now tell me."

"Were you checking to make sure Rex wasn't lurking around listening?"

"Yes. I guess considering that crowd out there today, I should sweep the place for listening devices, but they didn't strike me as sophisticated enough to even know one if they saw it, much less place some around the house."

Finally, Chyna was able to laugh. "For God's sake, Scott, you're acting crazier than I sound."

"At least you're smiling. Besides, I have my reasons."

Scott reached out and took her cold hand in his. "Hurry up before Rex comes back."

"Here goes." Chyna ran her tongue over her lips just as she always did before she launched into a long or complicated story. "The night Deirdre was taken, I was at Ned's handing out candy while Beverly took the children out trick-or-treating. Ned was at the car lot. When Bev and the kids came back, Kate was sick—vomiting, sweating—so Beverly and I rushed her to the hospital. I stayed in the waiting room with Ian. He was scared, so I got him to look out the window at that house across the highway where they never take down the Christmas decorations." She paused. "All at once, I started muttering 'Forever,' only I didn't feel as if I were speaking. I felt as if I was . . . well, channeling someone *else's* words."

She blushed, feeling as though she really did sound like a fool. Or maybe worse. But Scott watched her intently, no derision showing on his face or doubt in his eyes, so she continued. "Then I saw, or rather, whoever I was channeling saw something pale. Just a glimpse. And I said, 'A ghost?' "

" 'A ghost?' "

"Yes. But as I said, I didn't feel as if *I* were talking, but I must have been because I think Ian repeated 'ghost.' I'm not sure. Then I just dropped him."

"You *dropped* him!"

"Yes," Chyna said miserably. "He was wearing a Donald Duck costume with a pillow on his bottom, so he wasn't hurt. Just scared."

Scott grinned. "A pillow?"

"Yes. You know how ducks have a puffy rump? The pillow was under the suit and—"

"Never mind. I know what ducks look like. Poor Ian. Even at age three, I'll bet he was mortified." Scott got his grin under control. "Go on."

"I started flailing. I knew I was doing it, but I couldn't stop it. I felt something scratching my arms. Then I smelled something sweet. I kept thinking, Don't breathe! but I couldn't help it." Chyna paused. "Then I snapped back to reality when someone came up to *me* and asked if I needed help. Suddenly I was back in the reality of the waiting room and Ian wailing and some woman yelling at me." She shut her eyes. "Scott, *I* didn't see a flash of someone pale or mutter 'ghost.' Nothing scratched *my* arms. There's not a mark on me. And no one in that waiting room was wearing cologne. *I* didn't smell anything sweet."

"But you think someone was scratched and someone smelled something sweet."

"When I heard they found signs of a struggle by the rhododendron bushes at the house where the party was held along with Deirdre's shoe . . ." Chyna trailed off, looking down. "Well, I think I was sensing *her* experience. I think she was out there by those bushes—rhododendrons don't lose their leaves in the winter, you know. The leaves are leathery and the branches of the bushes are strong. I think someone hit her on the head and grabbed her out there. When she was fighting to get free, the branches scratched her arms. And I'm sure that sweet smell she was trying not to breathe in was chloroform. She was excellent in chemistry. You said she was. She would have known the sweet smell of chloroform. She would also have known not to breathe it in. That's why I kept thinking, Don't breathe! But of course she couldn't help it, and the drug made her lose consciousness."

Chyna finally glanced up again to see Scott looking at her, his face rigid, his own breath suspended. He leaned even closer to her and whispered, "Did you see who grabbed her?"

Chyna shook her head. "No, dammit. I saw so much else, but not the most important thing—the person who abducted Deirdre Mayhew."

2

Irma Vogel parked in front of L'Etoile, glanced in the rearview mirror to make certain her bright pink lipstick wasn't smeared, her broad nose wasn't shiny, and hair spray held her thin bangs in a perfect sausage roll high across her wide forehead. As satisfied with her appearance as she ever was, she emerged from the car and slowly climbed the stairs attached to the side of the restaurant and leading to the second-floor apartment where Ben and Deirdre Mayhew lived. The sheriff had told Irma Ben didn't want visitors, but she was certain he would be glad to see *her*. After all, she was like family.

She knocked on the door. Nothing. She knocked louder. Nothing. The third time she almost pounded, and yelled, "Ben, it's Irma!"

After a moment, she heard Ben's ragged voice: "Not today, Irma. Go on home."

Irma felt stung, then reminded herself that Ben was distraught. "Ben Mayhew, you don't need to be alone right now," she called. A teenage boy walking by on the sidewalk looked up at her and smirked, clearly understanding that her visit was being rejected. He needed a good smack, Irma decided, refusing to let him embarrass her into slinking away. Instead, she called, "Ben, you let me in!"

"Irma, *please* go home."

"No. Absolutely not. You need me. I'll sit on the steps until nighttime if that's what it takes."

After nearly three minutes, Ben opened the door with a weary I-know-you-won't-go-away look, which Irma decided was just the result of worry and fear. He needed her more than he realized.

Abruptly she threw herself against him, wrapped her arms around him, and wailed, "Oh my God, Ben! Poor Deirdre!"

Ben stood rigid, his arms hanging at his sides. After a moment, he lifted his hands and pushed Irma away. She'd expected him to hug her back, grateful for her presence, but he just stared at her, his hazel eyes bloodshot, his hair awry, and his breath smelling slightly of gin. Ben Mayhew was not a drinking man, she thought. He must have turned to alcohol in despair, and that was responsible for his cool behavior toward her. "Oh, Ben!" she cried, swooping in for another try at a hug. "I know there hasn't been any word on Deirdre yet and I'm *so* sorry!"

"Thanks for your concern and for coming by," Ben said flatly. "I have to go sit down now. I'm not feeling too well."

"That's why you shouldn't be alone." Irma, all five foot eight, 190 pounds of her, pushed past Ben and planted herself in the middle of the living room. He couldn't have gotten rid of her without dragging her to the door, shoving her onto the porch and down the stairs. "You need someone to talk to about poor Deirdre," she pronounced.

"I do *not* need someone to talk to about poor Deirdre," Ben said with an edge to his voice. "I've been talking to people about poor Deirdre since midnight. I searched for her everywhere I could think of for sixteen hours and I finally had to come home and rest."

"Of course you did!" Irma cried. "You're worn-out and you needed to get in from the cold. I mean, it's not too cold right now, but it was cold during the night when you were out searching for her, going around town and tramping through fields where you thought you might come across her body, all lifeless and staring up at the sky, maybe raped, naked, and mutilated, even decapitated—"

"Irma!" Ben shouted. "For God's sake! I don't want to think about Deirdre maybe being dead and mutilated and all that other stuff. That's part of why I had to get away to myself. People like you keep harping on the horrors that might have happened to my daughter. Can't you understand that I needed a little peace right now?"

"And apparently more than a little gin!" Irma returned, insulted and hurt that he didn't appreciate her concern.

"Yes, I had a couple of gin and tonics. I might have another one."

"You don't need alcohol; you need hot food and coffee." Irma was already shedding her bulky pink, down-filled jacket. "I'll fix you a nice meal—"

"I don't *want* anything to eat!"

Irma recoiled, looking as if she were going to cry, and some of the tautness left Ben's wide face, puffy from exhaustion and what were obviously tears of fear and frustration and, no doubt, self-flagellation for letting Deirdre go to the party.

"I'm sorry," Ben said weakly. "I didn't mean to hurt your feelings. But I'm tired, I'm worried sick, and I can't even think rationally right now. Besides, you look a little tired yourself. Or . . . not well. Your cheeks are almost glowing."

"I'm fine," Irma protested quickly, feeling her cheeks growing even pinker as she remembered the fracas at the Greer house, picking up the rock and slamming it through the window, the things she'd screamed to Chyna. Irma's cheeks were hot pink because of the excitement of the near riot, but she wasn't ashamed of herself. Still, she didn't want Ben to know what had happened earlier. He might not understand what she'd done, and he definitely didn't like scenes. "I'm just worried about Deirdre," she sniffled.

"Yeah, well, me, too." Ben took a deep breath. "I need to lie down for a while, Irma. Maybe have a nap. . . ."

"Yes, yes, that's what you need," Irma announced promptly. "A nap. Put down that glass of gin; get in bed. I'll tuck you in and stay right by your side—"

"Right by my side?" Ben sounded horrified.

"I meant in a chair." Irma was insulted again, but she recovered quickly. "I'll be in a chair beside your bed watching over you, getting you anything you need, answering the phone and the door. You can just close your eyes and dream of Deirdre safe and sound back here with you in your little apartment, not lying out somewhere—"

"Irma, stop. I'll take a nap; I promise. But I don't need someone to watch over me."

"I insist!" Irma began nudging him toward his bedroom like a sturdy little tugboat guiding an ocean liner into port. "Get right in bed. Get under the comforter. Put your aching head on a soft pillow. I'll pull the curtains against the sun, not that we've had much today, and what we did have is failing, which will make looking for Deirdre even harder. . . ."

Ben groaned in misery and allowed the implacable Irma to jostle him into his bedroom, nearly push him onto the bed, and pull a comforter all the way up to his unshaven chin.

Twenty minutes later, Ben Mayhew lay in a muttering, restless half sleep. Irma, who had lugged a heavy armchair from a corner to the side of the bed, leaned over Ben and looked at him fondly. She hated to see him suffering so much, but she couldn't help her pleasure at being near him under such intimate circumstances.

This would never have been possible if Deirdre were around, Irma thought. Deirdre would have taken care of her father, just as she did when Ben's wife finally died after a two-year bout with cancer that kept her an invalid. Ben had gotten sick then, too. Irma remembered Deirdre saying he'd lain feverish yet racked by chills for nearly a week after the funeral. She'd been so frightened of losing her father, too, that she'd barely left his side and refused to let anyone come in to "help out," as Irma had tried to do. "I can take care of Dad," Deirdre had firmly told Irma. "*I'll* make him drink some broth to keep him hydrated. Thank you, but I don't need your help," Deirdre had insisted when Irma continually offered her services. "*I* can change Daddy's sheets. *I* can take his temperature. *I'll* get him to the hospital if he seems to be getting worse." Refusal after refusal after refusal. That's all Irma had gotten from Deirdre when she'd offered, nearly pleaded, to be near Ben in his time of need.

Irma looked at Ben's pale, perspiring face. She bent over him, gently touching his forehead with a cool, wet washcloth, wiping it down his cheeks, and finally reaching into her purse for her lip balm. She scooped out a bit with her index finger, then slowly and sensuously smoothed the scented ointment onto his dry lips with pudgy, loving fingers. If Deirdre had been here, Irma couldn't have done that for Ben.

But Deirdre wasn't here anymore.

CHAPTER ELEVEN

1

Gage Ridgeway pulled into the Greer driveway, stopped the truck, and looked balefully at the smashed living room window. Rex Greer had called Gage's father several hours ago, asking that someone come and board up the broken window. Peter Ridgeway had immediately called his son, Gage, who said he was busy and someone else would have to handle the job. But two hours later Peter called again, said no one else was available on a Sunday afternoon, and insisted that Gage take care of the matter *immediately*. After all, Peter had said tartly, they got too many good referrals from the Greers to make enemies of them.

Normally, Gage would have come to board up the Greer window as soon as he'd heard about the rock-throwing incident, but he hadn't been able to forget the way Chyna had looked at him the other day when he'd been standing on the ladder. Everything had been fine and then suddenly she'd seemed jumpy. Or was it something else he'd seen in her eyes? Fright? Horror?

Gage shivered slightly as he climbed out of the truck. Now Deirdre Mayhew was missing. A friend of his had called him early this morning to warn him of the hue and cry raised over the girl and told him to expect a visit from the police. The police hadn't come because even if the girl hadn't been found yet, which Gage had a feeling she hadn't, she wouldn't have been missing for twenty-four hours. If she wasn't found by tonight, though, Gage would be expecting to see flashing lights coming up the road leading to his house. Dammit.

Gage was relieved to see Rex Greer come out of the house and walk toward him, smiling. Gage managed a tentative smile of his own and Rex shook his hand. "Glad to see you, Gage. It's been a while."

"At least three years." Gage's mouth felt dry. He wished he had the nerve to ask for a soft drink or even a glass of water, but he didn't want to appear flustered. "You haven't been around when I was here doing work for Mrs. Greer, and they stopped having the Fourth of July parties after . . ."

Gage trailed off, wishing he'd stopped talking at least a minute sooner. But Rex was as usual smooth and unflappable. "After Zoey disappeared." He smiled again and Gage noticed how much younger Rex looked than his own father, Peter, who was nervous and peevish and always in a dither about either Gage's behavior or something having to do with the business.

"I was afraid we were going to have to sleep with that window wide open tonight," Rex went on easily. "Either that or pile boxes in front of it, and they wouldn't have done much to keep out the cold."

"Sorry it took me so long to get here," Gage said quickly. "It's my day off and I thought one of the other guys was going to handle it."

"No problem. We survived." Rex smiled. "So how are things going at Ridgeway Construction these days?"

"Just fine. Better than ever, really." Gage caught himself. "Not that Grandpa didn't do a fine job of managing the place. And of course Dad is a good manager, too."

Rex laughed. "Your grandfather had a big heart that overruled his business sense. He was always doing jobs for free. That doesn't improve the bottom line, but he kept the business going anyway. Your father?" Rex lifted his shoulders. "Everyone knows you're the power behind Ridgeway Construction, Gage, and doing a fine job of it."

Gage said without conviction, "Oh, I don't know about that."

"I do. I don't live around here, but I keep up. I have old friends, and of course there was always Vivian, who knew everything about the town."

"I'm sorry about Vivian—Mrs. Greer, sir. I thought a lot of her."

"It's 'Rex,' and I thought a lot of her, too. She'll be missed, that's for sure. Chyna is broken-hearted. And Ned—well, Ned's always been harder to read. I'm not saying he didn't love his mother, but I'm not proud that he's pushing off everything on poor Chyna—funeral arrangements, that kind of thing." He paused. "But I didn't arrive in time to help her myself, so I shouldn't criticize. And if Vivian's death weren't enough, now we have new trouble."

Gage nodded and glanced over at the window. "Damn," he burst out in surprise. "I knew you had a broken window, but I didn't think someone had broken out the whole *front* window. It was a bay window, too. Expensive to replace."

"Yes. The rock that broke the window also hit the marble mantle over the living room fireplace. That's not going to be easy or cheap to replace, either."

Gage didn't know whether to ask what had happened. His father had given him a breathless, garbled tale of a crowd descending on the Greer house, making it sound like the rabble that had stormed the castle of Victor Frankenstein. It couldn't have been *that* bad, Gage thought. Still, the lawn was badly trampled and a few signs bearing crude pictures of what he guessed represented the devil still lay on the lawn. And the strong glass in that big bay window had taken quite a blow.

Rex seemed to sense that Gage didn't know how much to ask, and began talking casually. "I missed all the action, but I hear Chyna came home from a little picnic with her niece and nephew to find a bunch of people out here. One of the sanctimonious gang had blocked the road and she had to walk up the hill. Some of the uninvited guests were shouting that Deirdre Mayhew had disappeared just like the other girls over the years and the girls only vanished when Chyna was home. They'd decided that two and two makes four, so obviously Chyna abducted and probably murdered all of the victims. I hear she's 'death incarnate.' "

"Good God," Gage murmured, clearly shocked. "They didn't come in the house and hurt Chyna, did they?"

"It seems Scott Kendrick had come with the crowd, pretending to be one of them but really just trying to get here to protect Chyna. He's without a car right now. Anyway, I'm glad he was here when I wasn't. No one came in even though it seems the cops took their good old time getting here."

"Was anyone arrested?"

"No. Nor was the rock thrower identified. I don't think the local law enforcement even tried to do much of anything except break up the crowd. The sheriff is going to hear about that from both Kendrick *and* me. God knows what would have happened if that bunch of kooks had been around for much longer."

"It's Sunday and not many cops are on duty," Gage said, wondering why he was defending the very people who'd harassed him in the past and were bound to harass him again if the Mayhew girl didn't show up soon. Maybe he was thinking they'd go easier on him later if he supported them now, he mused. "The few cops who were working might have been handling something else—a domestic violence case or . . . hell, I don't know."

Rex shrugged. "I seem to forget we're not the only game in town. But considering the circumstances, I still think they could have given Chyna a little more help. If there weren't enough *city* cops on duty, they could have called in the state police for help."

Suddenly Rex and Gage heard a car speeding up the road to the house. With a squeal of tires, Ned stopped his white Mercury right behind Gage's truck and jumped out. He wore jeans, and his blond hair looked as if he hadn't combed it since morning. "What the hell is going on here?" he shouted. "Did someone try to hurt my sister?"

"Settle down, Ned," Rex said calmly as Ned sprinted across

the front lawn to the broken bay window. "Apparently, while Chyna was out with Beverly and the children, a crowd gathered down on the main road. When she got back, they'd blocked the driveway. Scott Kendrick was kind enough to walk her up the hill and make sure she got in safely."

"Who broke the window?" Ned demanded.

"We don't know. Several courageous souls climbed the hill, yelled a few nasty things at Chyna, and threw a sizable rock through the window. It hit that marble mantle your mother loved so much and broke off a corner. Gage is here to board up the window until we can get a glazier to replace it."

Ned glared at Gage. "Thanks for tearing down my clubhouse earlier this week without my permission."

Gage gave him a deadpan look. "Sorry, Greer, I didn't know you and your gang were still using the place."

"During her last call to me, Vivian told me the building was nearly destroyed by the storm and she'd asked Gage to finish it off and haul away the wreckage," Rex said casually, then turned to a scowling Ned. "Quit acting like a seven-year-old, Ned."

Ned threw his uncle a scathing glance, then demanded, "Why were people here yelling at Chyna?"

Rex sighed. "Use your brain, Ned. They came because Deirdre Mayhew is missing." Rex sounded patient, but Gage thought the patience wasn't coming easily. Earlier Rex had sounded annoyed that Ned had left all of the funeral arrangements for Vivian to Chyna. Maybe Rex was still annoyed with his nephew. "They've come up with the theory that it's no coincidence every time your sister comes home, a girl goes missing."

Ned looked at his uncle incredulously. "And they think Chyna is responsible?"

Rex nodded. "Irma Vogel seems to be the ringleader."

"I remember when that bitch worked here. She's always been jealous of Chyna." Ned glared at Rex. "Where were you when all of this was going on?"

"Visiting a friend," Rex returned calmly, then with an

edge to his voice, "Where were you and what took you so long to get here?"

"I was at the car dealership. That accountant messed up the books again. I'm going to fire him tomorrow." Ned turned on Gage. "Were you here earlier with the crowd?"

"Of course not!" Gage's face reddened. He looked both angry and offended. "Do you think I'm a kook like those others? I *like* your sister."

Ned closed his eyes and took a deep breath. "Oh damn, I know you do. Sorry, but this has been one hell of a week. Beverly just called me and told me someone else had called her and told her something bad had happened up here. I just lost my mother. I panicked over Chyna. I didn't mean to fly off the handle at you, Gage."

Gage shrugged. "Well, I do have the reputation of being a town bad boy, although I'm getting a little old to be called a boy anymore. Mr. Greer says your sister is okay, though."

"She's in the house with Scott Kendrick," Rex said. "Why don't you go in and see for yourself that she's fine?"

"Yeah, all right," Ned said distractedly. "I just can't believe people would act this way."

Rex raised his eyebrows, glancing first at Ned, then at Gage, and said in a half-amused, half-intimidating voice, "You'd be amazed at how crazy some people can be under perfectly normal façades."

2

"Wow, Rex, that was a comforting," Ned muttered bitingly as he stalked toward the front door. Things were bad enough. Did his uncle have to make statements that seemed to have a dangerously underlying meaning? He probably believed it was funny, Ned thought. He certainly hoped Rex hadn't tried out his wit on Chyna.

As soon as Ned stepped into the house, he called, "Chyna? It's just me—Ned."

"We're in the kitchen," Chyna called back.

Ned strode in to find Chyna and Scott sitting at the big, gleaming oak kitchen table. Michelle lay by Chyna's side and raised her head to give Ned a wary look until Chyna rubbed her behind the ears for a moment. Ned supposed Michelle took this as a sign that he was not a danger, because she laid her chin on her paws again and let out a sigh.

"Good lord, Chyna, I just heard what happened up here." He walked straight toward her and gave her a hug. "I'm sorry I wasn't around to help you."

"Why would you be?" Chyna asked lightly. "You don't live here."

"No, but I took plenty of time getting here. I was at the dealership. Bev didn't call until about fifteen minutes ago, so I wasn't even here to help you."

"Help with what?" Chyna smiled at him, but he saw the false bravado behind the smile. "Scott was with me, thank goodness. He's the one who called the police. No one was hurt." She paused. "Our mother would be a wreck, however, if she saw her window and her mantle."

"Well, yes, but they can be fixed. If they'd hurt you, though . . ."

Chyna peered closely at Ned. He looked tired and flushed. Sweat beaded his forehead and upper lip, and his blue eyes were fever bright.

"Are you all right?" Chyna asked. "You look sick."

"Thanks," Ned returned curtly.

"Well, you do." At that moment, he sneezed, then coughed a couple of times. "Okay. I don't feel great. I woke up late, but I hadn't felt like I'd slept all night, and I seem to have been losing ground ever since. Maybe I'm coming down with something."

Chyna nodded. "You're definitely coming down with something. You've always been prone to getting the flu in autumn and this is how it starts out—sweating, sneezing, coughing. Maybe you should go to the emergency room at the hospital."

"I don't feel *that* bad," Ned snapped. Then he looked at

Scott, sitting with a glass of iced tea in front of him. "Thanks for taking care of my little sister."

"It was my pleasure, although I'm not sure anyone finds me much of a threat with this damned walking stick." Scott threw the stick, propped against the wall, a glare that seemed to say it had seen its last day as his companion. Chyna glanced at it, too, noticing tiny bits of rust-colored stain in the deep ivory engraving of Henry VIII. Scott's mother would have a fit if he'd damaged her antique, Chyna thought. Scott went on, "And of course Chyna had Michelle."

The dog raised her head and looked around fearfully, as if someone were going to ask her to do something brave. Even Ned grinned and said, "It's okay, girl. Your mistress is safe. You can go back to sleep."

"Don't expect her to fall into an immediate snooze," Chyna said. "She's spooked again."

"I thought dogs were supposed to protect you," Scott said.

"A dog's duty is first and foremost to be your best friend," Chyna told him. "Some of them are asked to protect their owners. Mine are not. I can take care of myself."

"I'm not so sure about that." Ned opened the refrigerator door, stared at the contents for a minute, then withdrew a can of 7UP. "Chyna, considering what happened here today, don't you think you'd be safer staying with Bev and me?"

Chyna frowned. "Ned, you don't have room for me."

"Sure we do. We have three bedrooms."

"One of which you turned into a playroom for the kids. The second is their room, with bunk beds. Are you going to kick one of them out of a bed and give it to me? Or do you want me to sleep with you and Beverly?"

Ned popped open the can and downed at least a third of it. Chyna knew this meant he had a sore throat and felt dehydrated. "You and me and Bev in one bed?" he asked after a noisy gulp that Chyna thought would end with his getting choked. "I don't know about that. You two would talk about hairstyles and boys and giggle all night. I wouldn't get *any* sleep." Chyna made a face at him. "I guess either you or I could sleep on the couch."

Chyna tried for the least insulting words she could muster, but she knew she'd never had the finesse of her mother when it came to not insulting people. "Ned, thank you so much for your offer, but I'm not going to kick you out of your bed, especially when you're getting sick, nor am I going to sleep on the couch, either. I don't mean to hurt your feelings, but your couch feels like it's filled with gravel."

"Bev's mother gave it to us and she'd be crushed if we got rid of it, although I know it's hardly the most comfortable piece of furniture in creation," Ned said dolefully.

"Mom did a good job of picking some furniture on the basis of beauty rather than comfort, too," Chyna reassured him. "Those armchairs in the living room, for example. If that rock someone threw today had hit one of them, it would have ricocheted right back out the window."

"And hopefully it would have hit one of the Black Willow Crusaders on the head," Ned returned fiercely. Then he sighed. "You really just don't *want* to leave this house, do you?"

Chyna frowned and said slowly, "No, even in spite of the ruckus today. Maybe it's because I don't want to desert Mom's house. Or maybe I just feel her presence here." She realized both Ned and Scott were staring at her uneasily. "I mean, I don't think I see her ghost or anything," she added hastily. "I don't go around talking to her essence, not that I think her essence is hanging out here or . . ."

She took a deep breath. "I sound like a lunatic. What I am trying to say is that there are things I need to do here, like . . . like clean out the refrigerator and pay that stack of bills I saw on her desk and gather up the personal papers she didn't put in the safety-deposit box. I should also go through her clothing to see what needs to go to Goodwill and what maybe Beverly would like to have. I need to do at least a dozen things around here. After all, Mom wasn't in the hospital or a nursing home for a long time. We made no preparations for closing up this house or . . ." Chyna felt her throat closing up. "Or disposing of her belongings," she choked out. "Besides, Rex is here."

"Bev can help you with all that stuff," Ned said. Chyna

caught Scott flashing her brother a stern glance. Ned had offered his wife's services but not his own, and clearly Scott didn't approve. Ned didn't seem to notice, though. "And I wouldn't count on Rex to be your protector. He's never here. But if you really don't want to stay with Bev and me, we can't make you."

"It was a kind offer, Ned, but it's really more practical for me to stay here. Especially because I have Michelle. The children would never give you and Beverly a moment's peace with a dog around."

"Yeah, they would go crazy over the dog. The poor thing would probably have a nervous breakdown." Ned took a sip of his soft drink, then said, "If you're determined to stay, I guess there's nothing I can do. You always were the bravest woman I ever knew. And the most stubborn."

"Good heavens, Ned. I'm the smartest, the bravest, and the most stubborn woman in your universe. You're giving me too many crosses to bear."

"You can bear all of them and probably more."

"Everyone has their limit." Scott's sharp voice grabbed everyone's attention. "She's not invincible, Ned, even if she seems to think she is."

"Well, I can't make her come to my house if she doesn't want to," Ned flared. "What do you propose, Scott? That you stay here with her?"

Chyna felt her cheeks flush at the possibility, particularly because Ned knew she'd had a crush on Scott since she was a kid. "I love it when everyone talks about me like I'm not in the room," she said loudly to cover her embarrassment. "You two are making me more jumpy than that crowd did earlier. Quit worrying about me. Both of you."

"Spoken exactly like Mom," Ned mumbled in annoyance.

"Good. She was a wonderful example," Chyna shot back.

"If you're talking about Vivian Greer being a good example, I couldn't agree more."

Chyna, Scott, and Ned looked up to see Owen Burtram standing in the doorway with Rex. While Rex looked casual in khakis and a yellow cable-knit sweater, Owen wore gray wool dress pants and a black cashmere coat over a dark blue silk shirt. Every dyed hair was in place—in fact, it looked as if he'd used hair spray. Above a black eyebrow he had what seemed to be a small bruise that he'd tried to hide with a concealer too light for his skin tone, but otherwise he looked perfect, his expression carefully arranged to show just the right amount of both anxiety and compassion.

"Chyna, dear," he began in his loud but carefully well-modulated voice, "Russell and I just heard what had happened here earlier and we came to see if you're all right."

Rusty Burtram, still wearing the jeans and parka he'd had on in the park across from McDonald's earlier, leaned around his father and said, "Hi, Chyna. Scott. Ned."

The elder Burtram held firm, blocking the door into the kitchen, and Rusty disappeared behind him again. Chyna was on the verge of asking Rusty to enter the kitchen, too, when Owen began another soliloquy. "I do not know what has gotten into some of the members of this community, but it is a disgrace. Unforgivable. They have destroyed property, not to mention frightened a poor, recently orphaned girl." He paused to let the drama of this last image sink in, Chyna of course being the "poor, recently orphaned girl."

"I will be speaking to the mayor tonight about this deplorable occurrence. He and I are close friends," Owen confided self-importantly. "I have a great deal of influence with him, and together we will see that people are punished for wreaking havoc at the home of one of the community's finest families!"

Owen sounded so ridiculously egotistical and pompous that Chyna almost burst into uncontrollable laughter. Ned had opened the refrigerator door again, behind which Chyna knew he was snickering. Owen looked at Scott, who stared back unflinchingly, his gaze clearly letting Owen know Scott thought the man was acting like an arrogant bag of wind. Owen haughtily swept his gaze back to Chyna, symbolically banishing Scott to a corner with his face to the wall.

"Thank you, Mr. Burtram," Chyna choked out past incipient giggles. "That is very kind of you. Very . . . solicitous."

"Nonsense! We simply can't allow people to get away with this kind of heathenish behavior!"

"Oh, well, I guess not . . . ," Chyna said faintly.

Rex obviously sensed that Owen was not only making a fool of himself but also throwing everyone else into a tailspin, including the dog, who was scooting farther under the table. "Owen, come take a look at the mantle," Rex said, grasping Burtram's shoulder and spinning him around. "I want to know if it can be fixed properly, and in your line of work you know much more about marble than I do."

"I know about marble for headstones, Rex," Owen protested. "Not the kind of marble meant to be kept in a house or church."

"I'm sure you know much more about all kinds of marble than you think you do," Rex insisted, propelling Owen toward the living room. "You can at least give me a *few* pointers. I'm absolutely clueless."

After they'd disappeared, Ned closed the refrigerator door, still grinning, and looked at Scott. "I'm leaving now. Chyna's right—I'm coming down with something and I need to get home before I get too sick to drive. I know your car isn't here. Can I give you a ride? I promise I'm not too bad off yet to drive a car."

Scott hesitated. Chyna didn't want him to leave and she didn't believe he wanted to leave now, either, but Owen would surely know Ned would offer Scott a ride home. An insistence by Scott on staying would be noticed by Owen and duly reported all over town.

"Thanks, Ned," Scott said, rising slowly. "I rode out here with Irma. I'm without a car. I'm going to get a new one, though. Maybe you can give me some pointers on the way home."

"Glad to," Ned said heartily. He walked over to Chyna, started to kiss her, then drew back. "I don't want to spread any germs I'm carrying, even though I could shake you for being stubborn enough to stay here. I love you. Take care of yourself, little sister."

"I will." She gave him a bright, brave smile. "Those people won't be back."

"Is that your second sight talking?"

"It's common sense talking. Although the police have already run them off once today, if they give it a second try, especially with Owen Burtram bringing all of his considerable influence to bear on the situation, I'm sure they won't dare to bother me again."

Ned winked at her. Scott grabbed his walking stick, giving it another glare. He was frustrated and angry, Chyna thought, whether about needing the stick or nearly being forced from her home by the booming man in her living room she wasn't sure. "If you need anything, call me," Scott said, then grimaced. "Physically I don't look like I could be much help, but my brain is still working."

"Thank you for everything you've done today, Scott. In spite of what you think, with all of those people out there shouting at me, I don't believe I could have walked up that hill alone." Scott's smile bore a touch of gratitude. Gratitude and something else extremely pleasant Chyna wasn't quite secure enough to acknowledge. "But you've managed to get the engraving on the top of that stick stained. You'd better clean it off before your mother sees it."

Scott jerked the walking stick to eye level, staring at the stained engraving. His face turned white and rigid. Certainly he wasn't *that* worried about his mother's reaction, Chyna thought. For a moment, he looked as if he were going to pass out. What in the world was wrong with him?

And then with something close to horror, Chyna realized the stains buried in the engraving looked exactly like dried blood.

CHAPTER TWELVE

1

Deirdre knew she'd dozed sometime during the morning. She could only tell time of day by temperature and a couple of muted sounds that penetrated her prison—birds chirping nearby and distant church bells. At first, she hadn't been certain the bells she'd heard belonged to churches; then she reminded herself that she'd been taken on a Saturday night. She would have liked to believe the sound of the bells meant she wasn't far from Black Willow, but churches seemed to be scattered every couple of miles throughout the whole county.

Deirdre wondered if people were looking for her the way they looked for other girls throughout the years, the way they'd looked for Heather Phelps. How many Christmases ago had that been? Deirdre was too tired and cold to remember. She'd known Heather—not well, but enough to talk with casually on a few occasions. Heather had been smart and pretty. Very pretty, but shy and something of a Goody Two-shoes.

Deirdre hadn't known Edie Larson at all, but most people believed the same thing had happened to her that had happened to Heather. Then there was Zoey Simms.

Deirdre could remember hearing her parents talk about Zoey when they didn't know she was listening. Zoey had been the first girl to vanish from Black Willow a long time

ago, when Deirdre was just a kid. Zoey had been Chyna
Greer's best friend who came to visit once a year. A lot of
folks believed Chyna had done something to Zoey, but
Deirdre remembered her parents saying they knew Chyna
slightly and she'd been sweet and kind. They'd said Chyna
would never have hurt Zoey and they'd get angry whenever
anyone implied Zoey's disappearance had anything to do
with Chyna.

And Scott Kendrick sure didn't believe anything bad
about Chyna, Deirdre thought, remembering how he'd
looked at her yesterday. Was it just yesterday? It seemed like
a week ago they'd come into L'Etoile and Deirdre had seen
that look in his eyes when he gazed at Chyna—a look that
said he admired more than her beauty. Deirdre had been
wounded even though she'd always known Scott had no romantic interest in her, even when she wasn't a kid anymore.
That's why she'd insisted on dressing up and going to the
party when she really didn't feel like it after Nancy Tierney's death. Deirdre had thought the party might make her
feel a little bit better about her lost friend Nancy and realizing with a jolt that afternoon that her dreams of someday
having a romance with Scott were beyond ridiculous.

Instead, Deirdre had been just as miserable at the party as
she would have been at home. And to top it all off, she
thought with macabre humor, she'd gone and gotten herself
kidnapped. Deirdre couldn't believe what an unfathomable
nightmare this week had turned into, not only because of
Nancy and Scott but also because, for the first time in her
life, she doubted her mother's wisdom. She had always told
Deirdre that God was a benevolent being who loved all His
children. Deirdre had clung to that belief when her mother
died. She'd even managed to hold on to it when Nancy died.
Now she wondered. How could He have let her mother suffer so much before snatching her away? How could He have
loved Zoey, Edie, Heather, and Nancy and still taken each of
them when they were so young? And how the hell could He
love *her,* even though she'd always tried to be the good girl,
just the way her parents had wanted her to be?

Deirdre felt tears forming in her tightly bound eyes. She was so frightened. She was so hungry. She was scared almost witless, and she was cold as ice. With her stripped naked, the worn wool blanket her abductor had provided was next to useless. What had the person hoped would happen? That Deirdre would get frostbite and not move around very much? Or was the reason something even darker? She'd read once that serial killers liked to take tokens of their kills. Her earlobe ached where one of her cubic zirconium studs had been ripped loose, but maybe he'd wanted more—clothing. Ludicrous as it seemed, she was embarrassed that the killer would remember Deirdre Mayhew in her mother's old "party" dress and some cheap cotton underwear.

A mouse ran over Deirdre's bare, numbing feet and she moaned, her urge to cry making her gag beneath her duct-taped mouth.

2

Chyna stood up and began clearing soft drink cans from the kitchen table. When she turned around, Rusty stood staring at her in the doorway. They looked at each other for a moment before he finally gave her a tentative smile.

"I'm really sorry about all you've been through today," he said.

"I'm fine." Chyna heard the wooden tone of her voice. Her mind was filled with the image of dried blood on Scott's walking stick. That and the vision she had when she clasped Rusty's hand in the park earlier that day when she'd known she was watching Nancy Tierney pounding down that path in the woods. She could still see the girl's navy blue running suit and shining ash-blond hair pulled back in a ponytail as she breathed rhythmically and kept her arms close to her sides, her form perfect for a professional runner. "I don't think those people would have really hurt me."

"I wouldn't be so sure of that." Chyna looked sharply at Rusty. "I mean, I think they only came here to scare you, but sometimes people get carried away and do things they wouldn't normally do. And there could have been an accident. That rock could have hit you in the head. . . ." His voice trailed off as his face paled.

"I guess you're right." Nancy hit her head on a rock, Chyna wanted to shout at him. You *saw* it happen. Instead, she asked, "Would you like something to drink?"

Rusty stared at her for a moment. Then he said in a rush, "What I'd like to do is talk to you. Privately."

"Privately?" Chyna tried to keep her voice light, but it didn't work. "What do you want to talk about?"

"I need to explain something to you. Can we go outside?"

"Outside? Why do you want to go outside? It's chilly. There's a breeze blowing up—"

"Chyna, *please*." Rusty's slender, earnest face and gray eyes pleaded with her although he kept his voice low and controlled. "I know this might sound silly. Or maybe it sounds threatening under the circumstances."

"Under *what* circumstances?"

"Just go out on the terrace with me for a few minutes. If you're uncomfortable, you can come right back in. Or even scream if you want. There are three other men here."

Rusty looked so pale, so pathetic, and so harmless that Chyna couldn't say no to him, although she knew she should. After all, she'd watched Nancy Tierney running down a path through *his* eyes—Nancy, who had fallen and smashed her head on a rock, causing a subdural hematoma that had killed her. Chyna knew she could have been seeing Rusty gazing at Nancy a week ago, two weeks ago, or even a day *before* she died. But something told Chyna that wasn't the case. Rusty had seen Nancy the day of her death. Minutes before her fall. And if he hadn't been the one chasing her, causing her to tumble as she fled from a pursuer, then why hadn't he called the Emergency Service when he saw she was badly injured? Why had he waited for hours until a search party had found her?

"Rusty, anything you have to say to me you can say right here." She heard the slight quiver in her voice although she'd been trying to sound stern. "If it's something private, you don't have to worry. The men are in the living room. They can't hear you."

"My father can walk like a cat when he wants to. He could be standing beside the doorway, listening, and neither of us would know it. Chyna, I'm not going to hurt you, but I *have* to talk to you and only you. For God's sake, I beg you. . . ."

Chyna could feel herself melting when she saw tears rising in Rusty's soft gray eyes. Good heavens, he's going to start crying, she thought in horror. Poor Rusty, with that gentle heart and that awful father, is begging to talk to me and I'm treating him like a pariah.

"Let's go out the back door and look at the fountain," she said casually. "Do you mind if the dog goes with us?"

Rusty looked so grateful, Chyna felt her throat tighten against her own tears. This day had been too much for her. She knew she was losing control of her emotions, doing things that weren't prudent or safe, but she couldn't seem to help herself.

Rusty asked, "Michelle is the dog, right?" She nodded. "Then I don't mind. I love dogs."

Michelle had fallen asleep under the kitchen table and Chyna nudged her awake and motioned for the dog to follow her. If Rusty was truly dangerous, she was quite sure Michelle wouldn't attack him—she was too timorous—but at least she would bark at any sign of trouble.

Rusty followed Chyna and Michelle onto the terrace. The air felt heavy and moist—depressing—not sunny and light as it had when Chyna had talked to Rusty in the park earlier today. She wondered if this was a portent. Was she about to meet her end just like Zoey and Heather and Edie? And maybe Deirdre, too? The rational part of Chyna told her she was being a fool, but her emotions were taking control.

She and Rusty walked slowly around the old fountain. "This fountain used to be beautiful," Chyna said, trying to sound offhand. She didn't want to pressure Rusty into talking before he was ready. "My grandfather designed it and I loved the angel on top. I thought of it as my guardian an-

gel when I was little. And there were goldfish. Huge goldfish. Only about a month after Grandfather died, the fountain
cracked. We came out one morning and the terrace was
covered with water and dead fish. I remember sobbing and
my mother told my father it had to be fixed immediately.
He had it patched and turned on the water every summer,
but he never replaced the fish. He said if it cracked again
and more fish died, he couldn't bear to see me as broken-
hearted as I had been that day."

"He sounds like a thoughtful man."

"He was."

"Were you . . . intimidated by him?" Rusty asked.

Chyna's gaze sliced to Rusty's. He'd said "intimidated,"
but he'd meant "afraid." Chyna sat down on the edge of the
drained pool beneath the fountain and looked at him. "No,
Rusty, I wasn't at all intimidated by my father. He was rather
remote, but always gentle and loving." Rusty nodded slowly,
clearly intending to say nothing about his own father. Chyna
asked softly, "What is it you wanted to tell me, Rusty?"

Rusty remained standing, looked at his shoes, looked
over at the nearly leafless trees, and finally fastened his gaze
just past her face. "When we were in the park this afternoon
and you took my hand, you had a vision or read my mind or,
well, you *saw* something about me, didn't you?"

"I had a . . . sensation," Chyna answered carefully.

"It was more than a sensation." Rusty finally looked directly at her. "I saw it in your eyes. I saw that *you* saw—" He
broke off and sighed wretchedly. "You know I was watching
Nancy the night she was killed."

Chyna hesitated. Was it wise for her to be honest? Then
she knew she had no other choice, because somehow Rusty
was already certain she'd had a vision of him and Nancy.
Maybe he was a bit psychic himself.

"I saw you in a group of trees watching Nancy running up
the path. As she neared you, you stepped behind one of the
trees."

"Is that all?" Rusty asked.

"Yes. It was just a flash. I didn't even know if it was a vision of the evening she died. It could have been a different evening."

"It wasn't. It was *that* evening—the evening of her death. But you didn't see her fall or . . . or anything else?"

The despair in his face grew and he sounded almost disappointed. "That's all I saw, Rusty. Honestly." Chyna paused, trying to decide if she should push the matter further. But Rusty obviously wanted to talk with her, maybe even confess. What kind of coward would she be if she fled from a murder confession when she was perfectly safe? At least, relatively safe, with the other men so close by. She tried to look composed and asked calmly, "Do you want to tell me about that evening, Rusty?"

"Yes, even though I'm sure you'll think I'm some kind of pervert." He jammed his hands into the pockets of his parka. "Maybe I am a pervert. I was acting like one that evening."

He fell silent, his vision turned inward. Should I stop him now? Chyna wondered. Or should I prod him to say more, even if I don't want to hear it? Her mind flashed to the beautiful young girl lying in a coffin, and Chyna knew she must try to find out what Rusty had to say, even if what he had to say was appalling.

"I don't think you're a pervert, Rusty," Chyna said honestly. No matter what had happened between Rusty and Nancy the evening she'd died, Chyna somehow knew this man was not depraved. Nevertheless, he looked at her doubtfully. "I'm not reassuring you so I can get information, Rusty," she said sincerely. "I'm telling you the truth."

His steady gray eyes seemed to search hers for a moment. Then some of the tension left his body. He looked beyond her at the sky that had turned the color of weathered tin. "I was years and years older than Nancy, but she'd fascinated me ever since she was a little girl. I didn't lust after her. Honestly, Chyna, I didn't."

Chyna was taken aback by the fervor in his voice. "I believe you."

"I guess you could say I envied her. I was never much to look at. You remember me in high school, before I had plastic surgery. I was ugly."

"You weren't ugly, Rusty."

"You don't have to patronize me."

"I'm not. I'll admit, you look better now, but you didn't look bad then." She paused. "I was an adolescent when I knew you, and most kids that age aren't known for their kindheartedness, especially when it comes to the looks of the opposite sex. But even then, I didn't think you were ugly. Not even close. You just weren't a heartbreaker."

"Like Scott Kendrick?" Chyna blushed and was glad Rusty was looking at the trees again. She couldn't think of anything to say and was glad when Rusty continued. "My family was disappointed with my looks, my shyness, my clumsiness. Mostly my father. Then along came Nancy. She was a beautiful baby who grew into a beautiful girl. Not just beautiful—extroverted, entertaining, athletic. As she grew up, I used to watch her a lot because everyone doted on her. I thought if I watched her enough, I could learn to be like her. Not feminine, but charming and accomplished—someone people admired." He finally looked at Chyna. "That was stupid, wasn't it? Traits like Nancy's can't be learned."

"I don't think it's stupid," Chyna said. "I used to try to copy my mother because everyone loved her."

"But you didn't need to copy *anyone,* because you were also beautiful, smart, admired."

"I don't think I was admired after I reached age seven and people started thinking I was a kook because the gossip was that I claimed to have ESP." She made herself laugh. "In fact, I don't think those people who gathered on my lawn today, pitched a rock through my window, and called me 'the devil's spawn' admired me one bit."

Rusty smiled faintly before his face once again fell into morose lines. "I know things have been bad for you lately. But still, you're special. Nancy was special, too, but in a different way." He looked back at the sky. "But back to my disgraceful tale. Once I got into the habit of watching Nancy, I couldn't seem to stop. I just wanted to figure out what she had that drew people to her when they seemed to avoid me, even when I had my looks improved."

He sighed. Chyna felt she should say something wise, but nothing came to mind. Besides, she didn't want to break Rusty's talkative mood. "I used to watch her run. She was so agile, so *elegant,* even when she was running and panting and sweating, that I was amazed. I knew where she went to every evening, and I'd hide and watch like some nasty voyeur, just to see how she could manage to be so charismatic even when she was just jogging."

A pinecone from a nearby evergreen fell and blew across the terrace. Rusty kicked at it and missed, although it was only an inch away from his shoe. "I started doing some soul-searching and decided I was acting stupid. Watching Nancy wasn't going to help me to be more charismatic. Besides, it felt weird, almost . . . dirty.

"So I started taking my evening walk down a different path," Rusty went on. "I'd been doing this for about two weeks when one evening I heard someone running behind me. Not close, but definitely running. Fast. I don't know what got into me." He paused. "Okay, I was scared. Another one of my admirable traits—I scare easily. So I got off the path and sort of hid behind some trees. In just a minute, *Nancy* ran by. At first she was running like usual, with that professional style. Then she started running like a regular person would if they were running *from* something. At least I thought that's how she looked. I didn't want to spook her, so after she passed by me, I moved forward and stood behind another tree. I just stood there."

"Nancy didn't see you?" Chyna asked.

"I don't think so. She was going so fast, mostly looking straight ahead, but a couple of times glancing over her shoulder. Her face . . ." He shook his head. "I only caught glimpses, but she looked alarmed. Panicked, actually. And then . . ." He broke off and closed his eyes. "And then she fell. Well, she didn't really just fall; she stepped in a hole in the path and crashed to the ground. I'm sure I heard a thump as her head hit that rock. I could swear I heard the bones in her ankle breaking, but maybe that's just my imagination. Before she fell, though, I heard something else. I heard someone running behind her. There were hard footsteps pounding down the path. They weren't as fast as hers. In fact, they sounded a little bit clumsy. But they kept coming. When she fell, though, they slowed, then stopped."

For a moment, Chyna fell silent. Rusty was lying, she thought. He was making up a story, covering for himself. He must be.

But something within her demanded, What if he isn't? You can't just dismiss what he's saying. You *can't.* Softly she asked, "Rusty, did you see who was running behind Nancy?"

"N-no." Chyna focused, trying to sense whether he was lying, but she failed. He sounded sincere, but she wasn't certain. "I didn't see anyone," Rusty said mechanically. "Only an empty path. No person."

"All right," Chyna said softly, determined not to sound as if she were interrogating Rusty. She instinctively knew that would send him into silence. "What did *you* do after Nancy fell?"

Rusty was silent, gazing into the distance as misery grew on his face. "I stood there behind that tree, looking at her. I just *stood* there! I didn't have my cell phone with me, but I could have gone for help. I could have, but I didn't!"

"Why not?" Chyna asked casually.

"Because then everyone would have known about me. Because everyone in my family, hell, everyone in town, would have said, 'There's that awful Rusty Burtram. He hides and *watches* girls.' I couldn't bear the shame. I couldn't bear my father's anger and indignity, I couldn't bear his disgust with me, and believe me, he would have been disgusted. He would have felt repulsion every time he looked at me, even more than there already is, and I just couldn't bear it."

"Would he have fired you?"

"Fired me?" Rusty almost laughed. "No. Worse. He would have stood behind me in public. The public image is what counts, you know. He would have praised me and made up some story about why I didn't do something for Nancy. But in private—"

Rusty shivered. He's like a little boy, Chyna thought. A little boy terrified of his father.

Rusty swallowed. "So I just stood still, watching her. I saw how her foot was twisted in a way that had to mean her ankle was broken, and I saw blood seeping from her scalp onto that rock. So much blood." He shivered again, then looked at Chyna. "I thought I heard the other footsteps running away, but I wasn't sure, so I waited for at least twenty minutes. And then I left. Nancy was still alive, breathing, bleeding, so badly needing help, and I . . . just . . . left!"

Rusty's voice had risen dramatically. His gentle eyes looked wild and he slapped a hand over his mouth, as if to choke back more words and maybe sobs. Sensing trouble, Michelle stood up and moved closer to Chyna, never taking her amber gaze off Rusty. Chyna didn't take her gaze off Rusty, either. She couldn't imagine that the cringing, tortured man standing in front of her now was the same nonchalant, smiling guy she'd seen earlier today in the park. She knew strong emotion could change a person's physical aspect remarkably, but the difference was almost unbelievable.

"I let Nancy die because I was worried about *me*!" Rusty ground out. "Don't you see how loathsome that is?"

Silence spun out for a few moments before Chyna managed to say, "I can't say it was heroic, Rusty." She was glad her voice was gentle and steady even though she felt as if she was quivering on the inside as hard as Rusty was on the outside. "But no one is perfect. We've all done things or *not* done things we regret."

"Like let someone die? Have ever just *let* someone die, Chyna, because you were afraid of what people would think of you?"

Chyna drew a deep breath and thought, wondering what harmless, soothing thing she could say to this hysterical man. But she didn't have to say anything, because Rusty went on in that awful voice turned gravelly by torment. "And the worst thing is that I know her death wasn't just an accident! When Nancy ran by me, she looked scared. After I heard the other footsteps, I knew why. She was fleeing. Good God, Chyna, Nancy was *chased* to her death!"

By now Rusty's face was crimson from the effort of speech, sweat pouring from his forehead over his slender cheeks, his hands held out to Chyna almost in supplication, as if he were asking her forgiveness for his cowardice. She sat rooted on the fountain rim, her dog pushing in alarm against her right leg, her mind blank, unable to come up with one consoling, calming word.

Suddenly Rusty's head jerked around to the kitchen doorway and his eyes filled with dread. Almost in slow motion, Chyna turned as well to see Owen, Rex, and Gage standing there, staring, motionless.

Then Owen, looking at Rusty with narrowed eyes cold as winter ice, said in a quietly furious voice, "It's time for us to go home, son."

CHAPTER THIRTEEN

1

By seven o'clock, darkness cloaked the Greer house and Chyna wondered if she hadn't made a mistake by not accepting Ned's offer to stay with him and Beverly. Then she thought of the children, who would no doubt expect to stay up later than usual because they had a special guest—Michelle the dog, not Chyna. Beverly would enforce bedtime, which would cause arguments and perhaps tears, neither of which Beverly needed when she was already upset about Deirdre Mayhew. Ned, in the meantime, would be watching any sports show he could find, not a difficult task, because they could get about two hundred channels using their satellite dish. Chyna didn't mind watching an occasional live ball game, but she couldn't bear Ned's whooping and yelling at the television.

No, she'd made the right decision to stay in this house tonight even if she felt slightly uneasy, she thought as she sank down on the couch, Michelle beside her. Chyna needed her dog, a light dinner, time to read or to listen to music, and, most of all, peace.

Peace. It sounded nice, but how could she have peace with her mother gone forever? They had been so close. They'd talked to each other on the telephone every three or four days. Sometimes, when Chyna had endured a particularly grinding shift at the hospital or a child she'd come to love had died, she'd called her mother, who always managed to make her feel better. If not better, at least calmer. And Vivian had always been there for her, day and night, knowing just what to say. Now they could never talk again.

Tears filled Chyna's eyes and her throat tightened. Never again would she hear her mother laugh, joke, console, praise, or pour out her love. Vivian was gone and for a few minutes Chyna felt as if she simply could not go on without her. Michelle, sensing her distress, laid her blond head on Chyna's knee. She rubbed the dog's ears and face, and in return, Michelle gently licked Chyna's hand. "I'm so glad I brought you," she said to the dog. Michelle licked Chyna's hand again and looked up at her expectantly. "And I'm showing my gratitude by not giving you your dinner. Are you hungry?" Chyna thought it might have been her imagination, but the dog suddenly looked joyful. "Dinner it is, girl," Chyna said. "Maybe some food will make both of us feel better."

Food seemed just the ticket for Michelle, who ate with gusto. Chyna, however, couldn't even finish a bowl of soup and a sandwich she'd made for herself. She'd thought she was hungry, but the food simply would not go down. Every time she tried to swallow, Rusty Burtram's tortured face flashed in front of her. Then she would remember Owen's hard, cold eyes gazing with disgust at his son. Chyna had felt afraid for Rusty when she'd seen Owen's face. Rusty had felt afraid, too. Hell, we were *all* afraid, she thought, remembering Gage's look of frozen helplessness and how Rex's customary expression of careless ease had vanished in seconds.

Chyna was glad Rex had made an excuse to follow Owen home for a talk about investing in the mortuary business. Rusty didn't live with Owen, but it was clear that Owen intended something nasty for Rusty—a punishment of some sort, as if Rusty were a little boy. Rex's excuse had been lame, but he'd skillfully managed to force Owen into accepting his company for the evening. Owen couldn't immediately vent his wrath on Rusty, thanks to Rex. That would probably come tomorrow, Chyna thought, and was proud of Rex for stepping in to delay or, she hoped, diffuse what could have become a disgraceful, even violent situation, at least for a while.

She'd watched the three of them leave, Owen walking toward his black Lincoln with a solid, measured step, jaw tight and lips clamped shut. Anyone could tell he was seething. Rusty had trailed behind, still shaking, his head hanging. He and his father had come in Owen's car and Chyna was cringing inside, thinking of what that ride home would be like for Rusty, when Rex suddenly grabbed Rusty's arm and said, "Why don't you take the wheel of my car? I've had a couple of drinks and I don't want to get arrested for drinking and driving. You live just a couple of blocks from your dad. You can get out at your house, and I can certainly make it two blocks without causing an accident." Rusty had looked as if he were going to fall at Rex's feet in gratitude.

Poor Rusty, Chyna thought, feeling almost sick as she thought of his agonized face and his uncontrolled shaking. He hadn't done the right thing when he saw young Nancy fall and he felt wretched about it.

Chyna suddenly dropped her soupspoon. Or did he?

She sat at the kitchen table, her bowl of soup growing cold, and replayed every word Rusty had said to her. First he'd talked about how Nancy had always interested him; "fascinated" was the word he'd used. He'd said he was homely and clumsy, a disappointment to his family. Chyna had no trouble believing Owen considered Rusty a letdown. The man thought he was perfect and would expect his child to be perfect. Suddenly she remembered Rusty asking her if she'd been intimidated by her father. The question had startled her because she'd focused on her own childhood. Edward Greer had been distant but always loving and accepting. Rusty's experience must have been different, Chyna realized. Growing up, Rusty no doubt had feared his father. The way he looked at his father standing cold and unyielding in the doorway today told her Rusty still feared Owen.

Nancy had been different. Rusty had said she wasn't just beautiful but also extroverted. She seemed to excel at everything she did. Rusty said he thought that if he watched her enough, he could learn how she managed to do everything right, to make people love her. He'd watched her all of her life. He even kept an eye on her when she went out running, because studying her had become customary for him.

Chyna sat up straighter in her chair. She understood how watching Nancy perform in society could have become a habit with Rusty if he wanted to see how she managed to charm people, to win them over with her wit and poise. But how could watching the girl run every evening possibly help Rusty? He didn't want to become a runner. But when she ran, especially in summer, she probably wore tiny shorts and a tight T-shirt over a sports bra. Could Rusty have been watching her run in the evenings because she looked tantalizing? After all, even the surgical improvements he'd made in his looks didn't seem to have made him more popular with women. He'd been stumped when Beverly had asked him to come to dinner and bring a date. He clearly didn't have a girlfriend now. Chyna wondered if he'd ever had a serious relationship with a woman.

Chyna sighed in sympathy for him. He'd had a lifetime of being thought of as awkward, homely, a disappointment at best, more likely an embarrassing misfit, by his father. No amount of plastic surgery could correct those mental scars. Rusty had probably been emotionally crippled for life.

But did his emotional scars make him an object of pity or one of danger? He'd watched Nancy constantly. That certainly wasn't normal. And in spite of what he'd said to Chyna on the terrace, he hadn't watched Nancy just so he could learn and imitate her style. At the funeral home he'd said, "Nancy did as she pleased. Always. I suppose quite a few people would consider her spoiled." And Chyna had known he felt the same way. He'd admired Nancy and hated her at the same time.

And then there was the matter of the path. Nancy had run on the same path for years. Rusty had said he'd always

watched her on that path. Then he'd suddenly decided his behavior was ridiculous and he'd started taking his evening
walk on a different path. And miraculously, just two weeks
later, Nancy ran down *that* path instead of her regular one?
Quite a coincidence. In fact, it was too much of a coincidence
for Chyna to accept. She was almost certain that Rusty had
not accidentally been on the path Nancy never used except on
the night of her death. And he'd said he hadn't called for help
because he didn't want anyone to know he'd been watching
her. If he'd used a cell phone or called 911 from home, his
call could have been traced. But he could easily have called
from a pay phone.

If he'd really wanted to help her.

If there hadn't been a mysterious, unseen person chasing
Nancy.

If the person responsible for Nancy's fall had actually
been Rusty himself!

Chyna stood up abruptly from the table. She'd felt sorry
for Rusty this afternoon. She'd been glad Rex had gone
home with Owen, a move obviously meant to protect Rusty
from Owen's fury.

But maybe Rusty didn't need to be protected from Owen.
Maybe Owen needed to protect other people from his own
son, and Rex had only managed to allow Rusty his freedom,
the freedom he needed to save himself because he'd seen
something in Chyna's eyes earlier today, something he'd
tried to fix by painting himself to her as a man who'd made
a terrible mistake and considered himself beneath pity. It
had actually worked for a while, but if Rusty had earlier
sensed that she'd been aware of his memories of that night,
then maybe he would realize that in spite of his efforts to
"explain" his actions to her today, she would later analyze
them and recognize that his story didn't make sense. What if
he decided he'd done more harm than good by spinning that
tale for her this afternoon?

Then he would conclude that she was a danger to him.
And here she sat in this big house, all alone, with a possible
killer thinking of her as his only real threat.

2

Deirdre awakened with a start. Waking up without being able to open her eyes felt beyond strange, but the odd sensation was quickly overwhelmed by the stiff, cold throbbing of her body. She was lying on her side, and drawing in a deep breath, she managed to flip herself onto her back. Pain shot along her backbone. She could barely feel her feet for a moment, which terrified her. Then the pins and needles of returning circulation stabbed them. She groaned partly from misery, partly from the relief of knowing that her feet weren't frostbitten. Frostbite could mean amputation. . . .

I'm getting out of here, Deirdre thought with sudden ferocity. I am not going to lie here on this cold floor, waiting for God knew who to come back and murder me. I *will* live!

She began violently twisting her wrists and ankles bound with duct tape. She could barely move her wrists, but it seemed to her that her ankles weren't as firmly bound as they had been last night, right after she'd regained consciousness to find herself lying on this concrete floor. She wriggled her feet, then tried jerking them up and down.

There seemed to be some movement, not just of her feet, but also of her ankles, which had been bound by what she knew was duct tape. She tried again. Yes! She could definitely feel movement in the area of her ankles.

The cold, she suddenly thought in triumph. The glue on the duct tape had grown stiff and begun to lose its adhesiveness in the cold. The tape around her wrists was almost unbearably tight, but it hadn't been possible for her abductor to tape her ankles as tightly because of the bone structure. The inside ankle joints, the tibias, were pressed tightly together, but above and below them lay small spaces where the cold air had crept in. If her captor had used more tape, firmly securing the ankles above and below the joints, all of the air would have been shut out. But maybe the person had been in a hurry. Or maybe careless. Or maybe just not aware that cold had any effect on glue. Maybe her captor wasn't a chemistry buff,

Deirdre thought with hope, and that simple fact might cause a plan to hold her until she could be murdered to fail for good. Neither she nor any other girls could be kidnapped and killed if she escaped and told everything she knew.

Deirdre took a moment to slow her breathing. She needed to concentrate, not hyperventilate and lose her focus. It didn't matter that she was cold and hungry and scared. All that mattered was the loose duct tape on her ankles.

She moved her ankles back and forth. The movement was so minimal that it almost didn't seem worth the effort. But there was movement, she reminded herself, and *any* movement at all was worth every bit of energy she had left.

Using her thighs, she began to move her legs up and down. Such tiny movements, she thought. Such pathetic little movements. But movements nevertheless. And unless her imagination was running away with her, the tape felt just a bit looser. Just a fraction looser, but still looser. Yes, there was no denying it. She was making progress. Slow, slow progress, but . . .

Deirdre heard a door squeak. Although she was already cold, even colder air rushed over her. She went perfectly still, like a young rabbit caught in the sights of a fox. If I hold still enough, maybe he won't see me, she thought wildly. Maybe he'll think I'm dead. Maybe he'll decide tonight is not the night. . . .

"Chilly in here." Deirdre's heart pounded at the sound of the casual voice. "Of course, it's chilly all over this part of the country considering the time of year. Nights don't usually get this cold until late November. Thanksgiving time. I've always liked Thanksgiving. I think it's funny, our giving thanks for all God provided for us. Actually, the Indians provided. We showed our gratitude by killing them. Of course, they got a few of us, too."

A sigh. "But it's the way of the world. At least, that's my opinion. What's yours?" A long pause. "Oh, you can't answer. I'll bet you have an opinion, though. I'll bet you have opinions on just about everything. You smart girls think you know it all. It's like being pretty. Pretty girls think they can get it all, too—everything the world has to offer. And there you are, Deirdre—both smart *and* pretty. You'd have an un-beatable combination if there weren't people like me to stop you from taking everything away from the rest of us."

Daddy, Daddy, help me, Deirdre thought wildly. I know you'd save me if you knew where I was. But you don't. And I don't, either. Only one person knows where I am. The person at the door. The person who's going to kill me.

"Bet it's been a long day for you," the voice went on re-lentlessly. "When you're just left to lie around and think about your life the way it used to be, to wonder what's going to happen to you eventually—well, that must be pretty tire-some. Not what you're used to. Not at all what a smart, pretty girl is used to doing with her time."

Deirdre had been aware of the voice drawing nearer. Now she felt a touch, fingers trailing over her forehead near her hairline, running down her temples, over her cheeks, across her throat. Lingering at her throat. She ex-pected to feel the fingers of a second hand brushing over the same area before the fingers moved back to her neck and hands tightened, cutting off her air, strangling her. Is this what happened to the other girls? she wondered. Had they all died by strangulation? If that's what is going to happen, please don't let it take a long time, she prayed. Even if I don't die quickly, please let me black out. Don't leave me conscious to feel every horrible second of what's to come.

But no second hand touched her. Instead, the first moved downward, pulling back the thin blanket. Cold air washed over her abdomen and she shuddered.

"So slender. Not an ounce of fat. And such soft skin," the person muttered. "The soft skin of a *young* woman. I hate old people's skin, all dry and wrinkled. And there's a smell about old people. The smell of decay." Deirdre felt a face touch just above her belly button, then heard a deep inhala-tion. "Sweet. Even after a night and day out here, you still bear the sweet smell of youth."

By now Deirdre was jittering. She tried to focus on a dif-ferent time, a different place. She thought of a picnic she'd gone on with her parents when she was about ten. Her mother had spread out a blanket and laid cartons and plates and containers all over it. "Good heavens, honey!" Deirdre's father had exclaimed, beaming at her pretty mother. "Are you a genie or something? How on earth did you get so much food in that little picnic basket?" She had only smiled. "We'll never be able to eat all of that," Deirdre's father had laughed. "We're going to have a ton of leftovers."

But there had been no leftovers. They'd eaten until they were too full to move. Then they'd lain on the ground, staring up at the sky, trying to make shapes out of clouds. "That one is an elephant," her mother had said. "And she has her baby elephant with her. Don't you see it, Deirdre?" And Deirdre had said she could, even though she hadn't seen anything except a big blob of a cloud. Her mother was the one who made even the clouds seem magical and fun. Her mother was the one who'd made the whole world seem magical and fun, for Deirdre and Ben.

Maybe I'll see her again if all that stuff about meeting your loved ones in Heaven is true, Deirdre thought as this creep hung over her, sniffing her "young flesh," flesh that now felt foul. Maybe death won't be so bad, she mused. It had to be better than this.

Suddenly Deirdre heard a noise. A car engine. A noisy car engine. The engine of an old car, not a new car whose engine purred. The fondling stopped. The person above her stiffened and let out one quick huff of air that signaled fear. Oh God, has someone come to save me? Deirdre thought desperately. Has something miraculous happened?

Warm breath in her ear. "Do not make a sound." All she could have done was squeal beneath her duct tape, but tempting as it was to let someone know she was here, Deirdre knew any move from her, any sound from her, would be fatal. The rumble of the engine drew nearer. Please, please, *please,* Deirdre's mind screamed. Voices. She heard voices. Male voices. The person above her seemed to have stopped breathing. This is it, Deirdre exulted mentally. I'm being saved! Mama sent someone to save me!

Deirdre's heart pounded so hard she thought it would burst through her ribs. And then, just as her jubilation grew almost beyond the point of endurance, she heard laughter, girls squealing in a tangle of fear and delight.

Who was out there? Deirdre wondered. A bunch of teenagers? A bunch of laughing teenagers just like the ones at the party last night when she'd been taken by this lunatic who now held her captive.

"I don't *want* to go in there!" a girl squealed. "I've heard the guy that owns this place has guns and if he catches us out here—"

"What? He's gonna *kill* us?" one of the guys challenged. "He might try to scare us, but he's not gonna let himself get arrested for murder. Come on, Cookie. You need another beer or somethin'? 'Cause you didn't used to be such a wimp!"

A girl began giggling wildly. "Okay, okay, if you're gonna get all jerked out of shape, I'll go. We'll *all* go, right?"

A car door opened and slammed shut. A cheer went up. A cheer of how many people? Three? No, four, Deirdre decided, and they said they were coming in! Someone had already gotten out of that car. Someone was going to come in? More than one person. Surely to God they'd do something. They'd *save* her!

Then she heard the engine revving. It slowed. More laughter. More of that infuriating squealing. A car door slammed again. Was it slamming because someone else was emerging from the car? Yes, that had to be it. That just *had* to be what was happening.

"Ah, it's not worth the trouble. I've got someplace better in mind for tonight," one of the guys yelled to the others.

"Yeah," the girl called Cookie agreed. "Let's go someplace better. Whatcha got in mind?"

"Someplace *spooky*!"

The girls shrieked and fell into nearly hysterical giggling. Then the engine revved. It slowed and revved again. Then Deirdre heard the spinning of gravel beneath tires. The engine rumbled again as the car spun away. Away! No! No, it was impossible that people had come so close and now they were going away. Speeding away! This couldn't be happening. They *couldn't* be leaving her!

But they were.

Was it one minute or five before Deirdre realized she couldn't hear the car at all anymore? She should have counted out the seconds, she thought. She should have kept track of how long the car had been here, because if it had only been gone a few seconds it might be còming back. Maybe they were just circling the building, trying to find the best way in. If the car had only been gone a minute, that's what they were probably doing. But if more time had passed . . . if even five minutes had passed, it could mean they were leaving.

Deirdre was furious with herself for a few moments. Then emotional darkness descended on her. What would have been the use of knowing how long the car had been here? No one had come to save her. The people who'd been in that car probably weren't even looking for her. They were just a bunch of teenagers, she guessed from the sound of their voices. A bunch of teenagers out having fun. And she was still here, on this cold concrete floor, with her eyes and mouth taped shut, her hands bound behind her. Everything was just the same. Just the same . . . except . . .

Deirdre held her breath, straining her ears, concentrating with every ounce of her being, until she was certain.

The car had gone, but so had her captor.

3

By eight-thirty, Chyna had completely given up on eating, although she knew her body needed nourishment. Well, what it needed and what it wanted weren't the same, she decided, so to hell with it. She gave the uneaten portion of her sandwich to Michelle and poured her cold soup down the disposal.

She sighed and looked at Michelle, who'd finished the sandwich in two bites and now sat patiently by her bowl, waiting for her after-dinner biscuit. "I wish getting my dessert was the only thing I had to worry about," Chyna told her. "Well, don't worry. I've been off-kilter the last few days, but I haven't forgotten *all* the important things in life."

Chyna went into the kitchen and found the bag of beef-basted biscuits Ned had brought along with the Gravy Train. He'd obviously remembered how much the Irish setter they'd had so long ago loved those biscuits. Ned had taught the dog all kinds of tricks, always rewarding him with one of them. The dog had been purebred and worth a fortune, but Chyna had always known Ned hadn't cared a thing about the setter's impressive lineage. He'd just loved the dog. Ned had even allowed the dog into the sacred clubhouse the wind had torn down this week. As far as Ned had been concerned, an invitation into the clubhouse was the ultimate honor. He hadn't even allowed Chyna to enter more than twice. "You'll mess up everything," he'd told her haughtily when he was ten. "Besides, this place was built for guys. I don't want you spreading around your girl germs."

She'd gone wailing to her mother, who'd laughed at Ned's reasoning but told Chyna she'd have to abide by Ned's rules. After all, the house had been built for him. After that, getting into the house had been one of her main goals in life, but Ned always kept it carefully locked and watched her like a hawk whenever she ventured near it.

Chyna walked to the back windows and looked out on the terrace—the terrace where Rusty had supposedly poured out his heart to her this afternoon. Fog was wafting in from the lake, frothing around the fountain, quiet and secretive and somehow frightening, as if it were hiding something from her. Maybe Rusty had been hiding something from her, too. Or maybe he *had* been totally truthful, just desperately needing a friend, someone to whom he could tell his demeaning story of going off and leaving Nancy to die because he didn't want people to think he was a pervert.

Because he was afraid of what his father would think of him. And what if what he'd told her was the absolute truth? What if someone had been chasing Nancy down that path? Why would they have done that?

To make her the next lost girl, Chyna thought abruptly. Deirdre Mayhew hadn't been meant to follow Zoey and Heather and Edie into oblivion. The next victim was meant to be Nancy Tierney. But something had gone wrong that night. Whoever had been chasing Nancy, whoever had meant to drag her into the void with the other girls, had run afoul of a watcher.

Rusty. In spite of the holes in his story, Chyna *knew* he was telling the truth about merely seeing Nancy run down that path and fall. He hadn't been the one chasing her.

But had he been absolutely truthful when he told Chyna he didn't see who was chasing Nancy? Had he seen who'd pursued Nancy to her death and was simply afraid of saying who it was?

Chyna felt cold. Cold and frustrated because she couldn't *feel,* she didn't *know,* whether Rusty knew more than he was saying. And knowing was important, she told herself. Knowing was—

The doorbell rang. That certainly wouldn't be Rex, Chyna thought, and she certainly wasn't in the mood for company. She thought about not going to the door until she heard Ned yell, "Chyna! Didn't want to take you by surprise after the day you've had, therefore the doorbell. But I used my own key. Where are you?"

Chyna hadn't realized until that moment how tense she'd been all evening. Her body suddenly seemed to unwind and she nearly ran into the living room to greet her brother. "Ned, I'm so glad to see you!"

Although his face was still flushed, his eyes slightly bloodshot, he looked at her with his old, familiar grin. "I didn't expect such a joyful greeting!"

"Rex is gone—as usual—and this hasn't been one of the best days of my life. You're a godsend!"

"Yeah, I always tell Beverly I'm a godsend, but she doesn't seem to agree."

"Of course she does. She's crazy about you. Come into the kitchen and keep me company for a while."

Ned's grin faded. "I'd love to keep you company, Sis, but

I have to get home or Beverly will divorce me. She says I'm gone all the time anymore. Besides, I'm really not feeling so good." Seeing his sister's crestfallen face, he worked up a smile again. "I just came by to give you something. I've been meaning to ever since you got home, but I keep forgetting." He pulled a small white box from his jacket pocket. "The morning I found Mom dead . . ." He swallowed and started again. "The morning I found Mom, she was wearing her engagement ring. The diamond and sapphires. Well, I don't have to tell *you* what it looked like. You always loved it and I knew Mom wanted you to have it.

"I know you're not supposed to remove anything from a body, but I was afraid the ring would get lost at the morgue or the funeral home," Ned went on, "so I slipped it off her finger that morning. I took it home, put it in this box, and now I want you to take it."

Chyna looked at the small white box as if it held something strange and forbidden.

"Oh, come on, Sis," Ned said, his voice a bit lighter. "Don't look scared. I didn't *steal* it. This is your ring now. Please take it."

Chyna felt her eyes fill with tears. She held out a slightly shaky hand and Ned placed the box in it. She didn't open the box. She just closed her hand around it. "Thank you, Ned," she said softly. "You don't know what this means to me."

He looked at her with sadness in his own watery blue eyes. "Yes, I do know what it means to you, Chyna. It's Mom's last gift to you. When you wear it, think of her."

"I always will," Chyna said. "You're the best brother in the world."

Ned left almost immediately and Chyna had just started upstairs to put the ring in her room when the phone rang. She jerked, pulled from thoughts—both happy and sorrowful—of the ring, and laid the box on the end table as she picked up the receiver. Rex, no doubt, she thought in annoyance. Rex who should have been back a couple of hours ago. She'd called Owen's house, ostensibly to ask when Rex would be home so she could fix dinner, but there had been no answer.

She fervently hoped Rex had only stayed with Owen half an hour or so, not long enough for the man to cool down after the scene with Rusty. And where the hell was Rex? What was he going to tell her when he finally dragged in? That he'd been with a friend who needed to talk? She wouldn't believe him. He wasn't being one bit of help during this ordeal, and she was suddenly furious with him.

Chyna grabbed up the phone and nearly snarled, "Yes?"

"It's Beverly. Are you all right, Chyna?"

Chyna immediately felt silly. "Yes, I'm okay."

"You don't sound okay. Ned told me about the crowd that came to your house. No wonder you're edgy. I wanted to come and be with you, but he said it wasn't safe for me or the children."

"He was right. I'm glad you stayed put. He was just here, he's on his way home, and I'm fine, really."

"Rex was here briefly. He said you'd been a real trouper."

"A real trouper?" Chyna repeated sarcastically. "Well, apparently he thinks I'm capable of handling anything, because he's never come back from Owen Burtram's house."

"He *didn't*!" Beverly exclaimed. "Well, he was here over an hour ago. He said something about Rusty babbling a bunch of nonsense and Owen getting mad about it, so he went home with Owen until the guy cooled down, but when he left, he said he was coming back to your house."

"Did he say if Owen did cool down?"

"He said Owen didn't mention whatever it was Rusty said—Rex wouldn't tell me—and then Owen got a call and had to go out. That's why Rex dropped by here just to say hi before coming back to be with you."

"Maybe he'll show up any minute," Chyna said, although she didn't have much hope of seeing Rex for a while, which made her angry.

"Those *awful* people!" Chyna realized Beverly had switched the subject back to the crowd that had gathered on her lawn. "Rex said Irma Vogel was a ringleader. I've never really liked her, although for some reason she seems to think I do. She calls me with every news flash she comes across.

But sometimes I've thought she seemed a little crazy. No, I'm *sure* she's crazy and I don't want anything more to do with her." Beverly changed the subject again. "Chyna, what did Rusty say to make Owen so mad?"

Chyna wasn't about to get Beverly upset by telling her everything Rusty had confided. "I think Nancy's death really just hit him. He sometimes runs on that path she was on, and he had some foolish notion that he could have helped her if his timing had been better, you know, if he'd been there."

The explanation sounded incredibly lame to Chyna and apparently Beverly thought so, too, because she asked, "Why would Owen get so mad about that?"

"I don't know. Sometimes I think Owen's as crazy as Irma. And you know how hard he's always been on Rusty." I can't keep acting so vague, Chyna thought. Beverly will know I'm keeping something back. "I'm really annoyed with Rex," Chyna snapped suddenly. "I would think that after a day like I've had he'd show enough concern to come stay with me. Instead, he's probably out at some bar surveying available women."

"Chyna!" Beverly laughed. "Well, you certainly have a head of steam built up." Then she sobered. "But I don't blame you for not wanting to be alone. When Ned gets home, do you want me to send him back?"

"No. I think he's getting sick. Maybe the flu. Make sure he drinks plenty of fluids, preferably orange juice, not beer. I'll take one of Mom's sleeping pills and go to bed early."

"Yes, Ned hasn't looked good all day. I'll—" Beverly broke off and yelled, "Ian Greer, you are supposed to be in bed!" Beverly lowered her voice and spoke to Chyna again. "I'm sure Rex will be home soon, anyway. If he isn't, you call and I'll come keep you company."

"I'll do that," Chyna said, knowing she wouldn't disturb Beverly no matter how uneasy she grew.

Forty minutes later, Chyna still sat alone, waiting for Rex but determined not to take a sleeping pill, so she'd be awake to tell him just how mad she was when he finally dragged himself home. Abruptly the phone rang again. "That's him calling with some stupid excuse," Chyna muttered murderously at the phone. She picked up the handset without even looking at the Caller ID. "Well, it's about time," she snapped. Nothing. "If this is you, Rex, I want you to come back home right now." Her voice was sharp and cold. "And if this is one of you idiots who were on my lawn today, defacing property, calling me names, thinking you *scared* me, then you have another think coming!"

Still nothing.

She heard the far-off windy sound of a long-distance call from the past. "Who is this?" Chyna demanded, trying not to betray the terror and dread creeping over her, although she managed to state staunchly, "You're not scaring me. What do you want?"

Another pause. Finally, she heard a voice: "Your help, Chyna. I need your help."

Oh God, Chyna thought. She was almost certain she heard Anita's voice again. The first time, in spite of the windy sound, the voice had sounded light and lilting. This time it echoed in weak, pathetic tones. It can't be, Chyna thought. And yet . . .

"You know it's me, Bubble Gum."

"No, Anita, it can't be you. It just can't be . . ." Because you're dead, Chyna almost said, but bit back the words. By this time she was trembling, her hands icy, her breath coming shallow and fast. "Anita, what do you want?"

"Star light, star bright, first star I see tonight . . ."

"Anita," Chyna got out in a strangled voice. "What are you talking about?"

"You'll figure it out, Bubble Gum." Chyna closed her eyes, her heart pounding. "You have to help Zoey. *Please,* Chyna." Another pause as the voice grew weaker. "Star light, star bright . . ." The voice began to fade as the windy sound grew louder, drowning out the last notes of Anita's pitiful voice. "First star I see tonight . . ."

Chyna clutched the phone long after Anita's voice had

disappeared, long after she knew no one of this world or another still clung to her, still tried to reach her through the clumsy, flimsy device called a telephone.

And then she fainted.

At first Chyna had the sensation that she was lying on a beach, feeling waves lapping gently over her face. Warm, caressing waves. She kept her eyes closed for a few moments, savoring the sensation, the feeling of love washing over her.

Then everything in her seemed to jump to attention. Was this dreamy, comforting feeling merely death sneaking up on her, charming her into unfathomable, inexorable darkness? Well, she wouldn't go. She *couldn't* go. She had something to do. She owed it to Zoey. She owed it to all the other girls who'd vanished like wraiths in the night. Zoey had said Chyna was the only one who could stop it. She didn't know *how* she could stop it, but she knew she would try with every ounce of energy in her body and mind.

The fire of resolve rushing through her body, Chyna opened her eyes. After blinking a couple of times, she burst into near-hysterical laughter. She wasn't lying on a beach with waves washing over her, pulling her into the ocean of death.

She was lying on the living room floor with Michelle licking her face.

4

"I have never in my life called a man and asked him to rush to my side because I was afraid," Chyna said as Scott stepped into the living room of the Greer home. "I'm almost ashamed of myself."

"I'm not. I'm flattered beyond reason." Scott was smiling, but his dark eyes were filled with worry as they searched her face and flicked over her body, as if he were looking for signs of injury. "Actually, Chyna, I'm just glad I had a car so

I could come when you called me. If it hadn't been for Ned, I wouldn't be driving that shiny new automobile in your driveway. When he took me home today, he stopped by his car dealership. He said, 'You mentioned you were thinking of buying a new car. Pick one out and drive it around for a couple of days. If you like it, I promise to give you a good deal on it.' So, that's why I'm not depending on free rides or the Black Willow taxi service tonight."

"Thank God. If you hadn't been able to come . . ." Chyna's voice lowered pitch slightly. "Oh, never mind me, Scott. I'm just frustrated with Rex, who is gone, as usual, and of course doesn't have a cell phone. One of those would make it too easy for the women in his life to track him."

"Well, I see Rex is out of favor tonight," Scott said drily. "Are you sure he's all right? No bad vibes?"

"No, I'm not sure he's all right. He should know I'd be worried, the jackass. But I don't have a bad feeling about his physical well-being."

"I wouldn't give a dime for his physical well-being if he came home right now," Scott grinned. "What about your brother?"

"Ned is getting sick and in my opinion also needs to spend some time with his family." Chyna paused. "Look, Scott, if I'm imposing on you—"

"You're not. I'm extremely glad you don't think of me as an invalid, that you felt you could call on me for help."

"Good, because I could *not* sit here for the rest of the night talking to ghosts."

"Talking to ghosts?" Scott asked cautiously.

"On the phone. Anita Simms, Zoey's mother." Scott stood still, staring at her. She shot him a sardonic look. "Yeah, I know she's dead. It's been that kind of evening."

"Wow, that's some kind of evening, Chyna."

"You're telling me." She tried to smile. "You look like you could use a glass of wine. Or maybe something stronger."

"Something stronger, please. Bourbon maybe? Or Scotch. Then you can tell me about your phone conversation with Anita."

"Don't look at me like that, Scott," Chyna warned. "You wanted to know what was going on in this mess of a head of mine. I'm just telling you what you wanted to hear."

"And I'm taking you seriously. Honestly. But I'm new to all of this, Chyna. Don't get mad at me if it throws me sometimes."

"It throws you all of the time. But I accept that." She shrugged. "Do you want your bourbon mixed with anything?"

"I'll take it straight. And I'd like a double, please."

Chyna laughed as she headed toward the kitchen. "I've thrown you that much, have I? Even after what you've been through in the plane crash?" She stopped cold and turned, her expression appalled. "My God, I'm so sorry, Scott. All I've been thinking about is what's been happening to me and I just blurted out a dreadfully callous thing about the most horrible event in your life. Please forgive me; I'm—"

"You're forgiven," Scott said evenly. "It's all right. I'm still on my feet, not crushed to the floor by a phrase that popped out of your mouth when *you* have obviously been through one of the most awful events of your life, too."

"Yes, I'm shaken to the core, but still . . ." She closed her eyes and hung her head. "Do you think either one of us will live to see Christmas?"

"Yes. We'll be a little rough around the edges, but we'll make it, unfortunately for me. I hate Christmas."

"So do I!" Chyna burst out. "I thought I was the only person in the country, maybe in the Christian community of the whole world, who couldn't stand decorating the Christmas tree, eating fruitcake, wrapping gifts, singing Christmas carols. Oh, what a relief! I'm not a weirdo, after all!"

"Oh, don't be too sure," Scott said solemnly. "You might be a weirdo. You just aren't the *only* weirdo who doesn't like Christmas."

They both broke into laughter, bending slightly at the waist, their eyes filling with tears. "It wasn't even that funny," Scott gasped out at last.

"I know. But it feels so good to let go. Oh, I let go sometimes, but not *with* someone." Chyna glanced over at Michelle.

"Except for her. She saw me really let go about half an hour ago after I got the phone call."

Scott wiped a tear off his cheek, sniffed, then looked at Chyna closely, his laughter turning into a smile that seemed to signal the return of restraint. "The phone call. You mentioned it when you called me." He stepped closer to her and gently put his hand on her shoulder. "Let's forget about those drinks and get away from here for a while. Then you can tell me all about the call."

"Where will we go?"

"Nowhere. We'll just take a ride in my shiny new car."

Chyna hesitated for a moment, then nodded. "Sounds good—on one condition. Michelle goes with us."

"Will she shed?" Scott asked.

"Who cares?" Chyna smiled. "The car still belongs to Ned."

"The car has a great sound system," Chyna said fifteen minutes later as they traveled north on the highway. "I love this song."

"So I guessed when you insisted on bringing this CD and turning it up so loud."

"Too loud?"

"No. Fine."

"I always listen to music when I drive. Especially at night."

"Well, you're not driving tonight, but I do the same thing. Great minds and all that," Scott said absently as U2's "With or Without You" washed over them in the warm duskiness of the car.

Black Willow was small and they'd left the lights of the town behind in minutes after they'd driven away from the Greer house. Now fields surrounded them—fields where stalks stood in the cool autumn night, the corn at least six feet high but dry and withered and brown, the knee-high soybean plants tan and leafless. Chyna shivered. "Do you think Deirdre is out here somewhere, still alive?"

"I'm not the psychic," Scott answered without sarcasm. "I thought you'd be able to sense whether she was still alive and where she is."

"That's the trouble with this fabulous ESP stuff," Chyna returned drearily. "It just turns itself on in your head when you least expect it, and usually never when you really *need* it." She rubbed a hand across her forehead. "It would be so wonderful if I could control the visions and the voices. Like Zoey's."

Chyna had already told Scott about the call she'd received earlier during which Zoey had once again told her she must help and then lapsed into that maddening rhyme in an ephemeral, singsong voice. "You and Zoey knew each other nearly from birth," Scott went on. "Are you sure you never chanted that rhyme to each other? Or maybe your mothers each said the rhyme to you when you were tiny."

"You think Anita Simms said the rhyme to Zoey and my mother said the rhyme to me when we were babies or toddlers?" Scott nodded. "That's possible, but what's the significance? Zoey is saying it to me for a reason, Scott, but for the life of me, I don't know what that reason could be."

"Were either of you particularly interested in the stars?"

"I wasn't. I think Zoey developed a passion for stargazing one year, but as soon as her parents bought her a telescope, she lost interest. She didn't think it was fun anymore when people expected her to actually study astronomy." Chyna smiled ruefully. "Zoey was smart, but she wasn't a good student. She was too restless to sit still reading books and doing research, and she hated discipline. I suppose she would have gone to college because her mother expected her to, but she never expressed an interest in any particular subject."

"Not like you with your enthusiasm for chemistry and physiology." He paused. "Deirdre had the same interests. She was mature for her age and a 'deep thinker,' Ben used to say, an intellectual. And she was especially pretty. The two of you are quite a bit alike."

"So it seems as if I'd be better at getting a bead on where she is." The fear that had gripped Chyna after the phone call

was now giving way to the despondency that had haunted
her all day. "God, I feel useless."

"You certainly aren't useless, Chyna. And don't give up
on your power yet. After all, you're almost certain you experienced Deirdre's abduction."

" 'Almost' is the key word. And even if I did, maybe that's
all I'm going to experience where Deirdre is concerned. It
wasn't helpful. I couldn't even see who took her."

"Okay, now you're sliding into a funk," Scott said. "I may
not know much about ESP, but I have a feeling funks aren't
conducive to inspiring visions."

"Funks aren't conducive to much of anything except
making you feel like a failure."

"No more talk about failure." The fields of dead corn-
stalks gave way to pieces of flat, empty land. Up ahead,
Chyna saw something large and square seeming to loom
over the landscape as it shone in the moonlight. "What is
that?" she asked, pointing.

Scott laughed. "Chyna Greer, don't tell me you've forgotten that we used to have a drive-in theater here!"

"Yes, I did forget," she said vaguely as they drew nearer.
"I never went to it."

"You were probably about seven or eight when it closed. I
doubt if you had too many dates who took you to the drive-
in under the guise of wanting to see a movie when what they
really wanted to do was . . ."

She raised her eyes at him. "Yes?"

"Pursue romance."

"Oh, we're into euphemisms," she said drolly. "And why
do I have the distinct feeling you brought quite a few girls
here?"

"Because you're psychic?"

"Because you were quite the Lothario in your teenage
years." Scott looked at her. "Your mother told my mother."

"And Vivian told you?"

"Well, I was sort of eavesdropping."

"Shame on you!" Scott laughed as they passed directly by
the drive-in. The old marquee still stood, surrounded by

dead grass and weeds. Moonlight shone on dozens of poles that had held the rusty, tinny-sounding speakers people hung on their windows so they could hear the dialogue as they stared up at the giant screen. Even the old concession stand remained, almost swallowed by heavy foliage and a tangle of ivy that looked as if it were trying to pull the building down beneath the surface of the earth.

"I can't believe that place has just been sitting there for at least twenty years," Chyna said. "I know we're not a Mecca for business around here, but surely some developer would have snatched up the land and found a use for it."

"I think the owner, old Mr. Dickens, had a sentimental attachment to the place, even though he had to close it when drive-ins went out of style. His daughter told me he was always certain they'd become all the rage again."

"Not with cineplexes everywhere offering six movies in the same building, comfortable seats, air-conditioning, not to mention surround sound."

"Yeah," Scott said absently as they passed the old drive-in, exceeding the speed limit by at least 15 miles an hour, but the state police rarely patrolled this part of the highway. Everyone in the area knew this and took advantage of it. "And speaking of Lotharios, Gage Ridgeway lives around here," Scott added. "A lot of people think he's crazy for living on all that land by himself, too, but Gage won't budge."

"He didn't used to be such a loner, or so I've heard."

"I think he changed after the whole Edie Larson business. Everyone was sure he'd done something to her."

"Are you certain he didn't?"

"I always got the idea he really cared about her—I think I teased him about it. But the cops had their minds made up he was their guy. They put him through hell. Couldn't find a shred of evidence, though. That didn't stop Edie's father, good old Ron Larson, from hounding Gage for years, even though people knew Ron didn't give a damn about Edie. I think he hoped Gage would be arrested and found guilty of murder so he could launch a civil suit against him."

"Always thinking ahead, our Ron Larson. There's nothing

like making a fortune off your daughter's murder," Chyna said distastefully.

"And I wouldn't quite put it past Ron to try something of the sort if he were smart enough to pull it off."

"You mean kill his own daughter?"

"I don't know if he'd actually have the nerve to kill her, but he could make it look as if she had been killed." Scott shook his head. "But like I said, he'd have to be smart and he'd need Edie's cooperation. He's not smart and Edie would never have helped her father hurt Gage."

"If Edie had just run away, no one could have blamed her." Chyna sighed. "But of course, she didn't run away."

"You're sure she didn't?"

"Yes, I'm sure she met with the same fate as Zoey and Heather. I haven't had any visions about her, but I'm sure." They remained quiet for a moment before Chyna caught sight of a side road flanked by white pillars. "Black Willow Cemetery," she said softly.

"I always thought that was a depressing name for a cemetery," Scott said.

"Are there cheerful ones?"

"Well, none that come to mind. But there are lots that don't sound so ominous."

"My father is buried there," Chyna said. "I always thought Mom would be beside him, but in the last weeks of her life she decided she wanted to be cremated and for me to keep the urn." Chyna shook her head. "I keep wondering if there was something wrong with her mind, as well as her heart, and that's why she made the decision. It seemed so abrupt. And, well, kind of selfish."

"Selfish?" Scott repeated.

"Daddy's in that cemetery all alone. Mom won't be beside him." When Scott said nothing, Chyna added, "I guess that sounded like a ten-year-old talking. After all, they're both dead."

"It did sound on the sentimental side for you, Chyna, but I guess when members of your own family die, you feel different than you do about strangers. No one close to me in my family has died." He paused. "But after the crash, they weren't able to find three bodies. A child and two teenagers. I always think about their parents. It's bad enough that three young people were killed, but they can't even be buried properly. That eats at me, Chyna, even though a proper burial wouldn't make them any less dead."

"I understand what you mean," Chyna said softly. "And I'm not going to say a burial would have given the parents *closure*. I hate that word. It makes it sound like you can just close the book on them and not think about them anymore when of course their parents will never stop thinking about them."

Scott looked at her. "So we agree about hating Christmas and the word 'closure.' Who would have thought?"

"We're two peas in a pod," Chyna said lightly. "The co-incidences are simply amazing!" Scott nodded, although she could tell he was still thinking about those three young, missing passengers who had been on the horrible flight he'd piloted.

Chyna decided to change the tone of their conversation. "Are you driving any place in particular, Scott, or are we just cruising and letting Michelle get nose prints on every window in the back of this car?"

"The nose prints don't matter, because I've decided I'm going to buy the car. *You* can clean them off with Windex."

"Oh, how chivalrous," Chyna muttered.

She could see Scott smiling in the glow of instruments on the dashboard. "And we also have a destination, Dr. Chyna Greer. Some place where you can have a little fun and stop dwelling on your lack of success in finding Deirdre Mayhew. *Yet.*"

Chyna forced herself to toss him a bright smile, but inside she felt dark and worthless, because she was certain she would fail to find Deirdre Mayhew just as she'd failed to find her beloved Zoey twelve years ago.

CHAPTER FOURTEEN

1

Rex had tried to keep up a casual conversation as Rusty drove him to Owen's house, but Rusty could barely answer, shame turning him mute. He wasn't certain how much any of the three men had heard of his story to Chyna out on the terrace about how he'd watched Nancy run in the evenings, right up to the last evening of her life. They'd all heard part of it, at least the part where he'd said he'd seen her fall and hit her head, then simply run away because he didn't want anyone to know he'd been watching her. Gage Ridgeway had heard part of it, because he wouldn't meet Rusty's gaze before he'd mumbled something and returned to boarding up the window in the living room. Rex acted casual, but then, Rex always acted casual. "Urbane." That was the word for Rex. "Urbane." And "opaque." "Opaque"? Rusty wasn't sure why that word had popped into his mind, but it had. It had always been hard to tell what Rex Greer was thinking.

Rusty's own father was another matter. Owen Burtram's every emotion showed somewhere, no matter how hard he tried to hide it—his eyes, his lips, the white lines between his nostrils and mouth, his throat that seemed to balloon, his *fists*. Rusty always shuddered when he thought of those fists, and when he'd seen them opening and closing in his father's coat pockets, Rusty knew Owen had definitely heard Rusty tell Chyna he'd seen Nancy fall and done nothing to help her.

But had Owen heard Rusty saying he'd thought Nancy was running away from someone? That he was sure Nancy was being chased by someone heavier, clumsier—more like a man in his fifties, Owen might think—and that the person who was chasing Nancy had left when she fell? Rusty burst into a cold sweat. Good lord, had his father heard him claim he had *not* seen who was chasing Nancy? Please, please, God, Rusty thought frantically as he broke into a cold sweat, please let Owen have heard him say he didn't see anyone except Nancy.

But if he had heard Rusty, would Owen Burtram believe his own son? If so, that would be a first, Rusty thought bitterly. Then fright overcame him. What if Owen had heard most of what Rusty had said and hadn't believed *any* of it? What would Owen do if he knew Rusty had routinely followed Nancy, watching, spying, peering into her most private moments? What if Owen guessed that Rusty even had lingered in the bushes outside of Nancy's home and watched at night as she undressed, often not closing her curtains?

But he wasn't the only one who had watched Nancy undress. There had been others. Many others. Some close to home.

Still . . .

Rusty had taken a Valium as soon as he got home. He'd paced and thought and practiced speeches he'd use on his father tomorrow or, if God was being particularly cruel, tonight after Rex left Owen's house. But none of the speeches sounded good. Of course, even if Rusty were Shakespeare, he couldn't come up with anything eloquent enough to quiet Owen's anger. No one could. Absolutely no one, which was why Rusty's beautiful, seductive mother had left when he was only fourteen. She'd left Owen and she'd left Rusty, too. He remembered that night so well—that night when she'd loaded three suitcases into her Cadillac, then turned to gaze at her husband and son with the dark, fathomless eyes that had always intrigued Rusty. "Don't look so crestfallen, Owen," she said in her sultry voice, her red lips smiling slightly, tauntingly. "You'll think up a good excuse for my leaving, something the neighbors will believe.

"And Rusty," she went on, "you won't have a mother keeping an eye on your every move, not that I would do so even if I stayed. I'm not that kind of mother. In fact, I was never meant to be a mother. Or a wife. Especially to you two." She smiled slowly, just a hint of cruelty lingering around her mouth. "Remember me fondly, guys. Or don't remember me. I really couldn't care less." And then she'd calmly climbed into her Cadillac and driven away.

Owen had stood as if carved from stone for at least ten minutes, the only sound emanating from him being his heavy breathing. Rusty had stood beside Owen, feeling like he should say something comforting, feeling like his mother's departure was all his fault because of the magazines she'd found in his bedroom yesterday, although when he walked in and found her leafing through his secret stash, she'd only looked at him and laughed, saying, "Like father, like son." Finally, Owen had stridden toward his own car and, without a word to Rusty, climbed in and torn off in the same direction his wife had gone.

Rusty had finally gone inside. He'd sat up all night, watching television. Sometime near dawn, his father had returned, looking disheveled, dirty, and almost wild-eyed. "Go to bed," he'd ordered. Rusty had immediately run to his bedroom, where he'd stayed for the rest of the day. Later he watched Owen from his window. The man had changed into a suit, combed his hair, and shaved. He'd left, then returned at six, the same time he always came home from the funeral home.

When Rusty had finally slunk down the stairs, his father had been sitting in an armchair reading the evening newspaper. "I brought home some hamburgers from one of those drive-through places," he said, not looking up from the newspaper. "They're not very good, but at least they're filling. I've already phoned in an ad for a housekeeper. It will take a while to find someone suitable, but it *can* be done, even in this town."

And Rusty had neither seen nor heard from his mother ever again.

He hadn't loved his mother, but he'd been fascinated by her beauty, her bold sensuality, her clingy clothes, her don't-give-a-damn attitude. She'd intrigued him, even though he knew she was as contemptuous of him as his father was. Sometimes, though, she hugged Rusty, kissed him on the mouth, and outright fondled him in front of Owen. Rusty had known she was only doing it to make his father mad, but he'd loved those sexually charged strikes at Owen anyway. When she left, Rusty had felt desolate because he knew no one would ever fondle him again. He'd also wondered what had happened to her. Had she simply outrun his father that night and gone on to live the kind of life she'd always wanted?

Or had his father—his domineering, strong, emotionally storm-ridden father—caught up with his escaping wife and she'd never gone *anywhere*? What if his mother, not Zoey Simms, had actually been the first of Black Willow's "lost girls"?

Rusty began to tremble and nearly ran to the drawer in his nightstand, searched wildly for the bottle of Valium he'd had in his hand not twenty minutes ago. When he finally found it, he popped another one into his mouth with shaking fingers. Then, as he choked while trying to swallow it dry, he stuck another pill in his mouth before rushing into the bathroom and drinking cup after cup of tepid water.

He went downstairs and slid a CD of classical music into his stereo system. Unfortunately, Mozart's Clarinet Concerto: Adagio filled the room, the same song that had played repeatedly in the "slumber room" where Nancy had lain right before her funeral. Rusty nearly broke the stereo, punching buttons wildly until the drawer holding the offending Mozart CD emerged. He grabbed out the CD and slapped it down on a tabletop, knowing he was scratching it but not caring. He, who was always so fussy about how his CDs were handled and stored, didn't care if he defaced this one. He hated it. He'd never listen to it again. Never!

He got control of himself before he snapped the disc in two, then looked at his collection for something with better memories. But he couldn't concentrate. He couldn't remember what songs he liked and didn't like. He grabbed up a CD his father had given him last Christmas: *Great Waltzes*. It had been Owen's only Christmas gift to his son and Rusty hated it. He decided to force himself to play it tonight, though, almost as a punishment.

After inserting the CD, Rusty nearly ran to the kitchen and found a bottle of sherry. His father said sherry was an old lady's drink and looked disgusted whenever he caught Rusty with a glass in his hand. But Owen wasn't here tonight. Owen was with Rex.

For the time being, at least.

Rusty poured the golden sherry into a glass and drank nearly half of it without stopping to take a breath. The liquor hit his stomach like a bomb, and for a moment Rusty thought he was going to vomit. Then his stomach slowly stopped cramping while the sherry spread through his system, warming him, easing him. "Nectar from Heaven," he said aloud, then almost slapped a hand over his mouth. His father hated when Rusty uttered what Owen called "sissy" phrases like that. Owen. Owen Burtram, always so perfect, so manly, so oratorical in public. In *public*. In private . . . well, that was a different matter. Defiantly, Rusty looked around his empty kitchen, raised his glass, and almost shouted, "Nectar from Heaven!"

He expected a rush of power to surge through him after he'd bellowed that phrase. Instead, he felt silly. Silly and small and scared. He closed his eyes in misery for a moment, then wandered back into the living room, glass in one hand, bottle in the other.

The room felt stuffy. He looked at the thermostat, which read eighty-four degrees even though it had been set to keep the room at seventy-two. Dammit, he thought. Furnace on the fritz again. Tomorrow he'd have to call the place that fixed things like furnaces—he couldn't remember the name of it now—and have a repairman come out for the second time since the new furnace had been installed in September. And he would refuse to pay them, he thought rebelliously, even though the last time the workmen had come, they'd told him the furnace was under a year's warranty and therefore he owed nothing. He supposed it was still under warranty.

However, this time they would try to charge him, he arbitrarily decided. Yes, they'd try to charge him a bundle. Rusty took a deep breath and narrowed his eyes into what he thought were dangerous slits. Well, they'd get a surprise! He wasn't a pushover like everyone thought. He'd put them in their place. He'd *report* them! Report them to whom, he wasn't sure, but the threat of being *reported* usually scared workmen to death. He'd seen his father use the tactic a hundred times.

Mentally practicing the tirade he would turn loose on the furnace repairmen tomorrow, Rusty unlocked and opened one of the sliding glass doors an inch. Cool air leaked into the room. It felt so good on Rusty's sweaty body that he slid the door open another inch. That felt even better. That felt just fine.

He wobbled over to the couch just about eight feet directly across from the open door and sank down on it. He was now nearly deafened by "Carousel Waltz" and he knew he should turn down the music, especially with the door open—neighbors and all—but he couldn't seem to make himself move from the couch once he settled onto it with his sherry. The Valium was beginning to work, the effect of three pills heightened by the sherry. Rusty took another gulp of the sherry, almost choking on it. "It's *not* an old lady's drink!" he declared to the empty room. "It's a gentleman's drink!"

The music roared on. Rusty emptied the bottle of sherry. Then, slowly, he felt sleep creeping up on him. Thank God, he thought. Sleep. Oblivion, at least for a little while. He slumped on the couch and his head fell sideways onto his shoulder. He dreamed of his mother, looking him up and down with her lazy, sloe-eyed gaze, and even in sleep he felt a thrill.

Maybe the sudden silence had awakened him, Rusty thought as he jerked to attention on the couch. *Great Waltzes* had mercifully ended and Rusty's CD player didn't simply repeat the same CD until it was removed. When a CD was finished, the player shut down. Otherwise, *Great Waltzes* could have gone all night. That could have caused a neighborhood uprising, Rusty thought, giggling at the scenario of the house under siege because of his father's favorite CD.

After Rusty stopped giggling, he struggled to sit up on the couch, yelping as pain shot through his neck, which he'd twisted in his sleep. He was also cold. He must have slept longer than he thought and the temperature had dropped, because the air coming in through the open sliding glass doors wasn't crisp, it was downright cold.

Rusty staggered to his feet and weaved across the room to the glass doors. One living room lamp burned behind him, casting his reflection on the glass and preventing him from seeing outside. He opened the door farther and leaned out to see that frost had turned the grass spiky behind his house. Damn, it *had* gotten cold tonight, he thought as he retreated into the home, then pulled the door shut. He was clicking the lock shut when he thought he heard a movement behind him.

Rusty looked up. He thought he saw a reflection in the glass—a large, hazy form a few feet behind him. Just as he started to turn around, he heard a rushing noise before something slammed into his body with such force he crashed through the sliding door and landed in a sea of shattered glass and sharp, frost-sheathed grass.

"My head," he muttered, although his head wasn't the only thing that hurt. His entire body seemed to sting. "Death by a thousand cuts," he murmured, remembering the phrase from a movie he'd seen long ago. The phrase had sent a chill over him at the time. Maybe it had been a premonition, he thought for a moment. But just for a moment. Then the instinct for self-preservation took over. He was badly hurt. He knew that. He needed help.

Rusty tried to call out, but his voice was weak. No lights in neighboring houses came on. Perhaps everyone had stopped paying attention to noises from his house after the blasting music that had lasted for nearly an hour. I need a phone, he thought in a growing fog of pain and confusion. Have to get inside to a phone and call 911 while I can still make sense.

Rusty reared up slightly, then nearly screamed as he felt warm blood flowing from his scalp into his eyes. His *eyes.* He lifted his right hand and gingerly touched his forehead, where he could feel the long slice about an inch above his eyebrows. His stomach roiling, he tried to wipe some blood away from his eye area, then place his hand tightly over the laceration to prevent more blood loss. Still, he could feel the warmth seeping between his fingers.

Supported by one elbow, he tried to rise even farther, hoping he could clamber to his feet. He could make it into the house, he told himself, even with his eyes closed. And the phone was right next to the sliding glass doors. Thank God. He could make it to the phone—

"Going somewhere?"

Rusty nearly screamed as a voice rumbled above him. He stifled back the embarrassing sound. An instant later he thought that might have been a mistake—maybe someone would come to his aid if he screamed, no matter how girlish he sounded. Then, intuitively, Rusty knew that screaming would end his life instantly. "*Please,*" he murmured.

"Please, what?"

"Please don't hurt me."

"Please don't hurt me," said the voice in a mocking, mincing tone before returning to normal. "Did Nancy say please? No, I'm sure she didn't say anything when she fell. That rock knocked her into immediate unconsciousness."

Rusty tried to swallow and couldn't. His throat muscles worked as he tried to stifle humiliating tears. His eyes were filling up again with blood and he tried wiping them clear so he could at least look his attacker in the eye, at least be that much of a man, but there was too much blood. Too much.

Someone stooped down beside him. "God, you're a mess. And after all that plastic surgery, too. What a heartbreak, kid." Suddenly Rusty felt something sharp, surely a long shard of glass, slide neatly along his neck, under his ear, and around to his throat. "You should be glad you're going to die, Rusty, because believe me, no plastic surgeon can help you now. You're going to look like the goddamned monster you are."

Rusty collapsed back onto the cold, stiff grass. A monster. He'd tried so hard to make his parents love him, always to be polite, to work hard at a job he hated, to *act* as a good person, even if he knew many people would find his peccadilloes disgusting. He even had spent thousands of dollars and undergone painful surgeries to look like the handsome son his father wanted. And it was all going to end here in his own backyard with him slashed, bloody, and repulsive.

Rusty could feel blood spurting from the carotid artery in his neck. He closed his eyes, oddly surprised that he didn't care that he was bleeding to death. In fact, he was oddly peaceful, almost glad that it would soon be over.

Yes, death would be a gift, he thought almost giddily in his last moments of consciousness. Death would be the wonderful gift of freedom, because he wouldn't have to *try* anymore.

2

Deirdre had expected to feel a rush of exultation if she managed to free her feet of the duct tape. When it finally gave way and she pulled her feet apart, though, all she'd felt was exhaustion. I'm going to sleep now, she thought dully. I've worked for hours and I'm cold, worn-out, and *so* sleepy. I deserve to sleep.

"Don't sleep!" an ephemeral voice nearby seemed to order urgently.

But I'm so tired, Deirdre mentally answered the urgent if ghostly voice. I'm too tired to move.

"Don't give up. Stay strong for a while."

Deirdre moaned, thinking, I don't know you.

"Trying to help. Chyna trying to help."

Chyna? Deirdre wondered. "Chyna Greer?"

"Chyna . . . trying to find you."

Deirdre shut her mind to the voice, marshaling her energy, her focus. She lay facedown, still as death, for a moment. Then she took a deep breath, rolled onto her left side, pulled her knees to her abdomen, rolled back to her original position, and rose up on her knees. Then she placed her right foot on the floor and slowly, stiffly, stood up, weaving for a moment as she tried to get her balance on stiff, cold legs she hadn't used for probably close to twenty-four hours. At least, Deirdre hoped it had been at least twenty-four hours, because that would mean it was night again. She was afraid to try to escape in the day. She believed she could only get out here, wherever *here* was, and make it to safety in the dark. If her abductor happened to be close by, he could be on her in minutes if it were light out. Night was her only refuge, her only hope.

If only I could have gotten my hands free, Deirdre thought in frustration. Then I could have gotten this duct tape off my eyes and seen where I was going. Escaping blind is impossible. No, it *might* be impossible, she said mentally, trying to adopt a bit of the confidence of the ephemeral voice she'd heard earlier. The voice had urged her to make an effort to escape because Chyna Greer was trying to help her. Deirdre was aware that the voice might have only been a hallucination, but it had still given her a morsel of faith. At this point, she was willing to believe someone like Chyna actually might be able to find her. Deirdre didn't know why she thought this, except that when she'd met Chyna, she'd felt something. What was it? Some kind of weird kinship?

You're losing your mind, Deirdre thought as she staggered around the building that held her captive. But if I'm going to die, it doesn't matter if I lose my mind, she mused. It doesn't matter one bit.

Abruptly she banged into a piece of equipment. She and it crashed to the floor with a clatter. She had no idea what she'd fallen over, but the sound it had made against the concrete let her know it was metal. She would have tried to discover what it was if she'd had use of her hands, but she wasn't going to waste precious energy rolling over and exploring the object with her bound hands. All that mattered was that she wasn't seriously hurt. She was shaken up and something had jabbed at her right thigh, but she didn't think she'd even been cut. She was lucky. Lucky.

I'm lucky, she kept telling herself as she slithered off the metal object and managed to get her footing again. I'm a very lucky girl. I will get out of this. I *will* get out!

CHAPTER FIFTEEN

1

"The Whippoorwill Grille?" Chyna asked as Scott pulled into a gravel parking lot. A long wooden building sat in front of them. Every window glared with a neon beer sign. Country music roared from the inside. A few people stood on the long porch outside, holding beer bottles and laughing uproariously. "Isn't this a roadhouse?"

"Don't tell me you've never been *here,* either?" Scott asked in feigned shock.

"I haven't."

"Boy, you really were all work and no play when you were a teenager."

"I was not! But this place has a bad reputation. You're always reading about patrons getting in bar fights and Hell's Angels come here when they're in town, and there's even a wet T-shirt night."

"Yeah. It's great. Got your T-shirt on?" She looked at Scott, slightly shocked. "Close your mouth, Chyna. I didn't bring you here to compete. Besides, this isn't even wet T-shirt night."

"Well, thank goodness!" Chyna exclaimed. "Do you really want to go in here?"

"Yes, I really do. You'll enjoy it, Chyna. Don't be such a prude."

"I am *not* a prude."

"Then come in with me, have a couple of beers, dance to some music, and forget your troubles for a while." She hesitated. "Look, not only isn't it wet T-shirt night, I don't even think we have any Hell's Angels here presently, not that there's anything wrong with them. In fact, they usually make things even livelier."

"I'm sure," Chyna said drily. "What about Michelle?"

Scott looked in the backseat. "She's sound asleep. Snoring even." Chyna double-checked. He was right.

"I don't know . . . ," Chyna still demurred.

Scott sighed hugely. "Well, if you're going to be a stick-in-the-mud, we can go back to your house and brood and wait for more eerie phone calls."

Chyna was already opening her door. "Not on your life, Scott Kendrick. I'd even compete on wet T-shirt night rather than go home right now."

"That's the spirit!" Scott said enthusiastically.

When he opened the roadhouse door, Chyna was hit by a barrage of light, cigarette smoke, the smell of beer, and the sound of loud music. She looked around to see a country band playing on a dais. The lead singer was obviously trying to be the next Shania Twain, with flowing brown hair and a midriff-baring top. She seemed oblivious to the fact that even heavy makeup couldn't hide that she was in her late fifties, and her short top revealed a wide, flabby waist whose loose skin hung over the top of her tight pants and jiggled when she bounced along to "Whose Bed Have Your Boots Been Under?" Nevertheless, she looked thrilled to be singing her heart out, and at least a third of the crowd inside danced to her music with abandon and sang along with her.

"Wow, have I been missing *this* all these years?" Chyna said into Scott's ear so he could hear her over the noise.

"Yeah, you have. Great, isn't it?"

Chyna started to say something sarcastic, then noted Scott's happy expression. She hadn't seen him look this jovial, this carefree, since she'd come home. "Actually, it

does look like fun," she yelled back at him. "Shoulder your
way up to the bar, cowboy, and get us a drink."

"Is beer okay?"

Chyna had never been fond of beer, but she doubted if
this place served Cosmopolitans. "Beer it is. I want to fit in."

"Oh, you do," Scott reassured her. It was meant as a compliment, but Chyna glanced with sudden insecurity at her
silk and wool blend slacks, blue cashmere sweater, and designer suede jacket. She also remembered that this morning
she'd slipped in her diamond stud earrings, last year's Christmas gift from her mother and each a full carat. Did she really look like all these other people with their worn jeans
and flannel shirts?

Suddenly she realized she'd really meant what she'd said
to Scott: "I want to fit in." She'd never felt like she fit in anywhere with her visions, her hearing of voices, her brushes
with other people's experiences. Ever since she'd been old
enough to realize her "sixth sense" made other people uncomfortable, even made them think she was something of a
freak, she'd constantly been on her guard. She'd tried to
hide from the things her mind told her that no one else knew.
She especially tried to hide her "power," or whatever it was,
from everyone except Zoey, gone long ago, and now Scott,
who she knew didn't completely believe she wasn't just hy-
perimaginative, no matter how hard he was trying.

No, tonight Chyna wanted to forget the bizarre side of her
life and just have a good time with all these "regular" folks
with their beer and country music. She'd never been in a
place where so many people looked like they were having a
wonderful time.

Scott came back with a pitcher of beer and two glasses. "I
see a table over there in the corner," he shouted above the
din. "Let's grab it. Everything else is taken."

He barged ahead of Chyna, holding the pitcher high so
beer wouldn't slosh out as people bumped into him. When
they did, Scott said, "Excuse me," the dancers said, "Excuse
me," and everyone smiled. Well, no fights yet, Chyna thought.
No one looked as if they were spoiling for a fistfight, either.

Who'd told her not much went on at this place except fighting? Ned? Her mother? Chyna couldn't remember. And it
didn't matter, because she saw Scott moving smoothly,
deftly dodging flying elbows and feet stomping to the music.
He wasn't limping anymore. His shoulders didn't have that
slight droop she'd noticed when she first saw him down by
Lake Manicora using the walking stick. Maybe the precrash
Scott was coming back, she thought, almost afraid to hope
for such a miracle. Maybe his spirit had been too strong even
for disaster to crush.

Once they were seated, Scott poured two glasses of beer,
each with a large, foamy head. "A lot of people tell you to
pour slowly so you get as little foam as possible," he said
loudly to Chyna, "but actually, you get rid of a lot of the car-
bon dioxide in the foam. Therefore—"

"You get less gas," Chyna said wryly. "How romantic."

Scott grinned. "That piece of information usually reduces
women to putty in my hands."

"I take it that piece of information, as you call it, is one of
your tried-and-true seduction lines."

Scott frowned. "Well, it's *one* of my best."

"I guess you don't date a lot, then."

Scott made a face at her. "I suppose you'd rather hear
about your beautiful eyes and silky hair."

"I wouldn't go for that one, either." Chyna took a sip of
beer. "And *please* don't say you really admire me for wanting to help people by going into medicine."

"I'll bet you've heard that statement a lot."

"Yes. Usually from guys who follow up by asking if I'll
make a lot of money when I'm a full-fledged oncologist."

"Then my approach that had nothing to do with your
beauty or your self-sacrifice or your money should have
been a real change of pace."

"Oh, it was. I congratulate you on your unconventional
approach to the so-called fairer sex."

"Thanks. I don't like to be obvious."

Chyna reached for her glass of beer just as a woman jos-
tled the table. She apologized profusely and Chyna smiled

and told her it was nothing, although beer had splashed on her new suede purse.

Scott made a face when the woman turned around. "Sorry."

"I'm sure I can find some genius who knows how to remove stains from suede," Chyna said, smiling, as she took the purse from the edge of the table and hung it on the arm of her chair next to the wall. A piece of white paper fluttered from a side pocket and Chyna reached to the floor and retrieved it. When she rose, her smile was gone. " 'Deirdre Mayhew. Five-five-five one-two-one-two. Any time after eight P.M.' " She sighed. "I never called Deirdre, Scott."

"You never got a chance."

"But—"

"But what? If you'd called her, she wouldn't have been abducted? That's ridiculous."

"I wasn't thinking—"

"Yes, you were. And I want you to stop it right now." The woman on the stage was now singing "Don't Be Stupid." "We're going to dance," Scott nearly shouted at Chyna, already rising from his chair.

"Are you up to dancing?"

"Of course I am."

"Okay," Chyna said listlessly. "But I'm not really in the mood right now."

"Sure you are."

"Besides, I'm not a very good dancer, Scott, so don't get carried away like some of those people."

Actually, Chyna had taken years of ballet classes when she was younger and usually loved to dance—rock, salsa, even still some ballet. She worried that Scott wasn't as strong as he thought, though, and they should take it easy. But when they found a small spot on the crowded dance floor, Chyna knew she didn't need to fret. So many people jammed the floor that there was barely room to move, but she did her best and Scott seemed to hold his own.

Chyna forced herself first to concentrate on Scott, then to relax and let herself move to the music. After about five minutes, she'd managed to edge Deirdre to the back of her mind. Then, on impulse, she twirled and, surprised, twirled again. A few people around her clapped as she felt her cheeks warm.

Scott looked at her, his eyes shining. "Having fun?"

"Either I'm having a ball or I'm drunk," Chyna laughed. "I think I'll start coming here every time I'm in town."

Scott grinned. "I just hope I'm here to come with you. Especially on wet T-shirt night."

2

Deirdre had no idea how far she'd walked. After her fall over the unknown metal object in her prison, she'd taken tiny steps because her hands were still firmly taped behind her back and she couldn't use them to make sure she had clear space in front of her. If she took only mincing, careful steps, she was bound to bump her foot, lightly, against any impediment. After all, she couldn't risk another fall. The last one had made a tremendous noise, but the crash hadn't brought her captor running because he knew she was partially free, and it hadn't hurt her. At least not much. But a bad fall could be the end of her. So she had to be careful, so careful.

When Deirdre brushed against a door, she would have let out a cry of joy if, mercifully, her mouth hadn't been taped. She turned her back to the door, then slowly brushed against it until her hands encountered a knob. It would be locked, of course, she thought. She'd have to take another snail's-paced tour around the building until she found something with which to pound it loose. . . .

Automatically her right hand clenched the knob and tried to turn it. This is silly, she thought. It won't move. It's locked.

The doorknob turned with only a slight squeak, the door flew open, and Deirdre, who'd been leaning against it, fell out of the building. She lay stunned for a moment. Why hadn't that door been locked? Certainly her captor wouldn't have just stuck her in an unlocked building.

Unless he'd left in a hurry, she concluded. She could feel the fingers caressing her face, the warm breath in her ear, the pressure of a body against hers—and then the car had driven up right next to the building. A car with at least four people in it. The voices had been young, but still—at least four people would have been up against one. And they'd said something about coming in. Someone had gotten out of the car. Deirdre realized now that the car had been on the opposite side of the building from the door. At the time, she had been concentrating so much on those voices, she hadn't noticed that no one touched her face or body anymore. Of course not. Fear of capture had sent her own captor scurrying quickly and quietly to the door, which, probably in a frenzy of fear, had been left unlocked.

The unlocked door would be remembered, though, and when all seemed safe, the teenagers long gone, a return visit would be in order. Maybe it would come an hour from now. Maybe it would come in just a few minutes. She had to get away from here fast.

Deirdre pulled up her knees again, rolled onto her legs, then dug her bare feet into the cold grass and gravel and heaved herself up to her knees, then stood. Once again, she weaved for a few moments without hands to steady her, without sight to help her focus on a point until her balance returned. She simply let herself weave, trying to make her body fluid. She knew if she went rigid, she'd slam to the ground again. The weaving slowed, and finally she was firmly planted on her feet.

Deirdre turned her head right and left, although she could see nothing. Which way should I go? she wondered. Where can I find someone to help me?

The car. When it had sped away, it had sounded like it was headed to her left. She thought. Yes, she was almost certain she heard it roaring off to the left.

Deirdre took a deep breath, told herself to ignore how cold and frightened she was, and began walking.

CHAPTER SIXTEEN

1

Chyna insisted they sit down after the third song. "I'm worn-out," she said loudly, the need for shouting temporarily unnecessary between songs. The Shania wannabe onstage was sweating profusely and taking a long slug of beer from a bottle. "I really need to catch my breath, Scott."

"No, you want *me* to sit down and catch my breath," Scott said, smiling. "You're right. I don't want to take a chance on injuring these dancing legs."

When they made it back to the table, Chyna grabbed her glass of beer and took three substantial swallows.

"Well, I guess you *were* tired," Scott said. "And thirsty."

"Both. I haven't danced in a long time."

"You don't regularly go clubbing in Albuquerque?"

Chyna laughed. "Are you kidding? I'm a medical resident, Scott. All I do is work and study."

"No time for a boyfriend?" Scott's voice was overly casual and he quickly lifted his glass to his lips.

"Nope. No boyfriend," Chyna replied, absurdly glad that he'd asked in a way that let her know it wasn't an off-the-cuff question. "Only Michelle."

"She seems like she'd be the perfect companion—sweet tempered and not overly hyper like this poodle my girlfriend has." Chyna's heart sank until Scott added, "I mean my ex-girlfriend. The trauma of the plane crash seems to have messed up my sense of time. We parted ways three months ago."

"Oh." Chyna, too, took a sip of beer and asked offhand-edly, "Do you miss her?"

"No, not much." He frowned. "Well, to be truthful, not at all. Admitting that just sounds so . . ."

"Cavalier?"

Scott nodded. "She was a nice woman, but we realized we were just marking time with each other because we were the same age and both pilots." He smiled. "Actually, I think she was really looking for a guy her poodle loved, and it sure wasn't me. I couldn't stand him, either, and I'm a dog lover."

"I could tell by the way you acted around Michelle when you first saw her at the lake." Chyna glanced at her watch. "I wonder if I should call and see if Rex is home?"

"Rex? Why? Do you have a curfew?"

"No, and neither does he, but something else happened today that involved Rex." She briefly told him about Rusty's admission that he'd seen Nancy Tierney fall during her run and he'd just taken off and left her there. Scott's forehead wrinkled and she knew his opinion of Rusty had forever been altered. "If he's telling the truth, I admit I'm disappointed in him for not doing *something* to help Nancy. But he may not have been telling me everything, Scott. He said someone was chasing Nancy and that's why she was going so fast and not watching her footing. He said he didn't see who was chasing her.

"But the worst part is that when he finished, we looked up and saw Rex, Gage, *and* Owen at the door," Chyna continued. "Owen looked ready to spit nails. He was furious. Rex made some excuse to go home with him. I think he was afraid that if he didn't keep Owen occupied for a while, Owen might beat Rusty to death or something equally awful."

Scott raised his eyebrows. "That was quite an admission for Rusty to make about watching her. Why was he telling you all of this?"

"Because I'd seen him earlier in the day. He put his hand on my back and I saw Nancy running down that path through *his* eyes. I suppose I started acting uneasy, he remembered all the ESP stuff from when I was young, and then he got nervous. Nancy's death must constantly be on his mind."

"So you think he was trying to keep you from suspecting him of having anything to do with Nancy dying."

"Yes."

Scott was quiet for a moment. Then he asked, "Do you believe Rusty?"

"That he just happened to be on the path where Nancy was running that evening? Not for a minute. That would be just too much of a coincidence."

"I mean about his not seeing who was chasing Nancy."

"Oh." Chyna thought. "Yes. I think she was being chased, but I don't think Rusty saw the person. I don't know why I believe part of his story but not all of it, but I do."

"But someone else might not have believed that either he wasn't chasing her himself or he didn't get a good look at who *was* chasing her."

"Exactly." Chyna frowned. "Either way, he didn't count on his father hearing him tell this tale, and you know how Owen is about the great Burtram family dignity. God, for him to know that Rusty was blabbing to me about going around watching Nancy . . ." Chyna shivered. "If I were Rusty, I certainly wouldn't want to face Owen after that scene."

"Well, even if Rex managed to head off old Owen for a while, the guy's not going to forget what he heard Rusty say." Scott paused and looked at her solemnly. "I'm sure you know Owen has a reputation for eyeing young women. *Very* young women."

"I've heard gossip," Chyna said vaguely.

"Well, it's true. Owen is a letch."

"And he's older," Chyna murmured. "Rusty said the footsteps following Nancy were heavy and *clumsy.*"

"Like an older person's might be compared to a fleet young thing like Nancy?" Chyna nodded, and Scott added,

"Owen is also one very mean son of a bitch under that unctuous manner of his." Scott shook his head. "Chyna, Owen is
going to make Rusty pay for what he told you, especially if
he was the one chasing Nancy and he thinks Rusty saw him."

2

Deirdre had walked gingerly on gravel and frosted grass for
a while, all the time thinking that her abductor was going to
jump on her any moment. After a while, though, she stopped
thinking about being followed or even watched. She was too
consumed with trying to keep herself on her feet and taking
small steps, not giving in to the urge to run, to worry about
anything else. So far, she'd stepped hard on a rock that had
left her right foot aching, tripped over cold, leafless vines,
and walked into a tree. She was sure she'd have a bruise on
her forehead tomorrow. If she was lucky enough to live until
tomorrow.

Her nose ran, her breath came hard and heavy, and her
feet felt so cold and sore she was tempted to sit down. But
she didn't give in to the temptation for rest. She was partly
afraid that if she did sit down, she wouldn't be able to make
her sore, exhausted body rise again, and partly frightened
that she had not gotten far enough away from her prison that
she couldn't be easily found. So she plodded on, her eyes
taped shut, her hands trapped behind her with several layers
of duct tape, and her entire body shivering in the cold night.
She had no idea where she was. She had no idea where she'd
end up if she kept going in this direction. But at least she no
longer simply lay on that concrete floor, a silent, helpless
victim waiting to be murdered.

She thought of the voice she'd heard, or imagined she'd
heard, in her prison. The voice telling her not to give up, that
Chyna was trying to help her. The voice had sounded young,
but not familiar—not the voice of anyone Deirdre knew. It
probably existed only in her mind. She'd heard so much
about Chyna Greer all of her life. Some people had admired

Chyna and completely believed she was good and blessed with a special and wonderful gift. Other people, particularly Irma Vogel, had hated Chyna and talked about her being unnatural and even evil. When Irma occasionally went on those rants about Chyna, Deirdre had thought with a chill that the woman sounded like a raving lunatic.

Of course, Deirdre thought Irma was fairly off-kilter about most things. She certainly wasn't the kind, helpful, caring woman she pretended to be. Deirdre believed Irma was small-minded, often vicious in her judgments of people, and, worst of all, secretly glad when Deirdre's mother had died. Irma had set her sights on Ben Mayhew as soon as she learned his wife was incurably ill. Deirdre could never forgive the woman for feigning sorrow and sympathy at her mother's funeral when she'd known that secretly Irma had been delighted.

And she doesn't like me any more than she liked my mother or Chyna, Deirdre thought as she inched along, still being as careful as possible so she wouldn't fall. She's probably glad I'm gone. Now, at last, she's got Daddy all to herself.

This last thought drew Deirdre up short. Irma had wanted her out of the way. She hadn't been able to hide her disappointment when she'd learned Deirdre wasn't leaving for college back in September. Deirdre knew Irma didn't stand a chance of winning Ben Mayhew's affection, but what if she thought she did if only he weren't both bolstered and protected by his daughter? And then, lo and behold, Chyna Greer's mother had died and Chyna had come home. Irma always said girls went missing when Chyna was around.

My, my, what a perfect time for me to disappear, Deirdre thought grimly as she nearly tiptoed her way out of a tangle of ankle-high weeds onto a swath of grass that had obviously been well tended, even recently. Although stiffened from cold, the grass was short and evenly cut. It lay thick and luxurious, the kind that had never been marred by crabgrass or dandelions, the kind that flowed over golf courses.

Lost in her thoughts, Deirdre had unconsciously picked
up speed and abruptly smacked into a tall piece of rock.
Stunned, she reached out and touched it. This was no ordinary rock. This had been honed into the shape of an obelisk,
a four-sided shaft that stretched high above her head. What
on earth is this? Deirdre wondered, after she'd bounded back,
checking to making certain she hadn't broken her nose.

She moved closer, then circled the obelisk, thinking it
seemed like something out of a science fiction movie, which
would have sent her into half-dazed, hysterical laughter if
her mouth weren't taped. Giddily she wished she could feel
the obelisk, but her hands remained trapped behind her
back. Taking a deep breath, she choked down her inner
laughter, forced herself to focus, inched her way forward,
and stood beside the stone. She leaned her head against it,
feeling it extend far above her own five feet, five inches.
Gently she touched it with her cheek. It was cold and
slightly rough. *Granite.* Then, with rising hope, she circled
it until her icy forehead brushed against what felt like engraving.

If Deirdre could have clapped her hands and let out a
whoop of joy, she would have. Finally, she knew where
she was.

3

They were up again, this time in the middle of the dance
floor, almost right in front of the band. Scott had found his
rhythm, and even if it was a bit slower than that of most
other dancers, he looked poised, almost polished.

"You used to dance a lot, didn't you?" Chyna called over
the music.

"How did you know?"

"Because now that you've gotten into the swing of things,
your natural grace is showing."

"Natural grace?" Scott grimaced. "You make me sound
like a girl."

"Pardon me. I meant your ease with dancing is showing."

"You want to see my Jerry Lee Lewis mule kick?"

"No, thank you."

"Chyna Greer, you're jealous."

"And you're crazy."

The fast song concluded and Shania's would-be twin broke into the ballad "From This Moment." "I don't usually like country music," Chyna said, "but this song . . ."

Scott smiled at her, his gaze softening. "It gets to me, too. We *have* to dance to it, Chyna."

"Yes, we do."

Chyna moved easily into Scott's arms. He held her close. He was very warm and she could feel his heart beating beneath his sweater. For the first few moments she was in his arms, Chyna felt stiff. She'd never been this close to Scott Kendrick—the Scott Kendrick she'd thought she was in love with when she was a teenager. The Scott Kendrick she couldn't stop thinking about all through college and medical school and her internship and residency. The Scott Kendrick who'd been so kind, so protective, so understanding, or trying his hardest to be understanding, since she'd come home. All of this in spite of his own recent tragedy.

In a moment, she realized she'd relaxed against him. His arms tightened around her and he bent his dark head, singing softly in her ear. The words were about love and commitment, and Scott sang them with a soft sensuality. His warm breath in her ear, his strong body so close to hers, his cheek rubbing her temple, almost had her hypnotized. For her, no one else existed in the room. Only her and Scott Kendrick. This is how it's supposed to be, she thought distantly, dreamily. This is how it's supposed to be with the man you love.

As Chyna floated through the dance, she kept her eyes closed, letting Scott lead her. I wish you were always leading me, she thought. Just like the song, I wish you were always leading me "from this moment on."

Slowly, Chyna opened her eyes. She blinked twice, but she felt as if her vision had gone fuzzy, almost as if someone had dropped a piece of gauze in front of her eyes. Around ten seconds later, the sensation passed. It's the atmosphere, she thought. All the noise, the cigarette smoke, being held so close by Scott. That's all it was.

But she couldn't dismiss the feeling that for ten seconds she'd been cold and barefoot and lost.

"Something wrong?" Scott murmured in her ear.

"No. Did I step on your foot or something?"

"You stiffened and then you tripped." Scott leaned back. "Are you tired? Want to sit down?"

"Maybe I should," Chyna said weakly. "I don't know what happened to me. I just—"

She went rigid, the dance floor, the entire roadhouse, disappearing from her view. She felt surrounded by a silver-washed landscape with statues and flowers and . . .

And a towering grave marker soaring smooth and gray in the cold moonlight. "The Sternhavens' family obelisk . . ."

"Just hold on to my arm," Scott soothed. "We're almost to the table."

"Somethin' wrong with her?" a woman with long, teased, bright red hair asked. "She don't look so good."

Chyna heard the woman, saw the woman, but she seemed far away, a dream image that peered and talked and took Chyna's other arm. Let go of me, Chyna thought almost wildly. I don't know you. Let go of me!

She shook free of both the woman and Scott and began mumbling, "I have to keep moving. I know where I am now. Just another mile—"

Abruptly Chyna sank to the floor. People scattered, but Scott instantly stooped and leaned over her, his face frantic. "Chyna, what's wrong?" he asked, holding one of her hands in his while with with the other he pushed her hair back from her forehead. "Someone call nine-one-one," he yelled.

Chyna suddenly felt as if she'd been hit by a jolt of electricity. The room came back into focus and she sat up, grasping at Scott's arm. "We have to go," she shrilled. "We have to go!"

Scott rubbed her arm. "Settle down, Chyna. The emergency guys will be here in ten minutes and we'll get you checked out. It's going to be all right, honey."

Chyna jerked her hand away from him. "I can't stay here, Scott. We have to help her!"

"Her?" Scott repeated blankly.

"A girl," Chyna almost wailed. "I think it's Deirdre. I believe I know where Deirdre is, Scott!"

CHAPTER SEVENTEEN

1

People made way for them as they rushed toward the door of the roadhouse. Chyna knew it was because they thought she was ill and she and Scott were leaving for the hospital. "What do I do about that nine-one-one call I just made?" a woman behind the counter asked.

"When they get here, send them to Black Willow Cemetery," Chyna said hurriedly. "Tell them to take the first left and head down the north side."

"The *cemetery*?" Chyna heard the woman echo incredulously behind her, but paid no attention. She simply clutched Scott's hand as they burst out of the doors and into the parking lot of the roadhouse.

"Chyna, what's going on?" Scott asked, alarm surging through his deep voice.

"I told you. I saw something. A girl, and she was falling."

"But you said to go to the cemetery."

"Yes. I know it sounds silly, but just do what I say, Scott. If I'm wrong, then I'm wrong, but I have to know if I was hallucinating or really seeing something." She paused, her head jerking right and left. "Dammit, where's your car?"

"It's at the end of the row." Chyna ran toward it, Scott rushing after her. When she reached the car, she saw Michelle sound asleep on the backseat. The doors were locked.

"Scott, the door—"

"Just a minute. I locked them so no one would take Michelle." He fumbled in his pocket, withdrew a key ring and unlocked the driver's side door, then hit a button that unlocked all doors. They both jumped in as Michelle awakened with a yelp.

"It's okay, girl." Chyna reached over the seat and rubbed the dog's ears. "Don't be scared."

Scott looked at Chyna. "Can I have one of those ear rubs, because I'm scared as hell." He started the car. "Why do we have to go to the cemetery?"

Chyna drew a deep breath, trying to slow her heart thumping far too fast. "While we were dancing, the room faded away for me. I felt cold and frightened. I felt like I was looking through someone else's eyes again—a girl's. She was so frightened—but still thinking that the grass was cold, but well tended. And I felt a gravestone. Or rather a tower. The Sternhaven family grave marker. It's an ornate obelisk, Scott, around twelve feet tall. Mom thought it was so pretentious and always joked that it should have a light on top to guide in aliens."

Scott snickered but still looked puzzled. "But what does that monument have to do with your vision?"

"The girl is at that huge grave marker! I *know* it. I *felt* it when we were in the Whippoorwill." Chyna paused. "Then I had a sensation of the girl falling."

"Like you fell on the dance floor?"

"Yes. I had no control over myself. I didn't even feel as if *I* were falling." Chyna winced. "I must have looked like a fool."

"No, you just looked drunk," Scott deadpanned.

"Oh, wonderful. How embarrassing, but a little embarrassment doesn't matter if what happened to me helps us find the girl."

Scott slammed on the brakes. Chyna's seat belt dug into her chest and waist, and Michelle was thrown forward onto the car floor. In the headlights, Chyna saw two large deer running in front of them. "Deer are always getting killed on this road," Scott said. "I usually go slower because of them."

The white tails of the deer vanished into a thicket on the other side of the road. "That was a quick reaction."

Scott half-smiled in the darkness. "Guess my reflexes are returning to normal. I was worried about them for a while. I always seemed to be moving in slow motion." Scott slowed the car and peered to the left. "There's the cemetery. Are you sure—"

"Yes! Scott, the girl I felt falling may be Deirdre and she could be hurt."

Scott turned into the Black Willow Cemetery. Just past the brick pillars, the road forked. "You said *north* in The Whippoorwill."

"Yes. The Sternhaven monument is about fifty feet further into the cemetery and beyond a few graves, not next to the road. As a matter of fact, my father's grave is right beside it."

"I know where your father's grave is. I came to the funeral, remember?"

Yes, she remembered. Barely. Deirdre had been so saddened and surprised by her father's death that for once in her life, she hadn't been throbbingly aware of Scott when he was near.

"Why would Deirdre or any other girl come to a cemetery at night?" he asked.

"I don't know. Probably she's lost, Scott."

Scott drove slowly over the white graveled road and Michelle stood, her hind legs on the backseat, her paws thrown over the front, her breath hot on Chyna's ears. "There!" Chyna exclaimed. "I can see the monument. Stop!"

As soon as Scott pulled the car off the side of the road and they clambered out, including Michelle, a cloud floated over the full moon. Even though Scott had left on his headlights, they seemed to do little to cut the gloom, their glow dulled by wisps of fog rolling in from the nearby river.

Fear suddenly spiked through her. "Oh God," she muttered.

Scott looked at her sharply. "What's wrong?"

"It's spooky out here."

"No kidding. Night in a cemetery isn't my idea of fun, either."

"I know, but . . ."

"But what?"

But something isn't right, Chyna thought, feeling inexpressibly wary. Danger was near. She knew it and for a moment she couldn't make herself take a step.

"Chyna, you wanted to come here," Scott said patiently. "What's wrong?"

She couldn't move and she couldn't tell Scott she felt surrounded by evil. Pure, malevolent evil. He'd think she was crazy. He'd lose all faith in her. "Uh . . . I just wondered if we had to lose the moonlight *and* get fog at the same time?" she managed.

"It's a little inconvenient but not a disaster. Don't worry—I always come fully prepared." Scott leaned into the car. As she stood still as stone, though, he opened the glove compartment and withdrew a flashlight. "Not sizable, but better than nothing. And we also have this." He reached into the backseat of the car and pulled out his walking stick. She hadn't even known he'd brought it with him. The stick she was certain bore traces of blood.

"Is this better?" Scott asked as he turned on the flashlight and a beam of white light pierced the darkness.

"Yeah, much better," she answered weakly.

"You don't sound like you feel better." Scott flashed the light around. "I'll be manly and go first. Besides, I have the stick in case we're attacked."

"You think we'll be attacked?"

Scott looked at her, his face weirdly shadowed and sharp-angled as he held the flashlight below his chin. "You're the psychic. Will we?"

"I don't know. I just feel . . ." She sighed. She hadn't been able to get him here fast enough. Now she was acting ridiculously timorous. "Just go ahead," she said, and added with what she hoped sounded like lightness, "but if you have to hit someone, do it with the flashlight. If you break that walking stick, your mother will kill you."

Michelle, a dog of many fears, did not prance ahead, ready to warn the humans of danger. Instead, she tried to walk between them and finally, after Scott had twice stepped on her paw, dropped directly behind Chyna.

The dark cloud had moved on and the moon now bathed the landscape with a cold, silvery sheen. It should have been beautiful, Chyna thought, but instead everything around her looked weirdly bleached and dead. The night seemed unearthly still. She didn't hear birds; she didn't hear small animals or deer moving in the wooded area beyond the cemetery; she didn't hear cars on the highway behind them.

To make matters worse, Chyna could not stop thinking of all the cold, decaying bodies lying here, bodies of people who'd once laughed, and eaten, had arguments, made love, gone to work, suffered sorrow, experienced joys. And now all of it had ended for them. The thought was almost more than she could bear, and she pushed it from her mind, telling herself she didn't have all the answers. Maybe death wasn't simply oblivion, as she'd always feared. After all, she was certain Zoey was dead, and yet Zoey had been speaking to her for days. The thought should have been comforting, but it wasn't. Chyna couldn't stand the thought of Zoey's spirit trapped in some netherworld, not at peace, not at rest, just talking to Chyna, begging her to help another girl as Chyna hadn't been able to help her.

"What about Zoey?" Scott asked.

"What?"

"You said 'Zoey' and 'netherworld' and—"

"I was just mumbling to myself." Chyna was embarrassed. Exactly *how* much did she talk to herself? A lot of the trick-or-treaters at Halloween had certainly noticed. Did she run around the hospital having long conversations with herself? Were people laughing behind her back and saying that she was strange and— "There's the obelisk!" she burst out, grateful both to find it and to keep her mind on a different track.

Forgetting her fear, Chyna ran ahead and touched the

marble "tower." Almost immediately Scott stood beside her, shining the flashlight beam on the engraving: *Sternhaven.*

Suddenly Michelle began barking furiously. Chyna jumped in surprise, sliding on the frosty grass as her gaze darted around, searching for an intruder, someone who shouldn't be in a cemetery at night. Scott's sharp gaze darted everywhere. In a moment, he said, "Chyna, come here!"

She turned around. At first all she saw was a large piece of plywood. Beside the plywood lay a beer bottle and a crumpled potato chip bag. Michelle barked again and, when she'd gained Chyna's attention, dipped her paw about two inches into a hole. "Michelle, get back!" Scott commanded.

The dog cringed at the harsh sound of his voice but moved away from what Chyna now saw was a large hole in the ground. A deep hole dug for a casket, she thought with a shudder. She would have expected Michelle to retreat to her after being spoken to so loudly by Scott, but instead she kept barking, circling the hole in agitation. There is something down there, Chyna thought. Something I probably don't want to see.

In fact, for a moment Chyna felt like bolting away from the scene. She wanted to run back to Scott's car, lock herself in, and drive away, Scott and Michelle in tow. But of course she couldn't do that. She wasn't *supposed* to do that.

She closed her eyes for a moment, trying to draw on the well of strength her mother used to say everyone had inside them. Then, with dread, Chyna crept closer to Scott, who was shining the flashlight into the deep hole.

At the bottom lay a girl, facedown, naked, her wrists bound with duct tape. Her right leg was flung out at an unnatural angle and her auburn hair spread in a tangled, stringy mess, blocking any view of her face. Still, Chyna knew.

"Deirdre," she whispered. "Dear God, I hope she's alive."

2

After looking at Deirdre for a moment, Chyna had begun to climb down into the hole to see if the girl still lived, but Scott had stopped her. "You could fall and get hurt yourself," he said, holding tight to Chyna's arm. "Or you could fall *on* Deirdre. If she's alive, you might make things worse for her, cause another injury."

Chyna pulled back from the edge of the hole. "You're right. It's just so hard to wait. Are you sure that woman at The Whippoorwill made the nine-one-one call and gave the right directions?"

"I'm sure she made the call, but I didn't hear her give the directions." Scott pulled his cell phone from his pocket. "I'll double-check."

While Scott called the Emergency Service, Chyna tried to get Michelle under control. She wished she'd brought a leash, but they'd left in a hurry and she hadn't bothered because Michelle so seldom needed a leash. At last, the dog came to her and Chyna knelt down, holding on to Michelle's collar. The dog panted heavily after running around and around the hole. Chyna had never seen her act so agitated. Or so driven. Chyna had a feeling Michelle sensed someone was hurt and actually wanted to help rather than hide, which was a first for the dog.

"The woman at the Whippoorwill told the Emergency Service to come to the cemetery," Scott said, putting his phone back in his pocket. "They're on the way."

"Thank God." Chyna glanced at Deirdre again. "Oh, Scott, she looks so tiny and vulnerable down there."

"She is." Scott frowned. "How long do you think she's been in that hole?"

Chyna looked at him in surprise. "She fell in the hole when I fell in the roadhouse. I was having her experience, Scott. I thought you realized that."

"Maybe, but you don't always experience things at the

time they're happening. Like with Rusty. You had the vision of Rusty watching Nancy when she died several days after she fell."

"Rusty was *thinking* about her falling at the moment I touched him. At least, I believe that's what happened. And in the Whippoorwill, I handled the paper Deirdre gave me in the café. Maybe that somehow put me 'in touch' with her this evening." She shrugged helplessly. "As I've told you, I don't know everything about how this power of mine works and often doesn't work."

"Do you see something over there?" Scott asked suddenly.

Chyna scanned the cemetery. Then she saw it. A movement in the trees about forty feet from them. Was it one of the deer? She squinted. Maybe. Or maybe it was a person, she thought in dread. Someone else out in the cemetery at night, perhaps looking for Deirdre or perhaps watching her and Scott.

She rubbed a hand over her tired eyes. "I see it, but I don't know if it's a person or an animal."

"I can't tell." Scott shook his head. "It's disappeared back in the trees."

"Was it coming at us?"

"It wasn't. Not *directly,* at least, but that doesn't mean it's not circling around—"

Fear swept over Chyna again. They should get out of here, because she was almost certain they hadn't seen an animal. But how could they desert Deirdre?

Chyna felt like she jumped a foot when Scott almost shouted, "Thank God! Here comes the cavalry."

Headlights sliced through the darkness. "An emergency unit," Scott said. He'd left on his own car headlights, so the unit, which turned out to be a fire truck, came directly toward them and stopped behind Scott's car. In a moment, an ambulance followed. Scott waved his flashlight and yelled, "We're over here! There's a girl in an empty grave!"

"God, that sounded ominous," Chyna muttered.

Scott shrugged. "Is there any way to make this situation sound *less* ominous?"

No, Chyna thought, especially because she believed the person lingering at the edge of the woods was Deirdre's abductor, arrived too late to catch his escaped prey.

CHAPTER EIGHTEEN

1

Rex pulled into the driveway of the Greer home, fumbled in his pocket for his keys, then went in through the side door. He headed straight for the kitchen, poured vodka in a glass, and drank it in two gulps. He was cold, shaken, and exhausted, but he knew he couldn't go to sleep. Not now. Not with all that was churning through his brain. For the first time in his life, he felt old and weak.

He poured more vodka, walked into the living room, turned on a lamp, and sat down directly across from the portrait of Vivian and Edward. How solid they looked. How privileged and poised, Edward strong and handsome with his patrician features and silvery hair, Vivian beautiful and vivacious, her blue-gray eyes glinting with humor and a confidence that said she could take on the world. That painting was only nine years old, but already they were both gone, each dying far too young. Vivian's death hadn't really hit Rex yet, still didn't seem real, but abruptly he violently missed his brother, a man whose quiet ways belied the strength and tolerance that had carried him through until the end.

It was long after midnight, hours later than when Rex had left with Owen and Rusty. I should have called Chyna, Rex thought with regret. He knew she'd sensed trouble when they left. She'd looked so worried. He should have let her know he'd deposited Rusty safely at his own home before he went to Owen's.

Not that his tactic had been very successful. Rex had intended to stay with Owen for at least an hour, maybe more. After twenty minutes, though, Owen had received a call and claimed pressing business at the funeral home before nearly pushing Rex out the front door. Rex had gone to Ned's for half an hour, but Ned had been called to the car dealership and Rex could tell Beverly wanted to get the children bathed and quieted before bed, so he hadn't stayed there long, either.

Rex had cruised past Rusty's and not seen Owen's car, but it hadn't been at the funeral home, either. So if I'd called Chyna then, Rex mused, what could I have said, where could I have told her I was going for the rest of the evening?

After his failure to locate Owen, Rex had felt overwhelmed and nearly incapable of thinking at all, much less of making up casual, believable excuses for Chyna about why he wasn't coming home until late. So he'd just left her hanging, not knowing where he was or when he'd return.

No doubt, Chyna was feeling abandoned by him, and with good cause. He hadn't really spent any time with her, even though her mother had just died. Instead, he'd been running willy-nilly, making up a lie about why he hadn't arrived as soon as he heard about Vivian's death, fabricating stories about visiting local friends once he'd gotten here. He was never around when Chyna needed him. She'd even had to face the crowd that had gathered in front of the house this morning—the crowd calling her names, making accusations, throwing rocks at the house. At least Kendrick had arrived, Rex thought with gratitude. It was Scott Kendrick, a man recovering from great emotional and physical trauma, who'd had to help Chyna ride out that storm. Meanwhile, Rex had been doing other things, things that would shock and sicken his lovely and extraordinary niece.

But maybe he hadn't let down Chyna as much as he thought he had, because she hadn't really expected much from him. She hadn't exactly been leaning on him since he arrived, maybe because she knew that trying to lean on Rex Greer would be like trying to lean on a pillar of whipped cream. Ruefully Rex felt that failing people had always been his forte. That and keeping secrets. He knew so much about so many things, things that could blow apart what was left of this family, things that could hurt or destroy at least a dozen people in this town. Sometimes his head pounded from the pressure of all he knew and of all he'd done. It would be so nice to be able to shed the compulsions that drove him, the obsessions that haunted him. At times like tonight, Rex didn't know how much longer he could continue to live life as he had been for years.

But he had a feeling he wouldn't have to maintain his façade for much longer, because after tonight, he knew with dreadful certainty that Chyna would soon end it all for him.

2

The fire truck and ambulance arrived with such fanfare Chyna wondered if the dead could sleep through it all. Sirens wailing, lights flashing, people yelling. Five minutes ago this area had been silent and dark and definitely eerie. Suddenly it had the air of a carnival.

"First, we'll lower ourselves into the grave on ropes and take her vital signs," one of the paramedics told Chyna and Scott.

"Don't you mean that first you'll see if she's alive?" Chyna asked in fear. "She hasn't moved a fraction since we found her."

The young, dark-haired paramedic smiled at her. "We always hope for the best, Mrs. . . ."

"Dr. Greer. Chyna Greer. This is Scott Kendrick." Chyna suddenly thought these formal introductions seemed silly and a waste of time. Another man was already lowering a rope into the grave. Two paramedics slid down the rope with tremendous speed. Chyna tensed and felt Scott's arm encircle her shoulder. Then she closed her eyes, unable to watch them check for signs of life in the girl who lay like a broken doll at the bottom of the cold grave. At last, one of them called, "She's alive!"

"Thank God," Chyna breathed, sagging in relief. Scott smiled at her as they waited for the paramedics to check Deirdre further.

"Pulse is a little thready, but no signs of serious trauma besides the lack of consciousness," one yelled up to the others. "Lower the backboard and the cervical collar."

"Did you hear that?" Chyna asked Scott. "No signs of serious trauma!"

He gave her a small, tight smile. "So far so good."

Of course they had to check for other damage, Chyna thought. Who knew how long Deirdre had wandered naked before she'd fallen into the grave? And what had her abductor done to her before she'd gotten loose? Raped her?

Once the cervical collar was in place and Deirdre had been strapped to the backboard, the men above used ropes to raise it. When they got her to ground level, they asked that Chyna and Scott look at her. "You said this was Deirdre Mayhew, but you couldn't see her face," one of them said. "Take a closer look now."

They both bent over and peered at the unconscious girl. She was extremely pale and Chyna's expert eye immediately discerned that she was suffering from hypothermia, but it was definitely Deirdre. "That's the Mayhew girl," Scott said firmly. "I've known her all her life."

"She needs IV fluids," Chyna directed, temporarily forgetting that she wasn't in the hospital. "And she's probably malnourished. Are you sure you have her spine immobilized?"

"Yes, ma'am, we know our jobs," one of the paramedics said patiently.

"Of course you do. I'm sorry," Chyna said quickly. "I'm a doctor—"

"You said that."

"Yes. I didn't mean to come off as a know-it-all. I'm

just . . ." Chyna swallowed convulsively, feeling as if she were going to burst into tears. She hardly knew Deirdre, but the emotional drain of feeling her walking on the cold ground, naked, blind, then falling into the hole—a grave, of all things—momentarily overcame her.

Scott tightened his hold on her and said to the paramedics, "I'll notify her father."

"We'll call the sheriff," one of the men said as they carefully loaded Deirdre into the ambulance. "We need to know why that grave wasn't covered. They *always* cover open graves. An open grave at night is just a lawsuit waiting to happen."

"Yes, I guess so," Chyna said absently, wondering how he could be thinking about lawsuits at a time like this.

Another paramedic looked at her and Scott and smiled. "There are going to be a lot of relieved people tonight. We were afraid we were going to lose another girl."

As the ambulance and fire truck drove away, Scott turned her around and hugged her tightly. "You did it, Chyna! You saved Deirdre."

Chyna felt relief and even a small flame of triumph. But greater than her sense of triumph was her regret that she hadn't been able to do the same for Heather and Edie, and especially for Zoey.

3

It was near two in the morning when Scott followed Chyna up to her house. Rex's car still wasn't in the driveway, and now Chyna was glad. If he was home and still awake, she was in no mood to talk to him. Chyna opened the front door, walked into the house, then turned around to see Scott lingering just outside. He smiled at her wanly and reached out to take her hand. "Well, I know you're exhausted," he said softly, somewhat self-consciously. "Get a good night's sleep, Chyna. You deserve it."

The glow from the outside carriage light beside the front door shone on his black hair, the finely chiseled features of his face with its two healing scars, one on the right cheek, one on the left jawline, leftovers from the crash that had almost claimed his life. Finally, she looked into his eyes— deep, dark, soulful eyes, still holding the horror and sadness of watching the fiery remains of the jet he'd piloted destroy seventy-two lives.

She'd had romantic feelings for this man since she was twelve—feelings she'd later dismissed as a teenage crush. At this moment, though, she knew that what she'd felt at twelve was just a younger version of what she felt for him now—love.

Chyna leaned forward, stood on tiptoe, and kissed Scott tenderly on the lips and the neck. Then she whispered, "I don't want you to go."

His right arm circled her waist, drawing her even closer to his tall, lean frame. "Is this because you don't want to be alone after finding Deirdre?"

"The way we found Deirdre was scary, but she's alive." Chyna had always been shy around men, always letting them make the first move, usually stopping them before things went too far. But now, almost against her will, her lips trailed down Scott's warm neck.

Scott drew a deep breath, wrapped his other arm around her, and pulled her so close she could feel his heart beating. His lips touched hers lightly at first, then pressed against them passionately, his right hand tangling in her long hair as they seemed to melt into each other as time stopped for Chyna. His tongue barely touched hers—warm, soft, almost teasing.

At last, he pulled away a fraction, his breath coming fast and hot against her face cooled by the evening air. His gaze held hers, his dark, penetrating eyes seeming to see all the way through to her soul. Chyna felt as if she'd never been kissed in her life, and she never wanted Scott's kisses to end. After what seemed like an endless moment, he asked softly, "Want me to stay awhile?"

"Oh yes, I want you to stay," Chyna said huskily, her face drawing nearer to his. "I want you to stay the night."

Their lips met again and Chyna gently pushed the door shut behind him.

4

Irma Vogel sneezed violently and wiped her nose on an already damp tissue as she looked in disgust at the screaming headline of the morning paper:

MISSING GIRL FOUND ALIVE

Irma knew calling Ben and pretending to be elated would be useless. He'd be at the hospital with Deirdre. Irma had no intention of walking into that lion's den full of Ben's friends and policemen and reporters. Besides, she'd called Ben on his cell phone around one in the morning, telling him she hadn't been able to sleep so she'd sat up, listening to her police scanner, and heard about the finding of Deirdre. "It was Chyna Greer!" he'd boomed at Irma in ecstasy. "Chyna Greer had a vision or something—I never understood what people said she could do, but she knew where to find Deirdre!" Then he'd told Irma that Deirdre was still unconscious, they didn't know a thing about who'd taken her, and now he needed to get back to his daughter and slammed the phone in her ear.

Irma now let the paper slide to the floor and walked over to a wall mirror. God, she looked awful, she thought. Her bulgy eyes were red, her nose was swollen, and her face bore a gloss of perspiration from a fever she knew was rising. Too much time out in the cold, she thought, often without a coat. She'd always been careful about keeping herself warm in the past. Lately, though, she'd been distracted, trying to do too much. Now, on top of all of her efforts, she was getting sick. Irma felt like crying for herself.

She shuffled to her chair and retrieved the newspaper. The

rescue of Deirdre Mayhew had been Irma's first concern, but she also wanted to read the piece on Rusty Burtram, who had apparently fallen through his sliding glass doors. One of the shards of glass had sliced his carotid artery and he'd died from blood loss. Irma lowered the newspaper and thought deeply. A person wasn't likely to just "fall" through his glass doors unless he was drunk or stoned, a conclusion Irma was sure most Black Willow residents would make. She had barely known Rusty, but she knew Owen and she could imagine the man writhing in embarrassment over this story on the front page of the paper. His son falling through glass doors because he was drunk? God, old Owen might have a heart attack from humiliation rather than grief, because it was plain to anyone who'd had more than the slightest contact with Rusty and Owen that Owen felt no love for his son. "Well, Mr. Owen Burtram, you won't have to put up with the big disappointment of your life anymore," she said, full of scathing disdain she'd never manage if Owen stood in front of her. Liking the sound of her voice, she spoke even louder to the nonexistent Owen. "You simply have to pretend you believe Rusty tripped and crashed through those doors and then act like you care that he's dead. Really what you'll be feeling is relieved that he's blessedly gone from your life forever, just like your slut of a wife."

If Irma hadn't felt so bad, she would have laughed at her own macabre assessment of the situation. She hadn't liked either one of the Burtram men, especially Owen. Smug, that was what he was. He'd always looked her up and down like she was a piece of garbage, and Rusty had acted half-afraid of her, like he sensed something was wrong with her and he should steer clear.

But *sensing* things was Chyna Greer's specialty. When Irma had talked to Ben, he'd said they hadn't a clue about who'd abducted Deirdre. She was unconscious and couldn't tell them anything. So because they didn't know who'd kidnapped Deirdre, Chyna obviously hadn't been able to *sense* that important information.

Irma went to the phone, looked up the number of the hospital, and put in a call to the third floor, asking for Nurse Tally Jones. When she heard Tally's familiar loud twang, she hissed, "It's Irma. I need information, but I don't want anyone to know I'm asking, so keep your voice down."

"Oh, okay, Irma," Tally hissed.

"And don't say my name! Has the Mayhew girl regained consciousness?"

"No, Deirdre's still—"

"Tally, keep your voice down!"

"Oh yeah." Tally went back to her hissing whisper. "No, she hasn't. Word is that she's in a coma."

"A coma!"

"Yeah. She knocked the dickens out of her head. She fell into an open grave! I think that is *so* yucky! Seems the grave had been dug for a service this morning and covered with a piece of plywood, but someone—probably some teenagers who were out tearin' around last night—moved the plywood. I think the cops found tire tracks and a beer bottle near the grave and—"

"Tally, I don't care about any of that!" Irma snapped. "Is there a chance Deirdre could die?"

"I dunno. I'm still in trainin'. The doctors don't consult with me. They think all I'm good for is emptying bedpans." Tally sounded deeply offended and her voice rose. "They think they're God Almighty. They'll go nuts if Deirdre dies and proves they can't really save anybody." She paused. "What do you want to know all of this for?"

"Her father and I are . . . involved."

Tally gasped. "*Really?* Are you sure? I heard he didn't even *look* at anyone since his wife died."

"Tally, lower that voice! And yes, Ben and I are *deeply* involved. We're simply keeping our relationship quiet for now." Mentally, Irma dared Tally to challenge her again. "I just didn't want to keep calling him because he's so busy with Deirdre."

"Doin' what? She's out like a light."

"I needed the information, Tally. I'm concerned, that's all."

"Well, if you two are an item, why don't you come and be with Mr. Mayhew? He'd probably appreciate it."

"I told you we're keeping our affair a secret. Besides, I have a terrible cold. I wouldn't want to give it to Deirdre or anyone else." Irma coughed and blew her nose to give her story credence. "Thanks for telling me about Deirdre and don't tell anyone I called."

"Why can't I tell anyone you called?" Tally twanged, but Irma had already hung up.

Irma slogged back into the living room and picked up the paper again, her gaze moving back to the story about Deirdre. Chyna wasn't mentioned, but the way news traveled around here, half of the people in Black Willow already knew she'd been the one to find Deirdre. They'd be thankful. They'd respect her. Hell, Chyna might even become some sort of hero.

Irma raised her head and smiled slowly. Yes, Chyna might be a hero *unless* people got the impression she'd found Deirdre because she'd already known exactly where to look for her. And how would she know that if she wasn't responsible for Deirdre's abduction and near death?

5

Chyna sighed and rolled over in bed, reaching for Scott as if he'd slept beside her for years. But the other side of the bed was empty. She glanced at the bedside clock. Four-fifteen. He couldn't be gone, she thought with a mixture of disappointment and embarrassment. He wouldn't have just had sex with her, waited until she drifted off to sleep, then left. *Left,* how about *escaped* before anyone saw his car in her driveway? Oh God, he wouldn't have, not after the things he'd said to her. Not after the tender yet passionate way he'd made love to her. Or would he? She'd cared about him for so long, had she been imagining he actually felt something for her other than momentary lust?

At that moment, Scott opened her bedroom door and walked softly to the bed. He was barefoot and wearing only jeans. In the dim light of first dawn, she could see his soft smile. He slipped off the jeans, then crawled into bed next to her and took her into his arms.

"Where have you been?" she asked, trying to sound casual.

"I had a nightmare," he said quietly. "They're frequent these days. I went downstairs, tossed cold water all over my face, and had a glass of warm milk."

"Warm milk? You wild man."

"I know." He made a face. "I hope that piece of information doesn't get loose at the Whippoorwill. I'll never be able to set foot in there again."

Chyna reached out and touched his moist, flushed face and his damp hair. "I thought you were gone."

He frowned. "Do you want me to leave?"

"Oh no!" She'd sounded frantic. "Of course not," she said in a more normal tone.

He smiled again, drawing her closer against him. "Good. Because at this moment, I'm happier than I've been for years."

"You are?"

"I am. Cross my heart and hope to die."

"Don't say that!" Chyna snapped.

Scott pulled back, looking deep into her eyes. "It's just a phrase."

"I know, but . . ."

"But what?"

Chyna buried her left hand in his thick, black hair, placing her cheek next to his. "I just don't want to think about dying right now."

Scott laughed softly. "Neither of us is going to die, Chyna. Maybe I'm the one with second sight today, because I'm certain we're going to be together for a long, long time. At least, if I get my way, we are."

Chyna relaxed, feeling as if her warm, naked body were sinking into his. "Then I hope you get your way, because I believe it's what I want more than anything," Chyna murmured as his lips closed over hers.

"Satisfaction . . . oh no, no, no! I can't get no . . ."

Chyna jerked awake, the words drumming in her head. The song by the Rolling Stones. The off-key voice. The good-looking man on the ladder. Gage Ridgeway!

Scott lay deep asleep beside her. His black hair had tumbled over his forehead, and one of his arms lay across her waist. His mouth was open slightly. The creases she'd noticed in his forehead and around his eyes seemed almost invisible in the morning sunshine. Except for the narrow, healing scars on his cheek and jaw, he looked the way she remembered him almost ten years ago—handsome, calm, at peace. She hated to wake him, but they needed to go someplace. *Now.*

"Scott," she whispered, not wanting to startle him. He remained motionless. "Scott," she murmured. Nothing. Finally, she said, "Scott," aloud while gently shaking his shoulder.

"Sleepy," he mumbled. "Ten more minutes, Mom."

"I am not your mother," Chyna said, a bit louder this time. "It's Chyna."

"Chyna," he slurred. Then his eyes flew open and he looked at her in shock. "Chyna Greer!"

"Yes, it is Chyna Greer. So glad you remembered who you slept with last night."

He was fully awake now and blushing slightly. "I didn't mean I didn't remember; it's just . . ." Scott blinked a couple of times, looked at her closely, then said, "Thank God. For a minute I thought you were still a teenager."

"Well, I'm not. Everything's perfectly legal, although I think Michelle is a bit put out with you for taking her side of the bed."

"Sorry, Michelle," Scott called to the dog who lay on the floor. Then he leaned over and kissed Chyna. "Did last night really happen or did I just have the best dream of my life?"

"It really happened and it was wonderful."

"We should have done this sooner."

"Oh, I agree. I've only been fantasizing about it for around sixteen years."

"That long, eh?" Scott grinned. "I made myself wait until you were legal before I started fantasizing."

"And then did nothing about it."

"I move slowly. Slowly and deliberately. And then . . . I pounce!" Scott did indeed pounce on her, tangling her in sheets and his arms, kissing her cheeks, her neck, her lips. "You beautiful, fantastic woman. Girl of my dreams."

"O Man of mine."

They were giggling at their own absurdity when Scott suddenly turned serious and shushed her. "Rex is in the house," he hissed. "I heard him when I got up earlier."

"For your milk, I remember." Scott blushed. "And you think Rex, the Playboy of the Western World, would be shocked that you spent the night with me?" Chyna grinned. "He's probably relieved. I believe he thinks I'm some strange creature who has no interest in sex, only books and hard work."

"Well, you certainly aren't the latter, I'm thrilled to say. Wait until I tell my mother!"

"Scott Kendrick, don't you dare!" Chyna laughed, then grew solemn. "My mother wouldn't have minded, as long as I wasn't a passing fling. . . ."

Scott's eyes widened. "I thought we got that straight a few hours ago."

"I know what we said, but one night together doesn't mean you owe me anything, Scott."

"How about if I *want* to owe you something? I told you—"

"You could have been light-headed from the warm milk."

Scott pulled the pillow from under his head and acted as if he were going to hit her with it. "Will you quit bringing up the warm milk?" She giggled. "How about if I want to give you everything I can, Chyna? Of course I'm probably scaring you, talking about giving you everything as if you even want everything, or anything, from me, especially since I'm not exactly at my peak—"

Chyna kissed his neck. "Scott, quit babbling."

"Babbling?" He drew back as if affronted. "I'm pouring out my heart and you say I'm babbling?"

Chyna began floundering out of bed, tossing back her thick hair, stepping over Michelle, and reaching for her robe. "I didn't mean 'babbling.' I loved every word."

"I could tell."

"But I woke you up for a reason. I dreamed of Gage Ridgeway."

"Oh great. You were in bed with me and dreaming of Gage Ridgeway."

"We have to see him because the dream has something to do with Deirdre." Chyna pulled a pair of jeans out of the closet and slid them on. "You said he lives near the cemetery. He dated Edie Larson and she went missing."

Scott squinted at the bedside clock. "Chyna, it's seven-thirty. You want to go see Gage at seven-thirty?"

"Yes." She struggled into a turtleneck sweater, realized she had it on backward, and turned it around. "I can go alone if you're too sleepy."

Scott threw back the covers. "I am not letting you go to Gage Ridgeway's house alone when you obviously think he had something to do with Deirdre's abduction. Maybe we should call the police."

"And say what? That I had a dream about Gage? I don't think so."

"What did you dream? Did you see him holding Deirdre prisoner?"

"No. I saw Edie Larson. She was with a man, arguing with him. Then I saw Nancy Tierney. She was lying naked on a bed and a man was standing over her. In both scenes, I saw the girls clearly, but the man was fuzzy. I kept struggling to see him and suddenly I did. He was up on a ladder, cleaning leaves and debris from a gutter. He was singing 'Satisfaction.' Scott, that happened the day after I got home. I heard singing, looked out, and Gage was cleaning the gutters and singing 'Satisfaction'!"

"And what are we going to do?" Scott was fastening his own jeans and reaching for a sweater. "Make a citizen's arrest? Drag Gage into the sheriff's office, where he'll spill his guts without asking for a lawyer?"

"We're going to sit on him for a while. Where are my boots?" She didn't notice Scott's quizzical look as she located the boots in a corner. "I have a feeling Gage won't be in his house or anywhere else around here much longer."

"You mean he knows Deirdre's been found. She's unconscious, but he's going to take off before she wakes up and accuses him?"

Chyna frowned. "I'm not sure. I don't know exactly what's going on." She closed her eyes and shook her head. "All I know for certain is that I feel compelled to go to Gage's house."

CHAPTER NINETEEN

1

The sun shone softly on the Black Willow Cemetery. In the daylight, the place looked sad but benign with its gravestones and flower offerings for the dead all set in carefully maintained grounds. Chyna thought of how it had looked last night—vast, moon-bleached, and cold. She shivered. She could not rid herself of the image of Deirdre's slender, crumpled body lying at the bottom of an open grave.

"I'll never be able to look at that place the same again," Chyna said.

"You should be proud of yourself," Scott countered. "Without you, Deirdre would have lain there all night and maybe died of exposure."

"I felt her being taken, Scott. I should have been able to find her then, before she spent a night God-knows-where, a prisoner, and got free only to wander around blind and freezing and then fall into that grave." She shuddered. "I wonder if she's still unconscious."

"I guess we'll find out when we finish whatever it is you have in mind for Gage." Scott turned off the highway onto a side road leading to the Ridgeway farm. "You still haven't told me your master plan."

"That's because I don't have one. I'm waiting for inspiration to strike."

"Well, can you do anything to speed it along? Because we're half a mile from Gage's house."

"Don't rush me. You're making me nervous."

Scott looked at her, half in amusement, half in astonishment. "I know you think Gage probably took Deirdre. Are you suddenly getting nervous about how *we're* going to capture him and turn him over to the police?"

"I didn't say he took Deirdre."

"You didn't *say* it, but I assumed . . ." Chyna looked at him. "I guess I shouldn't assume anything where you're concerned."

"Where my power, or ESP, is concerned, you shouldn't assume anything. Even *I* can't assume anything," Chyna replied, thinking of the things she'd said to him in the night. "Where my emotions are concerned . . . well, I know myself fairly well. I mean exactly what I say."

"Oh." She heard the poorly muted relief in his voice. "I'm glad you know where you stand emotionally." He looked straight ahead. "I've heard Gage doesn't like uninvited visitors and he keeps a shotgun by the door. He might not take too kindly to our just dropping by before eight in the morning. I really think we should call the police."

"Considering that Gage was a suspect when Edie Larson disappeared, I assume they went to Gage's right after Deirdre was found," Chyna said.

"So he might already be in custody."

Chyna shook her head. "I don't think so. And don't ask me how I know because I don't know how I know. I'm not even sure I know."

"That was too complicated for me. I'm not going to ask anything else," Scott said in a resigned voice. "I'm just going to take orders like a good soldier. I know when I'm out of my league."

"You're not out of your league."

"Oh yeah, I am. *Way* out. You're the one with the connection to the Powers That Be."

Chyna grinned. "The Powers That Be. I'll remember that. It sounds a lot better than 'the Spirit World.' "

Scott slowed down as they passed the large red barn and drew near the large two-story white house with green shutters. The place looked like it had been freshly painted in the summer and everything was in perfect repair, just as Chyna would have expected of a Ridgeway Construction owner. Gage's truck was parked in front of the house, and sparrows and cardinals took turns at a bird feeder a few feet away from the porch.

"Ready for the assault?" Scott asked, putting the car in park.

"I thought we'd just knock on the door first," Chyna said. "If we assault, Gage might get out that shotgun, and all we have is a flashlight."

"Excellent point." Scott turned off the car. "Sit still. I'll open the door for you and, once again, I go up to the door first like a true man protecting his woman."

His woman. Chyna felt a thrill run through her, but she tried not to beam at him. No sense acting like I'm sixteen, she thought, even though she felt sixteen. And happy. And in love.

Scott opened the car door with a flourish and she climbed out. He gently pushed her behind him as they climbed up the porch steps. Scott knocked and they stood, both staring at the door as if they were ready for it to fly open to reveal a wild-eyed man holding a shotgun. Instead, there was only silence.

"Knock again," Chyna said. "Louder, but not loud enough to scare him."

"Yes, ma'am." Scott knocked. They waited, both beginning to glance around the well-swept porch, the old barrels obviously used as planters in the summer, a gray wooden rocking chair sitting at the corner of the porch where Gage could look out over acres of land bearing no crops. "One more time?" Scott asked.

"Yes. A little louder."

The knock. The wait. No answer. "He's not here," Chyna said, reaching beyond Scott and turning the doorknob. The door opened. "He left without his truck or without locking his house door."

Chyna pushed the door open and leaned inside. Scott pulled

her back. "We can't go in there, Chyna. It's private property and we aren't law enforcement officers with a warrant."

"Of course we're not law enforcement officers. We're concerned friends. There's nothing wrong with concerned friends stepping into someone's house and calling for him, especially when the friends are afraid something bad has happened."

"Something bad?"

"I told you, Scott. I dreamed about Gage and I woke up feeling like something wasn't right. Maybe that feeling meant he'd been the person who took Deirdre. But maybe it meant something else, like *he's* in danger."

"From whom?"

"From someone who thought he took Deirdre when he didn't. Maybe from the person who did take Deirdre."

"I thought you believed the person who took Deirdre is the same one who took Zoey and Edie and Heather."

"I do." She looked at him. "What I never told you is that I'm not sure it was a man. Oh, it probably was, but no one has ever *seen* these girls being taken. Not even me. I *felt* Deirdre being grabbed, chloroformed, and dragged away, but I didn't see who did it." Scott was looking at her in astonishment. "Okay, odds are it is a man, but that doesn't mean another man is safe from him, especially if he thinks he's suspected as being the killer of those girls and the abductor of Deirdre."

"I can't imagine a woman . . . Chyna, why would a woman take these girls?"

"Jealousy? She picks out certain girls she hates? I don't know." She looked into Scott's eyes. "I'm just tossing out a theory that crossed my mind a few days ago when I was looking at a picture of Zoey and me taken at the Fourth of July barbecue the day before she vanished. The party wasn't only attended by men. I believe Miss Irma Vogel was there."

"You think *Irma* kidnapped these girls?"

"Even you said she's jealous of pretty girls. She's large, to put it politely. We saw out on my lawn that she doesn't have the sweetest disposition in the world. In fact, she might be crazy." Chyna lifted her shoulders. "I don't know, Scott," she said impatiently. "I haven't thought this through. I have no otherworldly knowledge on this particular matter. I'm just making a suggestion." Scott continued to stare at her and she leaned into the house again and shouted, "Gage!"

After thirty seconds, Scott asked, "You didn't really expect an answer, did you?"

"Are you reading my mind?"

"No. You just haven't acted like you were expecting him to be here."

"I was hoping he was." Chyna paused. "Maybe he's here, but he's hurt or something. Let's go in."

"Oh no, Chyna, that would be breaking and entering."

"We're not going to break anything—not a window, not a lock." Scott frowned. "Well, I'm going in," Chyna announced. "You can wait on the porch if you want."

"And act like a scared little girl?" Scott demanded in reproach. "I'm coming in, too. Ahead of you."

"I don't know why you always insist on walking ahead of me. You aren't armed, either."

"My mother taught me that when a gentleman is with a lady, he always walks nearest to the curb, in case a passing carriage splashes water, and he always leads the way into dangerous situations."

"I had no idea your mother was so wise," Chyna said lightly, although she had to admit she felt a bit nervous walking into Gage Ridgeway's house. She didn't trust him. At the same time, she couldn't shake the feeling that she was meant to find him, for what reason she had no idea. "Gage?" she called again. "It's Chyna Greer. And Scott Kendrick. Are you awake?"

They both stood absolutely still in the silent house. Chyna glanced around. The furnishings were old, the house not exactly dirty but not neat and clean, either. Sun shone through an eastern window and she saw dust motes floating in the air. She also noticed that the walls were bare. Gage obviously was not interested in interior decoration.

"I'm going upstairs," she whispered, although apparently they were alone.

"I don't think he's up there. He hasn't answered."

"Maybe he *can't* answer. Come on, Scott. It will only take a minute. Then we'll get out of here."

With a sigh, Scott led the way up the wooden stairs badly in need of refinishing. They walked down a long hallway, pausing to look into three bedrooms, each with the bed made and a layer of dust on the dressers. Then they came to the fourth. Gage's room, Chyna knew at once. It was the largest and the messiest, the dressers covered with keys, belts, boxes meant to hold tie clasps and cuff links Chyna was certain Gage never wore, magazines, shoelaces, and a couple of dirty glasses.

A wallet lay near the edge of the dresser, not ten feet away from her, with some bills stuffed carelessly at the top. Immediately Chyna saw that two of the bills were fifties. Glancing around the room, she also spotted a police scanner on a table near the window. The bed was unmade. In fact, it was badly rumpled, the top sheet and spread barely hanging on to one of the bed's corners. On the floor lay a lamp with a broken base and a shattered glass. Chyna tiptoed toward the lamp and glass.

"Chyna, don't," Scott said firmly. "I think this might be a crime scene."

"I won't disturb anything. I just want to see if there's any blood."

"Don't—"

"I won't touch anything! I watch TV, too, you know. I know not to contaminate evidence." She stayed a foot away from the lamp and glass but studied them carefully. Then she walked backward, keeping her feet in the prints she'd made walking toward the broken objects. "No blood that I can see."

Scott gazed at the bed, the lamp, and the glass. Finally, he said, "Do you think that after Deirdre was found so close to Gage's house, someone decided he'd taken her, came here, and dragged him away?"

"To kill him?"

Scott nodded.

"Who would get carried away enough to do something like that except maybe Deirdre's father?"

"The father of one of the other missing girls, assuming that if Gage took Deirdre, he also took Heather or Edie?"

"Maybe," Chyna said reluctantly, "but I think Heather Phelps's family moved out west. And can you see Ron Larson getting wound up enough to come after Gage? He was probably already drunk by the time any news of Deirdre being found went out even over the police scanner." She paused. "I'm going to touch the bedclothes."

"Chyna, *no*!"

She ignored Scott and once again tiptoed across the floor, a couple of times stepping in prints she'd already made, and reached for the sheet. "I'll just touch with my knuckles so I don't leave any prints. Of course, I don't want to disturb prints, either. . . ."

"Chyna, do you watch cop shows *all* the time?" Scott demanded.

"Only when I'm not on duty at the hospital," she said absently as her knuckles brushed across the low-thread-count sheet. Then she moved them slightly to the right, farther up, across from her—

Chyna's vision blurred, darkened, then cleared. She saw Gage almost writhing under the covers, his face sweaty and flushed. Slowly, his breathing returned to normal and he lowered his head, looking into the face of a girl with green eyes and thick, shiny ash-blond hair.

Although she'd only seen her in death before, Chyna instantly recognized the girl—Nancy Tierney.

"Oh!" Chyna jerked back her hand as if it had been burned. "My God!"

"What is it?" Scott barked.

"It was Gage, and he was making love to Nancy Tierney."

"Nancy Tierney!" Scott exploded. "Gage was in bed with Nancy Tierney?"

"Yes, but it couldn't have been last night. She's been dead for days. Still . . ."

"Gage was involved with Nancy Tierney," Scott said flatly. "I can't believe it. Gage and *her*?"

"Scott, you don't live in Black Willow and you barely

know Gage Ridgeway anymore." She paused. "And why are you so surprised that he was involved with Nancy? You said you didn't know her at all."

Scott gave her a startled look, then blinked a couple of times. "I was surprised because of her age. Gage is what? Thirty-two, like your brother? Nancy was just a teenager."

"That's not all you meant." Chyna looked at him steadily. "You know Gage liked younger girls. Edie was only sixteen when she dated Gage and he was only a month or two away from twenty. So why are you so surprised Gage was with Nancy?"

"Sixteen and twenty isn't seventeen and thirty-something," Scott replied vaguely. Chyna felt as if he was floundering for an answer to her question, not telling her the whole truth. "Uh, did Nancy look like she was being raped?"

"Not at all," Chyna said firmly. She stared at Scott, the feeling that he wasn't being completely honest making her want to draw away from him. She thought he was conscious of her wariness, but he determinedly stared back, almost as if he were daring her to ask him another question. "Nancy didn't look like she was struggling to get away from Gage," Chyna stated, "but I'll try again since you seem to have some doubt."

"You do that," Scott said with a trace of acid in his voice.

Chyna again touched the blanket with her knuckles. She expected to see Gage again having sex with Nancy. Instead, she saw him asleep in the darkened bedroom. Someone pounded on the door downstairs and Gage jolted up in the bed. More pounding downstairs. Gage half-climbed, half-fell out of the bed. And then . . . nothing. Chyna closed her eyes and concentrated, but she knew with disappointed familiarity that the vision had ended.

"Well?" Scott asked.

"I just saw him sleeping. Then heard the knocking," she said.

"That's all?"

"That's all. Sorry." Suddenly an awful possibility flashed into Chyna's mind. In her vision, Gage's curtains were parted to show the night sky. Someone had come to Gage's door in the night. Last night? Last night while Chyna slept peacefully, and alone, while Scott was supposedly in the kitchen drinking warm milk? But why would Scott—

"Well?" Chyna jumped as Scott turned his penetrating gaze on her. "Do you know who came to the door?"

"No," she said emphatically. "I don't see who was at the door."

"It was probably the cops, Chyna. Last night you said they'd probably go after him immediately."

"Yeah. The knocking must have come right after Deirdre was found. Ned said the cops put him through hell after Edie disappeared. They had to be looking at him pretty closely this time, too."

"Especially if anyone knew he'd been seeing Nancy." Scott shook his head. "God. Edie and Nancy. One definitely dead, the other missing for years. I sure wouldn't want to be in his shoes right now."

"I wouldn't, either, if he knew Deirdre had been found. But he was asleep."

"But you don't know if that vision was from last night," Scott said.

It was, she thought, remembering the chatter over Gage's police scanner saying that Deirdre Mayhew had been found, the dispatcher sending emergency vehicles to the grave site. But Chyna didn't want to tell all of that to Scott. Why? Because he'd left her bed in the middle of the night?

Chyna wrapped her arms around herself, glanced at the bed again, and said, "I want to look outside."

"Good. If we get caught in here . . ."

"I know. Twenty years of hard labor at a maximum-security prison."

"You're taking this way too lightly, Chyna. Don't forget that not everyone in this town is exactly fond of you." She looked at him, stung. "I don't mean to be cruel, but you have to watch your step. Don't forget that crowd outside your house yesterday. I don't think they were members of your fan club."

Chyna continued to look at him in injured surprise for a

moment, then glanced away and nodded. "You're right. A lot of people in this town think I'm a kook. A lot of people think I had something to do with the disappearance of those girls. It's so ludicrous, I sometimes forget that public opinion can get you in a lot of trouble."

"So let's get out of here," Scott said.

But as they started toward his car, Chyna stopped, looking over at a small aluminum building. "I wonder what's in there."

"I don't know. I don't care. I think this is a matter for the police now."

Chyna didn't seem to hear him. She walked to the building and opened one of the double doors. "More unlocked doors," she said. "Gage must be a trusting soul."

"Chyna, we are *not* going in there," Scott said forcefully as Chyna opened the door wider, letting sunlight flow into the small building, and stepped inside. Scott sighed, muttered, "Oh, hell!" and followed her.

When he reached the door, he saw Chyna standing motionless about two feet within the doors on a clean concrete floor. Well, we don't have to worry about footprints, he thought, unless they'd managed to pick up some mud on their shoes. But it hadn't rained for days. The earth was dry.

Finally, after watching Chyna for a couple of minutes, he couldn't stand it any longer. "Sense anything?" he boomed, startled by the volume of his own voice.

Chyna jumped and turned to him. "For heaven's sake, Scott, I'm right here. You don't have to shout."

"Sorry." He glanced around. A tractor, a ride lawn mower, and a motorcycle. Scott couldn't resist walking toward the motorcycle and lifting up the canvas. A blue Electra Glide. Maybe twenty years old, he thought, and an absolute dream! He'd wanted one of these for so many years, yet always found an excuse not to buy one. But Gage hadn't. It was all Scott could do not to swing his leg over the seat and—

"Found your one true love?" Chyna asked right behind him. "You should see the look of ecstasy on your face."

"Ecstasy? That's nonsense," Scott snapped, his cheeks

growing red. "This is a really nice model, a classic, kept in perfect condition. I was just admiring what good care Gage has taken of it."

"Um-hmm." Chyna smirked. "Scott, only sometimes I can read minds, but I can always read facial expressions. You were picturing yourself tearing down a highway with the wind in your hair and a girl on the back clutching your waist."

He grinned sheepishly at her. "Well, maybe you're right. But the girl was you."

Chyna cocked her head, narrowed her eyes, then winked at him. "Yeah. The girl *was* me. That makes it okay."

"Thank God," he breathed, dropping the canvas back in place. "Picking up on anything?"

"Maybe," Chyna said. She walked over to a dirty white blanket lying near a wall. The remains of a cobweb clung to one corner along with several small pieces of black grit. She stooped down and, avoiding the grit, placed her knuckles on the blanket.

A girl. So cold, so frightened. Her auburn hair spilled around her chalky face. The dirty blanket had scooted up to her calves, exposing bare feet and duct tape on her ankles, ankles she twisted furiously, obviously trying to loosen the duct tape. Got to hurry, the girl thought. Got to hurry while I still have time— Then one of the front doors opened.

Chyna gasped and jerked her hand away from the blanket. "It was Deirdre," she whispered almost convulsively. "Deirdre was wrapped up in this blanket, waiting for someone to come and kill her."

2

Chyna and Scott were getting into the car when a police cruiser pulled up with two officers inside. "Oh no, I knew it," Scott groaned.

"Don't look so guilty. We haven't done anything wrong."

"Except poke around another man's house."

The officer who had been driving tapped on Scott's window and he rolled it down, fixing his face in a tight, unnatural smile. "Yes, sir?" he asked in a bright voice that made Chyna want to cringe. He sounded guilty as hell of something.

"What's your business here, sir?" the officer asked.

"We just dropped by to see Gage Ridgeway," Scott answered. Chyna let out her breath. At least Scott's voice sounded casual. "Is there a problem?"

"You always go visiting at eight in the morning?"

"Is it that early?" Scott raised his arm and looked at his watch. Chyna noticed a fresh scrape on the side of his left hand that ran up under the cuff of his sweater. It had just begun to form a scab. At last, Scott's commanding spirit seemed to return. "It's eight-thirty, Officer, but I don't see what that has to do with anything. We had some work we wanted Gage to do and thought we'd catch him early." The policeman continued to stare at them. "Officer, is there anything special you want with us, or are we free to go?"

"I want to know if Gage Ridgeway is in that house."

"No, he isn't," Scott said. "We knocked on the door three times."

"Did you go inside?"

Fingerprints, Chyna thought quickly. She wasn't wearing gloves. "I tried the doorknob. The door was unlocked, so I stuck in my head and yelled for Gage. No answer. I also opened the door to that aluminum building over there. That's where he keeps his motorcycle. I wanted to see if he was out riding this morning." Chyna hoped her color wasn't rising to betray her lie. She hadn't even known until a few minutes ago that Gage still owned his motorcycle. "It was there."

"So where do you suppose he is?"

"We have no idea." Scott shifted the car into drive. "Sorry we can't be of any help, Officer, but we really should be getting home," he said almost curtly.

Scott didn't wait for an answer. He simply drove past the police cruiser and out the long drive to the highway. "We made a big mistake going into Gage's house without his or the police's permission," he said finally.

"If either the house or the aluminum storage building was a crime scene, it would have been marked," Chyna returned. "I think the police just wanted to question Gage."

"Or arrest him."

"With what evidence? His house hadn't been searched."

"Until we came along."

Chyna made a derisive face. "I'd hardly call that little glancing around we did a search and we certainly didn't disturb evidence."

"Didn't we?" Scott asked. "What about that blanket in the shed? You said Deirdre had been wrapped up in it. She wasn't one of Gage's girlfriends like Nancy. You said you felt her fear. She was held in that building, Chyna. Gage took her and he kept her prisoner in that building. Somehow, she managed to get loose and make it to the cemetery. Gage didn't know. I saw the police scanner in his room. He must have had it on, heard that Deirdre had been found, and run. It's obvious."

Chyna thought for a moment. "I don't think it's obvious at all, Scott. In my vision, Gage was asleep. He was awakened by someone knocking on his front door." She paused. "But if you're right and he ran away, why isn't there any sign of hurried flight in his house? His wallet was lying on his dresser. He'd need money. His truck was there."

"He wouldn't take his wallet with all of his identification in it, Chyna. And he sure wouldn't take a truck with 'Ridgeway Construction' plastered on the side of it."

Chyna had to agree with Scott, yet some things didn't add up. She'd seen two fifty-dollar bills in Gage's wallet. He would have needed cash. And naturally he wouldn't have taken the truck, but what about the motorcycle? Chyna made up her mind. Whether or not Gage had abducted Deirdre, he had not made a run for it after she was found. Something else accounted for his disappearance—something terribly wrong.

CHAPTER TWENTY

1

When Chyna and Scott reached the Greer house, both garage doors had been raised and she saw Rex's car sitting beside hers. "I didn't even notice earlier," she said. "When we left this morning, was Rex's car here?"

Scott shook his head. "The garage doors were down and my car was in the driveway. I didn't notice, either. I'm sure he didn't stay out all night, though."

"I'm not," Chyna fumed. "Honest to God, if he spent the night with some woman and left me here all alone . . ."

Scott looked troubled. "Don't blow a gasket yet, Chyna. You said he was going to Owen Burtram's, probably to prevent trouble between him and Rusty. Maybe something happened. . . ."

Chyna fumbled with her key, suddenly nervous, more frightened than she'd been invading Gage Ridgeway's house, and burst through the house. "Rex!" she yelled. "Rex, are you here?"

"In the kitchen," he called, but he didn't sound right. He sounded weak and . . . she didn't want to think about the possibilities. She grabbed Scott's hand and dragged him behind her as she ran for the kitchen.

When she reached the doorway, she stopped so fast Scott bumped into the back of her, knocking him back a step.

"Sorry," he said, but she didn't hear him. She'd fully expected to find Rex lying on the floor, probably having suffered from a heart attack just like her mother.

Instead, Rex sat at the table with a mug of coffee and the morning newspaper. He wore an old flannel robe over pajamas. In the many times Rex had stayed in this house, Chyna had never seen him in his nightclothes. He always came downstairs freshly shaven, his thick hair carefully combed, and wearing a shirt or sweater with designer jeans or khakis. This morning, stubble covered the grayish-tinted skin of his face. He looked up and Chyna saw that his eyes were sunken, almost lost in hollows and shadows. He didn't even nod a greeting to them. He just held out the newspaper and said, "Rusty Burtram is dead."

"Dead," Chyna repeated blankly. Then the import of Rex's words hit her. "Dead! How? Oh my God, not Owen?"

"I don't know." Rex's usually buoyant voice was flat. "Read the details for yourself, not that they'll tell you much."

Chyna nearly snatched the newspaper from Rex's hand. He was right. All she learned was that Rusty had fallen through a sliding glass door in his home and died of massive blood loss caused by lacerations. Not even a time of death was given, although a neighbor was quoted as saying she'd heard a "loud crashing sound" at Rusty's house around nine o'clock. Chyna looked at Rex. "How long did you stay with Owen?"

"Twenty minutes, tops," Rex said dully. "He got a call and said he had to go to the funeral home. I told him I'd wait until he got back, but he said he'd be gone quite a while. He obviously wanted to get rid of me. I went to Ned's for a little while, but he had to leave, too, and I could tell Bev was in a hurry to get the kids ready for bed, so I left there, too."

Chyna said sharply, "And just figured Rusty was safe and went off on another one of your mysterious jaunts."

"No, I did not!" For the first time, Rex's voice sounded normal. "After I left Ned's, I parked down the street from Rusty's house. Thought I'd do a little surveillance. I felt ridiculous, but I couldn't forget the look on Owen's face even after we got back to his place. It was scary, Chyna, and I don't scare easily. Anyway, after I'd sat outside Rusty's for over an hour, this woman kept looking out her window at me. Then she came out and glared at me from her porch a couple of times. I think it was the woman quoted in the newspaper as hearing the 'loud crashing sound' at Rusty's. I could tell she was suspicious of me—probably thought I was casing her house for a robbery–and she was going to call the cops.

"So I left," Rex continued. "I drove around for about twenty minutes with every intention of going back to Rusty's. Then the car began losing power. I barely got over to the curb before it went dead. I just bought a battery last month, so I knew it was the alternator and there would be no help until morning. No cab service in this town at that time either. I started walking and finally I stopped at Harlon Watkins's. Woke him and his wife up, but they were pretty gracious. They gave me a cup of coffee and she loaned me her car.

"I drove back to Owen's and saw his car in his driveway. Then I passed by Rusty's. Everything looked calm there, too." Rex grimaced. "No wonder. All the excitement had happened hours earlier. Rusty was already dead, the ambulance and police were gone, and the house was dark. The crime scene tape must have been in the back around the sliding glass doors and I didn't see it. So I dragged myself home, thinking everything was all right. Then the morning paper came and I read the headline." Rex smiled ruefully. "Some hero I am." He looked at Chyna. "Not like you. I saw the other headline, too. You saved Deirdre."

Chyna scanned the article, then said, "Uncle Rex, my name isn't mentioned. What makes you think *I* found her?"

He smiled at her. "Just a feeling, Chyna. As soon as I read the article, I knew it had to be you. But if I had any doubts, someone called here just before you came in. A woman. She said something like, 'Big miracle. Who does she think she's fooling? Chyna found Deirdre because *Chyna* took her!'"

"Someone thinks *I* took Deirdre?" Chyna exclaimed.

"You're surprised after that little scene on the lawn the other day?" Rex asked drily. "I'm pretty sure the woman on the phone was that awful Vogel creature, but you have other enemies out there, Chyna. You *must* be careful, honey."

"I will," Chyna mumbled, then couldn't help adding, "I guess you haven't been MIA so much because you were sneaking off to be with Irma Vogel, Mrs. Rex Greer number five."

Rex choked on his coffee and finally burst into the old, uncontrolled laughter she knew so well. In spite of her sadness and uneasiness about how Rusty had died, she was relieved to have her uncle acting normal, even though he suddenly looked old and haggard. "I'd swear off *all* women for good before I'd even touch her! Gee, Chyna, give me credit for having *some* taste!"

"I'm going to call Ben's cell phone and find out how Deirdre's doing," Scott interrupted. "She might be conscious by now."

Scott stepped into the other room, and in a moment, Chyna heard him speaking softly. She looked at Rex, whose laughter over Irma had disappeared. "Do you think while you were without your car, Owen went over and *killed* Rusty?"

Rex closed his eyes and shook his head, almost hanging it. "I'll never forgive myself if that happened. I knew there was going to be trouble. What's that song by Phil Collins you loved so much? 'In the Air Tonight.' Well, I felt trouble in the air last night. Serious trouble. I tried to stop it, but . . . well, making trouble, not preventing trouble, has always been my specialty."

Chyna reached across the kitchen table and covered his hand with hers. "Uncle Rex, you tried. You watched Owen; you watched Rusty. If your car breaking down prevented you from keeping an eye on Rusty, it's not your fault." She paused. "You could have called me. I would have taken up surveillance duties."

"Actually, I tried, Chyna. But you weren't home and I didn't know your cell phone number." She felt the blood

drain from her face, and remorse filled her. "Now, don't look
like that," Rex said. "We don't know anything except that
Rusty fell through those glass doors. Maybe he'd gotten so
scared he took pills or got drunk or both and just fell, without any help from anyone. Besides, you were out saving another life last night. If it weren't for you, Deirdre Mayhew
would probably be dead." A tear ran down Chyna's cheek,
though, as she thought of the agony of Rusty's expression
yesterday and the blind fear in his eyes when he saw his father at the door. "Chyna?" She looked at her uncle. "Not
even you, special as you are, can save everyone, honey."

When Scott came back into the kitchen, Chyna looked at
him hopefully. "Is Deirdre awake?"

Scott shook his head. "Ben's trying to sound upbeat, but I
can tell he's getting worried. He said the doctors claim she
hasn't suffered brain damage, but it's what he fears."

"Deirdre just can't have come so far only to slide away
into perpetual unconsciousness," Chyna said, "although as a
doctor, I know it's possible."

"I think I'll go over to the hospital and see Ben," Scott
said.

Chyna stood up. "I'll go with you."

Scott looked troubled for a moment, as if he was searching
for a kind way of saying something bad. Finally, he looked
her directly in the eye and said, "You going with me isn't a
good idea. A lot of people are there. You know the Black Willow grapevine—word was all over town long before the newspaper came out that Deirdre had not only been found, but
she'd been found by you. The trouble is that . . . well, it seems
some idiot has started the rumor that Deirdre was found by
you because you're the one who took her."

Chyna stared at him for a moment, her face frozen. Then
she spoke, her voice even. "Tell me truthfully. Does Ben believe that?"

"Oh God, no," Scott reassured her. "He's so grateful,
you'll probably be drowned in free pastries for the rest of
your life. But some of the other people . . ."

Chyna swallowed, then nodded. "This attitude isn't exactly

new to me, Scott. A lot of people thought I had something to do with Zoey's disappearance. And after the gang that gathered here on Sunday morning, I could hardly ignore the fact that bad feeling was building against me again."

Scott looked wretched. "The people who believe it are fools, Chyna. You can't let it trouble you."

"I won't." She paused. "Well, it will bother me a little bit. I can't help it. But I'll survive. You don't have to look like it's the end of the world."

He smiled. "Okay. I am going to the hospital to see Ben in a little while. I'll tell him you'd be there if you could." She nodded again. "And I have an appointment with my orthopedist in Huntington this afternoon. He wants to take a few more X-rays of me. I've had so many already, I feel like I should be glowing. Anyway, why don't you and I go out someplace quiet for dinner when I get back?"

"That sounds nice," Chyna said.

"Great. I'll pick you up around seven, all right?"

"I'll be ready."

She stood at the open door, smiling and waving as Scott drove away. As soon as he was out of sight, though, her smile disappeared. She hadn't wanted to let him know how much it bothered her that so many people in town believed her capable of hurting Deirdre or any young girl.

Also, Chyna didn't want him to know that she couldn't stop thinking of Rusty Burtram and Gage Ridgeway. One man appeared to have died in a fall, the other to have fled when the girl he'd kidnapped made her way to freedom.

Nevertheless, Chyna could not shake the feeling that neither scenario told the real story.

2

Rex sat at the table, drinking cup after cup of coffee until Chyna had to make a second pot. When it finished, she poured herself a cup and sat down with him. "I've never known you to just sit in pajamas and drink coffee most of the morning," she said. "What's wrong?"

"I think my age finally caught up with me," Rex said with a sad imitation of his insouciant smile.

"In twenty-four hours? Because you weren't like this yesterday."

"Maybe I just held on to youth, or the illusion of youth, too long. When you do that, it vanishes just like that." He snapped his fingers sharply and Chyna jumped.

"I would think vanishing so quickly would be caused by some precipitating incident," Chyna said easily, trying not to show that Rex was making her uneasy. "I'm sure it wasn't the death of Rusty Burtram. You hardly knew him."

"No, I didn't," Rex said casually, staring off in space. Then he looked at her. "Did you know your boyfriend was out and about last night?"

She looked at him in puzzlement. "Of course I know. He was out with me."

"No. Later. Or should I say earlier this morning? When I got home, I came in here to get a drink of water. I looked outside and there was Scott Kendrick, sitting on the side of the fountain."

"At four in the morning?"

"I didn't get home until shortly before five."

Five in the morning. She thought. She and Scott hadn't gotten home until two. They'd gone to bed, made love, and fallen asleep. She'd awakened to find him gone.

"What was Scott doing at the fountain?" she asked casually.

"I told you. He was just sitting there. Chyna, he was looking down staring at his hands as if they didn't belong to him. I opened the back door and said his name. He glanced up, absolutely expressionless, then went back to looking at his hands. I don't think he knew who I was. I'm not sure he even saw me, although I was standing in the light."

Rex paused. "Chyna, I have to say he gave me a fright, and I don't frighten easily. But Scott Kendrick spooked me.

I sat in the room next door until I heard him come in and go back upstairs. I followed him. I hovered for about five minutes, then peeked in your door and saw he was back in bed, murmuring to you, and finally you both went back to sleep. Sorry for the intrusion, honey, but I had to make sure you were safe."

Chyna took three sips of coffee before she could manage an easy, natural voice. "I'm sure there's an explanation, Rex. I'll ask him about it this evening."

"Are you sure you want to go out with him later?"

"Yes. Yes, absolutely sure," she said firmly, but all she could think about was the long, fresh scrape on Scott's hand that extended over his wrist and disappeared under the sleeve of his sweater.

It hadn't been there when they'd gone to bed last night.

3

Chyna felt as if this had been the longest day of her life. Rex finally showered and dressed, but his spirits didn't improve. He sat passive-faced in front of the television from morning into the afternoon. Around two o'clock, Chyna took Michelle for a walk, but the dog seemed to have absorbed the general malaise that consumed the Greer household. She ambled along, apparently uninterested in sniffing leaves and blasé about the ducks floating on Lake Manicora. When a daredevil squirrel ran about one foot in front of her nose, Michelle merely gazed at it, showing no excitement, much less an urge to pursue. "I know," Chyna said understandingly to the dog. "If the squirrel is that dumb, it's not even worth chasing."

When they returned to the house, the phone rang. Chyna answered and Beverly chirped excitedly, "Chyna, you found Deirdre! Why didn't you call and tell us? We had to hear it from neighbors."

"I was tired when we—I got home last night—"

"I'm sure," Beverly interrupted. "You found her in an

open *grave*. God, I get goose bumps just thinking about it. But you did find her. It's a miracle!"

"Not everyone thinks so. I hear there's a rumor going around that I knew where to find her because I abducted her. Apparently some people believe I was trying to get good publicity for myself."

"Oh, Chyna, anyone who thinks that is beyond stupid," Beverly said hotly. "I think I know who started the rumor. Miss Irma Vogel. She called here just a little while ago. I told her to *never* come near me or my children again. She acted dumbfounded, even after what she'd done at your house! And I'd bet a thousand dollars she's the one who started that awful rumor about you taking Deirdre. I think she's out of her mind."

"I do, too," Chyna said listlessly. "I just wonder how long she's been unbalanced, what other things she's done beside throw rocks at my house and start rumors."

Beverly went silent for a moment. "Oh, Chyna, I never even thought about what she might have done in the past, but then, I didn't think there was anything wrong with her except that she was a gossip and something of a pest, but considering how she's acted over this Deirdre incident, the hatred she's shown toward you . . ."

"Makes you wonder, doesn't it?" Chyna, who'd answered the phone in the kitchen, opened the refrigerator door, remembering that she hadn't eaten anything all day. As she scanned the contents, she asked, "Why did Irma call, anyway?"

"She wanted to tell us that Deirdre seems to be regaining consciousness. She's still really muddled, but they hope that by tonight she'll be able to say who abducted her."

4

Chyna had brought a couple of medical books home with her. Around five o'clock she sat down with them and attempted to read. Try as she might, though, she simply could not concentrate on arthropod-borne viral fevers or acute liver abscesses. Finally, in such a funk she childishly decided she didn't even care if she made it through her medical residency, she built a fire in the family room fireplace, went to the bookcase, found her old, well-worn copy of *Wuthering Heights,* and settled on the couch, pulling a colorful afghan over her, although the room was already warm. Michelle jumped up on the couch and laid her large blond head on Chyna's lap. Chyna rubbed the dog's ear with one hand and lost herself in the tragic, twisted love of Cathy and Heathcliff.

When the doorbell rang, Chyna looked up in surprise. She'd expected an influx of neighbors after Vivian's death, but there had been few. Maybe everyone had been too preoccupied by Deirdre's disappearance, she thought. Or maybe people had just wanted to avoid Vivian's daughter.

When the bell rang the second time, Chyna realized Rex wasn't going to answer it. She knew he was somewhere in the house, but perhaps he was taking a nap after having been awake all night. She gently moved Michelle's head off her lap, tossed aside the afghan and book, and hurried to the front door.

A young man dressed in a navy blue suit and coat stood on the porch. His cheeks were red and she had a feeling it wasn't from the cold. He was either embarrassed or uncomfortable. He held a large, sturdy brown bag in front of him.

"Miss—I mean Dr. Greer?" he asked.

"Yes. Chyna Greer."

"My name is Norman Holt. I work at the Burtram and Hodges Funeral Home."

"Oh!" Chyna uttered in surprise. "My goodness. I wasn't expecting anyone from the home. . . . I'm so sorry about Rusty."

"We all are, ma'am," he said dolefully. "Young Mr. Burtram was always good to me. Very patient, very kind. Not like—" He broke off and his cheeks grew redder. Not like the elder Mr. Burtram, Chyna thought. "Anyway, the funeral home is closed today because of Russel's—Mr. Burtram's—

death, but this was ready and I thought I'd just deliver it instead of making you come down to the home tomorrow or the next day, whenever Mr. Burtram—Mr. Owen Burtram—decides to open again." He thrust the bag at her. "Here."

Chyna took the bag, surprised by its weight. "What is this?"

Norman Holt went from red to fuchsia. "It's your mother, Dr. Greer, all cremated and tucked away in her urn. I'm sorry for your loss." With that he turned on his heel and walked quickly to his car, never looking at Chyna again as he backed out of the driveway.

She stood motionless, holding the large, weighty parcel, until Norman Holt's car disappeared. Then she looked down at the bag, slowly stepped back into the living room, and closed the front door. Once again, Michelle had drawn near her, so close her body pushed against Chyna's leg. "You always know when I'm upset, don't you, girl?" she muttered to the dog.

Chyna walked on stiff legs to the couch, held the bag for at least a minute, then slowly withdrew the heavy gold-plated urn that held the ashes of Vivian Greer. This could not be, Chyna thought. Ashes in an urn could not be the remains of her beautiful, loving, vivacious mother. Although no tears came to Chyna's eyes, a wave of desolation swept over her. "Dust in the wind," she murmured, and then in a strangled, agonized voice, "Mommy!"

This was all that was left of Vivian Greer. It seemed impossible to Chyna. This urn, heavy though it may be, could not contain the only earthly remnants of her mother's body. The thought was too bleak, too desolating.

Chyna leaned forward and set the urn on the coffee table. A flash of light from the fading sun caught its bronze luster and sent out a tiny beam of light—a beam that fell on the white box Ned had brought her. The box containing her mother's engagement ring. Chyna hadn't even looked at it yet.

Slowly, she removed the lid of the box. There on a square of cotton lay the beautiful platinum ring. Chyna slipped it on

the third finger of her left hand, holding it up to the light.
The two-carat center diamond gleamed amid its bed of platinum filigree and sapphires. She still thought it was the most
beautiful ring she'd ever seen. In fact, it looked even more
beautiful than ever. Chyna stared at it, mesmerized as it
sparkled and flashed with an almost unnatural brilliance. . . .

Vaguely, she became aware of Michelle beginning to
tremble. Then, slowly, the room darkened. For a moment
Chyna thought she was passing out. Then, like a bolt of
lightning, the room seemed to fill with golden sunlight. She
stiffened, blinked, then abruptly turned to look at the secre-
tary desk in the corner. After a moment, she saw the figure
of a woman writing on her blue-gray stationery.

"Mom," Chyna mumbled to the oblivious figure she knew
was only part of a vision. Her mother wore beautiful brown
slacks and a matching sweater, but her hair was drawn back
sloppily with a rubber band, her face was white and without
a trace of makeup, and her hands shook. She was writing furiously, as if she might not have enough time to finish all she
had to say, and beside her lay a pile of trinkets and a plastic
bag of the type usually used for leftover food.

I'm in the past, Chyna thought foggily. I'm in the past on
what I *know* was the last day of my mother's life.

Chyna sat frozen on the couch, staring at the desk where
she could see her mother writing frantically, nervously, stopping only occasionally to wipe her face with a tissue. She
was crying, Chyna thought. In all of her life, she had never
seen her mother cry.

Finally, Vivian had folded the sheets of stationery, then
reached for the plastic bag in which she placed the trinkets
that lay on the desk along with her letter. Vivian then picked
up a roll of tape and walked over to the portrait of her and
Chyna's father, the one in which Edward had looked so dis-
tinguished and she had looked so beautiful, confident, and
happy. Her face glistening with tears, Vivian took down the
large portrait and propped it against the wall with the back
facing outward. She then taped the plastic bag to the back of
the portrait, touched it once almost as if she were tempted to

remove it, then shook her head and said, "No," aloud. Vivian turned the painting around and, with an effort that betrayed her failing strength, lifted it and hung it back on the wall. Finally, she touched a spot on the portrait—her beautiful diamond and sapphire engagement ring, the ring she had promised Chyna would one day be hers—and said, "Find this package, Chyna. It's meant for you because you're the only one I trust to know what must be done."

As the vision faded, Chyna felt air leave her body in one long, profound sigh. The first day she'd been home, she'd looked at that portrait of her parents. They'd both seemed young and good-looking less than ten years ago. Vivian even had a twinkle in her beautiful blue-gray eyes.

Chyna had also looked at the ring—the ring given to her great-grandmother and passed through generations, the gorgeous platinum ring with the two-carat center diamond with four sapphires set in filigree on either side. She always gazed at that portrait when she came home and commented on what good-looking parents she had. Her mother had usually stood beside her, given her a nudge, and said playfully, "How you love that ring, little daughter. Don't worry. It will be yours someday." Vivian had known Chyna loved the portrait, so that's why she'd put something especially for her in that particular spot, Chyna thought. Behind the portrait Vivian had placed the letter she'd written so hurriedly, so emotionally. But Chyna had no idea what other trinkets Vivian had put in the plastic bag with the letter. There was only one way to find out.

With shaking hands, Chyna lifted the portrait off the wall and set it on the floor, the back side facing outward. The bag hung there, securely held by several strips of tape. Painstakingly, Chyna began to remove each strip, although she felt like ripping the bag off the portrait. She didn't want to damage anything, though. Both the painting and the bag were important, she reminded herself. She must be careful, careful.

When at last she'd freed the plastic bag, she looked at it with a pounding heart. No definite images came to her from it, yet it seemed to emanate an aura of despair and tragedy.

I don't want to open it, Chyna thought almost childishly. I don't want to read Mom's letter, and I don't want to touch those trinkets.

But she knew she had no choice. They had been left with urgency and only for her.

Her fingers trembling, Chyna withdrew the stationery and unfolded it to see her mother's handwriting. The letter was dated the day before her death:

> *My Dearest Daughter,*
> *This is the hardest letter I have ever had to write. You have always been the most precious person in my life and I have thanked God for you every day. I have felt that you truly love me, too, but after you read this, you certainly will never feel the same about your mother. The truth must be told, though, my confession made.*
>
> *Almost six years before your birth, I met your father. We began to see each other and I soon realized Edward loved me. I did not take his love lightly, but I was young, gregarious, some said wild, and Edward was too "tame" for me. I was still dating him, though, when he introduced me to his younger brother, Rex. Rex seemed just the opposite of Edward and, in terms of personality, almost a mirror image of me. Within a month, I had broken off things with Edward and had begun seeing Rex, with whom I quickly fell in love.*

"Fell in love"? The words echoed in Chyna's head. She'd always known Rex and Vivian were fond of each other. When Rex had come to visit, Vivian had acted even younger than usual, with her spirits always high. The two had talked and teased, obviously enjoying each other's company. And Chyna's father, Edward, had simply looked on, not showing the least bit of jealousy or competitiveness. In fact, now that Chyna remembered those visits, her father had acted as if he were benignly watching two high-spirited children when Vivian and Rex were together. But what had he really felt? Chyna wondered. She had never been able to read her father's thoughts and moods, though. He had been an enigma to her. Intrigued, she read on:

> About five months into my relationship with Rex, I learned I was pregnant. I knew Rex certainly wouldn't be pleased—he was still in college, still really just a high-spirited boy. I told him and he had the reaction I'd expected. He did not want me to have the baby. He offered to see me financially and emotionally through an abortion. I was surprised to realize I had a moral problem with it. I refused to have the abortion, which threw Rex into an agony of fear and stubbornness. He told me quite plainly that although he loved me, he simply could not bring himself to marry me at that time in his life.
>
> I felt lost, frightened, rejected, overwhelmed. I knew I could not turn to my mother—my father had long ago deserted her. For some reason I never understood, Mother blamed me for Father's desertion and had little love or generosity in her for me, his child. Edward had finished law school and had just begun his career at the bank then, and in desperation I turned to him. Maybe I thought he could talk Rex into marrying me. Maybe I just remembered his unfailing kindness and tenderness toward me. Even he could not move Rex into marrying me, though. Instead, he finally asked if I would be his wife. Chyna, I honestly had not gone to him in the hopes that he would propose, but I had no trouble accepting his offer of marriage, and not just because I was in trouble. I knew I needed his strength, his goodness, his maturity, and his unselfishness. We were married within a week, and eight months later your brother was born. Thank goodness he was late. He made it easier for us to pass him off as a premature baby.

Chyna stopped reading, stunned. Edward Greer Jr., Ned, was Rex's biological son? She'd noticed before how alike their bright blue eyes were, how they both possessed the same occasional joie de vivre, the same casual attitude toward life, but she'd always thought Ned had simply inherited more of the personality traits of some of the Greer family than had Edward. How wrong she had been.

> *Ned was not a happy baby. In fact, whenever we held him, Ned would scream until he was almost blue. We took him to a number of medical specialists, but none could find anything wrong with him. Edward suggested that somehow Ned realized Edward was not his real father, and believed it a good idea if Rex came to see the baby. Edward and Rex had not been in touch since my marriage.*
>
> *Anyway, Edward's parents had recently died, leaving him this house because they knew Rex never wanted to return to Black Willow to live, and we had moved in. With my permission, Edward invited Rex to come for a visit both to see the baby and to "keep the family together," he said.*
>
> *To my surprise, Rex came and, although the atmosphere was tense, at least a tenuous bridge had been built among us again. Rex paid the baby a great deal of attention and Ned seemed calmer in Rex's presence than in Edward's or mine. Although at the time I still resented Rex mightily, I did my best to hide my feelings because Edward was obviously glad to have his little brother back in his life. I decided I would never let my personal animosity come between the men.*
>
> *More and more, Edward invited Rex to our home. Rex and Ned became pals, and when I saw that Rex truly cared for the child, I couldn't help letting go of the rage I still bore toward Rex. I became calmer and more settled in my new life. By the time I announced that I was expecting another baby, your father and I were elated. I looked forward to giving Edward, that wonderful man, a child who was his in every way.*

So Daddy was happy when Mom told him she was pregnant with me, Chyna thought. He'd usually been so reserved around her, so different in his outward affections than her friends' fathers were, that at times she thought he'd been disappointed in her or that maybe he hadn't wanted a second child. But apparently, he had wanted her as much as her mother did. Chyna continued to read:

> *Edward was thrilled when his beautiful baby girl was born. You were a beauty, happy, quiet, and never seemed happier than when you were in your father's arms.*

I made Daddy happy, Chyna thought, tears rising in her own eyes. The thought that she had pleased him, even then, made her feel both happy and sad. At that time in his life, although more reserved than Rex or Vivian, Edward had been able to let loose and act "thrilled." Later he became self-contained. Chyna hadn't thought about it until this moment, but she never remembered her father even laughing out loud, not like her mother said he had when she was a baby.

> *Ned accepted his new sister with as much grace as a three-year-old can be expected to have. I didn't think Ned felt neglected. Now I know different. Over the next few years, he grew into a feisty child, usually happy but prone to occasional black moods when he seemed to shut out the world around him.*
>
> *Ned's moodiness didn't begin to show itself until you were around three. Your father and I knew even before then that you were special—not just pretty and smart, as most people believe their children to be, but gifted. At four you were already reading and better in math than Ned. When you were five, you began to play chess with your father, a game Ned never mastered.*
>
> *Ned always acted pleased by his little sister's accomplishments, but I sensed in him a feeling of inferiority. All of us—Edward, Rex, and I—made a great fuss over Ned's own special gifts, like his exceptional coordination and quickly blooming expertise at sports, and for long periods at a time he would seem satisfied with himself. Then you would do something remarkable, such as read a book with ease that he'd stumbled over in spite of being three years your senior, and he would draw in upon himself again. He was never*

t to you, but some special feat you performed would usually be followed by Ned starting a fight with a neighbor's child or getting in trouble at school. We knew he felt overshadowed by you and none of our praise could make him believe he was equal to his sister, either in his accomplishments or in our hearts.

After you both entered school, the old pattern persisted. Ned made passing grades, but only with the help of tutors. Meanwhile, you were blessed with an insatiable curiosity and an ability to soak up any subject placed in front of you. At the end of second grade, they placed you in fourth. We were informed you had nearly the IQ of a genius, a fact we never told Ned. But he knew. And even when you were only seven and eight, when children are losing teeth and not always looking their best, you looked like an angel. Ned, however, went through what we secretly called his "ragamuffin" stage. His front teeth were slow in growing in, he had acne, and he nearly always sported a black eye from one of his many fights.

Chyna put down the third page of stationery and began reading the fourth, noticing that with each page, her mother's usually beautiful handwriting had become more unsteady.

Edward had Ned's clubhouse built when he was nine. He felt giving the boy a place that belonged to him alone might draw him out of his increasing depressions, his aggressiveness toward other children, his feeling of inferiority to you. For a while, it seemed to work. Ned spent hours in the building, which eventually became known as the clubhouse for the Black Willow Warriors, the gang of boys who were brave enough to be Ned's friends. As Ned grew older, he spent less time in the clubhouse, but he always kept it locked, making certain everyone knew it was his.

Then came the teenage years. Ned's looks had improved dramatically, as had his personality. He became popular and excelled at sports, although his poor grades often had him teetering on the edge of losing his place on various teams. Also, there were several acts of vandalism around town at that time and Ned was suspected of being involved in some of them, but he was always cleared, sometimes because of Edward's influence.

But in spite of Ned's many friends, and girlfriends, he was still prone to those dark moods that worried me so much, times when he barely spoke, spent hours staring at television, and seemed removed from his family and the world around him. Once I went into his room while he was at school. I admit to snooping, and what I found shocked me. In a metal box he'd forgotten to lock, Ned had a collection of stories about serial killers and what I had no doubt were staged photos of naked girls who had been brutally murdered. Still . . .

I was deeply shaken but couldn't bring myself to tell Edward. Instead, I called Rex—a man I am ashamed to confess to you had become my lover again when Ned was about eleven. I had a bond with Rex I never had with Edward, and Ned was Rex's son. But perhaps those are just excuses for not doing what I should have done, which was get professional help for my son. When I told Rex about Ned, he assured me I was overreacting—that many teenage boys became fascinated by tales of horror and pornography. He insisted Ned was just going through a "stage." Maybe I accepted Rex's diagnosis of Ned's behavior because I wanted to believe him. More likely, I was running from an appalling fear that had been haunting me for months. I probably don't have to warn you of all people, Chyna, that you should never ignore your instincts about people. If only I hadn't ignored mine.

Around this time, a girl was gang-raped by four boys. The girl was able to identify two of the boys. Both were part of a group Ned considered his best friends. Ned was questioned in relation to the rape, but he had an alibi, although it was shaky at best. We tried to keep as much of this ugliness from you as possible, Chyna.

Of course Chyna had heard rumors of the rape at school, but several conflicting stories existed and soon the whole matter seemed to have become top secret. No one knew who had been raped, and no one had been charged with the rape. It had all seemed so horrifying, so far from her own protected world, that Chyna had not let herself dwell on the matter. She didn't want to spark the visions she had been trying hard to suppress for over a year.

> I don't need to tell you the next tragedy we suffered—the loss of dear Zoey. Had she been killed, the incident would have been awful, but to have her just vanish, to not know if she was dead or alive being starved and tortured, was to that point the most horrifying time of my life. Of yours, too, Chyna. I don't think you'd ever known true grief until then, but it was at least a year before I saw you genuinely smile again.
>
> I desperately didn't want to suspect Ned. I didn't try to find out where he was that night. And later, when he'd go out at night, I never asked him where he went and he never offered an explanation. Then, near Christmas over a year after Zoey, I happened to be awake, sitting in the dark in the living room, when he came in at two in the morning. I turned on a lamp and he stood in front of me, sweating and disheveled, with what I can only describe as a feral look on his face. He didn't say a word—he just went up to bed. The next day I learned that Heather Phelps had gone missing, just like Zoey.

Only one more page of the letter remained, but Chyna couldn't even look at it. She felt dizzy and slightly nauseated. She wanted to stuff the letter back in the bag, throw it into the fireplace, and set the biggest fire she could manage. But she knew this horror was not over. The trinkets still lay in front of her like small, pathetic offerings begging for her to touch them, pleading with her to let them tell *their* story.

Slowly, Chyna reached out and touched a slender silver bracelet bearing the initials "HCP." "Heather Carol Phelps," Chyna said aloud, although she had not known Heather's middle name until that instant. Then the vision hit so hard

Chyna thought she'd be thrown from the chair. A blond teenage girl after dark on a deserted side street. On one corner of the street Chyna could see a lighted Christmas wreath decorating a mundane streetlight. The girl walked slowly, looking in all the windows, smiling occasionally, looking happy, excited, young.

She had reached the end of the street and stood for a moment on the corner, waiting to cross to the other side of the sidewalk, when a figure stepped out of the darkness behind one of the buildings. Chyna couldn't tell much about the figure with a parka and ski mask, but it was around six feet tall, obviously a man, and slender. He crept up on the girl so quietly she barely had time to let out a squeak before he had one gloved hand over her mouth and an arm around her midriff. She wriggled in his grasp, but in a moment he'd jerked her onto the heels of her shoes with her legs stuck straight out in front of her and lowered her so close to the sidewalk she didn't have room to kick.

Chyna could feel the girl's heart pounding. She could feel her confusion, her terror. Then, in what seemed only an instant, the man dragged the girl behind a building and covered her face with a cloth—a heavy, sweet-smelling cloth.

The vision ended as abruptly as it had begun. Chyna sat rock-still in her chair, sweat covering her face and her palms, her hands shaking, her breath coming deep and rough. The abduction of Heather Phelps, she thought dully. Heather out Christmas shopping, having a good time that ended so tragically.

"Oh God," Chyna moaned, then folded her arms and put her head down on them. She knew Heather hadn't been killed immediately—otherwise he would not have needed chloroform, just like he did with Deirdre. No, this person, this monster, as Chyna now thought of him, liked to keep them alive awhile. He enjoyed their fear. He reveled in their desperation.

Next Chyna picked up a slim length of red velvet ribbon. She saw it drawn through thick, dark hair, hair shining even in the moonlight. The girl with the ribbon walked quickly,

nervously looking at a cheap watch on her left wrist. She
wore a thin coat and she carried a backpack. Edie Larson,
Chyna thought with dread. Edie walking home after play rehearsal on a narrow path beside the highway. Suddenly a
black Lincoln pulled in front of her.

Edie stopped abruptly. Then the front car door opened and
a young dark-haired man wearing sunglasses and a suit
stepped out. He smiled. "Edie Larson?" She nodded. "Don't
look so afraid, dear. I only wanted to tell you I watched your
rehearsal of *Our Town* and I thought you were wonderful."

Edie looked flustered. "Thank you. I messed up a line in
one scene, but I'll have it down by next week. No mistakes."

"I'm sure there won't be." The man took one tiny step toward her. "My name is James Chadwick and I work in the
theater circuit, especially around New York," he said. "I'm
what in the old days they called a talent scout. I was traveling through Black Willow, and when I heard there was going
to be a play rehearsal at the high school, I decided to drop
by." He smiled conspiratorily. "Actually, I thought I might be
stopping in for a few laughs. Some of these high school pro-
ductions . . ." He shrugged. Edie giggled guiltily, a bit nervously.

"I was particularly impressed with the way you could
project your voice without losing any nuances of the character's speech," he said quickly. Another small step toward her.

"Really?" Edie breathed, thinking he looked vaguely familiar, except for the dark hair.

"Yes, really. I believe with just a few acting lessons and a
little more experience with stage movements, you could be a
star. Of course, that may not appeal to you at all."

"Oh yes!" Edie trilled. "I want more than anything to act
in Broadway plays, even though I haven't seen any Broadway plays."

"There's a lot you haven't seen." In a flash, he was behind
her, his hand over her mouth, leaning her back just like he
had Heather. "There's a whole world you haven't seen, Edie."
He placed the white cloth over her face. "And I'm going to
show it all to you."

Suddenly Chyna was back at her mother's desk, holding the red ribbon from Edie Larson's hair in her hand. She dropped it as if it were a poisonous snake. Sweat poured down the side of her face and her heart beat so hard it felt as if it might fracture a rib. Daylight saving time had ended and already the evening was closing in, a soft gray evening pressing at the windows, shadows lurking in the corner. Michelle had curled up at Chyna's feet and she reached down, rubbing the dog's ears. Michelle licked her hand. This was how they sat most evenings, with Chyna reading medical books and Michelle right beside her, waiting for the occasional pat or ear rub and, at the end of study time, a beef-basted biscuit.

And that's how it should be tonight, Chyna thought. I can't go on with this. She was tired, she felt sick physically and emotionally, and her head was beginning to ache fiercely. But no matter how she felt, one more object on the desk seemed to call out to her, and she was helpless to resist holding it in her hand—a four-leaf-clover necklace. Zoey's necklace.

Zoey had bought them matching necklaces when they were fifteen, and Chyna had worn hers faithfully ever since Zoey's disappearance. She wore it now. All of these years, she'd pictured Zoey wearing her own necklace, even if she were nothing except a skeleton by now. Instead, here it lay, still clean and sparkling, right in front of her.

Chyna's hand crept toward the necklace almost as if the hand belonged to someone else. Finally, her middle finger touched the chain and she quickly grabbed it before nerves overtook her.

Chyna expected to be rocked by a vision as soon as she touched Zoey's necklace. Instead, she seemed swallowed in cloying, complete obscurity. Puzzled, she closed her eyes and tightened her grip on the clover pendant so tightly she could feel the edges jabbing painfully against her skin. The smothering, unnatural gloom lightened into the sweet, warm, velvety darkness of a summer's night, and suddenly Chyna could see what had happened twelve years earlier.

Moonlight danced off the waters of Lake Manicora and the night seemed full of fireflies. "It's almost like a firecracker display!" Zoey was saying, her voice gleeful, her brown eyes filled with delight. "I think this is the most beautiful, wonderful night of my whole life!" And then she looked up at the face of a man.

Gage Ridgeway.

Chyna was so shocked she dropped the necklace and opened her eyes. She'd remembered that earlier in the visit Zoey had run into Gage Ridgeway. He'd greeted her, told her she was "lookin' good," and Zoey had been transported. Apparently, they'd talked again and set up a rendezvous at the lake, a rendezvous kept secret from Chyna.

Everything in Chyna rebelled against picking up that necklace again, seeing what had happened to Zoey at Gage's hands, but she knew Zoey wanted her to see. Zoey had wanted her to see since the first time she'd spoken to Chyna at the lake. "I owe her that much," Chyna muttered, and again clutched the necklace.

More darkness. The fireflies. Then Gage bending down and kissing Zoey deeply. After the kiss, she'd looked at him with tears in her eyes. "I won't get to see you again until next summer," she'd said mournfully.

"Next summer isn't so far away. And by then you'll be seventeen and I don't think Vivian Greer will object to you going out with me. We won't have to sneak around like this."

"Maybe you're right." Zoey had looked at him with pleading eyes. "Will you write to me?"

"At least every two weeks. And I'll use a fake name on the return address. How about 'Irma Vogel'?" Zoey, who had met Irma, laughed delightedly. Gage had smiled and leaned down to kiss Zoey's freckled nose. "Everything is going to be fine, Zoe. I promise."

And you had no idea to how many girls he'd made that same promise, Chyna thought. Gage simply could not resist girls of sixteen or seventeen. She sensed that he already had been feeling relieved that Zoey was leaving tomorrow. There were so many other girls to conquer.

They hugged. And now he's going to grab her, Chyna thought with dread. Now he's going to put a hand over her mouth and pull her backward. . . .

Instead, Gage had begun walking away from the lake toward the parking lot. Zoey had stood still, watching him climb onto his motorcycle, throw her a casual wave in return for the kiss she blew to him, and roar out of the parking lot. Then, wiping tears from her cheeks, Zoey had begun to climb the hill up to the Greer house, the hill on which Chyna slept peacefully in the grass by the road.

"No!" Chyna cried, making Michelle jump. "No. That's not what happened. She was killed by the man she met at the lake!"

Except she wasn't.

Chyna squeezed her eyes shut. Her head was pounding now, her neck grew stiff with tension, and her entire body felt damp with perspiration in spite of the comfortable temperature of the house.

She'd dropped the necklace in shock when she'd seen Zoey, healthy and only unhappy about parting from her "big love" of the summer. Zoey had been headed back to Chyna, who lay sleeping between Zoey and the house. Zoey had been *fine*. It couldn't be possible. Chyna's vision of that night was "off." With determination, she picked up the necklace one last time.

This time the vision was not slow in coming. She felt as if she were flying through time, back twelve years, to that warm, beautiful July night. Zoey was humming to herself as she climbed the hill. She was humming and smiling and touching the four-leaf-clover pendant on her necklace—

When Ned stepped out from the woods beside her. She squealed slightly in surprise. Then they both laughed as Ned said, "Geez, Zoe, I didn't mean to scare you!"

"I thought you were a bear or something," Zoey giggled self-consciously. Chyna could feel that the girl was actually afraid she'd been caught doing something she shouldn't. "It was so hot tonight and Chyna and I couldn't sleep, so we decided to take a walk. . . ."

Zoey seemed to run out of breath and her smile was stiff and unnatural. But Ned looked completely at ease as he said, "Sometimes I need to get out of the house, too. I get, I don't know, claustrophobic at night."

"Is that why you quit listening to your music and came out?" Ned looked at her quizzically. "You said you were going to listen to music with your headphones on all evening so you wouldn't bother anyone."

"Oh yeah."

"You were lying that night, Ned," Chyna now murmured. "You'd heard Zoey make plans with Gage. . . ."

Back in the past, Chyna could see Ned looking around. "You're all alone except for Chyna?" Zoey nodded. "Well, she's asleep in the grass on up the hill."

"Asleep? Well, I'll have to wake her up." Zoey looked at him pleadingly. "You won't tell on us, will you?"

"'Course not." A tight, narrow smile appeared on Ned's face. "You can count on it."

"Oh God," Chyna moaned as in her vision she saw Ned grab Zoey in the way she'd already come to know—hand over mouth, arm around her midriff, and tilting her backward as he dragged her off into the woods. "Zoey, I'm so sorry," Chyna said aloud. "I should have been there for you."

"But you weren't."

Chyna whirled around to see Ned standing right behind her. "N-Ned!" she blurted in a bright, brittle voice. She tried to casually push the letter and trinkets aside. "I didn't know you were coming by. Did you bring Bev and the kids?"

"It's too late to try to act natural, Chyna. I've been standing here for at least five minutes." Her heart felt as if it were plunging to her stomach, but she could think of nothing to say. "I see you have a letter. No doubt it's from Mom, and hidden someplace only you could find, hidden because it told you all her secrets. Where was it, Chyna?" She stared at him. "Oh, come on. It can't hurt to tell me now."

Chyna felt as if her mouth were so dry she could barely speak. "It was behind the portrait of Mom and . . . Dad."

"Don't you mean Mom and *your* dad?"

Ned grinned. She'd always thought he was so good-looking—blond, blue-eyed, even-featured, with that slightly lopsided, charming smile—but he wasn't good-looking now. Now he looked pale and flat-eyed and his smile had turned into the slit of a shark's mouth. Something about him didn't even appear human anymore. "The man in the portrait isn't *my* father, Chyna."

Should I bluff or be honest? Chyna wondered. But something in Ned's expression told her they were beyond bluffing. "Did Mom tell you Edward wasn't your father?"

Ned looked away from her for a moment, those awful, flat eyes focused on the portrait of her parents. "Vivian didn't tell me when I was a kid. But I knew. You're not the only one who can sense things, Chyna. I think I was about nine when I began to wonder if Rex was my father instead of Edward. When I was old enough to know anything, I thought it was odd that I was a seven-and-half-pound premature baby. Then I read a book about a boy who thought one guy was his father and he found out another guy was. All at once . . . *bingo*! I knew I was just like that boy in the book." He gave her a weird, crooked smile. "Bizarre, isn't it?"

"Very. And pretty flimsy evidence, if you ask me."

"Oh, you mean I should have checked with you? Gotten a reading from the walking ESP machine? Oh, but you were only six then. It was a whole year before the boating accident that triggered your visions." He paused and smiled. "You didn't have the slightest idea that it wasn't just one boat banging into another that sent you over the side of the *Chyna Sea,* did you?"

"W-what?" Chyna was flabbergasted. "Do you mean . . ."

"That you had a little help? Yes. When the boat jerked, I was standing beside you. In a flash I just put my hand on your back and sent you right over the side."

Chyna felt as if she could hardly get her breath. "Then why did you save me?"

"Oh, Chyna, don't act stupid. If there's anyone in the world who's not stupid, it's you. You were everyone's little darling. So pretty, so smart, so accomplished. Everyone's golden girl. Oh, Ned was okay when he was behaving himself—average intelligence, good sense of humor, temporarily gawky looks he was bound to outgrow—but Chyna! Well, she was another matter altogether.

"You got all the attention until that day when her brave, athletic brother risked his ten-year-old life to save his sister and succeeded! Wow, was I the glory boy for a while. It felt so good, Chyna. It felt so very, very good. Even Edward looked at me differently. Not that he'd ever let anyone else see the coolness in his eyes when he'd looked at me earlier, but after that day even he let a little warmth show—warmth he usually reserved for you."

"Ned, Dad never treated you different than he did me."

Ned smirked at her. "He never treated me different, but treating us the same was an effort for him because he *felt* different. I didn't have to be a psychic like you to know. Kids sense those things. Edward Greer did not love me. He resented me with every fiber of his being."

"No, he didn't!" Chyna and Ned both stiffened when they heard Rex's voice as he descended the stairs from the second floor. Chyna had forgotten he was still in the house. "You weren't Edward's biological child, but you were Vivian's child and my child, and he loved both of us. He loved you, too."

Ned nearly spat, "He hated me from the minute I was born because I was the child of Vivian and *you!*"

"When you realized you weren't Edward's child, you made up this whole fantasy about how you were unloved, resented, maybe even hated," Rex lashed back. "You were jealous of your sister, but you couldn't admit that. No, Ned, you've always had one thing your sister doesn't—a huge ego. You couldn't admit to feeling something as petty as jealousy of a little girl, so you invented reasons to explain all the foulness that's festered inside you since you were a child!"

"That is a damned lie!" Ned snarled. "You—you got Vivian pregnant and then you deserted her. And after your own brother saved her from disgrace, you had a soul rotten enough to betray your brother and start up with her again. I remember the first time I saw you two together. I came home early from school. I heard noises in the guest room and I peeked in and there you were, you and your brother's wife, heaving and sweating, riding each other, grunting like a couple of animals—"

"Shut up!" Chyna realized she'd screamed at Ned. Michelle had nearly entwined herself around Chyna's legs and she could feel the heat of the dog's fear, a fear that almost equaled her own. She'd had no idea Vivian and Rex had carried on an affair, but the reality hadn't hit her yet and she couldn't make herself be quiet. "Just stop talking, Ned!" Her voice cut through the air like a knife. "What Mom and Rex did was wrong, but it's over. I don't want to hear any more about their affair. I don't want to hear about how Dad hated you. He didn't, but even if he had, it doesn't matter anymore. Dad's been gone a long time. And now Mom is gone, too." She paused, feeling as if lights were flashing behind her eyes. She could see Vivian standing at the top of the stairs. She saw Ned standing only a couple of feet away from her. And she could see Vivian's face—flushed and horrified but absolutely determined and relentless as she threatened her son.

Chyna held her breath for a moment as all three of them stood as if frozen. Meanwhile, evening fell early without the benefit of daylight saving time. The only light came from a small lamp on the desk, a lamp that sent wavering shadows crawling up the walls and across the ceiling. Chyna felt as if a ball of ice had settled in her stomach. At the same time, sweat slithered from her hairline to the neck of her sweater like a slender, treacherous snake. Still, she managed to find her voice, even though it emerged thin and raspy. "You admitted to pushing me off that boat when I was seven, Ned. You know that *I* know you're responsible for the deaths of Zoey, and Heather, and Edie. Probably Nancy, too." She paused. "Now tell me what happened to Mom."

"She had a heart attack," Ned said flatly, his gaze never leaving Chyna's.

"The medical examiner says Mom did have a heart attack. But I can see you with her, Ned. I can see the two of you at the top of the stairs. What happened that morning, Ned? You might as well tell us. You have nothing to lose now."

"Nothing to lose?" Ned repeated. He glanced at Rex, then back at Chyna, and started to laugh. "Well, I guess I don't. I was always afraid you'd figure it out one day, little sister, although I thought your so-called visions were just the result of intense scrutiny. You were constantly observant, never missed a trick, even when you were young. I wasn't absolutely sure, though. That's why I've avoided touching you ever since you came home. Did you notice that?"

Chyna quickly cast through her memories. The night she arrived he hadn't hugged her when he and Bev came over. He hadn't even laid a hand on Chyna's shoulder after the crowd had gathered on the lawn. He seemed to see the dawning comprehension in her gaze and smiled ruefully. "I didn't count on having to tell Rex everything, but maybe it'll be entertaining to describe to him exactly how his paramour, or more aptly his whore, died."

Rex winced and briefly closed his eyes. It had hurt him to hear Vivian called a whore, Chyna thought. Even though he'd turned his back on Vivian when she needed him before Ned was born, even though Rex had only dallied with her when he came to visit between wives, he had cared for Vivian. Somehow, as disappointed as she was in her mother, knowing Rex had at least cared made the pain a bit less sharp for Chyna.

"Sometimes I noticed Mom looking at me like she didn't know me," Ned began. "There was all this speculation in her gaze. I don't know if she said anything to Edward or he just started to wonder about me, too, but I saw the same look in his eyes." Ned grinned. "I'll tell you, it freaked me out. Scared me. And I don't like being scared. So, I thought that if they *were* on the scent, if they thought their Edward Junior might be the killer of young girls, what better way to make them think I was just a normal guy than by getting married to a sweet, pretty girl from a nice family, a gentle girl they knew and loved, a girl they would have picked for a daughter-in-law? So I proposed to Beverly."

"You used Beverly as a *cover*?" Chyna asked, appalled.

"Yeah. Why not? She loved me. She was thrilled when I asked her to marry me. Vivian's eyes lost that strange look right about the time of the wedding. But Edward's didn't." Chyna remembered how withdrawn her father had seemed during the wedding festivities. She'd *thought* he was troubled, but she hadn't known why. Now she did. "Boy, was I relieved when he kicked off two weeks later," Ned ended casually.

"Please tell me you didn't kill him," Rex said in an old man's voice.

"I'd planned to if he didn't quit looking at me like he suspected something. But luckily, I didn't have to. He just went on his own. Or almost on his own." Ned raised his eyebrows. "Don't look so relieved, Rex. He found out about you and Vivian. When my wedding didn't seem to settle his mind about me, he learned about the two of you in an anonymous letter complete with photos." Ned stretched his mouth in that awful grin again. "He found out his brother and his wife had been sweatin' up the sheets, banging away for years, right under his nose. The shock, the hurt, threw him right into a stroke."

"Oh God," Rex moaned. "I never meant . . ."

"You never meant for him to find out?" Ned asked. "Well, I guess you didn't. You didn't mind screwing your own sister-in-law; you just didn't want him to know it. Very noble, Rex. Shows how much you loved your brother."

"And you were the anonymous informant," Chyna said dully.

Ned nodded. "Sure was. I was particularly proud of the photos. When those two were going at it, they didn't notice me opening the door just wide enough to get a few excellent shots of them. Anyway, you asked about Vivian, not Edward. Well, of all the damn luck, we had that big windstorm when I was in Pennsylvania at Bev's sister's wedding. It wrecked my old clubhouse—the place I'd always kept padlocked. Vivian had always been suspicious of how protective I was of the place, and with one side of it blown out, she went tearing out there to nose around. That's when she found my memorabilia tucked carefully away in the old chest."

Chyna felt sick. "Your mementos of the girls you'd killed."

"Yeah. When I got home, I was furious that she'd had the place torn down and carted away. She tried to act blasé about it, but I wasn't convinced. I came back the next day and confronted her. She'd been in bed and she met me at the top of the stairs. She looked weak and sick and she completely broke down. She said she'd found all my 'grotesque treasures.' She told me she'd suspected for years that I'd killed those girls, but she'd kept her mouth shut because I was her son, as if she ever gave a damn about me!"

"She did, Ned," Chyna ventured.

"Shut . . . your . . . mouth," he returned coldly. "She and Edward cared about you. *Only* you. But we've been over that and I hate having to repeat myself. Anyway, she gave me this ghastly hollow-eyed look and said, 'For once in my life, I'm going to do the right thing before you kill another girl, or Beverly, or your own children. I kept those things that belonged to the dead girls, and don't bother looking for them because you'll never find them. I'm going to show them to the police and say where I found them. Then I'm going to tell the authorities everything I know about you. I don't know a lot, but I know enough to get them started on an investigation. I've already called Rex. He's going to help me.'"

The extra food in the refrigerator the night she'd gotten home, Chyna thought. Her mother had been expecting Rex, but he'd been delayed by the flu.

"Vivian pushed past me and started down the stairs," Ned continued. "All at once she gasped and grabbed at her chest. I already knew she had heart trouble. She was having a heart attack. So, since opportunity was right in front of me, I just gave her a nice, hard push down the stairs. Then I went down and studied her closely to make sure she was dead. Her neck was twisted at this god-awful angle and—"

"Stop!" Chyna cried. "For the love of God, don't describe it!"

"For the love of God?" Ned asked. "I don't love God and he doesn't love me, but in honor of your sensitive nature, I won't go into details. I hung around the house for a half hour or so, then called nine-one-one. I wanted them to think she'd been lying there for a while before I found her. And lucky for me, the autopsy showed she'd had a heart attack. The conclusion was simple. She was at the top of the stairs, had the attack, and fell to the bottom, where she broke her neck, which finished her off. I did a fine job of sounding like the stricken son when the Emergency Service got here. Then I called you, Chyna. Don't you agree my grief sounded genuine?"

"Yes, you son of a bitch," she ground out.

"Son of a bitch. Well, that would be accurate."

"Why, Ned?" Chyna and Ned both looked surprised to hear Rex speak. He'd come down the rest of the stairs and now stood in the shadowy living room. "Why did you kill those girls?"

"Why, why, why?" Ned chanted. "Why does a serial killer want to kill? Well, usually they have a type in mind. In my case, I always chose young, pretty, smart girls, girls everyone knew would *do* something beyond the usual with their lives, girls who were *special*. . . ."

"Girls like your sister," Rex said flatly.

"Exactly. I admit, I failed to get rid of her a long time ago, but I was only ten at the time and my desire for admiration outweighed my better sense. Then Zoey came along. She was cute, sort of smart, would surely go to a good school because her parents had money, but she wasn't special except for one thing—she was Chyna's best friend. If I couldn't get at Chyna directly, I'd do it indirectly, through Zoey. And I did it, didn't I, Sis? I tore your emotions to shreds when I killed Zoey."

"Yes, you did," Chyna said brokenly. "And the girls after Zoey—I didn't even know them, but to you, they were like me. Symbolically you were killing me over and over."

Ned cocked his head. "Well, I never thought about it like that—you're the deep thinker in the family—but I guess you're right." His gaze drifted from Chyna as if another thought was dragging away his attention. Then he looked at the gold-plated urn sitting on a cherry end table. "Well, Mom's home again." He looked at Rex. "I don't think there will be any fun and games in the bedroom this time, though."

Rex stood by the wall, looking as if he were made of stone. His once-brilliant blue eyes moved from Ned to the urn, though.

"Vivian called me and told me what she suspected about you, Ned," Rex said in an odd, detached voice. "She told me about the 'trophies' she'd found in the clubhouse—the velvet ribbon, a pair of panties, a copy of the playbook for *Our Town,* other things. She told me how you looked the night Heather Phelps vanished. She said she was going to turn you in to the police and she begged me to come, to help her. I couldn't accept what she wanted me to do and I delayed a day, for which I'll never forgive myself. Then I realized I had a duty—you're my son—and I forced myself on a plane. I rented a car at the airport, drove here, and just as I got to the house, I saw an ambulance in the driveway. I saw someone being carried out on a gurney, and even though the face was covered, I knew it was Vivian."

Rex looked coldly at Ned. "And I saw you, trailing along behind it with that hangdog expression on your face. Maybe you fooled the cops and the paramedics, but you didn't fool me. I knew Vivian was dead and I knew you had something to do with her death. I couldn't prove anything, though, so I didn't stop at the house. I followed you around for a couple of days, hoping I could catch you at something. But I couldn't. I also couldn't put off Chyna any longer. So I finally showed up and made an excuse about being delayed because I was sick. But I didn't stop following you, Ned. I haven't stopped for days. That's why I was never here, Chyna."

"Well, I can't say much for your skill as a private investigator, Rex," Ned sneered. "Look what happened to Deirdre Mayhew and Rusty Burtram."

Chyna looked in despair at the man she'd loved as a brother her whole life. "When I got home, you were limping and Bev said you strained a muscle in your leg by tripping over a water hose at the car dealership. But you actually strained it chasing Nancy down that path. She tripped and hit her head before you caught her, but not before you saw Rusty watching. That's why you killed him."

"I don't think he saw me." Ned shrugged. "But I wasn't absolutely sure and I wasn't going to take any chances. Besides, I did him a favor. That pitiful guy wasn't destined to have one happy day in his whole goddamned life."

"You weren't even here when Rusty told me he'd seen Nancy running down that path and he thought someone was chasing her," Chyna said.

"No, but Gage was, and he made the mistake of telling me about the whole scene—Rusty pouring his heart out to you, trying to convince you he wasn't some kind of pervert, his father overhearing him and ready to explode like Mount Vesuvius. The funny thing was, Gage didn't know whether to believe Rusty was innocent. He told me because he was pondering the whole thing, trying to figure it out."

Chyna said evenly, "Yes, that must have been hilarious to you." She hesitated. "Ned, where *is* Gage Ridgeway?"

"Why, he took off, little sister, when you found Deirdre in the cemetery so close to his house. After all, you found the blanket she'd been wrapped in on his property."

"Stop playing games. You planted the blanket at Gage's. Even when I found it, I knew something was wrong. It was dirty. It had pieces of grit and grime on it. But the floor of Gage's storage building, where you planned to have the police believe he was keeping Deirdre prisoner, was spotless." Ned merely smiled at her. "You put the blanket in that building and I'm sure a couple of other items that belonged to Deirdre will turn up at Gage's, too. As soon as you heard on your police scanner—the scanner you listen to constantly

that drives Beverly up the wall—you were out of your house
like a flash. You went to Gage's and you planted evidence.
But what did you do with him?"

"What would you expect me to do with him?"

"You want me to think you killed him, Ned, but you
didn't." Chyna tapped her temple. "ESP, remember? I *know*
he's alive."

"You're guessing."

"Oh no, I am not guessing." Although everything inside
Chyna felt as if it were quivering, she maintained a strong,
steady voice. "Gage Ridgeway is alive, Ned. You have plans
for him."

Ned's gaze wavered slightly. Then he looked at her with
eyes as cold and emotionless as a snake's. "You're right. I
have plans for Gage." He paused. "But I also have plans for
you, Chyna dear. Plans I'm afraid will end in your tragic de-
mise."

"You're going to kill your own sister?" Rex asked in his
old man's voice.

"Yes. Don't sound so shocked. I've tried it before, remember? Only this time I'll be successful."

"The hell you will," Rex snarled, and charged at Ned. But
Rex was slow and Ned was not. So fast it almost seemed a
blur, Ned pulled a gun from beneath his jacket. Chyna
screamed as the gun went off. Rex went completely still.
Then, slowly, he looked down at the blood spreading across
his abdomen. His glance met Chyna's one last time before
he fell with a crash onto the glass-topped coffee table.

"Gut shot," Ned said. "It's a painful way to die."

"Oh my God!" Chyna screamed. "What have you done?"

"Looks obvious to me."

She started to run to Rex, but Ned turned the gun toward
her. "Stay where you are." Rex moaned and Chyna moved
again. This time Ned shot. The bullet hit the wall not a foot
from her head. "I missed on purpose, but I won't the next
time, so it'll be in your best interest to stop being so sentimental. I told you getting gut shot was a painful way to die.
It's also a slow way to die. Old Rex here will be moaning

for quite a while, but you can't do anything for him. Nothing, Chyna. The only way you can save your life is to do what I say."

She met his eerily inhuman gaze. "You intend to kill me, too. Why don't you just get it over with?"

"Because this is not the way I planned it. It's perfectly obvious there isn't one thing you can do to save yourself now. But . . ." Ned lowered the gun and pointed it at the trembling Michelle. "You can go along with me and save your dog. Most people wouldn't think that was much of a trade, but I know how you love that dog."

"Come on, Ned. You'd kill her; then you'd kill me, too."

He shrugged. "You're right. So think of it this way instead. If I shoot you now, it's all over. If you give yourself some time, that big brain of yours might provide you with a much-needed inspiration." He kept the gun pointed at Michelle but never took his eyes from Chyna's. "So what'll it be, Chyna doll?"

She swallowed convulsively, pressing herself against the desk, keeping her hands behind her so she wouldn't make some instinctive move that might startle Ned into shooting her. "I'll do what you say." Her hands, slippery with sweat, slid along the top of the desk. Stop it, she commanded them silently. Don't *move*. But her hands kept sliding. They were moving against her will, she suddenly realized. It was almost as if something, or someone, were moving them for her. And then they touched it. Zoey's four-leaf-clover necklace. Chyna clutched it in her left hand and continued to look steadily at Ned. "I said I'll do what you want. Just don't shoot me. Or the dog. Please."

"Don't shoot the dog. Please," Ned mimicked, then laughed. "Okay, you idiot. My kids love that dog, too. They'll be only too happy to care for it when poor Aunt Chyna dies. Now, I don't think anyone is outside, but considering that a few people believe you're a bad witch or a demon and might be hiding out there, waiting to drive evil from their town, I'm not going to tie you up or in any way make you look like a prisoner. You're going to walk out to my car just as calmly as you normally would. The only difference will be that this time, I'll be behind you with a gun pointed at your back."

"Where are you taking me?"

Ned was speaking, but suddenly Chyna couldn't hear him. Instead, she heard a sweet, light voice singing, "Star light, star bright . . ."

"Are you listening to me?" Ned demanded.

"I-I'm sorry. I'm scared. What did you say?"

"Is this your way of stalling? Because it's not going to work."

"I'm not stalling. I said I'm sorry. I . . . I . . ."

Again it came. "Star light, star bright . . ." Abruptly the room disappeared. For a moment, Chyna saw only darkness. Then, in a burst of color, she saw a neon sign, an old sign she hadn't seen lit up in over twenty years: STAR LIGHT DRIVE-IN THEATER.

The scene changed. No longer did she see the theater in its heyday. She saw it as it must have looked after it had been closed, the stars and moon providing the only light shining down on the poles holding rusting speakers, and the deserted concession stand, surrounded by weeds, ivy creeping up its sides, although the place did not look as if it were nearly devoured by flora as it did now. It looked—

Like it did twelve years ago! Suddenly Chyna knew this was where Ned had taken Zoey. Zoey and Heather and Edie and Deirdre. And this was where he was taking her.

"Goddammit, Chyna, I said *move!*" Ned shouted. "Right now or—"

"All right!" she cried. "We're going to the Star Light Drive-In, right? The old concession stand? That's where you took all the others, isn't it, Ned? If you're going to kill me, you can at least answer one question for me. You're taking me to the old drive-in theater on Route Five?"

"You just have to show off, don't you?" Ned said in disgust. "Well, genius, you're right. That's where I'm taking you. Another proof of your amazing sixth sense. The only trouble is, it came a little too late to save you." Ned sounded

completely exasperated, verging on desperate, and his eyes
no longer looked flat. They'd seemed to go wild, almost as if
they were full of fire. He grabbed her shoulder and whirled
her around, jabbing the barrel of the gun in her back. "Now
get moving!"

As she moved away from the desk, Chyna kept a tight
grip on Zoey's necklace. They walked toward the door, Ned
right behind her. Rex was still moaning, and Chyna tried to
shut out the sound. "How do you plan to explain your uncle
lying shot in the living room?" she asked Ned. "You can't
just hide the body. There's way too much blood to clean up."

"Thought I got mad and lost my head when I shot him,
don't you?" Ned asked smugly. "Well, you don't know
everything. It was all part of the plan."

"I see." She reached out toward the coat tree and Ned
jabbed her with the barrel of the gun. "You wanted this to
look normal, Ned. It's forty-five degrees outside. I wouldn't
normally be going out without a coat on. Or didn't you figure
that into your brilliant plan?"

Ned allowed her to slip on the coat, but when she reached
for her purse he hissed, "Forget it. Do you think I don't know
your cell phone is in there? That you think you're gonna secretly click it on, auto-dial someone like Kendrick, talk loud
until you hear him say hello, then ask me again if I'm dragging you to the Star Light Drive-In? Give him a clue? Well,
it's not gonna happen. Just get out the door."

Chyna felt tears rising in her eyes and she blinked furiously. She would not let Ned know he'd guessed exactly
what she planned to do. She did have Scott's cell phone
number on auto-dial. Two flicks of a button and he could
have heard every word she said. But now she was helpless.

As they left the house, she walked straight and tall, knowing Ned couldn't see her tear-filled eyes. He was never more
than a couple of inches behind her as they walked to his car.
"Open the door," he said as they reached the passenger's
side. "Then scoot on over to the wheel." She looked at him.
"Did you think I was going to let you just climb in, shut the
door, and wait like a good little girl for me to amble around

to the driver's side? Get behind the wheel and keep in mind
I'll have this gun pointed at your head every moment."

Chyna slid across the seat. Ned had left the keys in the ig-
nition. She turned on the car and put her hand on the gearshift.
"Don't get any ideas about ramming the car straight ahead and
wrecking us. You'll have a bullet in your brain before this car
ever hits the garage door."

And he means it, Chyna thought. He had a plan, all right,
but he wasn't figuring on letting her go free if things didn't
go perfectly. He was beyond being careful. He'd probably
gone beyond being careful as soon as he heard Deirdre Mayhew had regained consciousness and would soon be identi-
fying her abductor, if she hadn't already. Now Ned cared
about only one thing—the thing he'd cared most about since
they were children—killing Chyna.

They'd ridden for about ten minutes in silence before
Chyna finally asked, "What gave you the idea to use the
drive-in?"

"The place had been closed down about six years when
one evening a bunch of us guys drove up there. Weeds were
already taking over, growing everywhere, especially around
the old concession stand. It was locked. We didn't break in. I
didn't push it because I wanted to come back in and break in
by myself. I wanted to explore every inch of that big place
because it just . . . well, I hate to sound like you . . . but it
just spoke to me. Especially at night. We were two abandoned souls, things nobody cared about, things left to rot
while everyone concentrated on what was younger and better and sparkling." He sighed. "It's the only place where I
ever felt entirely at peace."

"At peace?" Chyna repeated, amazed. "You took the girls
you planned to murder there because it's where you felt at
peace?" Ned nodded casually. "But you didn't kill them immediately, did you? After you broke into that concession
stand, you liked it so much, you decided to keep your victims in there and torture them for a little while, didn't you?"

"Torture them? I never thought of it that way. The concession stand was my secret place where I could . . . enjoy them for a while before we had to say good-bye."

Enjoy them? Bile rose in Chyna's throat. She closed her eyes and swallowed hard a couple of times. How had her brother "enjoyed" Zoey and the others? Chyna wouldn't ask. She didn't want to know.

"And do you plan to enjoy me, too?" she asked instead.

"I'm afraid there's no time." He looked over at her, one side of his mouth lifting in that strange, feral smile that let her know he'd finally lost the control that had protected him since he'd tried to kill her when he was ten. "Besides, Chyna, we're brother and sister. It just wouldn't be right. Now get out of the car and keep in mind that I will be directly behind you. If you try to run, you won't make it more than six feet."

Intellectually, Chyna knew that she should be thinking at top speed, trying to come up with a means of escape. Emotionally, though, she felt that her only chance lay in trying to cut as many analytically chattering thoughts from her mind as possible. Still clutching Zoey's necklace, Chyna believed her only hope lay in what came from outside her small realm of reality, in what answers existed in the huge world that existed beyond the circumference of the five senses.

But the other girls had not entered the concession stand as she was, Chyna thought. They'd all been unconscious. Ned had opened the door, dragged their limp bodies from his car, and carried them inside. And then . . .

"Key to the padlock," Ned said, waving a key in front of her while holding the gun in his right hand. "*You* will use it to open the padlock."

"So you're not trying to open a lock while holding a gun on me," Chyna said. "Ned, you really are brilliant."

"Stop patronizing me."

"I wouldn't bother. It's too easy."

"One more comment like that and—"

"And you'll blow my head off right out here in the open? That can't be part of your plan, Ned. It's too crude. Lacks your usual finesse."

"I know what you're doing," Ned snarled. "You're trying to get me so enraged that I'll completely lose my head, blow the whole damned thing, and you'll have a chance to get away. But it's not going to happen, Chyna. I'm too close to the end to let *anything* you say fluster me into making a mistake."

"Well, whatever you say." Chyna tried to sound maddeningly offhand. She had a feeling what Ned wanted most was to see her reduced to a shaking, fear-addled adolescent, barely more than a child. Her brother fed on fear, he "got off" on terror, he lived for control, and the ultimate control was the power of life and death. The problem was, for Ned, the high that he got from killing never lasted long enough. He needed fix after fix after fix. Oddly, she believed he thought his constant need for fixes would end when he killed her, but she knew that it wouldn't. As long as Ned lived, so would his hunger for destruction.

She unlocked the padlock and pushed open the door. Small windows lined the upper edge of the one-story building and they let in a small amount of moonlight, but not enough to be much help. Then Chyna heard a click behind her and the beam of a flashlight cut through the darkness and fell on a huddled figure in the corner. A blanket had been thrown over him, but part of his beaten, bloodstained face showed clearly. Gage Ridgeway. He blinked in the sudden blaze of light and ducked his head, but not before Chyna had seen the duct tape across his mouth.

"So here he is," Chyna said somberly. "I knew you hadn't killed him, Ned. Mind telling me why?"

"Because *he* is going to kill *you.*" Ned pushed shut the door, but he didn't turn off the flashlight. He didn't need to be careful, Chyna thought. They were quite a distance from the highway, and no houses or businesses sat near the drive-in. "Want to know *why* he's going to kill you?"

"I'm dying to know."

"Cute, Chyna. Sit down."

"I don't want to sit down."

Ned pointed the gun at her head. "I said to *sit down.*"

Chyna sighed as if thoroughly exasperated. Actually, she felt as if she were on the verge of fainting and was only too happy to sink down to the cold concrete. She just didn't want to look as if she were collapsing from fright. "Okay, I'm down," she said coolly. "Please continue enlightening us with your brilliance before you burst."

Ned shot her a knife-edged look, clearly infuriated that she was showing neither fear nor the proper respect for his power. "I'm about ninety-nine percent certain Deirdre didn't see me. I was dressed like a ghost when I took her—keeping in costume like everyone else so I wouldn't be noticed. Afterward, I wore a ski mask around her. But just in case she recognized my voice or something, it won't matter. There is so much evidence pointing to Gage as the killer of all those other girls *and* Rusty Burtram that everyone will convince her she was so befuddled by terror and chloroform she got confused and mistook me for Gage. After all, I'm the upstanding family man. While Gage here—well, we all know Gage Ridgeway's reputation even without the evidence."

"So Gage is going to trial and take the fall for all the murders you've committed." Ned nodded. "What if the jury isn't convinced beyond a reasonable doubt that he's the killer who's prowled Black Willow for twelve years?"

"There won't be any trial because Gage is going to disappear. He's already disappeared. You saw that for yourself when you and Kendrick went snooping out to his house this morning. The cops had already been there last night. Of course, as usual, it took them too long to get there. While they were all standing around watching Deirdre get pulled out of that grave, I was already forcing Gage away from home. Using one of his own guns, by the way," Ned said, looking at the .38 revolver in his hand.

Chyna frowned. Then she understood. "Of course. Rex was shot with Gage's gun."

"Yes. Gage shot poor old Rex when he stupidly tried to defend you."

"If Gage was hell-bent on simply disappearing from Black Willow, why would he have come after me?"

"Because you were the only person he had to fear. He could hide anywhere from anyone. From anyone except Chyna Greer. After all, you found Deirdre. That had to shake him up. So he decided to kill you, the last threat to his freedom, before he vanished." Ned looked over at Gage, whose eyes had not been covered with duct tape. They were blackened and a streak of dried blood ran beside the right one, but their green depths burned with hatred. "They'll never find you, Gage, but eventually they'll find Chyna's body and those of the other girls."

"You're going to kill me and bury me in the same place you buried them," Chyna said. Ned nodded, smiling, but almost instantly his face faded from her view. She didn't see Ned; she didn't see Gage; she didn't see the filthy interior of the concession stand. She saw Zoey, dressed in her white jeans and her blue top, standing in the lot of the drive-in, the screen looming behind her.

Her voice rang sweetly in Chyna's ears, "Star light, star bright . . . ," as her right arm swept gracefully over the moon-washed, graveled remains of the theater lot. "The last star I see tonight . . ." The rhyme said: "The first star I see tonight," Chyna thought. But Zoey sang, "The *last* star I see tonight." And then, with sickening clarity, Chyna knew what Zoey was telling her. The Star Light Drive-In Theater was the last symbolic star that had shone upon her before she was buried.

"They're all here, aren't they, Ned?" Chyna said stonily. "Zoey, Heather, Edie . . . they're all buried here at the theater. 'It's the only place where I ever felt entirely at peace.' That's what you said to me about this place, Ned. So it's where you gave your victims peace, too, isn't it? A peace they didn't want. A peace I don't want."

Ned looked at her in surprise for a moment before that chilling smile returned. "Now see why I have to do away with you, Chyna? Why *Gage* has to do away with you? You're just too smart for your own good, little girl. Always were."

"No, I wasn't, or I would have caught on to you a lot sooner. I don't know why I didn't," Chyna said sadly. "Maybe it was because of our blood relationship or because I loved you too much."

Ned's smirk faded. He looked at her gravely, almost affectionately, and at that moment Chyna knew that her brother had felt something for her besides jealousy and resentment all those years. But he'd never let that better side of him flourish. Instead, he'd tried to keep it buried with the fires of hatred, and tragically, he'd done a damned fine job of it.

"Why did you bring me out here, Ned?" Chyna asked. "If my death is going to be blamed on Gage, you could have killed me and left me anywhere."

"Old man Dickens has owned this place for fifty years. Even when it closed down, he wouldn't sell it. But he's dying. As soon as he's gone, his children are going to sell it to a company planning on turning it into a shopping mall. Digging will probably start on it next spring. Then they'll find the skeletons. Naturally, Gage would put his last Black Willow victim here with all the others, knowing they wouldn't be discovered for so long. It's so much safer to shoot Gage out here in the middle of nowhere before I haul him away." Ned looked at her with a strange, skewed tenderness. "And I want to bury you with Zoey, Chyna. That will please both of you."

Ned took a deep breath, stood up, and stretched. "Well, I think we've talked long enough. I can't be gone half the night again. Beverly's going to start thinking I'm having an affair." He laughed. "Gage, since you enjoy looking at women so much, I'm going to let you watch me kill my sister before I kill you. Special treat since you're being good enough to take the blame for me." Ned looked at Chyna. "Take off your clothes."

She sat perfectly still, staring at him. No, this can't be happening, she thought. I know that he's sick, I know he's done unspeakable things, but not this. Please, Zoey, Mom, somebody, *help* me . . .

"I said, 'Take . . . off . . . your . . . clothes,' " Ned repeated evenly.

Gage made a raspy, growling sound and began thrashing

beneath his blanket. Ned whirled on him. "Think you're going to save her? You can't even save yourself, so shut up and
quit distracting me or I'll go ahead and kill you first."

Gage grew quiet, but his eyes continued to burn at Ned.
He would kill Ned if he got the chance, Chyna knew with
absolute clarity, as much for his long-lost Edie as to save his
own life. But he wouldn't get the chance.

Chyna started to stand. "You don't have to stand up to
take off your clothes," Ned snapped.

"No, but I can get them off twice as fast this way, and if
this is inevitable, I'd like to get it over with quickly." The
words came out in Chyna's voice with just the right mixture of
fear and resolution, but she had not meant to say them. Someone else had said the words in her voice. Someone else was
with her, maybe even within her, she realized. Should she try
to figure out what was going on? No. The thought went off
like a gong in her head. No. Let go. Let someone else take
control.

Chyna took off her coat, then pulled off the heavy
sweater she wore over a lightweight blouse. She still held
Zoey's necklace in her left hand, so she began unbuttoning
her blouse using only the fingers of her right hand. She let
the blouse slide off, then stepped out of her shoes. The cold
concrete floor seemed to bite through her thin trouser socks,
but she tried to show no discomfort. She unbuttoned and un-
zipped her jeans, then pulled them down to her ankles. It was
then Ned asked sharply, "Why are you keeping your left
hand clenched? What do you have in there?" He jumped up,
pried open her hand, looked at the necklace, then threw back
his head and laughed. "Oh God, Chyna, I know you're a
freak, but really! What the hell good do you think dragging
Zoey's necklace around is going to do you? Are you going to
jab me in the eye with it? Or is she sending you secret sig-
nals through it?"

"The latter," Chyna replied calmly though truthfully. But
Ned only continued to laugh. Then, abruptly, he stopped.
"Drop it."

"I thought you thought my holding it was stupid."

"I do, but . . . well . . . just drop it."

"What's wrong? Beginning to get a little spooked by my supposedly crazy ESP?"

"Drop it!" Ned snarled. "Drop it this instant or I'll shoot Gage."

Much as she feared losing contact with Zoey, Chyna did as Ned said. She didn't like the look in his eye or the sweat beginning to run down his face even though the little building was growing colder by the minute. She kicked the jeans away, took off her socks, then stood in front of her brother wearing only a lace bra and bikini underpants. "Will this do, or are you going to insist on full nudity?"

"Gage and I would like to see everything," Ned said. "After all, Kendrick has. We don't want to be left out."

Chyna reached behind her and began to unfasten her bra when suddenly the light of the flashlight dimmed. She thought the battery was giving out until she noticed that Ned hadn't even glanced at the instrument. And just a moment ago she'd been able to hear Gage breathing, his breath roughened, no doubt, by the cold and dehydration. No, the room was changing for no one but Chyna, she realized as the room darkened even more and finally disappeared to be replaced by the sight of cars racing up the highway—two police cars with lights flashing and sirens wailing and a new blue Mercury with Scott Kendrick behind the wheel. Was she seeing reality or only a wild delusion of hope?

"What's the matter?" Ned demanded. "Does it always take you this long to get undressed?"

Chyna fumbled with the clasp, then felt the bra fall away. She could not see her brother, though. She could not see Gage or the room. She only saw the cars on the road. But she couldn't let Ned sense that anything was happening to her except that she was beginning to be afraid. He'd like that. It's what he wanted most. To inspire fear.

She slid her right thumb down her abdomen until it touched the elastic top of her panties. She did the same with her left thumb, then curled her fingers over the material. Her body was covered with chill bumps from the cold. She could

feel the bumps, but she could not see them. Only the cars.
She saw them pass a huge billboard advertising the country
fair, a billboard she knew to be only about a mile from here,
and a new fear hit her. The sirens. Cut the sirens, she thought
desperately. Cut the sirens!

"What's wrong, Sis?" Ned asked. "Looked like some
kind of spasm crossed your face. Are you suddenly getting
as scared as you should be?"

Chyna heard Ned, but just barely. He'd said something
about being scared. She blurted out, "I'm cold. I'm embarrassed. I'm scared. Satisfied?"

"Yeah, but you don't have to shout. Nice body, wouldn't
you say, Gage? Except that you can't say anything. However,
I'd rate it an eight on a scale of ten. Maybe a nine? No, let's
not go overboard because she's my sister. An eight. Now
Beverly . . ."

The sirens. The sirens. Oh God, the sirens! Maybe she
could only hear them because of what Zoey was allowing
her to experience, but Chyna had seen the billboard. She
couldn't let Ned hear the sirens. "I'm cold!" she screamed.
"Damn it, how long do I have to stand here freezing to
death? You've seen me, Ned! You've humiliated me! Why
don't you get the hell on with whatever you're going to do?"

"Good God, Chyna, shut your mouth!" Ned yelled. She
heard him perfectly. She heard nothing else. She nearly
fainted with relief. They'd turned off the sirens. "You want
me to get on with things? Fine."

Ned laid down the flashlight, its light still glowing, stood,
and came toward her. She knew running toward the door
would be useless. Two steps and he'd have her. Chyna shut
her eyes. Where were the police cruisers? Where was Scott?
Nothing. She saw nothing but darkness. Heart seeming to
drop into her stomach, she continued to stand as tall and motionless as possible, her entire body quivering from cold and
fear. Automatically her arms covered her breasts. Her eyes
were still shut tight when she felt her brother slide his arm
around her face and slap his hand over her mouth just like
he'd done to the other girls.

Then she smelled the chloroform. She wouldn't breathe, she thought wildly. She held her breath for as long as she could. She tried to jerk her head from side to side. But Ned was strong. He pushed down on the cloth so hard she thought he was going to break her nose. And, involuntarily, her oxygen-deprived body drew long and hard on the cloth. Immediately the world felt fuzzy. She tried to cough and couldn't. She tried to hold her breath and couldn't. She gasped, inhaled, then felt her body begin to sag. . . .

Shouting. Outside. Inside. A gun went off. Dizzily she looked over and saw Gage slump against the wall. Another blast. The door flew open. Ned leaped away from her and she sank to the floor, raising her head just in time to see him hurl himself at a policeman. A gun went off. Again. Again.

A moment later, someone was beside her. "It's all right, sweetheart," a deep, familiar voice murmured in her ear. "I don't think you're hurt. Just cold. Put my coat on."

"S-Scott?" Chyna murmured. "My brother?"

Scott's arms tightened around her, and he pressed her head to his shoulder. "I'm sorry, Chyna, but it's for the best. Your brother will never hurt anyone again."

EPILOGUE

Beverly carefully laid a folded comforter in a packing box along with sheets and blankets and closed and taped the lid, then stood aside as Chyna wrote "bedding" on the top. Beverly looked at the word for a moment, then glanced up at Chyna. "We've been packing for two hours. I think we deserve a refreshment break."

Five minutes later, the two women sat at the kitchen table sipping soft drinks. "I thought I'd be living in this house for the rest of my life," Beverly said, looking around the small kitchen with its bare counters. "I can't believe that in less than a week my whole world has changed and I'm moving to Albuquerque, of all places."

"Would you rather go somewhere else?" Chyna asked gently.

Beverly shook her head. "As young as the children are, people are already saying things to Kate about Ned. I know I'll have to explain everything to them someday, but not now, not for a long time. They're still reeling just from their daddy's death. If they knew *why* he died . . ." Beverly's eyes filled with tears and Chyna reached over and took her left hand, a hand still bearing her gold wedding ring. Beverly swallowed. "I hope you don't mind that we're trailing after you to Albuquerque. My parents are dead, Vivian, Rex and

Ned are gone, and my sister is a newlywed with all the problems that entails, but I feel the children need to be near *some* family besides me."

"I'm glad you feel I might be a help," Chyna said. "But I think the biggest help won't be me—it'll be Michelle."

Beverly erupted with a tearful laugh. "I don't mean to insult you, but I believe you're right. They're crazy about that dog."

"And she can't get enough of them, so that relationship will work out fine."

Beverly took a sip of her Diet Coke and straightened the sleeves of her navy blue sweater. Bev's hair was sparkling clean, but for once she wore no jewelry or makeup. "Chyna, are you sure that even though we're going to get our own place, we aren't going to be a bother to you? I know how hard you work at the hospital, and with Scott coming down, too—"

"Scott is moving to Albuquerque for the climate," Chyna said. Beverly grinned and rolled her eyes. "Oh, okay, his doctors say he needs a couple of more months to heal because he's decided to go back to flying, thank God. But he feels he can do that best in a place far away from Black Willow. He says this place gives him the creeps now. He'd been sleepwalking for weeks before the incident at the drive-in. He said the morning after Deirdre was taken, he woke up with scratches all over him and rust-colored stains in the engraving on that ivory-topped walking stick of his. He was afraid he'd hurt someone with it, but the blood was his own from all the scratches and cuts on his hands. He says he woke up and found himself sitting on the edge of our fountain the night Gage disappeared. That scared the hell out of him." She smiled faintly. "He was driven to drinking warm milk."

"Oh, good heavens," Bev played along with a weak smile.

"Scott thought maybe he'd been so traumatized by the crash, he'd been doing awful things to people in the night. He'd been getting counseling, but he was on the verge of going to a psychiatric ward within the next couple of days.

Thank goodness that isn't necessary. He's mentally sound, but you can see how he really needs a change of scene, a completely different place, to get back both his complete physical and emotional health."

Beverly's mouth pulled to the right as she tried to hide a grin. "Chyna, honey, he's going to Albuquerque to be with you. Why can't you just admit that?"

Chyna felt her cheeks warm and finally said, "I don't know. Because I'm afraid this is all too good to be true? Because I'm scared that my relationship with Scott is only based on the ordeal we went through together, not anything *real*?"

"It isn't based on the ordeal," Beverly said firmly. "You've had feelings for him for years. And I know he's felt the same way—he just got into the habit of thinking of you as a kid, so you were hands-off. He sort of missed that you'd grown up." She smiled. "Men can be slow sometimes."

"Yeah. But Scott certainly wasn't slow when it came to saving me. I'd forgotten that he said he'd stop by the house when he got back from his doctor's appointment. When no one came to the door and he found it unlocked, he came in and saw Rex on the floor. Thank God Rex was still alive and conscious enough to tell Scott that Ned had shot him and taken me to the Star Light Drive-In. Poor Rex. He was in such agony before he died, but he saved me." Chyna sighed. "It almost makes me forgive him for how he betrayed my father with Mom for all those years."

"Rex saved you and so did Scott. Scott saved Gage, too. I heard he only got a shoulder wound."

"Yes. And freedom from the cloud of doubt that's hung over him ever since Edie Larson disappeared."

Beverly's eyes filled with tears again. "Now everyone knows Ned killed her. And Zoey. And Heather. And Rusty. And, if it hadn't been for you, Deirdre. You said you kept hearing Zoey singing, 'Star light, star bright,' and Deirdre worked in her father's café, L'Etoile, French for 'star'. Do you think that was a coincidence?"

"I have no idea," Chyna said sincerely. "I guess I have

this gift, or burden, whatever it is, but I can't explain it. And I can't control it, either. That's the most frustrating part of the whole thing."

"You can't explain your gift; I can't explain how I married a man, had two children with him, loved him dearly, and had no idea he was a serial killer. God, that sounds like a tabloid headline, but it's true. Chyna, I never had a clue."

"Of course you didn't!"

Beverly hung her head for a moment, then said, "That's not quite true. Now that I look back on our marriage, I see things that didn't quite add up—the amount of time Ned was gone, the way he looked sometimes when he came home from working late. At first I was just so in love with him I wanted to believe anything he said, and later I got so involved with the kids that I stopped paying as much attention to him as I should have." She gave Chyna an agonized look. "Do you think that's what caused him to do the things he did? My failings as a wife?"

"No, Beverly, absolutely not!" Chyna answered vehemently. "You were a wonderful wife. You always amazed me with how well you balanced Ned, and the kids, and a house, and did it all with such patience, such love. Besides, you know Ned tried to kill me when he was ten years old! There was always something wrong with him. I know he wanted to blame it all on my parents and Rex and even on me, but in spite of all the mistakes Mom and Dad and Rex made, and my colossal blunder of supposedly being smarter than Ned was, those weren't the cause of his problems. At least, they weren't the only cause.

"I've never been able to decide whether to believe in nature or nurture—that we're born a certain way or we turn out the way we do because of how we're reared," Chyna continued. "Now I think it's probably a combination of both. In Mom's letter, she talked about what an unhappy baby Ned was, how even as a little kid he was prone to these awful, depressed moods. I think there was something lacking in Ned at birth. Add that to the tangled mess of my family and we ended up with the Ned who died last week."

"I guess," Beverly mumbled. "But Chyna, Ian and Kate are Ned's children. Do you think that if something was wrong with him at birth it was passed on to them?"

At that moment, Beverly and Chyna heard the front door open. Next followed the voice of Scott yelling, "Bev, Chyna, we're back from the park!" Then he spoke to the children. "Hey, you two, chill out! We're home now. Time to behave."

Michelle barked raucously and ran into the kitchen, where she made a beeline for Chyna. Chyna slid out of her chair and sat on the floor, letting the big golden dog clamber onto her lap. Ian and Kate were quick to follow, and within a minute the three of them were floundering on the floor, petting the dog, kissing one another, laughing from the depths of their being.

Chyna glanced up at Beverly, who was looking down at them with the first genuine smile she'd managed since Ned's death. "He *never* acted like this when he was young," Chyna said, knowing the kids were paying no attention to her. "In spite of everything, you have two healthy, happy, *normal* children, Bev. And I call that being one of the luckiest people in the world."

Beverly smiled at the same time tears ran down her cheeks. Scott draped his arm over Beverly's shoulder and he looked down at Chyna with love in his eyes. "You can trust what she says, Beverly, because my darling Chyna knows more and senses more than we can ever imagine."